SPY
OUT THE
LAND

Acclaimed author of both fiction and non-fiction, Jeremy Duns is British but currently lives and works in Finland. Visit him at www.jeremy-duns.com and find him on Twitter @jeremyduns and on Facebook.

Also by Jeremy Duns
Free Agent
Song of Treason
The Moscow Option
Dead Drop: The True Story of Oleg Penkovsky and
the Cold War's Most Dangerous Operation

SPY
OUT THE
LAND

JEREMY DUNS

**SIMON &
SCHUSTER**

London · New York · Sydney · Toronto · New Delhi

A CBS COMPANY

First published in Great Britain by Simon & Schuster UK Ltd, 2016
A CBS company

1 3 5 7 9 10 8 6 4 2

Simon & Schuster UK Ltd
1st Floor
222 Gray's Inn Road
London WC1X 8HB

www.simonandschuster.co.uk

Simon & Schuster Australia, Sydney
Simon & Schuster India, New Delhi

A CIP catalogue record for this book is available from the British Library

Paperback ISBN: 978-0-85720-971-9
eBook ISBN: 978-0-85720-972-6

Typeset in the UK by Hewer Text UK Ltd, Edinburgh
Printed and bound in Great Britain by CPI Group (UK) Ltd, Croydon, CR0 4YY

Simon & Schuster UK Ltd are committed to sourcing paper that is made from
wood grown in sustainable forests and supports the Forest Stewardship Council,
the leading international forest certification organisation. Our books
displaying the FSC logo are printed on FSC certified paper.

For Johanna, Rebecca and Astrid

1969

Chapter 1

Gunnar Hansson peered through his binoculars at the islet a few hundred yards to his north, and watched the bullet tear into the man in the diving suit.

He'd set out from the lighthouse half an hour earlier, having been woken by a noise he had gradually realised was a helicopter passing overhead. That had suggested some kind of emergency, most likely an operation by the coastguard patrol – and yet the radio set hulking in the corner of the room had been silent. He'd forced himself out of bed and over to the telescope, waking Helena as he did and telling her to double-check the receiver. But there was nothing, just the harsh hiss of static.

So he had scanned the sky, finding the helicopter after a few minutes and shifting his stance rapidly to keep it in sight. It had reached an area where visibility was poor, with layers of mist moving over the water,

3

but it looked like it was coming down to land somewhere in the skerries behind Örö.

'What's happening?' Helena had asked, an edge of
panic in her voice.

He took his eye from the telescope. 'I don't know.
I'm going out to see.' He began dressing, pulling on a
pair of waterproof trousers, a thick sweater and his
oilskin cape. 'If I'm not back by five, call Bengt.'

Bengt Hagerlund manned communications for the
coastguard in the area. Gunnar didn't want to sound
the alarm prematurely: a patrol could be in the midst
of an operation or conducting an exercise of some sort
and he might interrupt something important by
panicking. He found a torch and a pair of boots, kissed
Helena on the lips and clambered down the staircase.

It had rained earlier in the night, so it took him a
few minutes to walk the short distance across the
rocks and down to the jetty – one slip and he could
break his neck. The small motorboat rocked gently
against the lapping waves. Once he had loosened the
chains he threw them ashore and stepped in. He had
glanced up to the tower: Helena stood by the lens
watching him, as she did whenever he left the island,
and for a moment he'd pictured her pale grey eyes
imploring him to return quickly. Then he had headed
out towards Örö.

Now he sat with the engine idle and his mouth
agape. He had arrived a couple of minutes earlier and
watched as some sort of argument had broken out
between three men on a tiny islet whose name even he

didn't know, leaving him wondering what the hell they were shouting about and why they had chosen such a place to do so. Then suddenly there had been a gunshot, and a prick of blood had appeared in the forehead of one of the men, the one wearing the long coat. An instant after that a second shot had been fired, and the man in the diving suit had also fallen to the ground.

Gunnar had immediately reached for the revolver he kept in a locker in the stern, but he knew it would be suicidal to approach. The Finnish coastguard had helicopters with orange and green livery, but on the way in he had seen that this one, parked on the eastern edge of the islet, was khaki-coloured with side-mounted machine guns, and had a large red star painted on the clamshell door of the rear fuselage.

Russians.

Gunnar detested Russians. He was fifty-eight years old, as strong as a bear, a Swedish-speaking Finn who had lived in this part of the archipelago all his life. His father had been one of the first lighthouse-keepers on Bengtskär, and he had taken over from him. In the war against the Russians, a Finnish garrison had been stationed there to observe naval movements from the tower, until one night in 1941 the Soviets had landed with patrol boats. Gunnar and several others had been caught in a fierce fire-fight on the upper floors, while others had engaged them among the crevasses below. The Russians had eventually been repelled with the help of the Finnish Air Force, but thirty-one Finns died in the battle.

Gunnar had suffered only minor injuries, but he hadn't forgotten those brutal hours and the friends and colleagues he had lost in them. He had stayed on at Bengtskär for several years, until the coastguard had converted it to an unmanned station and he and Helena had moved a few miles west to run the smaller lighthouse on Utö.

He watched as the shooter and another figure carried the man in the coat over to the helicopter. He expected them to return and repeat the process for the other man, but instead the helicopter's rotors started up and it lifted into the air, a gust shaking it for a moment before it righted itself and swung east. Gunnar watched until it was no longer visible, then started up the motor and pointed it towards the skerry.

The man in the diving suit had been shot in the stomach, and Gunnar couldn't feel a pulse. He considered leaving him there, but something about that seemed wrong so he picked him up by the arms and started carrying him to the boat, dragging him on his heels. It was difficult work, and he had to stop for breath several times on the way. To his surprise, once he had eventually managed to deposit the man into the front bench of the boat, he opened his mouth and spoke, although his voice was barely a whisper.

'*Jag är Engelsman.*'

Gunnar nodded, although he didn't understand why an Englishman would be here, speaking Swedish, with a bullet in his stomach. In a compartment in the rear of the boat he found a blanket. He bound it around the man's abdomen as best he could, and watched as the cloth bloomed a brownish red. He was about to cast off and head home when he noticed that the man's right hand was bent strangely, waving in the breeze, and he realised he was trying to tell him something. He followed the line of his forefinger, and saw a fallen log lying against the edge of the water on the far side of the islet.

He jumped overboard and trudged back over the rocks. It wasn't a log. It was a woman, the back of her head a mess of blood and matter, her dress clinging obscenely to her young body. He heaved her from the water and began carrying her back to join the Englishman.

Chapter 2

It was cold in Kievskaya metro station, but Victor Kotov was sweating beneath his overcoat. He had spent weeks preparing for this moment, but he was still terrified something would go wrong. And failure meant a firing squad.

Something moved in his peripheral vision and he looked up, but it was just a bulb flickering in one of the nearby chandeliers. The long marble hall was deserted but for him seated on this bench, trying to stop his legs from shaking. He glanced at his watch for what felt like the hundredth time. If his calculations were correct the man should be on the next train. Just three more minutes.

He marvelled for a moment that he had been brought to this point by a passing remark. He had long known what they called him in the office: 'Akula' – the Shark. Over the years a few subordinates had mistakenly used it in his presence, but he had liked that they feared him.

8

Taken pride in it, even. But three months ago he had overheard Masevnin explaining the origins of his nickname to a pretty new secretary in the typing pool. 'No, no, it's not because he's dangerous – he's a pushover. It's because of how he looks. The sheen on those two sad grey suits he wears has become so worn over the years they look like the skin of a shark. And the eyes in that great meaty face of his, have you noticed? Tiny black pellets with no apparent feeling or intellect behind them, just a dull malevolence towards the world. That's why we call him the Shark!' And the girl had laughed loudly along with Masevnin.

Kotov had immediately ordered a new suit from GUM, a blue Western-style Super 100 he could barely afford. But the comment had cut him to the quick. His eleven years as the directorate's respected security chief had crumbled to ashes. He wasn't respected at all: he was a laughing stock.

He had started copying down documents a couple of weeks later, scribbling notes straight from the cipher machines whenever he could. Then last week Proshin had asked him to install one of the new safes in his office, and he had seized the opportunity. He had stayed behind two evenings in a row and photographed every scrap of paper he could find.

There was a rumbling in the ceiling, and Kotov looked up expectantly. Passengers began flooding down the staircase and into the hallway. And yes, there he was. Kotov jumped from the bench and hurried towards him.

'Sir!' he whispered in English, reaching out a hand and gripping his sleeve. The man swivelled round, his face frozen with fright. 'I'm not a thief,' Kotov assured him. 'A friend. We met before at your embassy, remember? You are Mister Peem.'

Third Secretary Angus Pimm nodded slowly, and Kotov gestured to the bench. 'Please,' he said. 'I just need a few moments of your time.'

Pimm glanced around anxiously, but the swathe of people were focused on one thing only – getting home as soon as possible. Kotov nodded at the rapidly emptying hall.

'No one watches us. And you know who I am, yes? I mean, who I really am?'

Pimm nodded dully. He knew. He'd been introduced to Kotov as a press attaché, but he was GRU: Soviet military intelligence. He'd been assigned to feel him out last year but had got nowhere and had been under the impression the man wasn't even aware he was approaching him. It seemed he'd been wrong about that, but what madness was this, to accost him in a metro station?

'And I know who you are,' said Kotov. 'Please, we don't have much time,' he continued. 'I wish to defect to England, and I have many secret documents on me.'

'*On* you? Christ! Where?'

Kotov was moving his hand to his coat pocket.

Pimm looked at him, aghast. 'Christ!' He couldn't think of anything else to say. He tried to remember the procedures for such an occurrence. Stay calm was the first, but he wasn't managing that very well.

There was another rumbling sound from the ceiling. It was time. Kotov removed the envelope from his pocket and placed it in Pimm's hands.

'This is my first gift to you,' he said. 'Please make sure it reaches the right people.'

He turned and walked hurriedly up the staircase to the platform.

Chapter 3

Monday, 17 November 1969,
Century House, London

'You can go through now.'

Rachel Gold walked across the plush carpet and pushed open the large mahogany doors. There were two men in the room: Edmund Innes was seated behind his desk, wearing a herringbone suit and drooping polka-dotted bow tie, while Sandy Harmigan was stretched out in one of the leather armchairs by the sideboard, looking as louche as ever.

Innes looked up. 'Good afternoon, Miss Gold.' He got to his feet. 'A glass of sherry, perhaps?'

'Yes, please.'

He walked to the sideboard, and she glanced around the room nervously. Harmigan smiled at her and she looked away, her gaze finding the window offering a skyline of grimy rooftops. All the mahogany in the world couldn't disguise the fact they were in the drab end of Lambeth.

Innes handed her the glass. 'Something's come up.'

He ambled back to his desk and picked up a brown folder, which he handed to her with a tight smile.

She removed the band around the folder and a crisp page of glossy black Cyrillic type stared up at her. Her eyes scanned it hungrily. At first blush, it looked like an internal report from GRU – specifically from its Second Chief Directorate, the department in Moscow responsible for counter-intelligence against the United States and Britain. In other words, gold dust.

She lowered herself into one of the chairs and started reading. The document was dated 3 November, and described a GRU special forces operation to apprehend a man and woman who had escaped from custody in the Lubyanka. The team hunting them had been led by Colonel Fedor Proshin, but the report was written by his son, Alexander. It seemed the man being hunted had once been a Soviet agent, and that Alexander Proshin had been his handler. In keeping with protocol, the agent was referred to throughout by his codename, NEZAVISIMYJ, meaning 'Independent', but the report revealed several details about him: he was forty-four years old, had been a high-ranking British intelligence officer and had been in Nigeria and Italy in the previous six months.

Rachel realised at once why they'd summoned her. It could only be Paul Dark.

She thought back to June, when Innes had first called her into this office. At twenty-four, she was one of the Service's youngest officers, and the only woman at her level of seniority, mostly as a result of being a mathematical prodigy. But she was dissatisfied nonetheless. She had been recruited by GCHQ a few months after finishing her degree at Cambridge, when she had been filling in as a junior don in the maths department at King's – a pale ferret-faced man in a green duffelcoat had appeared at her rooms one afternoon and asked if he could have 'a quiet word'.

GCHQ had reminded her of Cambridge in many ways, perhaps because several of her colleagues had been former academics, and she had soon been itching to tackle something more concrete than patterns on a page. As a child, she had devoured books of puzzles and codes her father had bought her, but the two that had most fascinated her were *Spy-Catcher* and *Friend or Foe?*, the wartime memoirs of the Dutch counter-intelligence officer Oreste Pinto, who had worked with MI5 in interrogating suspected double agents. The BBC had made a television series a few years later, but for her nothing could match the magic of the books, which had transported her into a world where solving puzzles was not simply an intellectual pursuit but a form of combat on which the fate of nations could hinge. It had led her to GCHQ, but she was still a long way from the sharp end – she yearned to be out in the field, testing her wits against others, face to face in the great game of espionage.

After asking around the office as discreetly as she could, she had eventually been introduced at a dinner party to someone from the Service, and in the spring of 1968, when many people her age were busy dropping acid, she had finally joined. She had started out in the Communications Section, where despite her youth and inexperience she had quickly become known as the 'crypto queen'. But barely a year and a half into the job it had already started to feel like she was treading water – and the problems she was dealing with felt as abstract as they had done at GCHQ, or King's.

Her first meeting with Innes had changed all that. She had been indoctrinated into one of the Service's greatest secrets – that it was about to be closed down.

Rumours had been circulating for months that the agency was in crisis. There were even whispers that the previous Chief, Farraday, had died during the memorial service for his predecessor in St Paul's, and if one stayed long enough after hours one heard talk of a sniper, an Italian terrorist group, of manhunts across Europe. It had all sounded too fantastical to be true, but there had been nothing imaginary about Innes' grim expression.

He had been appointed Chief a few weeks earlier, but nobody believed he'd last long. He had previously been head of Western European Section and was regarded as a forensic intelligence analyst but a weak politician. Rachel had only ever seen him once before, catching a glimpse of a top hat and tails as he climbed into a limousine outside the building, like a figure from a Trollope novel. Up close, she found he had unexpectedly kind eyes, and had felt herself wanting to please him: that sense of loyalty she had sometimes experienced with very good teachers, and with her father when she was a child.

That afternoon, he had explained to her the true state of the Service's predicament, which turned out to be far worse than even the wildest basement bar gossip. Farraday *had* been killed by an Italian group, but they had been sponsored by the Russians and the assassination was tied to the disappearance of Paul Dark, the former head of Soviet Section. Everyone had been told Dark was on extended leave, but the truth was he had been unmasked as a traitor that spring and gone on the run. The suspicion was he'd defected to Moscow, but nothing had been confirmed.

Rachel had listened in shock as Innes outlined the fiasco surrounding Dark. Several pieces of intelligence suggested the Sovs had recruited him as long ago as 1945, meaning that over two decades of high-level secrets could have been betrayed. Worse still, the Americans had got wind of it and were furious, threatening a permanent cessation of all intelligence-sharing unless the Service could put its house in order, and fast. It was just the latest in a long string of British spy scandals that had begun with Guy Burgess and Donald Maclean in the fifties and had been followed by Kim Philby and George Blake's defections. Dark was seen as the final straw. The prime minister had swiftly responded to the Americans' objections, threatening to shut the Service down completely and handing its responsibilities to Five until a new, 'untainted' agency could be formed.

This was the doomsday scenario, and Innes had been determined to stop it. He had promised to deliver the prime minister a thorough report into all the agency's security lapses before the year was out. Innes was moving thirty officers into a small command centre in Warren Street to form a new department, Review Section. He'd asked Rachel to lead the group analysing Dark's career, reporting directly to the head of Soviet Section, Sandy Harmigan.

Since then she had eaten, slept and breathed little but Paul Dark. Working through the files with four others, she had retraced as much of his life as possible: his racing-car driver father, his mad Swedish aristocrat of a mother, his string of girlfriends – 'Dark's dolly birds', Harmigan called them – all of whom seemed to be damaged in one way or another, and all of whom seemed to have come to a sticky end. She'd worked long into the night, fuelled by a steady supply of coffee from the vending machine downstairs and St Moritz menthols from an all-night offie across the street. In her more sombre moments, she despaired at the magnitude of the task. It could take years to assess what the man had done, and even then a thousand questions might never be answered.

Guiding her through the maze of the investigation was Sandy Harmigan. He was a daily presence in the command centre, and at six foot four, with a mane of silvery hair framing a long, lean face and dressed in bespoke Harris tweed, impossible to ignore. He was a war hero, having gained an MC at Saint-Nazaire – in the latter stages of the raid, he'd carried out a solo reconnaissance mission in the port. He had then been captured and imprisoned by the Germans, but had broken out of his camp with a group of POWs. After the war he had written a memoir, *Safe Conduct*, which had been filmed by Hollywood with Dirk Bogarde portraying a sensationalised version of him. Rachel had read the book in her teens – it wasn't quite as thrilling as Oreste Pinto, but it was close. Now Harmigan was the spook's spook: in the corridors of Century House, he was discussed in hushed, almost reverent tones, and was widely regarded as Innes' inevitable successor. Rachel had found, to her dismay, that she was falling in love with him.

But the work came first, and it had borne fruit: by August her team had pinpointed several contingency plans they felt certain Dark had betrayed to Moscow, all of which were changed accordingly. At the same time, ties had been severed with nearly a hundred agents and assets around the world. They had also discovered the true identity of Dark's handler, Alexander Proshin, who as 'Ivan Dimirov' had worked as a lecturer at UCL. Unfortunately, they hadn't got a lot further than that, as interviews with former students and tutors had turned up precious little concrete intelligence about him. He kept to himself. He liked Dave Brubeck records. He collected stamps. Proshin had become her second obsession: the man behind the curtain, the puppet-master, the great spy-handler.

Now, thanks to the document Innes had just handed

her, she finally had some answers. It seemed that Paul Dark's long run of evading justice had come to an end, and it had ironically been at the hands of Proshin. In the final paragraphs of his memorandum, Proshin described how he and his team had tracked Dark and an unnamed British woman to a small island between Finland and Sweden. A gunfight had ensued in which three had died: Colonel Proshin, the woman, and Dark. Alexander Proshin and his radio operator had flown his father's body back to Moscow, but had left the Brits to rot on the island – 'I decided that the birds there deserved some meat,' was how he had chillingly put it.

Rachel closed the file and placed it on her lap.

'Where's it from?'

Innes nodded at Harmigan, who set his glass to one side.

'A Russian chap approached Angus Pimm in the Moscow metro on Wednesday evening. Name of Kotov – a GRU security officer. He passed Pimm an envelope, saying it was his "first gift". It contained microfilms of twenty documents, of which this was one.'

'Wednesday?' She looked between them. 'Why are you showing it to me only now?'

Both men smiled tersely, and she blushed at her own impertinence. But Dark was hers, they knew that.

'We were looking into it,' said Innes gently. 'We've been stung with dangles before.'

She nodded. The Soviets would sometimes send an officer to a foreign embassy claiming to want to defect.

If accepted as genuine, he could feed them disinformation for months, or even years.

'Moscow Station have interviewed Pimm extensively,' said Innes. 'They think Kotov's the real thing, but as you're the expert on Dark we wanted your view before we decide how to proceed.'

The two men were looking at her expectantly. Innes had phrased it to flatter, but she suspected they were simply looking for confirmation of what they had already decided. If she agreed Kotov was genuine, they would then have more support for their case. It would mean they could justify running Kotov, but also that they could sign off the report to the prime minister saying Dark had been killed: 'But that was in another country, and besides, the traitor's dead.' She was tempted to disappoint them on principle, but that would be unprofessional. Still, they were putting her in an unpleasant situation, essentially asking her to gauge the worth of the report on sight, and devoid of any surrounding context.

'What are the other documents Kotov handed over?'

'Solid stuff,' said Harmigan. 'Most of it new to us, if not earth-shattering.'

'Can I see them?'

'We wanted your view on this first.'

She took a sip of the sherry. Vile, she thought – far too sweet.

'All right. Well, it could be disinformation, of course: Moscow's found Dark alive somewhere but they want us to believe he's dead so they've concocted this report and sent their man along with it to convince us. But I think that's rather unlikely. If they knew for certain he were alive that would suggest they had him in their custody, in which case they'd get much more mileage out of him by holding a press conference, like they did with Burgess and Maclean, or at least allowing him to be spotted by Western journalists, like they did with Philby in '63. Then there's the mention of the woman with him. Unfortunately, that sounds very much like it's Sarah Severn, who we know disappeared from Rome Station at the same time as Dark was there. Finally, the memorandum claims to be written by Alexander Proshin, and it seems to me that it is. We've already determined that this man was Dark's handler, and I very much doubt they'd word disinformation as callously as they have here. It has the unpleasant ring of truth. The details he gives of handling Dark in London also fit with the other information we have. It seems he's now relocated to Moscow and has become fairly senior in this directorate. You may remember my reports about his father, who used to be one of Andropov's closest advisers and has been missing for some time. His death as described in this report and the son's ascendency in Moscow explain a large part of what we've been missing.' She took a breath and gave a brief smile. 'So – pending further analysis, of course – my assessment is that the report is real.'

Both men looked relieved, and she wondered how to word her next sentence. Harmigan noticed her hesitation.

'Is something wrong?'

She shifted in her seat for a moment, then took the plunge. 'Yes. There's another possibility. The document could be genuine, but Dark and Severn might nevertheless still be alive. It doesn't need to be an attempt to feed us disinformation – Proshin could simply be lying on his own account.'

Innes' head snapped up. 'Why on earth would he do that?'

She gave a thin smile, unwilling to lecture the head of the Service. 'There could be any number of reasons, sir. Political infighting we don't know about, or simply to cover his own back. If he and his team lost Dark in Finland, for instance, writing a report admitting it would be tantamount to signing his own death sentence.'

Harmigan reached for his drink. Innes sighed, then offered her a polite but distant smile.

'Thank you, Miss Gold. We'll take this from here.'

She gave a brief nod, stood and walked out of the room.

Innes wandered to the sideboard and poured two more brandies, then headed back over to Harmigan and handed one to him.

'Well? What if she's right?'

Harmigan looked up at him, surprised. 'She isn't. She's just become too attached to the chase. And it helps if the person you're chasing is tangible.'

Innes took a sip from his glass, swirling the liquid in his mouth before swallowing.

'What about her idea it could be some kind of internal intrigue we don't know about?'

The other man let out a derisive snort. 'Edmund, you know as well as I do you can send yourself mad applying that sort of thinking to everything.' He nodded at the dossier on the table. 'It's all there in black and white.' He tipped his head back and downed the rest of his drink, then slammed the glass down on the sideboard and made a short chopping motion with his hand. 'Dark's dead. Good bloody riddance.'

Chapter 4

It was approaching dusk by the time the dilapidated Nissan Cedric came to a stop outside the house in Kenny Hill.

'This the one, *lah*?'

Rachel consulted her map and nodded. She paid the driver, peeling off notes from the bundle she had exchanged at the airport, and stepped out of the car. She watched as the car turned round and headed back down the hill, leaving the street empty but for her. After the cacophony of the city centre, with the beeping horns and roaring exhausts of buses and vans and motorcycles, the neighbourhood was eerily quiet.

She walked up to a set of iron gates. Beyond it, a gravel driveway led to a long white villa, its red roof tiles and black slatted windows giving it an incongruously Tudor look. She was reminded of her father's favourite pub, The Swan in Newtown.

A small card in a pillar to the right of the gates read 'Gadlow', and she pressed the button beneath it. In the dim light, she watched as a man in a belted uniform and peaked cap emerged from a cabin on the other side of the gates.

'I'm here to see the Gadlows.'

He nodded and placed a key in one of the gates to let her through, raising a hand to indicate the entrance of the house.

She thanked him. In the driveway, a small man in a safari suit was polishing the bonnet of a black Mercedes sedan with a chamois cloth. She said 'Good evening' and he looked up for a moment, then returned to his polishing.

Feeling slightly foolish, she approached the front door, which was a grand oak affair with a large bronze knocker. Her stomach was roiling. Was it simply nerves, she wondered, or was this part of the jet lag phenomenon she'd been warned of? When she'd left her flat in London it had been shortly after dawn. Now it was quarter to seven in the evening and she was suddenly just a few hours away from a new decade.

It had also been damp and cold in London, while here it was in the high twenties, and she could feel the beads of sweat forming on her skin, stinging her eyes and pooling in the ridge of her upper lip. She wiped it away with her hand. The humidity had hit her like a solid wall on walking out of the terminal building, and her neck still ached from having slept in an awkward position on the flight. The drive through the city had only made her feel more jumbled up. As well as the noise, the landscape had been an incoherent mixture of wide boulevards and palm trees, concrete tower blocks and ornate mosques. Billboards and signposts were often in several alphabets, including the Latin one, with many words near-phonetic spellings of the English equivalent. But you had to be in the right frame of mind to see this, and it had even taken her a few seconds to twig the sign reading 'Teksi' in the airport. Not a good omen for the supposed crypto queen.

She rubbed her eyes and took a deep breath. *Pull yourself together – you've come a long way for this.* She swung the bronze knocker. After a while, an elderly Chinese woman in a plain blue housedress and slippers opened the door a fraction and peered out. On seeing her, she gave a sharp nod and immediately turned and shuffled away again.

Rachel was debating whether to follow after her – and marvelling at the number of servants she had already encountered – when another figure stepped into the doorway. She was an attractive woman in her late thirties. Thirty-eight, Rachel remembered from the file. Her fair hair was swept back from her forehead and she wore a turquoise shantung silk evening gown that showed off long, tanned arms and accentuated her bust. Rachel was suddenly conscious of the wildness of her own dark curls and the pale angularity of her body beneath the cheap cotton dress she'd bought in Gamages a few days earlier.

'Hello? May I help?'

The voice was a bright English trill, the kind that would suit a speaker at a debutante's ball or the presenter of a children's programme on the BBC. Rachel straightened her back and pasted on a smile.

'Yes, hello. I'm looking for Tom Gadlow.'

'And you are . . .?'

'Rachel Gold. I've just flown in from London.' She stuck out her hand.

There was a momentary hesitation, of the type she was used to whenever she said her name with its 'biblical resonances', as her brother, Danny, euphemistically referred to it. And then she felt the tips of her fingers being gently shaken.

'Oh, yes. The office told us you were coming. I'm Eleanor, Tom's wife. He's out on the veranda. Do come in.'

Rachel followed Eleanor Gadlow through to a spacious living room: it was filled with several brightly coloured sofas, modern abstract oil paintings and cabinets housing glass ornaments. How much of it had been paid for by the Sovs, she wondered. The house and servants came with the job, but the décor looked a little too flashy for a Head of Station – perhaps Gadlow had a numbered account in Zurich. Was Eleanor in on his treachery, or did she not know where the money came from?

Three weeks earlier, Rachel had been reviewing the latest batch of material passed to Moscow Station by Victor Kotov when she had discovered something extraordinary: one of the microfilm reels had contained the minutes of meetings that had taken place in the secure room of the British embassy in Bangkok in the late fifties. Over the course of nine days, she had mapped out everyone who had had access to those documents until she had narrowed the list to just one person who could have seen them all: Tom Gadlow, who had since become Head of Station in Kuala Lumpur.

It had taken her several more days to persuade Sandy Harmigan she was right about Gadlow. Although Review Section had been set up for precisely this sort of breakthrough, nobody on the Fourth Floor had welcomed the news of another double agent in the ranks. Perhaps because of her insistence that Paul Dark might still be alive, Sandy had been especially sceptical. But after several meetings, at which section heads had been brought in and charts had been set up and explained, she had convinced Sandy and the others that there could be no other possible explanation.

Once they had accepted Gadlow was guilty, the next question had been how to get him back to London for interrogation without tipping him – or the Soviets – off. Sandy had decided to send Rachel out to fetch him. It was a risk – she had little experience in the field and he was still troubled by her refusal to back down over Dark – but she had all the details fixed in her mind and, more importantly, wouldn't get cold feet about bringing him in.

There had been similar missions, the most notable

being the attempts to bring George Blake and Kim
Philby back to London. Blake had come willingly,
having been summoned by telegram for a possible
promotion, and had eventually cracked and confessed
all. But Philby had managed to fool the officer sent
out to fetch him into giving him time to arrange his
affairs before flying home, and had promptly fled to
Moscow instead. Some felt that the officer in question, one of Philby's oldest friends, had deliberately
bungled the operation through a sense of personal
loyalty. 'Whatever happens,' Sandy had said with
startling ferocity in her last meeting with him, 'we
can't have a repeat of that fiasco. We need to know
precisely what Gadlow's done, so don't let the bastard
out of your sight and bring him back in one piece.'
And then he had smiled, and his usual smooth demeanour had been restored.

'How was your flight?'

Rachel snapped out of her thoughts. 'Oh, it was fine,
thank you. But rather long – the furthest I've been
before is Gibraltar.'

She winced at how provincial she sounded, but
Eleanor Gadlow gave her an indulgent smile. 'You
were lucky this afternoon's storm died down – sometimes they drag on for hours, and that's no fun to land
in, believe me.'

Rachel made further polite noises, wondering if the
chattiness was her natural state or a sign of anxiety.

They reached a glass door at the far end of the room.
Beyond it, a grey and mauve sky stretched above a

landscape of rolling hills that even in the twilight looked lush and alive.

Eleanor Gadlow caught the expression of awe on her face and smiled. 'Yes, we're very lucky. It all used to be plantations, of course.' She slid the door open and called out. 'Darling? The girl from London's here.'

Rachel noted the dismissive description and stepped out after her, her skin prickling as the hot damp air again swathed her like an invisible blanket. A dark plume of smoke emerged from a coiled device placed on the tiles, and she realised it was to ward off mosquitoes.

A figure rose from a scoop-backed rattan chair in the far corner of the veranda and walked towards her. He was broad-shouldered and beefy: he'd been a rugby blue, and his face bore further testament to that fact, with a conspicuously broken nose set in an otherwise handsome, hearty face. He wore a crisp white shirt paired with a bright pink and green patterned sarong and a pair of highly polished sandals, and his dark hair was greased back with pomade. Rachel tried not to show surprise at the absurd outfit and braced herself for the usual masculine glazing of the eyes once he had taken her in, but instead he gave her a dazzling smile of such apparent sincerity that for one horrifying moment she wondered whether she had got everything wrong, and was here in error.

She blinked, forcing herself to picture the chart on her desk with the row of distribution lists, and his name at the top of every one of them. No, he was guilty, and she could prove it. She *had* proven it, to the satisfaction of Sandy and everyone else who'd read her report. It was incontrovertible – and one may smile, and smile, and be a villain.

He leaned forward and took her hand firmly in his grasp. 'Tom Gadlow. You must be Rachel. The office cabled to say you were on your way a few hours ago. Though the message was rather vague.'

Rachel glanced over at his wife, and Gadlow caught it.

'Oh, you can speak freely – Eleanor's fully cleared.'

She was Gadlow's secretary at the station – it was how they'd met – but Rachel had wanted to speak to him alone. An awkward silence stretched out as she wondered how best to broach the subject. On an impulse, she walked over to the stone balustrade and leaned across it, looking out onto a large garden. Beds of vivid orange and red flowers – cannas, she thought – were dotted around a small swimming pool that had been lit up from within, like a diamond glowing in a velvet cushion. What a life: servants and evening gowns and swimming pools. She thought of her tiny kitchenette in Holborn: Danny's books and papers, the sink so small it was an engineering job to wash the dishes, the malfunctioning radiators. A few weeks earlier it had been so cold at night that she'd taken to spinning her legs around beneath her quilt, as though riding a bicycle, to generate some heat.

She turned back to the Gadlows, and the business in hand.

'I'm sorry to barge in on you both like this. I take it you're on your way out somewhere?'

Gadlow nodded. 'Yes. The Harrisons – colleagues from the High Commission. They have an open house every year.'

'It's the best New Year's Eve party in KL,' added Eleanor. 'Joan works with a local catering chap – what's his name again, darling?'

Gadlow smiled tightly. 'I don't remember.'

'Yes, you do. She was telling us about it the other day . . . Mister Kong, that's it! She goes on a little sortie with him through Chinatown, and she samples all the hawker stalls and chooses her favourite dozen, the *crème de la crème*. Mister Kong then makes all the arrangements and they relocate their stalls, just for the night, in the Harrisons' garden. They're all decorated with lanterns, and you wander through helping yourself to *kway teow* or soup or whatever you fancy – your own little Chinatown for the evening. Isn't that marvellous? Tom always gorges himself at the *mee* stall – it's those thick noodles, you like, isn't it?'

Gadlow nodded, Rachel thought a little embarrassed by his wife's loquaciousness. She gave what she hoped passed for a rueful smile. 'Well, I'm afraid he's going to have to give the noodles a miss this year. He's needed back in London.' She addressed Gadlow. 'We're flying back tonight, and you're expected at a meeting at headquarters as soon as we arrive.'

Eleanor Gadlow spoke first, her face now devoid of the brightness of a few moments earlier.

'Tonight? What's going on – is there some sort of emergency? And why've they sent you all the way out here to escort him back, rather than just telling him to book a flight out?'

'I've no idea. I'm just following instructions.'

Eleanor Gadlow shook her head in a small gesture of bafflement. 'But they must have told you *something*, surely?'

Rachel didn't reply. Don't get drawn in, Sandy had told her. Avoid all confrontation. But the mood had shifted: she was no longer a guest to impress with tales of lavish parties, or 'the girl from London'. She was an intruder.

Gadlow placed a hand on his wife's arm. 'It's all right, darling, I'm sure they'll have their reasons.' He turned to Rachel. 'What time's this flight?'

'We're booked on the BOAC leaving at three a.m. We'll arrive in Heathrow in the early afternoon and you're due at headquarters straightaway. You'll fly back out on Monday.'

She did have a ticket for him on the return flight, but he was never going to use it. The schedule had been worked out to give him the least possible time to think, let alone contact his handler or a cut-out.

Gadlow glanced at his watch. 'You have to check in at one for that flight, which is, let's see, in . . . six and a half hours from now. All right. I've got an overnight bag prepared upstairs. I take it you won't mind if I pop by the Harrisons' with Eleanor anyway – just for half an hour or so? I don't care for "Auld Lang Syne" personally, but it's the social occasion of the year in these parts and it would look odd if I didn't at least show my face. Eleanor would be fielding pointed questions from first attachés all night.'

He had played the hand well, she had to give him that. Concerned, polite, and there was nothing she could object to without seeming unreasonable. She didn't know if he was acting alone or with his wife's help, but even without the prompting he must have suspected her real reason for coming out here – why send an escort, indeed? But Rachel's objective was not simply to get him back to London, but to do so without the Sovs noticing. Once a few days had passed and he hadn't shown up at the High Commission or made contact, they would naturally worry he had been blown – but they wouldn't be sure of it. He might simply be attending a training course or being briefed for a future posting. After a few weeks they would realise there could be no other explanation, but by then the Service would have had a chance to place surveillance on every agent and case officer he'd identified in the interim, and perhaps even to feed them some disinformation.

She somehow doubted that a no-show at a New Year's Eve party would seriously perturb anyone, let alone the Russians – but it was a nagging possibility nonetheless. It was a deft hand in other ways, too, as he had instantly put her under pressure. *Don't let the bastard out of your sight.* Well, that had been easy enough for Sandy to say from the comfort of his enormous office in London, but if she insisted Gadlow didn't attend the party she would merely confirm his suspicion that he'd been detected, meaning he'd have even less to lose by trying to make a run for it. And she had no way of preventing him from going to the party, or anywhere else for that matter. She wasn't even armed.

She felt like a fool. All her planning had been undone in seconds. And as much as she wished she had brought a gun with her, she knew it wouldn't have helped, as she could hardly have just shot him if he failed to do what she said. That was something for the pictures.

And perhaps he had another motive. Was it simply the condemned man's last request, but rather than a cigarette or a rare steak, his favourite dish of noodles and perhaps the chance to save face with his wife and friends? The idea made her unaccountably sad. It was easy to hate traitors on paper. Far harder in the flesh.

Her mind raced through the possibilities, calculating her next move. Eleanor Gadlow was watching her intently, but her husband was now looking out into the garden, as though not especially interested in how she would respond. She cleared her throat.

'This party. Do you think the hosts would mind if I came, too?'

Gadlow turned to her and held her gaze for a fraction of a moment, then broke out his charmer's smile again. 'Of course not. You'd be our guest. Akib can drive us all there, and then he can take the two us on to the airport when the time comes. How does that sound?'

'Wonderful.'

At precisely ten o'clock, Udah Atnam walked through the front gates of the Harrisons' property and glanced at the gathering of cars parked in the drive. Most had diplomatic plates and small flags attached to the bonnets. The chauffeurs were smoking and talking among themselves.

He walked past them, down a narrow path in the grass that led to a servants' entrance. He parted a beaded curtain and entered the hot, steam-dense kitchen. The Harrisons' *amah* was working with members of Mister Kong's catering staff, preparing cold cuts and snacks. None of them paid Udah Atnam any mind, as he was dressed, like them, in a white smock with a checked blue and white sash and matching forage cap.

'It's like a paper-chase, only with crates of beer at the end of it. You really should try it if you ever get the chance.'

Rachel was half-listening as Simon Harrison explained to her the history and rules of the Hash House Harriers while she took tiny sips from the glass of advocaat he'd foisted on her. A blend of aromas – peanut sauce and chilli and coconut milk and fried meats – wafted over from the stalls in the garden, and somewhere over to her right a jazz quartet was playing an instrumental rendition of 'It Was a Very Good

Year'. Every few seconds she glanced towards Tom Gadlow, who was standing a couple of feet away, talking with Eleanor and a Spanish military attaché about the riots that had taken place between the Malays and Chinese the previous spring, and which had apparently led to the decision not to have any fireworks at midnight this year.

A mosquito whined in her ear, and she shook her head in an attempt to evade it. She was being bitten to death by the things. Harrison broke off his exegesis to commiserate.

'Ah, you're fresh blood. I'm afraid they love newcomers, although you do become hardened to it. How long are you out here for?'

'Oh, just a flying visit.'

He bowed his head. 'What a shame – both for us and the mosquitoes.'

She forced a smile, grateful for the kindness but now a little weary of the flow of expatriate charm. This was what she had to look forward to if she was ever posted to a Station, she thought. Christ. She caught Gadlow's eye and looked down at her wristwatch meaningfully. He broke away from his discussion, and she quickly disentangled herself from Harrison.

'We need to get going soon.'

'I know. Thank you for letting me show my face – I hope you can understand why it was necessary.'

She nodded, although she understood no such thing. But she was relieved nevertheless – he seemed to be taking his fate with a certain dignity. They were nearly there, and no Russians in fedoras had turned up to spirit him away on a freighter bound for Vladivostok. Only a few minutes to go now.

'I'm just going to grab my annual bowl of noodles, and then we can head off.'

She looked at him. A last-minute attempt to run?

'I'll come with you.'

They headed into the garden, towards the replica Chinatown.

Udah Atnam walked through the kitchen and into the narrow corridor leading to the dining room. Halfway along, he opened a door that had a card reading 'Staff Bathroom' taped above the handle.

He locked the door behind him, then took a small passport-sized photograph from his jacket. It was of a man, a European. He held it between two fingers and examined it for a few minutes. Once he was sure he had committed every aspect of the features staring back at him to memory, he tore the photograph into tiny pieces, lifted the seat of the toilet and dropped them, fluttering, into the bowl.

He reached behind the cistern and slowly pulled out a small dark wooden container resembling a cigar case. He clicked open the latch and removed the inner and outer barrels of a bamboo pipe. He fixed these together, then attached the small ivory mouthpiece that sat in an indentation in the case. He placed the assembled pipe inside a thin pocket that was sewn into the lining of his right jacket sleeve.

There was now just one item left in the case: a small dart. Its tip had been dipped in a mixture of strychnine and the boiled-down resin of an *ipoh* tree, and was protected by a wooden sheath. He made sure the sheath was clipped tight, then placed the dart in the pocket sewn into his other sleeve.

He stood, flushed the lavatory and walked back into the kitchen. On one of the counters he spied a tray of drinks. He picked it up and headed outside.

Rachel was panicking. She'd actually lost sight of Gadlow. The cardinal bloody sin. Sandy was going to kill her, string her up outside his office as a warning to others.

How had she let it happen? They'd been standing in line at his beloved noodle stall, and after she had given her order to the smiling stall-holder she had turned so he could do the same, only to find he'd vanished.

She had been paralysed for a moment, but then the magnitude of the situation had registered somewhere and she had started running through the small warren of stalls, searching for him among the party guests, of whom there suddenly seemed to be hundreds. Faces blurred into each other and snippets of laughter seemed to mock her as she rushed past, caroming into people. A babble of voices called out to her, in English, Malay, Tamil and who knew what else, and she felt her head spinning. Her sandals were slowing her down so she kicked them off, feeling the blades of the coarse grass digging into the soles of her feet as she did. He had to be here somewhere, he couldn't simply have disappeared . . . Through a cloud of steam she glimpsed a flash of pink.

There.

It was him. He was about twenty yards away, talking to someone. A servant holding a tray. Could it be a contact?

She started running towards him, abandoning her English restraint and knocking over people's drinks and plates in the process, her pulse racing as she tried to keep her panic from rising and focus on the figure ahead: white shirt, pink and green sarong, *get to him, get to him . . .*

A chit-chat scuttled in front of Gadlow's feet as he hurried through the stalls. He had to get out of the villa. If Kolya had received the message he'd transmitted that afternoon, there should be a car waiting in the street. If . . .

'Sir!'

Gadlow turned sharply, his shoulders tensing. A kitchen boy was standing near one of the *satay* stalls, beckoning him. Gadlow hurried over.

'Yes?'

The boy nodded in a small gesture of supplication. 'I have been sent to assist you.'

Gadlow peered at the boy in the darkness. 'By who?'

'Your friends in Moscow.'

Gadlow exhaled deeply as the relief flooded through him. Thank God. Kolya had received the message, and delivered. He wondered how they planned to get him out? Submarine? He had a brief stabbing memory of that first glimpse he'd had of the *Thule* from the beach in Tanjong Siang in 1945, and then the descent from its conning tower into the wardroom, the thick slabs of bread and English beer laid out on a vast white tablecloth like manna from heaven after all the years in the jungle. Well, no English beer would be waiting for him in Moscow, but he could live with that if he could only escape the jungle one more time.

He glanced behind him at the cluster of stalls. The bluestocking bitch from headquarters was pushing through the crowd and heading straight for him. He turned back to the servant.

'What about my wife – when will she be able to join me?'

The boy gestured that they step away from the lanterns that lit the maze of stalls. Gadlow followed him through until they emerged into the unlit part of the garden. The boy placed his tray on the grass and gestured at the slope, which led down to a wire fence. Gadlow nodded: there must be a way through to the street from there. He started negotiating down the slope using one hand to steady himself.

The dart thudded into the back of Gadlow's neck. He experienced a moment of realisation – the thought 'Kolya' flashed through his mind – before he grunted and fell forward, his knees hitting the grass and then his forehead joining them. Udah Atnam rushed towards him. He plucked the dart from his neck and slid it back into his sleeve, then rolled the man's body into the bushes and started walking back up to the house.

Rachel emerged from the stalls, her heart pounding as she scanned the throng of guests milling around the garden. She had lost him again. She saw one of the waiters passing and stepped forward to speak to him, but he wasn't holding a tray and didn't appear to understand what she was saying.

She glanced at her watch. They were going to miss the flight. What was the bastard playing at? She was about to return to the house to check there when she thought to look elsewhere in the garden – there was a lower tier to it. And what was that . . . a slash of whiteness glowing in the darkness?

She tumbled down the slope, her legs numb as she reached the bushes bordering the road. Gadlow's head was bent over his chest, as though he were sleeping. For a moment she thought he was – he had become drunk and taken a nap in the bushes – but then she kneeled down and tilted his chin back and saw his eyes had rolled up into the skull.

Footsteps padded behind her, and she heard Eleanor's contorted cry as she caught sight of him. Rachel would never forget that sound.

Udah Atnam walked at a brisk but steady pace through the kitchens. In the driveway, the chauffeurs were still smoking and talking among themselves. He passed them and walked through the gates, where he climbed onto a parked Yamaha motorcycle. It was a job well done, he thought, and he had repaid the debt.

He placed his helmet on his head, fastened the strap, and turned the key in the ignition.

1975

Chapter 5

A stream of notes travelled through the ventilation shafts of a small nightclub in the city's old quarter and drifted onto the maze of narrow alleyways. Peter Voers, a stout, crimson-nosed engineering salesman stumbling from a restaurant with colleagues, caught the notes on the air and recognised them at once: the opening bars of 'Night Time Is the Right Time'. Voers loved Ray Charles, and loved that song in particular. He couldn't resist.

The others in the delegation were heading back to the hotel: six hours of discussion on international drill-bit standards followed by some heavy Swedish cuisine could make even the liveliest executive drowsy. As they approached the turning that would lead them out of Gamla Stan, Voers announced that he fancied taking a stroll through the area and bid them goodnight. After a few friendly exhortations not to get into too much trouble, he began walking in the direction of the music.

He suddenly felt well disposed to the world, buoyed by the shafts of sunshine still creeping over the tops of the buildings and the melody drifting through the air.

After a few minutes he was sure he had located the source of the trumpet in a small street called Trångsund. About halfway down, he found confirmation in a poster stuck to a seventeenth-century buttress that read 'Jazz & Blues'. He handed ten kronor to a young man at the door, and with a nod was let past into a narrow hallway. It took a few moments for his ears to adjust to the abrupt rise in volume and his eyes to the enveloping darkness, and then he saw the flight of stairs and started descending. At the foot of it was a baize-covered door, which he pushed open.

The place was a brick-lined cellar packed with punters, most of whom were seated at small tables circling the stage. He made his way to the bar, glancing around to make sure nobody had followed him in from the street – no one had. The bar was staffed by a willowy blonde in skin-tight jeans and a beaded kaftan. Voers ordered a beer, paid the exorbitant sum for it, and found a spare table with a decent view of the stage.

The band had launched into another Charles number, a rendition of 'Drown in My Own Tears' played at a slightly faster pace than usual. They were a tight outfit: the lanky trumpeter, whose playing had pulled him in here, was in perfect lock with the drummer and bassist, both young men sporting sprouts of beard beneath their lower lips, while the singer, a silver-haired Swede wearing horn-rimmed glasses and a floppy beret, pounded a baby grand and sang his heart out in a creditable imitation of Charles' style.

But Voers was drawn most to the two backing singers at the rear of the stage, who were harmonising as well as he remembered from the record: unsurprising, perhaps, as both were *munts*. He smiled at the way his mind had leaped to the word, which he never used these days: his colleagues wouldn't understand it.

He had never liked the word himself, but had used it profusely in the old days to allay suspicions he was weak. Voers regarded blacks as inferior, but saw no contradiction in his love of rhythm and blues, nor in his attraction to black women. That they could sing powerfully and were often physically beautiful was undeniable – but that didn't mean they knew how to run a country, or that he wanted to hand over his to them. He had once made a joke on the subject to a couple of colleagues, but they hadn't appreciated it and some of the others in the unit had for a time openly questioned his commitment and principles as a result. So he had joined in their little games and used their sad names for the blacks. But he knew that he was above all that: his distaste was political, not personal.

He took a draught of his beer and savoured the coolness as it travelled down his throat, then turned his attention back to the singers. One of them was a little too plump for his taste, and her mouth overly rouged, but the other was stunning, with a perfectly oval face, almond-shaped eyes, and hips moving sinuously in time to the beat. Voers licked his lips as he took her in. He noticed that she had a mole just below her left eye, which reminded him of a young girl long ago, crouching in the darkness of a farm outside Bulawayo, her eyes widening as she realised what he meant to do to her . . . He froze as the realisation seized him. She didn't simply resemble that girl.

She *was* her.

He scrabbled around the table for some kind of leaflet or programme, but there was just a small card with the name of the group – 'Jan Karlssons Orkester' – and no further information. At the bar, the waitress was serving another customer, and it wouldn't be a good idea to draw any attention to himself.

He took another swig of his beer and looked at the stage again. Could he be mistaken? A trick of the light? No, it was definitely her. The same high cheekbones, now a little more refined, the same shape of the lips and nose, the long neck. He lifted his hand to his face and felt the small indentation beneath his chin where she had caught him with her kick all those years ago before fleeing into the night. She had been a strikingly attractive seventeen-year-old. That meant she would be twenty-seven now. She had become a beautiful woman.

The next realisation came not as a freezing moment, but as a warm glow that spread through his stomach. There wasn't simply an opportunity to exact revenge here. If he was careful, and if he was clever, this was a prize. But as soon as the thought had lodged in his mind, a cautionary note sounded. Not too fast. He needed more information than this. His table suddenly seemed far too close to the stage: he couldn't run the risk of her seeing him. As soon as the song ended, he found one a little further away and ordered another beer. It was a waiting game now.

Claire arrived home at just before two o'clock. Everything was quiet in the building, just the humming of a washing machine in the communal basement below – no doubt there would be a stern note from Fru Wallén on someone's door tomorrow morning.

She took the lift upstairs and quietly unlocked the front door, then slipped her shoes off and walked into the living room. Erik was asleep on the sofa, the left side of his face lolling on one of the cushions, a reading lamp next to him highlighting the flecks of silver in his beard. She leaned over and kissed him gently on the lips and he woke with a start. For an instant, fear registered in his eyes, and then they softened and he kissed her back.

'He's asleep.'

'What about—'

He placed a finger to her lips. 'He was an angel. And he ate and drank like a little king.'

She smiled.

'Let me just check on him.'

She tiptoed across the living room and carefully

opened the door to the small bedroom. A glow lamp hung over a wooden cot, inside of which a three-year-old boy was curled up in the foetal position, a thumb lodged firmly in his mouth.

She remembered how wildly he had been running around the same room a few hours earlier and smiled, relieved. One of Janne's backing girls had been taken sick at the last minute, and he had asked her to fill in for her. The opportunity had been too good to miss, but she had been stupidly torn about leaving the house for the evening. She hadn't been away from Ben for more than a few hours since his birth, and it had almost become a superstition for her: she had an irrational and almost paralysing fear that something terrible would happen to him the moment she turned her back, and began imagining all kinds of nightmare scenarios: his falling through a window, or being burned in the kitchen, or stumbling headfirst against a pair of scissors.

But once she was away from the flat, she had managed to hold the panic at bay. She had never told Erik about her singing, and had instinctively felt he wouldn't understand why she would want to do it again, so she had instead told him she wanted to meet up with an old friend who needed comforting after a messy break-up. A white lie. Not the only one she had told him, either.

Still, it had been worth it. It had been exhilarating to bask in the heat of the stage again, Per's trumpet blaring beside her, performing for an audience like she had done when she had first arrived in Stockholm, before Erik and before Ben. She had almost forgotten what the city looked like, as her life had been reduced to attending Ben's every need, especially as Erik worked night shifts twice a week. The two of them and this flat had become her bubble of existence, and when she'd walked into the club for the rehearsal she had momentarily felt like a visitor from another planet.

'How's Marta?'

Erik had come into the room and placed his arms around her waist. He rested his chin on her shoulder, staring down at their child.

She snapped out of her thoughts and turned to him. 'Oh, you know . . . she's Marta. She'll be fine.'

Erik was friendly, if a little remote, with her friends, but he had made no secret of the fact he found Marta Österberg insufferably self-absorbed. She worked for a local refugee organisation, which was where Claire had met her, but Erik thought she and her boyfriend were *bourgeois* playing at being radicals, which was harsh if not entirely untrue. Claire hadn't thought he was likely to check up on her, but she'd called Marta and warned her of their 'meeting' just in case. 'We went for a drink after dinner,' she added, suddenly conscious of the need to bolster the story – Janne had insisted on a celebratory round in the green room afterwards.

Erik smiled. 'Yes, I can smell it on you. Red wine?'

She nodded, and craned her neck up at him. 'I might even be a little drunk.'

'Oh, really?'

He leaned in and kissed her on the mouth. She drew away, flushed, and glanced back down at the cot. Ben was still fast asleep, his tiny chest gently rising and falling beneath the woollen blanket. She turned back to Erik.

'Are you trying to take advantage of me, Herr Johansson?' she said, her expression deadpan.

He gave her a mock-serious look and stretched out his hand. She followed him into their bedroom and drew the curtains, then stepped over to the bed and placed a hand inside his shirt, feeling the warmth of his chest.

In the street below, Voers considered his next move. Once the Ray Charles set had ended, he had waited outside the club until he had seen the girl – as he still thought of her – emerge from the artists' entrance.

He had been worried she might drive home or take a taxi, but instead she had walked to the nearby Slussen underground station: the network ran until three o'clock. He had followed at a discreet distance and bought a single ticket. It had been several years since he'd tailed anyone, but there had been a throng of young people making their way home to the suburbs after a night on the town, which had given him a lot of cover. He had stood at the far end of the carriage with his back facing her, watching her through the warped reflection of an advertisement for a modern art exhibition.

She had got off at Vällingby, and he had followed her out of the station and through a paved square surrounded by shops and concrete office and apartment blocks. He had taken up a sheltered position in the shadows outside a women's clothing store on one side of the square, and watched as she had approached a block of flats directly opposite. The block looked very much like those he had seen at a conference a few years earlier in East Berlin, *Plattenbauten*, but like many buildings in Stockholm it had been painted a bright shade of yellowy orange to mask the brutalism of the architecture.

Once she had entered the building, he had looked for signs of movement in the upper windows. Sure enough, about thirty seconds later shadows had flitted by on the second floor, and he had caught a glimpse of her at the curtains just before she drew them.

He had lit a cigarette then, savouring the taste of it and letting his pulse return to normal. Then he had started walking back towards the underground: there was nothing more to be done tonight. He would have to delay his flight tomorrow and rearrange his appointments for the next couple of weeks, but that was no great trouble. He knew where she lived now. He would hire a car, buy a decent camera, and stake out her place until he had photographs of her and anyone she was living with. His whole body was tingling with anticipation.

This was his ticket back in.

Chapter 6

Saturday, 12 July 1975,
Rhodesia–Mozambique border

The Unimog approached the outskirts of the camp at just after two o'clock in the morning and came to a standstill. A few moments later, the other vehicles in the column drew up behind it.

On a bench in the rear of the Unimog, Captain John Weale smeared a fresh coat of greasepaint on his face and hands. He considered the irony that he was disguised as a black man in order to capture black men. His father certainly wouldn't have approved, had he lived to see the day.

Weale was in command of a detachment of forty-eight Selous Scouts, the most secretive and deadly of the Rhodesian special forces groups. The regiment was named after the British game-hunter Frederick Selous, a fact of which Weale approved: his grandfather had fought alongside Selous in the Second Matabele War. Weale's great-grandparents had settled in Britain, but he'd lived all his life in Africa and regarded himself as entirely Rhodesian. He was proud of his grandfather's legacy, but since his country's declaration of independence from the Queen a decade before he'd come to hate the British with a fiery intensity that was second only to his hatred of the black terrorists fighting to wrest control from the minority white government.

Weale had joined the Scouts from the regular army within a few weeks of it being formed. The regiment's ethos was inspired by the British SAS, with whom several of its senior officers had served, either during the Second World War or in the Malayan emergency or both, but the selection process was even more gruelling: it took seventeen days, the first five of which required living entirely off the land at a training camp on the shores of Lake Kariba. On the fifth day, candidates were given the rotten carcass of a baboon as a reward for making it that far. The few who remained after that – usually around 10 per cent – were given the most meagre of rations to survive the rest of the course to supplement their diet of living off the land. A further four weeks' training followed, during which they were still monitored for suitability. Successful recruits therefore started out with a strong sense of camaraderie and great pride, as each man knew that the others had also gone well beyond the norms of human endurance and behaviour to become a Selous Scout.

Within the Rhodesian military the regiment had adopted the cover role of a reconnaissance and tracking unit, but in reality it was a counter-insurgency force. Its mission was to obtain intelligence on the terrorists, who were divided into two main groups, the Zimbabwe African National Liberation Army, ZANLA, and the Zimbabwe People's Revolutionary Army, ZIPRA. These were the armed wings of the black nationalist movements ZANU and ZAPU. The Scouts had become expert on the differences between them, as a large part of their job consisted of impersonating them in the field. To accomplish this, most members of the regiment were black: soldiers from the Rhodesian African Rifles whose salaries had been doubled for volunteering, and captured rebels who had been turned, or 'tamed'.

The black Scouts usually headed up small teams, making contact with rebels in the bush while the whites hung back. White Scouts operating in the field had to be fluent in at least one African language, and usually blacked up with burned cork or greasepaint and wore floppy hats and beards so that from a distance they too could pass as insurgents. Weale was fair-haired and ruddy-complexioned, but unless you were standing within a yard of him, he was now indistinguishable from the rest of the men.

The secrecy around the Scouts was to protect its methods being compromised, but also because impersonating the enemy in such professional ways was arguably against the Geneva Convention, even if the guerrillas rarely used established flags or uniforms. The Scouts' 'pseudo' teams had already captured dozens of rebels, and even when operations had failed had managed to sow confusion and paranoia among the 'terrs', as they referred to the guerrillas. In turn the guerrillas called them *Skuz'apo*, a Shona expression often used of pickpockets that broadly meant 'Please excuse me for having just slipped a knife between your ribs'.

Weale's current operation had involved weeks of planning at the Scouts' headquarters in Inkomo. Multiple reports from captured ZANLA members had led to the identification of a training camp a few miles from the border with Mozambique. Intelligence from another Scout unit indicated that several members of ZANLA's Central Committee were currently staying there.

The plan was simple: drive into the camp and capture or kill as many terrs as possible. Looking over his men, Weale was confident of their success. All were dressed as ZANLA terrs, down to the tiniest detail, and were armed with AK47s, RPD light machine guns and RPG-7 rocket-propelled grenade launchers. A Unimog led a column of Ferrets and homemade armoured vehicles known as 'pigs', all painted in ZANLA's camouflage patterns and with a few of their flags flying. Twenty-millimetre Hispano cannons were mounted on the front of the pigs, supported by twin MAGs on swivel mountings on the sides.

Weale gave the order for rations to be distributed, and the men ate in silence. After a few minutes, he looked at his watch. It was time. He gave the order and the convoy drove back onto the track. Twenty minutes later, they drew up to the main gates of the camp. Weale looked across at Corporal Sammy Oka, the man he had chosen to trigger the operation. Oka nodded, a gleam in his eye, and Weale nodded back in approval. Oka was quick, clever, athletic – one of the best. He clambered out of the back of the vehicle and Weale watched him run towards the boom, waving his arms wildly, just as they'd rehearsed dozens of times back at headquarters.

A few seconds passed and then two guards emerged from the hut to see what the fuss was about. Oka gestured frantically at the convoy.

'Let us through,' he said in Shona. 'We have casualties and need to get them to the clinic at once!'

The guards peered at the trucks behind him.

'Which camp are you from?' one asked. 'We've heard nothing about this.'

Oka had been expecting the question. 'We were on our way here but had no time to radio in – we were ambushed on the road. Comrades, open up, our men are going to die if they don't get medical attention very soon!'

One of the guards raised his machine-pistol and nodded in the direction of the convoy.

'Show us.'

Oka ran back to the front truck and parted the tarpaulin. The guard stepped forward and shone his torch. Several men were laid down on the flatbed, all wearing ZANLA uniforms and blood-spattered bandages. A few groaned with pain.

Convinced by the display, the other guard ran to the boom and raised it. Oka climbed back into the truck and the driver pressed his foot to the pedal. As the truck passed the boom, the bandaged men suddenly all stood, revealing their weapons, and fired through the rear of the truck at the guards, cutting them down. The convoy swept into the camp.

Chapter 7

He was walking down a passageway, the walls lit by candles set in sconces, and she was walking in front of him, dancing almost, wearing a white evening gown that clung to her figure, laughing as she looked back at him. White teeth, flowing hair. A beautiful young woman, her eyes only for him. But soon, he knew, she would be kneeling on a small spit of land, a pistol pressed against the back of her head, the hair matted to her scalp, sobbing with desperation and fear. He knew how it ended, because he had seen it before. It was always the same: the man with the gun didn't even flinch as he pulled the trigger, and then her cranium exploded and the spray of blood stained the water . . .

He woke, his body soaked with sweat. He opened his eyes. Claire and Ben were walking through the doorway of the bedroom. She was carrying a tray with a cake lit with candles, and both of them were singing:

'Ja, må han leva!
Ja, må han leva!
Ja, må han leva uti hundrade år!
Javisst ska han leva!
Javisst ska han leva!
Javisst ska han leva uti hundrade år!
Hurra! Hurra! Hurra! Hurra!'

Ben bounded onto the bed and wrapped his arms around him. 'Happy birthday, Pappa! You're halfway there.'

Claire laughed, placed the tray on the sideboard, and kissed him. 'Happy birthday, darling.'

He sat up and wiped the sleep from his eyes, banishing the nightmare. His birthday had in fact been six days ago, but he had altered it on his papers: if anyone ever suspected his true identity, keeping the same birthday could confirm it.

'Would you like to see your card, Pappa?'

'Of course I would.'

Ben took an envelope from the tray and handed it to him triumphantly. Inside was a card he had made himself, with '*Grattis Pappa!*' scrawled over a stickman illustration of him.

'It's lovely.'

Ben grinned with pride. 'Would you like your present now? Mamma bought you something expensive.'

He looked up at her. 'Really? You needn't have.'

'It was nothing.' She handed him a small blue box with a red ribbon around it. On it she had written 'To Erik – with all my love, Claire'.

He unwrapped it, to accompanying cries of encouragement from Ben. It was a small black leather wallet, and he recognised it as one he had looked at in a department store a few months earlier when they had been shopping for clothes for Ben. She must have spotted his interest in it and bought it when his back was turned. He opened it up and saw that she had pasted a photograph inside. It had been taken at the hospital when Ben was just a few hours old. They were both looking down at Ben, cradled in Claire's arms. He leaned over and kissed her.

'I love it. And I love you. Thank you.'

She beamed and returned his kiss. He blew out the candles and began to carve the cake, watched keenly by Ben.

Chapter 8

Sunday, 13 July 1975, Salisbury, Rhodesia

Major Roy Campbell-Fraser, known to his men as 'The Commander', was the first into the room after the security check. He poured himself a cup of tea and looked through the windows down at Jameson Avenue. The jacaranda trees were bare on the street, and he missed their lilac bloom. Cars and bicycles passed by in a gentle flow, metalwork and chrome gleaming in the morning sun.

An athletic 52-year-old with crew-cut white hair and the stark features of a buzzard, Campbell-Fraser was the commander-in-chief of the Selous Scouts. Once a month, he drove down to Salisbury for a briefing with the prime minister and his counterparts from the Central Intelligence Organisation, Special Branch and the army.

He glanced around the boardroom. How quickly one tired of the pomp and circumstance, he thought. He remembered how thrilled he had been the first time he'd had an audience with the PM two years earlier. Now it was an irritation. The security measures conducted before each meeting were time-consuming and tedious, and had been made worse since Special Branch had discovered a plot by the guerrillas to blow Smith up with a grenade as he left the building. Campbell-Fraser itched to be back in Inkomo, planning operations against the enemy instead of engaging in bureaucratic nonsense. He was particularly anxious to learn how Johnny Weale was getting on with his team's raid of the ZANLA training camp near the border with Mozambique. The last he had heard they were just about to go in. He thought of the boys in the operations room manning the radio sets at that very moment, sweat prickling their temples as they listened in wait for the call signs to come through to confirm that all was well. That was where he should be.

The others had now entered the room, and Campbell-Fraser took his place in a chair at the large leather-topped conference table. On the wall facing him was an oil painting of two Spitfires taking off, a none-too-subtle reminder of the prime minister's war record for the British, his having flown for their air force. The painting had been a gift to the PM from a group of British supporters a decade or so earlier. A lot had happened since, although there were still a few in Britain who believed in white Rhodesia. The rest of the room was decorated in the usual heavy government style: wall-to-wall red carpet, curlicued lintels over the door and, despite the heat, thick curtains in a hideous floral pattern framing the windows.

Smith was the last to arrive. He was wearing a dark tailored suit with a white shirt and a maroon tie. Campbell-Fraser thought he looked a very long way from the war. He took his place at the head of the table and nodded at the men seated around it.

The main item on the agenda was the discovery by the spooks that the South African government was secretly sounding out ZANU and ZAPU about the possibility of a new round of talks on 'the Rhodesian question'. The men listened intently as Willard Shaw, the chief of the Central Intelligence Organisation, presented the evidence. Shaw was a pudgy sunburned man with wisps of dun-coloured hair parted so severely to the left that it gave his entire face a lopsided look. Campbell-Fraser generally didn't judge men by their appearances – it could be fatal to underestimate people on such a basis – but he hadn't trusted Shaw from the moment he had set eyes on him. His instincts had proven correct. In the early days of the Scouts, he'd worked closely with the CIO on operations, but he had soon found Shaw obstructive. Campbell-Fraser's guess was that it was simply because the other man didn't like a newcomer infringing on his intelligence-gathering patch, but in his view this attitude was potentially dangerous for the security of the country.

The animosity between them had reached boiling point three weeks earlier, when Shaw had informed him that in March two of his operatives had assassinated Herbert Chitepo, one of the founders of ZANU and the head of its military high command, with a bomb placed in his car outside his home in Lusaka.

Campbell-Fraser had been furious that the operation had been carried out without his knowledge, but also that the CIO men – both former British SAS officers – had planted evidence at the scene that had suggested someone in ZANU could have been responsible. Shaw had thought this a brilliant way to sow dissent within ZANU, which had split from ZAPU several years earlier following power struggles within the movement. But Campbell-Fraser felt the manoeuvre had been politically naive: he would have either clearly incriminated specific targets within ZANU or left it open enough to suggest ZAPU might also have been involved, thereby creating a much wider field of suspicion.

Instead, Shaw had fumbled it with a halfway house, with disastrous results. One of ZANU's founders, Reverend Ndabaningi Sithole, had left to form a more moderate group, while a firebrand figure within ZANU, Robert Mugabe, had consolidated his power by accusing rivals of collusion in the assassination. Far from fostering divisions, Shaw's unsanctioned operation had made ZANU stronger, more militant and, worst of all, united behind Mugabe, who Campbell-Fraser felt was much more of a threat than Sithole had ever been, let alone the murdered Chitepo.

Now Shaw was crowing over his outfit's latest

intelligence haul. Through an asset in Lusaka, they had obtained a copy of a secret memorandum drawn up by the South Africans and Zambians. Grandly titled 'Towards the Summit: An Approach to Peaceful Change in Southern Africa', the document proposed 'a new spirit of co-operation and racial harmony' across the region, with Zambia, Botswana and Tanzania pledging to use their influence to find 'a political solution in Rhodesia'. In return, South Africa would withdraw its military assistance from Rhodesia and pressure Smith to release more political prisoners.

Photostats of the document had been handed around the table, and Smith grunted with barely suppressed anger as he read through it. According to Shaw's source, the document had been written by a special adviser to Zambian president Kenneth Kaunda in collaboration with the head of the South African spy agency BOSS, Hendrik van den Bergh, who was very close to South Africa's prime minister, John Vorster.

In recent years, Vorster had launched a charm offensive on black African leaders in an attempt to ease the international isolation South Africa faced as a result of apartheid. His idea was to rebuild diplomatic and trade links by exploiting Western fears of a Soviet takeover in the region, presenting himself as a statesman who could come to peaceful terms with his black neighbours. This stuck in Smith's craw, as during the war Vorster had been a general in the Ossewabrandwag, a South African paramilitary group that had been so pro-Nazi it had even adopted their salute. It was there that Vorster had first met and befriended his spy chief van den Bergh. Smith hated the British with an implacable intensity, but they had at least been on the right side together during the war with Hitler.

Despite his white supremacist past, Vorster had succeeded in persuading some that he had changed his spots. Chief among them was Zambia's Kaunda, who had referred to one of Vorster's speeches as 'the voice of reason for which Africa and the world have waited for many years'. The wider international community had been slower to proclaim Vorster a new messiah of moderation – the United Nations had even suspended South Africa from the General Assembly – but he wasn't giving up yet. Since the collapse of Portuguese rule in Mozambique, he'd redoubled his efforts, and he had South Africa's old ally Rhodesia firmly in his sights. Slowly but surely, he had applied pressure on Smith, taking advantage of the fact that Mozambique's fall meant he now depended much more on South African help. Vorster had already scaled back his military support to Rhodesia and forced Smith into releasing several guerrilla leaders from prison.

Smith closed the dossier and sighed. The document confirmed his worst fears about Vorster. If he didn't play by South Africa's rulebook, they would withdraw more military, weapons and oil shipments, isolating Rhodesia further and making life easier for the guerrillas. Smith felt as if a noose was tightening around his neck, and unconsciously loosened his tie.

Campbell-Fraser was the first to speak.

'This is sickening reading, Willard, but it seems very broad. Do you have any intel about specific plans for talks?'

Shaw shook his head. 'Just whispers at the moment, I'm afraid. But several credible sources have told us they're discussing it. One asset has told us Vorster offered the Zambians a million rand to host the talks and give them more credibility.'

Smith gave another snort of anger. He stood abruptly and wandered over to the windows, looking down at the scene Campbell-Fraser had earlier.

'Well done on getting this, Willard,' he said. 'I think we can be in no doubt about Vorster's game here. He wants to set up talks and then go public at the same time as he informs us of them. That way, if we agree to take part he gets the glory of having arranged it, but if we refuse we'll look like we're turning our back on negotiations for no good reason in the eyes of the international community. Teaming up with Kaunda would make us look even worse for turning it down, as he would have gone the extra mile to reach out to a black leader. What a devious little bastard.'

He turned to face the room, and nodded at Shaw. 'I need you to keep a very close eye on this. Apart from their going behind our backs, I don't like being blackmailed, especially by an ex-Nazi. And despite all the platitudes about peace and harmony in this –' he picked the document up from the table and waved it scornfully – 'I don't think we're at a point where another summit would be fruitful. None of the current crop of black leaders is up to the job, as they're all much more concerned with securing their own positions than any sort of reasonable and mature policy regarding the future of this country. More to the point, none of them is prepared to budge an inch right now. They have too much to lose with their own people, and they know if they concede even the tiniest thing to us they could be deposed, or perhaps worse. And of course we can't get any agreement on the big sticking points without wider black approval.'

He pursed his lips in a sour smile, and everyone in the room understood the reason for it. The last serious attempt at talks had been arranged by the British four years earlier, and had ended in farce. All sides had signed up to the idea that anything agreed at the negotiating table would then have to be ratified by a vote from the country at large. An agreement had eventually been reached – majority, i.e. black, rule was postponed for around a century – but unsurprisingly this had fallen apart as soon as it had been put to that same population, who had rejected it virtually *en masse*. Since then, there had been little appetite for another round of talks.

Smith turned to Shaw again. 'You mentioned at our last meeting that new rifts might be emerging in ZANU's leadership. Perhaps that's something we should be cultivating, in the hope of forcing a new attitude?'

Shaw nodded. 'I'll consider how we can do that, Prime Minister, and report back at our next meeting.'

'Excellent.'

They moved to the next point on the agenda. Campbell-Fraser listened in silence. His expression was neutral, but inside he was seething. ZANU's leadership was now looking more united, not less, and it was largely thanks to Shaw's own meddling. And he recognised a ball being kicked into the grass when he saw it. Smith was discussing vague long-term possibilities, when what was needed was immediate and concrete action. Familiarity had bred Campbell-Fraser's contempt for the empty routines of bureaucracy, but also for the prime minister personally. Outside Rhodesia, Smith was widely viewed as a monster, a cold-blooded racist who was refusing to budge on the matter of majority rule. In international circles, 250,000 whites leading a country with over five million blacks was manifestly unfair and needed to be rectified. But the country's white minority, naturally, viewed Smith very differently. He was their protector and indeed saviour: 'Good Old Smithy', standing up to the wily, hypocritical Brits and the rest of the world.

Campbell-Fraser didn't subscribe to either view. There was something twisted about Smith, he thought: in public he came over as all hail-fellow-well-met, the decent, principled chap, but close-up he cut a creepier figure, with skin like sandpaper, a bulbous nose and one glass eye staring out at the world with disdain.

Campbell-Fraser had no reason to doubt Smith's patri-
otism – he'd seen him at a garden party the previous
summer, drunkenly singing along to the rousing pop
hit 'Rhodesians Never Die' with tears welling in his
eyes – but he detested the way the man had painted
himself as a war hero for political ends. Through his
own research, Campbell-Fraser knew what most
didn't: that Smith's military career had been unexcep-
tional. He'd simply crashed a couple of planes and
been injured as a result.

Having observed him at close quarters for two
years, Campbell-Fraser had concluded that Smith
might once have been a half-decent if unlucky pilot,
but was now just another ineffective politician. He
could certainly be stubborn, but he was also self-important and unimaginative, and far from being
intransigent Campbell-Fraser felt he had been far too
soft when negotiating with the blacks. He'd kowtowed
to Vorster's demand for him to free terrorist leaders
from prison, and was now surprised that they might
try to seek concessions through talks. What the hell
had he expected? From Campbell-Fraser's vantage
point, Smith's image as a strong negotiator was a
sham, and he was losing the diplomatic battle in
imperceptible but nevertheless real increments. If it
carried on this way, one day soon they'd all wake up
and find the blacks in charge.

No, Campbell-Fraser thought, he no longer had any
sense of loyalty to Ian Smith. His loyalty was to
Rhodesia, and he would do whatever it took to ensure

it remained under white rule – 'in civilised hands', as Smith himself had once put it. And Campbell-Fraser was prepared to work without Smith's knowledge, or even against him, if he felt it was in Rhodesia's best interests.

Chapter 9

Paul Dark lit a cigarette and raised it to his mouth. The moment the tip glowed, he inhaled deeply and leaned back on his elbows. He squinted in the afternoon sunshine, taking in the view that stretched out before him. The hillside was dotted with squares of brightly coloured blankets, each of which was home to a Swedish family with young children – like small islands of social democratic prosperity, he thought. A few feet away, Ben was running around pretending to be an aeroplane with another boy, while Claire was seated cross-legged next to him on their blanket, one finger entwined in her hair as she browsed the arts section of *Dagens Nyheter*, a pair of sunglasses perched on her head. He leaned over and found his own pair, which he pushed tight against the bridge of his nose.

So here it is, he thought. Fifty. Half a century.

He realised with a start that he was now older than

his father had been at the time of his death. He took another drag of the cigarette as he let the thought sink in.

He didn't deserve to have outlived him; indeed, he was lucky to be alive at all. If it hadn't been for the Hanssons, he would have died out on the ice in the Finnish archipelago six years earlier. Even with Gunnar's intervention, had the lighthouse happened to be just a few miles further out he would have lost too much blood by the time they'd reached it. It had been touch and go as it was: Gunnar had wanted to evacuate him to a hospital on the mainland, but Helena had persuaded him that it would take too long so they had instead called in a doctor from a nearby island, who had given him a strong shot of morphine and cleaned and dressed the wound. Eventually, he had set up a makeshift operating table on the ground floor of the lighthouse, and removed the bullet.

Once Dark had regained consciousness, he had explained that he and Sarah were British diplomats who had escaped from imprisonment in Moscow, only to be chased by Soviet secret police across the border. They asked how it was that he spoke Swedish that sounded local to the region, and he told them his mother had been Erika Nordstedt of Åbo.

They hadn't questioned his story much further after that. He was one of them, a Swedish-speaking Finn, a Nordstedt no less, and Gunnar had seen the Russians try to kill him with his own eyes. That was enough. Dark had asked them not to inform the coastguard about him, because the presence of an unidentified foreigner might reach the ears of the Russian consulate in Mariehamn and renew the hunt for him, and they had agreed. For this, and much else, Dark would be forever grateful.

It had taken him six weeks to recover. In the meantime, he had drunk Helena's tea and her fish soup, and slept as much as possible, although he had often woken in the night, shaking and feverish. Gunnar discreetly arranged for Sarah to be buried in the island's cemetery in an unmarked grave, and late one night Dark accompanied him there so he could pay his respects. Otherwise he had kept to the upper floors of the lighthouse: even on an island of forty inhabitants, it hadn't been easy to keep his presence there a secret.

As soon as he had regained some measure of fitness, he had offered to repay the couple's kindness by helping out with the work around the lighthouse until he fully recovered, repairing broken machinery and lending a hand with the cooking and cleaning. They had agreed, and this arrangement had continued from one day to the next, until he had gradually become an integral part of their lives and nobody had mentioned that, physically at least, he was healed. They were a quiet, contemplative couple, and he'd sat in companionable silence with them through the long winter nights as the storms raged outside, playing backgammon and drinking rosehip tea or, when they had ordered it from the mainland, whisky.

He'd spent nearly eight months on Utö before

deciding it was time to leave. The Russians had evidently believed him dead when they had left him, and there had been no indication that they had revised that view. After so long undisturbed, it seemed likely that the Service would by now have come to the same conclusion. Although the Hanssons had protested at his announcement, he felt he was intruding too much and couldn't offer them enough in return. He had no right to ask them to shelter him for the rest of their lives – they had done more than enough in saving it, in burying Sarah, and in looking after him for so long.

He had weighed his options carefully. He wanted to live somewhere he wouldn't be reliant on anyone else, and where he had a decent chance of never being discovered. After much deliberation, he'd decided that Stockholm would make a good starting point. He had visited it several times with his parents and knew it as a small and rather anonymous city, and as he spoke Swedish he felt he should be able to find some form of work there and carve out a quiet, unobserved existence.

So early one June morning, Gunnar had taken him to the harbour in Mariehamn and bought him a ticket for the ferry across to Sweden. 'You are welcome back any time, Englishman,' he had said with a sardonic smile, before giving him the briefest of claps on the back and clambering down into his boat. Neither man had showed the other the tears welling in his eyes. And Dark would never know that Helena had woken to watch them leave from the lighthouse, but hadn't been able to bear the idea of saying goodbye to him.

Dark had found work within a few hours of the ferry arriving in Stockholm. On the crossing he had realised that some of the passengers were Swedish dock-hands heading home after a weekend cruise, and he'd approached their table and asked if they knew of any available casual work. They'd given him the name of a firm with offices in Värtahamnen, the city's main port, and he had headed straight there from the ferry. By the end of the afternoon he'd been paid thirty kronor to carry some crates onto a tanker. Enough for a slice of bread, a cup of bitter coffee and a room for the night above a local bar.

The next day he'd found similar work, and the day after that, but after a couple of weeks he had become anxious. Too many people came in and out of the bar and he felt exposed, so he'd moved to a basement squat in Södermalm populated by middle-class drop-outs and artists, none of whom had been in the least interested in who he was or where he'd been.

He soon realised that he hadn't been alone in his assessment of Stockholm's advantages as a hideout. As a result of a government prepared to look the other way, or at least not too closely, left-wing radicals from around the world had flocked to the city as a safe haven, attracted by the combination of a flexible attitude towards refugee status and a generous welfare system.

After a few weeks, Dark discovered that there were also some more serious operators around, on both the left and right. In April 1971, a fascist Croatian group had strolled into the Yugoslavian embassy and assassinated the ambassador, and since then there had been a spate of hijackings and bank robberies across the city.

For Dark, the fact such groups were living in Stockholm was an opportunity. Criminals and revolutionaries usually came with a retinue: couriers, explosives experts, forgers. After a few months of saving his wages, he set about trying to find documents in case he was ever discovered and had to escape in a hurry.

It had been a delicate process, as it had involved dealing with people whose true agendas were difficult to determine. The Soviets indirectly sponsored several leftist groups in Europe, and the slightest of missteps might mean word getting back to Moscow that he was still alive. Dark had made cautious progress, frequenting a succession of grubby cellars and marijuana-laden parties to get the lie of the land, until eventually he had become an accepted part of the background in the underground scene.

Towards the end of the year, he had heard whispers about a group of Palestinians who had set up base in an old villa in one of the quieter suburbs, where they were said to have an arsenal of explosives and sophisticated electronic equipment in the basement. These were the big boys: well-trained professional freedom fighters, or terrorists, depending on your particular 'bag'. In the circles Dark was now hovering around, the Palestinians were most people's bag.

He had bided his time before approaching one of

their acquaintances and mentioning that he was looking to obtain some supplies. Nothing big: just a couple
of forged passports. He had felt his way forward until
that winter he had finally been given – casually, a joint
waved in the air by a sallow young man wearing a
denim suit and pointed cowboy boots – the name of
an elderly gentleman in Gamla Stan, who had given
him a series of perfect documents in exchange for
three weeks' hard-earned wages. Dark had used one of
them under the name of a Swedish-speaking Finn, Erik
Johansson, to obtain from the tax authorities a *personnummer*, the ten-digit identification number that was
the key to living legally in Sweden.

In the following months, he had supplemented these
documents with other material, including a Zastava
M57 pistol, the brutish-looking Yugoslavian copy of
the Tokarev TT-33, and one of Husqvarna's discontin-
ued bolt-action rifles, both of which he'd bought
through the Palestinians' circle. Along with three more
passports and a bundle of cash, he had buried it all in
a hide in a cemetery on the outskirts of the city.

Confident his counter-measures were as secure as he
could make them, he had slowly slipped into a routine
existence. The biting winter hadn't helped – more than
a few times, he found himself wondering why he hadn't
fled to the Bahamas or Monte Carlo, like the jewel
thieves in Hollywood films. Stockholm was comfortable but conformist, and its long dark nights seemed to
drain all meaning from life. He was finally free from the
British and the Russians – but for what purpose?

In the evenings, he'd wander around the city looking at people, trying to fathom what drove them, inspired them – what they were *doing*. Since the war, his life had been an unbroken sequence of deception, and it had been disorienting to let go of the daily machinery of the espionage world: the dead drops, assignations, photographed documents and intense internal manoeuvring that had accompanied it all. Over the years he had become accustomed to the pressure weighing down on him, the ever-present dread that at any moment he might be discovered – with it removed, he discovered that a part of him strangely missed it. All he had to contend with now were his memories, which weren't pretty. In prison, he'd managed to stave them off with dreams of survival, escape, even revenge. Now he had nothing to focus on but a stretch of cold grey days in Sweden until death.

And looming over everything was guilt: for the lives he had taken directly and for those that had been taken as a result of secrets he'd betrayed. One evening after work, he had found himself walking in the diplomatic quarter of the city and passed the British embassy. He'd been oddly gripped by the urge to walk in and give himself up. It would be so easy, and would solve so many problems. 'My name is Paul Dark.' And then it would all be out of his hands. A secret trial, a long sentence . . . well, so? He could cope. And it would be just: he'd be repaying his debt to society, as they said. He'd stood across the street for several minutes, on the verge of making a move, but in the end he'd turned away and taken the bus back to his tiny flat, and the soul-crushing despair that was weekday evening Swedish television.

With the return of spring, he had found a way to keep his blackest thoughts at bay. He'd volunteered at a soup kitchen near Centralstation, and although he knew it was hardly a suitable penance there was some small comfort in seeing gratitude in the face of a hungry stranger. And it was there that he'd met Claire, the beautiful Zambian woman who now sat on the blanket beside him. Her passion for life had snapped him out of his limbo, and he'd been smitten. The city had thawed under her guidance, and life had begun for him again.

That summer he had moved into her flat in the suburbs, and soon after she had raised the topic of children. The thought had terrified him: he was already anxious enough at the possibility of her being used as leverage if anyone were to discover him, and had transferred his emergency cache from the cemetery to below the floorboards of her building's basement as a result. Sometimes it was her face he saw in his nightmares, the gun placed to the back of her head instead of Sarah's.

He had known that he owed her an explanation of his past so she could make her own choice about whether to stay, but he'd reasoned that simply telling her might itself put her at greater risk. And so he had said nothing, and then she had become pregnant and it had been too late. The whole world had changed, and sometimes he hardly recognised himself. Now he woke in the night, panicking that Ben might have unaccountably stopped breathing, only to pad over to look at him and see his soft pudgy cheeks squished up against the pillow, the gentle rise and fall of his chest, the tiny curled fingers, the sheer immense wonder of him – and the fact that he had brought this wonder into the world.

He turned his face to the sky. A cloud had moved across the sun, throwing a shadow over their section of the park, and he suddenly felt very old and out of place, the winter feeling creeping over him again. Yes, he had survived, he had outlived Father, he had fallen in love and started a family. But he was still a man on the run, and he always would be. He had no right to smoke cigarettes in the sunshine, watching a boy who called him 'Pappa' and giggled when he rustled his head against his stomach. He should be dead, or rotting in a cell, or at the very least pissing his days away in a frozen little flat in Moscow. He remembered Donald Maclean's sad long face, the expression of bitterness he'd had in his eyes . . .

'Are you okay, darling?'

He took Claire's hand in his, intertwining their fingers. 'Yes, fine. I was just thinking.'

'About how decrepit you are, no doubt. *Du gamla, du fria.*' He smiled. It was the opening line of the national anthem – 'You ancient, you free' – and she often used it to tease him. 'Are you having a nice day?'

'Lovely.'

He took off the sunglasses, tossing them on the blanket, and glanced down at his wristwatch. It was five o'clock – soon time to start heading home. He looked over at Ben, who was now pretending to be a charging bull, and as he did he noticed a man on one of the benches a few yards away, holding up a camera in their direction. A thought hit him: *Was he taking photographs of them?* And then another followed: *Or of Ben?*

Dark leaped to his feet, dropping his cigarette and stamping it out on the grass. The man was middle-aged: sturdy, with a reddish nose and sandy-coloured moustache, wearing a checked shirt, denim shorts and a large sunhat. He didn't flinch when Dark approached, just kept pointing his zoom lens at Ben. Dark hovered over him.

'*Vad gör du?*'

The man looked up, a puzzled expression crossing his face. 'I'm sorry, I don't understand Swedish.'

Dark couldn't place the accent – Dutch, perhaps. 'What are you doing? Why are you taking photographs of my son?'

Puzzled turned to startled. 'What do you mean? I was just trying to get a picture of the willow warblers.' He pointed towards a group of tiny birds pecking at food a few yards from Ben. Dark glanced down at the bench: on it sat a rucksack and a small hardcover book bearing the title *Birds of Europe*.

He nodded curtly, apologised for the trouble, and headed back to Claire, who was peering at him anxiously.

'What was that about? You ran off very fast.'

He shook his head. 'Nothing. Just a misunderstand-ing.' He pointed at the clouds. 'The sun's going in. Why don't we head home?'

She looked at him, her eyes searching his for trou-ble, then folded her newspaper and stood, propping her hands against her back and arching it. 'If you like. Time for some coffee, perhaps.'

Dark crouched down and started gathering up Ben's toys. When they left the park a few minutes later he looked back and saw that the man had moved from the bench and was crouched on his haunches by the birds, still clicking away. Was it a ruse? It was possible – it was an old surveillance trick to pose as an amateur snapper, and the book on the bench had seemed rather neat. Or was he overthinking, becoming paranoiac? Yes, he thought, it was surely nothing. Just a tourist photographing some birds.

Chapter 10

Thursday, 17 July 1975, Salisbury, Rhodesia

In a suite on the first floor of the Meikles Hotel, Major Roy Campbell-Fraser listened as Pete Voers explained how he had conducted his surveillance on the woman and her child in Stockholm.

'What about the boy's father?' he asked when Voers had finished. 'Still in the picture? Another *munt*?'

'No, a Swede. I got some of him as well.' Voers removed several glossy black-and-white photographs from the briefcase on his lap and handed them to Campbell-Fraser, who held each up to the light in turn.

'Looks like a hippy.'

'An old one. He's fifty. Name of Erik Johansson.' Campbell-Fraser looked surprised and Voers gave a ferrety grin. 'I made some enquiries about him through the tax office, posing as an accountant. It's all public there, no questions asked. He works for a haulage firm in the centre of the city, and volunteers for a charity a few nights a week.'

'Do you know which nights?'

Voers took a small notebook from his trouser pocket and flicked through the pages.

'Tuesdays and Fridays. He usually starts at five and comes home at around midnight.'

Campbell-Fraser continued to examine the photographs. Then he gathered them together into a tidy bundle and placed them on a side table.

'Thank you for this, Peter. I'll have to look into it more closely, of course, but it certainly seems interesting. We know how to reach you if need be. That will be all.'

'Sir.'

Voers saluted curtly and left the room. Campbell-Fraser picked the photographs up and lowered himself into an armchair near the window to look through them again. He was excited by the possible ramifications of them. He hadn't indicated this to Voers, partly for security reasons and partly because he was unsure what to do about the man. He'd dismissed him from the regiment a year earlier when he had discovered he'd raped a guerrilla's wife in a raid on one of the villages across the border with Mozambique, and as a result had been in two minds about whether to meet him when he had called his office that morning claiming he had valuable intelligence. But if the information was correct – *if* – it was undeniably a breakthrough.

After a few more minutes of contemplation, Campbell-Fraser packed the photographs into his briefcase and left the room, switching off the lights. He took the stairs down to the lobby, paid for the room, and walked out into Cecil Square to find his car.

Chapter 11

Joshua Ephibe grasped his ribs under the thin sheet and shivered at the sight of the man who had just walked into the ward. It was Sammy Oka, whom he had last seen four years earlier at the training camp in Mgagao. Oka had been one of the more impressive recruits, and Ephibe had earmarked him for fast promotion in his passing-out report. Now he was one of his gaolers. He looked in good shape, too, his muscular physique encased in a camouflaged T-shirt, faded khaki shorts and plimsolls, all of which presented an accurate impersonation of their own haphazard 'uniform'.

Oka approached the bed and smiled – for all the world as though they were meeting on the street on a Sunday morning in the marketplace, Ephibe thought.

'Hello, Joshua. It's been a long time.'

Ephibe didn't respond, but under the sheet his hands were trembling. How dare this man pose as a friend? How many operations had he destroyed?

Appearing oblivious to the snub, Oka looked

around the room until he caught sight of a wooden stool beside one of the basins. He carried it over to the bed, set it down, seated himself on it, and faced Ephibe again. 'How are you feeling? Have they mistreated you at all?'

'They' had treated him remarkably well, but Ephibe wasn't about to admit it.

'Where were you injured – your kidneys, wasn't it?'

Silence again. Oka took a pack of cigarettes from a pocket and shook two into his hand. He offered one to Ephibe, who finally erupted in anger.

'Why the hell are you here? Did they send you to try to persuade me to turn traitor like you?'

Oka replaced the proffered cigarette in the pack, then lit the other one, rocking back on the stool as he took the first draught. His face had assumed a puzzled expression.

'A traitor? But who have I betrayed?'

Ephibe looked at him in disgust. 'The movement, of course. *Chimurenga!* Zimbabwe!'

'Ah yes. "Zimbabwe".' Oka said the word as if it were the name of a land in a children's fairy tale. 'Well, my family sees things a little differently. Yes, I'm married now, with a little boy: David. You must come and meet my family. If you want to, of course.'

'I'm not a traitor.'

Oka ignored him. 'Clarissa and David live here while I'm out in the field. Her parents, too. Nobody can touch them, and my boy gets to be with his family, safe, secure, warm and well fed. There is a very good school here and, as you can see, the best medical facilities.' He indicated the state-of-the-art intensive care unit next to the bed.

'And who pays for all this?'

'The Scouts. I realise it is a blow to your pride to be captured, Joshua, but there's nothing to be ashamed of. We aren't the devils you make us out to be, you know. We're just soldiers. Many of the whites have become like brothers to me.' He ignored the expression on Ephibe's face. 'Yes, we're brothers fighting together, black and white alongside each other, for a common cause. There is no discrimination whatsoever – we eat and drink together every day, every night. And we get proper equipment, not like the crap you're using. You've already seen some of what we have: machine-pistols, grenades . . . whatever we need. And our leaders fight beside us. They don't sneak off to Botswana or Zambia to spend the money their supporters have raised for weapons on champagne and whores. My family is safe and looked after, I'm paid well—'

Ephibe looked up sharply. 'They pay you, too, to murder your own people?'

Oka slowly blew smoke from his mouth, watching as the cloud circled above the bed. The doctor had confirmed that Ephibe was still a smoker. Oka's pleasure in the cigarette was genuine, as Weale forbade any of the team from smoking on operations – the scent travelled easily.

'Listen, Joshua, I asked if I could come and visit

93

you, because I saw your name on the list of captured men. For old times' sake, you know? And because you were one of the better instructors. Of course I am paid. We are all paid. We're soldiers.' He clicked his teeth as though in thought. 'You know, this "Zimbabwe" you still believe in. It's just a dream, my friend – or rather a nightmare. You think those fools can run a country? Not a chance. They're at each other's throats already, and they'll be worse if their revolution succeeds. They're bloodthirsty, the lot of them.'

'So they're savages? *Murungu* trained you well.'

Oka shook his head. 'No, not savages. Ordinary men corrupted by power, leading others who have turned bloodthirsty through a lack of discipline. Through fatigue and desperation from fighting a war they cannot win. You know this as well as I do. What do you think would have happened to me if I had been captured by your men?'

'You would have been killed, of course.'

'Yes. At last we are being honest with each other. I would have been shot in the back without a trial, then left to rot where I fell. Compare that to your situation at the moment, Joshua. You were captured at a terrorist camp in possession of illegal weapons, in the very act of training terrorists to attack this country. You've committed treason by the laws of this land, and yet here you are talking to me. Why are you not dead?'

It was a question Joshua Ephibe had already asked himself many times.

'Not only are you not dead in a ditch,' Oka

continued, 'but you are lying here in this bed, with doctors and nurses waiting on you day and night, and with your own family on their way to see you.'

Ephibe's head jerked up. 'My family?'

'Didn't they tell you? They're sending a team to Caponda to get them. Your sister and your parents will be here in a couple of days, and after you've spent some time together they will stay in some very nice accommodation here while you are out in the field. That is, if you want to, and can pass the training.'

Ephibe sighed. 'I told you – I'm no traitor.'

'I see.' Oka pushed back the stool, retied the laces of his plimsolls in a few swift gestures, and stood. 'Well, it's a shame you see it that way. Of course, you will be hanged under the Law and Order Maintenance Act. I'm disappointed, Joshua: I told my comrades you were precisely the calibre of soldier we were looking for. It seems I was mistaken. If you're determined to die for a hopeless cause, I can't stop you. I'll let them know your decision. I don't think the team has set out for Caponda yet.'

He replaced the stool by the basin and walked out of the room, leaving Joshua Ephibe alone with his thoughts.

Chapter 12

Captain John Weale spent as little time in his office as he could, but was pleased with its setup. When he had first taken the job he'd made the mistake of not decorating it at all, but he had soon realised that the captured terrs had felt like they were being interrogated in a cell, so he'd persuaded the Commander to ship in a comfortable armchair, a few rugs and some soft lighting. He felt he now had the right balance: enough warmth to loosen them up, but not so much as to obscure the importance of his questions.

He walked to the filing cabinet in the corner of the room. It was filled with captured documents, photographs, and other snippets of information, all of which could be cross-checked. These question-and-answer sessions rarely elicited any useful intelligence, but they were often a helpful gauge of the current state of the terr's loyalty. Would he be prepared to identify his former commander? How about his best friend? So far, Joshua Ephibe seemed willing to help, having identified many of the other men they had captured and given their ranks and roles in the ZANLA structure.

Weale took a new dossier from the cabinet. 'Might be nothing,' the Commander had said when he'd handed it to him a couple of weeks earlier, 'but Pete Voers thinks he's spotted Charamba's daughter in hiding in Sweden. We need confirmation. Show it around.'

Weale was wary of using intelligence from Voers, who had left the regiment under a cloud, and didn't understand why Campbell-Fraser was interested in Charamba anyway – they knew where the man lived in Lusaka, but he was a thorn in the side of ZANLA and ZIPRA alike so they'd deliberately left him alone. But it wasn't his job to question the Commander's orders.

He walked back to his desk and removed a sheaf of photographs from the dossier, spreading them in front of Ephibe. All of them showed a park on a sunny day, with most of the people in them rather glamorous-looking whites. But every photograph also featured a striking young black woman with a pair of sunglasses on her head.

'Recognise her?'

Ephibe leaned forward to examine the image more closely, and let out a small gasp.

'Yes, that's Hope Charamba. She's older, but it's her.' He looked up at Weale. 'Where did you get this photograph?'

'Never mind that. Are you sure it's her?'

'Yes, I'm certain. I grew up with her. I was her first boyfriend, back in secondary school. We were inseparable.'

Weale nodded, and lifted his pen.

'Tell me more.'

Chapter 13

Friday, 22 August 1975, Stockholm, Sweden

Paul Dark stood perfectly still. With his index finger, he drew the curtain by a fraction of an inch.

The car was parked on a street east of the square, just beyond the children's playground and largely obscured by a row of elm trees. But it was definitely the same car.

He had spotted it three days earlier, when he had driven Ben and Claire in their VW Beetle, Ben to the kindergarten and Claire into town to the offices of *Aftonbladet*, where she worked as a picture researcher. He had caught it only by chance – on stopping at a traffic light he had glanced in the rear-view mirror and seen a muddy green late-model Opel Kapitän. For no particular reason, it had brought to mind one he'd seen several years earlier, in a traffic jam in Nigeria. And now here it was again, parked fewer than a hundred yards from his flat.

He walked to the other side of the room. It could

mean only one thing, he decided: he'd been spotted. Some time ago, too, probably – he remembered with a flush of self-recrimination the 'bird-watcher' in Haga Park a few weekends ago. What a bloody fool he'd been to ignore the signs. Not that he could have done much anyway: once you'd been spotted, you stayed that way. Was it the Russians, he wondered, or the Brits? Well, it hardly mattered. Either way, the game was up.

The question was what to do about it. He lowered himself into the armchair to think it through. Yes, someone had spotted him – but he had been very careful with that curtain. Even if binoculars had been trained on it at that very moment, they wouldn't have been sure that he hadn't simply been drawing them closer. And other than that, he hadn't reacted at all to the car. Conclusion: they didn't yet know that he had realised he was under surveillance. Could he use that?

The problem was he had no idea what they had planned. Was it a snatch team? A hit squad? And what was their time-scale? He'd spent fifteen days tracking Cheng before he had made a move on him in Hong Kong all those years ago. How long had they been watching him for – before the park, even? And how long did they plan to continue to do so before they made their move?

These were unanswerable right now. At best, they were in a stage of provisional surveillance, perhaps even still uncertain whether he was who they suspected.

At worst, they'd break into the flat in the next thirty seconds while he was sitting here thinking about it.

No, he decided, that was unlikely. It was only five o'clock and the shops were still open – people were milling around in the square and on the surrounding streets, and the underground station was starting to spill out commuters arriving home. Far too crowded for either a snatch or a kill. If they were planning to move on him today, they would at least wait until dusk.

What were his options? He could run, of course, but the same disadvantage they had also worked against him. The whole area was too exposed: even if he took the fire escape they'd see him the moment he landed. There was no way out of the building without them seeing him. He was like a rat in a trap.

Even if he could get out of the building, what about Claire and Ben? Ben was asleep in his bedroom, and Claire would be home from work soon. He couldn't leave them behind. Who knew what the men in that car might be capable of? Taking his family would be the obvious way to stop him running, and he didn't think they would hesitate to use it.

He would stay in the flat, he decided. They might not come tonight, and they might not come tomorrow. But sooner or later they would come, and he'd be ready for them.

But first he had to get Claire and Ben to safety.

He carried out a rapid but thorough search of the flat, looking for any sign of disturbance. He checked above and below every surface, and detached the telephone receiver to check for bugs. When he was satisfied that everything was clean, he went down to the basement and prised the holdall from the space beneath the floorboards. He unzipped it, and the blued finish of the ridges on the butt of the M57 gleamed in the dim light. Beneath it lay the reassuring shape of the Husqvarna, and next to that were the passports and several thousand kronor wrapped in rubber bands.

He closed the bag and carried it upstairs, then went back to the telephone and called a number he had long since committed to memory. Perhaps someone else would pick up, he thought. Perhaps they had moved, or died.

'Hello?'

Dark exhaled, and felt his shoulders relaxing marginally at the familiar voice.

'Gunnar. It's the Englishman.'

'Is it her?'

'I think so. It's hard to tell from here. Can't we move any closer?'

'No.'

Sammy Oka glared at Joshua Ephibe, fidgeting in the passenger seat next to him, and cursed himself for having persuaded him to switch sides.

For his part, Ephibe was equally ambivalent about having been 'tamed'. Thanks to the Selous Scouts' medical facilities and the food in the mess his ribs had fully healed and he felt physically fitter than he had in years, since his first days as an instructor. Oka had also delivered on the promise that he would see his parents again. But while it had been wonderful to reunite with them after so long in the field, the hurt of leaving again so soon afterwards had been almost more painful than if he hadn't seen them at all. But he knew it was too late to back out. Although Oka and the others had given him several loyalty tests, including sentry duty at the barracks in which he'd been given what he had correctly guessed was an unloaded rifle, he had no weapon now. Oka clutched a nine-millimetre Makarov pistol in his right hand, and although it wasn't aimed at him Ephibe had no doubt it would be if he tried to escape or hinder the mission in any way. And, of course, his parents were being looked after only so long as he co-operated. In effect, they were now hostages. And after the operation was over, he would have been drawn even deeper in by having taken part in it – even if he deserted, his old comrades would shoot him on sight. He had nowhere to call home now but the Selous Scouts, and the sooner he got used to the idea the better.

He lifted the binoculars to his eyes again, and at that moment the woman turned towards the street and he saw her face straight on. His stomach coiled in on itself.

'It's her.'

Oka looked at him.

'Are you sure?'

'Yes.'

Oka whistled to himself. He picked up the Pye Pocketfone and held down the button.

'Leopard One, this is Leopard Two. We have visual confirmation of Target One entering the building. Over.'

She knew something was wrong the moment she entered the flat. Then she saw the drawers askew in the bureau and the holdall on the floor and her pulse started racing. Erik was standing by the window. He walked to her and they kissed, but he drew apart abruptly and she saw his face was stark and drawn.

'Darling, what is it? Tell me!'

He took her hands in his, then breathed in deeply.

'Everything's fine. Ben's asleep. But something's come up – something urgent. It's going to be a little difficult and confusing, but I need you to trust me completely. Can you please do that?'

She nodded. 'Of course. But what—'

'I'll explain everything later, I promise. But we don't have the time now. I've packed some clothes for you and Ben. In a few minutes, you're going to go downstairs with him and get in the car. You're going to drive to Värtahamnen, as fast as you can without drawing the attention of the police. It's a short drive, just twenty kilometres away. As soon as you get there you're going to go to the port and find someone with a motorboat – look for a sturdy one with a lower deck – and pay them to take the two of you to the

Finnish archipelago, to a small island called Utö. I've marked it for you.' He took a tourist map from the coffee table and placed it in her hands.

She made to speak again, but he put a finger to her lips. 'This will be more than enough for the journey and anything else you might need on the way.' He peeled off the notes and held them out. She took them, staring at him with incomprehension.

'Where did you get all this from? And where are you going to be?'

'Here. I need to deal with something. I hope it won't take me long. Once you get to Utö you'll be met by a couple, Gunnar and Helena Hansson. They know me, and they'll look after you and Ben for a few days. You'll be safe there. Now can you go and wake Ben up while I make sure everything's ready?'

She looked into his eyes for a long moment. 'I need to know more about what's going on, Erik. I need to know how you got all this money.' There was an accusatory edge to her voice – they could have used it, for food, or clothes for Ben. Then her voice softened. 'You can tell me. I won't judge you. I also have secrets. I think—'

He grabbed her by the shoulders, his face suddenly so fierce that for a moment she was frightened of him. The outline of his skull was visible beneath his skin and the muscles in his jaw were clenching and unclenching manically. She winced from the pressure of his hands, and he took them away.

'I'm sorry. But we just don't have time.' He looked

into her eyes, and his expression was now pleading. 'You and Ben need to get out of here *now*. We can talk about it later, when we're all safe. But please. You need to leave.'

She looked at him for a moment, then nodded and walked towards Ben's bedroom.

Captain John Weale sat in the kitchen of the flat on the southern side of the square and stared at the clock on the wall. It was ten past six. He was tired and hot and uncomfortable in his own skin, ironically because it was his own skin, which he hadn't fully inhabited for a very long time – even when back in Inkomo, Scouts changed their field appearance as little as possible to help maintain their cover mentality – but he had now bathed and shaved off the beard he had spent nearly six months growing in the bush and felt almost effeminate as a result. He'd also thoroughly scrubbed away the greasepaint and make-up, although he was still finding bits of it in his ears and in his hairline.

But his discomfort was also because of this operation. He was trying to keep at bay the nagging thought that it was a mistake, but it kept wriggling back into his mind. The Commander had been his usual confident self about its chances, but this was a far cry from kidnapping a few terrs in the bush, or even across the border in Botswana. They were in the middle of a Western European capital, and because of the Scandinavian latitude the best they could hope for was twilight. The fact he had to operate unseen made it even more frustrating: he didn't even have a sightline to the targets' flat in case he was spotted.

He was also finding it increasingly irritating to be cooped up with Pete Voers, whom he had always found to be small-minded and boorish. He'd banished him into the living room so he could concentrate, but he could occasionally hear him shuffling around the place, and each movement was like nails dragged across a blackboard – he was used to being able to control every movement his men took, but Voers didn't take orders well.

Still, Weale thought, he had to admit the man had done a good job of setting them up, especially as he'd done it in just a few weeks. Usually, putting together a safe house like this would have involved a cell of five or six and taken a few months. Voers had been working with just one other man, a Selous Scout who spoke some Swedish as he'd once been married to a girl from Gothenburg, but had nevertheless managed to find a flat just around the corner from the target, and which had three entrances to boot.

Weale was working with a four-man team, the minimum possible for such a job. The weak point was Joshua Ephibe, the terr they'd captured in the raid near Mozambique and turned, but they needed him as a spotter for the girl and Weale had every confidence Sammy Oka could keep an eye on him. The other two members of the team were Corporals Abel Makuba and Peter Tandi, both highly experienced and trusted officers. Makuba had recently been part of a team that had abducted a ZIPRA official in Botswana, while Tandi was an expert marksman, and had spent some time in Europe as a youth.

For cover, Pete Voers had established locally that he was the manager of a jazz band on a small Scandinavian tour, and they'd flown into Arlanda eight days earlier with instrument cases in hand on expertly forged passports. Weale was a Brit named Frederick Collins, supposedly a booking agent, while the others were Tanzanians. The jazz band was good cover for a group of black men in an overwhelmingly white city, and it also gave them a good reason for irregular movements in and out of the building.

Voers had bought clothing locally so they would blend in. Weale's slacks and shirt were both a little too close-fitting for his own comfort, and it was peculiar seeing the men dressed in European fashions after so long in the bush in camo gear, but even there Voers had picked well – nothing too shabby, but nothing too flashy, either.

The safe house itself had also been well selected. The block of flats had only two other tenants, one of them a middle-aged businessman who worked in the city centre and the other a self-employed electrician. Neither was home much, and the cell members had quickly established polite but distant relations with them, jokingly promising not to rehearse in the building.

Voers had paid the rent in cash, and had also bought

cars from a second-hand dealer in the area and, from a contact in the north of city, several Makarovs with the numbers filed off, which they had stored in a lock-up garage less than a mile away. They had used the guitar cases to bring them into the flat. So Weale had to hand it to Voers: he'd done a thorough job in a short period of time. But he nevertheless couldn't wait until Sunday, when the man was due to travel on to Copenhagen and leave them in peace.

Weale glanced at his watch. It was time to check in. He reached for the Pocketfone and held down the button.

'This is Leopard One to Leopard Two – what's the current situation, over?'

He removed his finger and waited. There was a screech of static, and then a tinnier version of Sammy Oka's voice burst into the room.

'This is Leopard Two. Targets One and Two are still inside the flat with Hippy. Over.'

Going by Voers' schedule, the boyfriend should already have left for his shift at the soup kitchen. Why hadn't he? Weale didn't want to ask more questions than necessary – Oka knew what he was doing. He hoped he did, anyway.

He pushed his anxieties aside.

'Report back as soon as you know more. Over and out.'

Ben was still wiping sleep from his eyes as his parents ushered him into the hallway of the flat. He looked up at his father as Claire helped him put on his shoes.

'Pappa, aren't you coming with us?'

Dark crouched down and smiled at his son. 'No, I have to stay here for a short while, but I'll come out and join you very soon. Look after Mamma for me, won't you?'

Ben nodded solemnly. 'Will I have to be brave, too?'

Dark forced a reassuring laugh from his lips. 'I don't think so. But if you do, remember what we always say. You might *look* like a little boy –' he stretched out a hand and placed it gently on Ben's chest – 'but in here . . .'

'I've got the heart of a lion. I know, Pappa.'

Ben had always been small for his age, and it was advice Dark had given him in his first week at kindergarten, repeated often since.

'Good. You'll like the island, I promise. Some friends of mine live there. Now before you go, do I get a hug?'

'Leopard One, this is Leopard Two. Targets One and Two have left the building, and are heading for their car. Please advise, over.'

'Any sign she might be on to us? Over.'

There was silence for a few seconds, then: 'She's carrying a shoulder bag, but it doesn't look substantial. Over.'

Weale closed his eyes and considered the information. It was tricky. It was risky to move now – there were far too many people around. They had decided to move at eleven if she was identified, and barring an emergency that was when they would do it. The bag might mean she had spotted them, or simply that she was on an errand – going shopping for groceries, for example – and she'd taken the child along because the boyfriend had insisted, or perhaps because she wanted to calm him down. Weale remembered his daughter's temper tantrums at that age, before things had gone sour between him and Mary, and how he would drive her around the farm in the Jeep until she'd fall asleep. So it was probably something like that.

On the other hand, it might just be something else. He pressed the button and leaned into the micro-phone.

'Leopard Two, stay in position for the moment. Leopard Three, follow her at a discreet distance and report every five minutes. Over and out.'

Dark watched from the window as Claire bundled Ben into the Beetle and accelerated down the street. By the trees, the Opel remained in place.

He drew the curtain and sighed with relief. They were away, thank God.

He looked around the room, which suddenly seemed desolate without them. A few of Ben's stuffed toys were lying in the middle of the floor, and he picked them up and put them in his room. Then he walked into the kitchen area and found the bottle of *akvavit* he had bought from the government shop a few months earlier. It was strong stuff, reminiscent of the

Czech haymakers his old boss Templeton had once favoured – perhaps that was what drew him to it, a hair-shirt reminder of his past.

He cleaned a shot glass in the sink, poured himself a large portion, and knocked it back. It went down smoothly enough, the herbs filling his mouth, but it was like dousing a sauna with water: you had to wait a second or two for the full impact. And there it was, starting with a pleasing heat and then rising rapidly until he grimaced and wondered if he hadn't overdone it – the back of his throat would now burn for the next ten minutes.

Well, good. Pain was good. Pain was welcome.

He poured another dose, then walked back to the living room. He took the rifle out from beneath the sofa, then seated himself in the armchair and set the glass on the side table next to it. Pain was good, but he didn't want to get drunk. He had to stay alert. But the glass would keep him company: the glass and the rifle.

He sat there, ruminating on this, his throat torn. Best not to think at all. Focus on the sounds, and on the changes in sound. *Focus*.

She looked across at the map on the passenger seat and took the turning Erik had indicated. Once she was on the main road, she glanced in her mirror towards the back of the car. Ben was asleep, his head tilted back, his mouth agape and his left eye ever so slightly open. Keeping one hand on the wheel, she fumbled in her bag with the other. She found the pack of Prince and, in a practised move, slid a cigarette out, lit it from the lighter on the fascia and took a deep draught.

The trembling in her lips slowly abated, and her head began to clear. She had been so caught up with Erik's insistence that they leave that she had barely had time to consider what was happening. For a dreadful moment when she had come into the flat she had thought he had discovered her past and was leaving her, but it hadn't appeared so after all and she had agreed to follow his instructions almost blindly. But now she was away from the flat her initial questions returned, with a few new ones. What the hell had he been so afraid of? He had been desperate to place her and Ben out of harm's way, it seemed. But why?

Who was *he* running from?

'This is Leopard One. Please report on the situation, over.'

'Leopard One, this is Leopard Two. All quiet here. Hippy's lights are now out. Over.'

'Stand by for new orders. Leopard Three, do you read me, over?'

There was a crackle of static and Corporal Abel Makuba's voice came on the line.

'Leopard Three. She's just taken a turning for somewhere called Värtahamnen. We may soon be out of range. Over.'

Weale had already spread out the large map of the city on the kitchen table, and after a few seconds he had located Värtahamnen. 'It's a harbour. She could be on to us and planning to catch a boat. How busy are the roads? Over.'

Makuba looked out of the window at the traffic, and the tankers and cranes of the port coming into view ahead. 'Fairly busy. Over.'

'All right, use your discretion. But if she gets on a ferry, get on it after her. If it's some other form of boat, find someone in the harbour who you can pay to follow her. But only do that if it looks to be absolutely necessary, otherwise you might have the coastguard on your tail. She can't be planning on going very far, and eventually she'll be somewhere there aren't many people around. Call me when you can. Do you read, over?'

'Loud and clear. Over and out.'

Weale placed the intercom on the table and took a breath. After a moment, he picked it up again, switched channels and told Sammy Oka to follow the other car to Värtahamnen.

Dark walked to the window. He had avoided checking the curtain in case the repeated movements were registered, but it had now been some time since Claire had left with Ben. He pushed it aside with one finger.

The Opel had gone.

Why had they left? A horrid thought crept into his mind, and lodged there.

What if it wasn't him they were after – but Claire?

He walked back to the armchair and sank into it, the taste of vomit rising in the back of his throat.

I also have secrets.

Christ, what had he done? He looked at his watch. It had been two hours and fifty minutes since they had left. He might already be too late. He picked up the empty shot glass and hurled it across the room, letting out a cry of anger and despair as it smashed against the wall.

Stay calm, he told himself. Think of a plan, then enact it. He had to get to Utö, and there were only two ways there. By boat, as he had told Claire to go – or by air.

And air was quicker.

It was his only chance to make up the time, but even then he would have to be fast. He took the M57 and the passports from the holdall and placed them in his jacket, then raced down the staircase and out into the square. Most of the shops had closed, but the fruit and vegetable stalls and fast-food kiosks were still open, and there were plenty of people around: teenagers laughing, children licking ice-cream cones, pensioners seated on benches. Pigeons strutted around the fountains like sergeant-majors at a passing-out parade. By the cinema, a young man was parking his motorcycle and Dark ran towards him, waving his arms. When he was very close, he drew the gun from his jacket. The man's eyes widened in fear and he dropped the bike and ran.

As she came into Värtahamnen, the screech of seagulls and the smell of fuel woke Ben up, and he started crying. She switched the radio on and turned the dial, looking for some music to soothe him. She went past a drama of some sort, an exchange of urgent male voices, then with a start realised they were speaking in English and quickly dialled back to it. The voices were sharp and had the tinny quality one heard on frequencies used by taxi drivers and the police.

'*Target One is approaching the harbour now. Over.*'
'*Has she seen you, over?*'

Her entire body froze, gooseflesh forming on her skin, and almost without thinking she jerked her neck back to check the road behind her. The voices on the radio were unmistakably those of Rhodesians.

And they were talking about her.

'What are those men saying, Mamma?'

She glanced in the mirror at Ben.

'Nothing, darling. It's just a story in English. We'll be there soon.'

She drove down a ramp and onto the asphalt of the pier, her eyes flitting between looking for motorboats and the cars in her rear-view mirror.

Dark skidded to a halt in the skirting area outside the main terminal of Bromma airport. Once he had found the signposts, he started the motorbike up again and rode it down a narrow concrete passageway towards the flying school. The reception area was in a large Nissen hut and he braked the bike, climbed off, and ran into the building. A young woman in a smartly pressed white blouse was seated behind a marble desk, strands of bright blond hair emerging from beneath a beret with the flying school logo fixed to it.

'Do you have any helicopters on the premises?'

She stared at him, taking in his frantic look. 'Just the one, sir.'

'Where?'

She pointed out the window towards a hangar, and Dark made out the front of a Bell Jet Ranger. 'You have to book, Herr . . . ?'

But he was already running back out of the hut and heading towards the hangar.

Corporal Abel Makuba tapped Peter Tandi on the shoulder and pointed. A few hundred yards ahead, a red Volkswagen Beetle was parked beside the pier, its rear wheels skewed at an awkward angle.

Makuba drew his weapon, and Tandi took the car down a gear.

'Wait!' shouted Makuba as they came up by the Beetle.

It was empty, the key still in the ignition and the back door not fully closed.

The men jumped out. Makuba was the first to see the motorboat speeding from the shoreline.

He reached into his jacket pocket and felt for the wad of Swedish notes.

Ben was finally asleep on a bunk below deck. He'd had a tantrum about getting in the boat, but had finally become so tired he had dropped off again. A bottle of *välling* from her bag had done the trick – she'd been trying to wean him off the wheat-based milk for months, but now wasn't the time to worry about that.

When she walked out on deck, she found the fisherman she had hired looking through a pair of binoculars at the waves behind them. He seemed to be focused on a grey speck in the middle distance. He handed her the binoculars and she peered through. The speck came into focus, and she saw it was a motorboat of a similar size to their own. She handed the binoculars back and asked him what was going on.

'I think they might be following us.'

She took a deep breath. 'Can we go any faster?'

He grimaced. 'Not really.'

'Try anyway, please. Have they gained on us at all?'

'Not as far as I can tell, so it could be nothing. Or it could be that they're waiting for us to land.'

Paul Dark looked down at Utö, glittering in the twilight. He was still several miles away, but he could make out the jetty and the lighthouse. As he approached he saw that a large motorboat was moored to the jetty, and a man he didn't recognise was on the deck. A few agonising seconds passed, and then Claire emerged, clutching Ben in her arms, and he felt the relief flood through him.

The motorboat turned and headed back the way it had come, trailing a thin wake of surf behind it. Then Dark registered another disturbance in the waves, and his eyes followed it out until he saw the other boat, which was fast approaching the jetty. His heart heaved again, and he pushed the stick forward and started to descend.

Claire and the other man were now running towards the lighthouse, Claire slowed down by having to carry Ben in her arms. The second boat reached the jetty and a group of men disembarked. They wore black clothing and face masks, and one of them started firing up at him with a machine-pistol. Dark swerved out of the way and came in again, lower this time, and he noticed that the men were also wearing gloves. Then he realised that they weren't gloves, but that it was their skin – they were black men.

One of them threw a grenade into the air and a few seconds later it exploded below him, buffering the helicopter off course and sending spasms through Dark's neck as he crashed into the side of the cockpit. He righted himself and pulled back on the stick. Once he had managed to steady the helicopter, he stuck his head out of the window and looked down again.

Now the men had reached the entrance of the lighthouse, and Dark fought a feeling of helplessness as he watched them enter it. He had been so intent on getting here that he hadn't really considered what he might do once he had. He had thought he would be able to land on the jetty, but now he saw that the idea was madness: five winters had taken their toll on it and the strip of wooden planks looked much thinner than he remembered. The roof of the lighthouse was far too narrow, and the only other alternatives were to try to land on the water or to run aground on the rocks, both of which could easily kill him. The jetty was his only hope, but could it take the weight? He slowly started to bring the helicopter down vertically, craning his neck muscles so he could see below to position the skids directly over the planks.

In the corner of his eye he caught a blur of movement by the lighthouse – the men were coming out. One of them held Ben, who had started screaming, and the others had Claire, who was doing the same, her face twisted with fear as she looked up at the sky, searching for him.

Dark watched with horror as Gunnar and Helena came running out behind them, waving their arms. One of the men holding Claire turned and fired at Gunnar, hitting him in the chest. As he fell, a volley of further shots peppered him. Then there were more shots, and Helena fell too, her body and Gunnar's now suddenly horrifyingly still as they lay next to each other.

The men reached the boat and stepped aboard with Claire and Ben, then set off in a wide arc, leaving a wake of surf churning behind them as they headed back the way they had come.

Dark looked down and realised with a jolt he wasn't going to be able to land the helicopter: he was coming down too fast to judge the angles correctly and it was going to hit the jetty. He unstrapped his belt, grabbed the pistol from his jacket and dived out of the cockpit, stretching his legs as far as he could to clear the rocks surrounding the jetty.

He came to the surface with his head pulsing from the shock of the impact and the cold. The M57 had fallen out of his hands, and he couldn't see it anywhere. He wiped his eyes and blinked up to see the landing skids crump into the rear of the jetty, and then the tail rotor tipped back and unbalanced the rest. He went back down and swam towards the rocks, pushing against the weight of his clothes. He scrambled ashore and limped over to where Gunnar and Helena lay. Both were dead, their blood staining the ground. Seagulls wheeled overhead, shrieking.

Dark looked back at the jetty and felt the heat as the rear of the helicopter caught fire. A few moments later, an explosion rocked him onto his back.

When he sat up again, he thought for a moment he was hallucinating, as he heard the sound of rotors and saw the silhouette of the helicopter emerge, totally intact, from the smoke of its own explosion. Then he saw that it was a different colour, orange and green: the Finnish coastguard had arrived. A voice shouted down at him through a loud-hailer and men in dark fatigues rappelled from the cockpit to where he was crouched. They removed the rifles strapped to their backs and pointed them at him. He saw himself reflected in their face visors.

Dazed, he placed his hands above his head. His mind was still on the motorboat speeding away from the shoreline back towards Sweden, and he was wondering whether he could somehow reach the coastguards' helicopter and catch up with it. But even as he thought it, in the pit of his stomach he knew that it was useless. He'd come too late, and they were gone.

Ben and Claire were gone.

Chapter 14

Claire woke into darkness.

She was lying on a low cushioned bench, her hands and feet tied tightly with rope and her mouth bound with tape. The rocking motion beneath her and a throb of pain in her left bicep reminded her of what had happened: she had been dragged on board a boat, and one of the men had sedated her with a needle.

She heard a muffled whimper from nearby, and knew instantly that it was Ben – no doubt that was what had woken her. She sat up and hopped on her buttocks towards the sound. It seemed to be coming from an adjacent room. It didn't sound like he was in pain, but she winced inwardly. Would they feed him, and if so, what? Suddenly, his whimpering stopped. Milk? A biscuit? Or had they perhaps given him another shot with the needle?

Her eyes were slowly adjusting to the darkness and now she could see the door of the small room. She moved towards it and pressed her back against it, but it was, of course, locked. She lay on the floor and tried to clear her head.

Someone had found her. It had been her greatest fear, the background noise to her life for nearly a decade, ever since she had fled Rhodesia. She had been escorted across the border to Zambia by men loyal to her father, and from there she'd been placed on an aeroplane to Geneva with a wallet filled with dollars and a false Zambian passport. Looking up at a departure board in Geneva airport, she had chosen Sweden as her next destination – one of her fondest memories from childhood was reading the Pippi Longstocking books her father had brought back from a trip to London, which had taken her to a distant fantasy-land that had blossomed in her mind.

On arriving in Stockholm she had claimed refugee status under her new identity. That first harsh winter hadn't at all resembled the carefree summers of pancake-making of Astrid Lindgren's books, but she had nevertheless felt a little like Pippi, dreaming of her father the pirate on the other side of the world. And then she had met Erik, and everything had changed.

Yes, now she had finally forged a new life for herself, found someone, and started a family with him, someone had found *her*. She didn't know who they were, but she presumed they were enemies of her father. He'd had plenty of those, but she had been happy to place all that in the back of her mind. In Rhodesia she had been a girl whose only responsibilities had been to her father's household, and she had barely thought for herself. In Sweden, she had studied at night school, explored the worlds of art and literature, begun a career at a newspaper and eventually settled into society, earning her own keep in the process. She hadn't forgotten her past, but she had grown up and become someone else. She felt guilty at the realisation, but part of her resented not just the kidnappers but her father for having dragged her back into his world. She chided herself immediately. Of all the selfish reactions to have! After all he had done for her.

Her thoughts turned to how Erik had reacted. The more she pondered it, the more it seemed to her that his insistence she and Ben leave Stockholm was important. He had acted almost as though the men were after him – indeed, that must have been what he had believed. In a strange way, the realisation didn't surprise her as much as she thought it would. Something un-communicated had always lain between them. She had presumed it was the shadow of her own past that hung in the air, that he could sense she was withholding information from him, but now she knew she had deluded herself. He had been hiding secrets from her, too, and somewhere deep down she had known it. She had simply never let the idea form in her mind for fear of sabotaging their relationship.

He would be suffering, too, she knew, for the mistake he had made. And he would do everything in his power to put it right, she was sure. He would come and get them.

He had to.

Chapter 15

They searched his clothes, removing his sodden jacket, then directed him to the ropes and up into the helicopter. One man took the stick, while three others sat in the rear of the cramped cockpit and covered him with their rifles.

Dark did as he was told with a mounting sense of despair. Every second that passed was taking him further from Claire and Ben, but his entreaties that they turn round because his girlfriend and son had been kidnapped and were heading in the opposite direction were met with silence: either they couldn't understand Swedish, couldn't hear him over the noise of the engine, or were pretending not to. Their expressions were invisible behind their visors, and it was like shouting at statues. After a few minutes he fell silent himself, his thoughts spinning helplessly.

He had never panicked before. He'd been frightened, even terrified, many times, but he had never experienced sheer, blind panic. Now he found he couldn't think coherently for more than a couple of seconds before he was flooded with the reality of what had happened again. And it was his fault. It was his stupid, thoughtless, arrogant fault that Gunnar and Helena had been murdered, and that Ben and Claire were now in the hands of . . . whom? He had no idea.

The helicopter juddered along the coastline. After around twenty minutes, the outskirts of Helsinki hove into view below. In normal circumstances, Dark would have found it beautiful, the trees and lakes bathed in the dusk. But now the sight sickened him. He knew he had to formulate a plan, fast, but he was coming up empty. Surrounded by this sort of firepower, there was nothing he could do.

The helicopter landed on the roof of a large brick building, which he guessed was the coastguard's headquarters. They hurried him out, and he watched as the pilot took off again: another avenue closed. He was taken down a metal staircase into a boxlike room, where they positioned him in front of a camera on a tripod. The flash blinded him momentarily, and then they were on the move again, the men frogmarching him down another flight of stairs and along a narrow corridor, past a succession of heavy steel doors with small grilles in them.

They unlocked one and pushed him into it. Concrete walls, a metal-framed bed and a bucket in the corner. The sharp vinegar reek of urine rose into his nostrils. He asked if he were under arrest, but they ignored him and marched back out. The door slammed shut, and he banged on it with his fists and called out in protest until he realised it was futile.

Chapter 16

John Weale paced the floor of the living room, glaring at the members of his team.

'Is there any chance they might survive?'

Peter Tandi shook his head. 'But we had no choice. They could have stopped us taking the targets.'

'Two elderly lighthouse-keepers?' Weale laughed bitterly. 'Now we're going to have the whole of Sweden looking for us.'

'Finland,' said Makuba. 'We were in Finnish territory, and the helicopter that picked the boyfriend up headed that way.'

Weale stopped pacing and fixed his stare on him, unimpressed. 'So the Finns *and* the Swedes will be looking for us.'

He walked to the trestle table by the sofa and picked up the bottle of Hine VSOP that Voers had bought from the government shop when they'd moved in. He had been looking forward to toasting the success of the operation with the team, but now that idea seemed spoiled. He found a glass anyway and poured himself a measure, then tilted his head back and gulped it down. The others watched him in resentful silence, as he knew they would, and as he had wanted them to. Operating out of uniform could give the impression that rank didn't matter, but right now he needed them to understand he was their leader, and even such small gestures helped. And he had needed the drink.

He reached inside his pocket and found a pack of cigarettes. He drew one out and lit it, then walked over to the sole armchair and lowered himself into it.

'So what tipped her off?'

The men shifted on their feet. Weale waved the cigarette in the air, indicating he expected an answer. It was vital for it to appear that black Africans had been responsible for the kidnapping – the point of using black Scouts with him keeping out of sight for the duration was so that even if they were spotted suspicion would fall on ZANLA, ZIPRA or one of their splinter factions. Any indication of involvement by the Rhodesian government would be catastrophic both domestically and internationally, so if someone was on to them he needed to know.

Tandi glanced at Makuba, then decided to speak. 'I don't believe anyone tipped her off. We were as careful as we could possibly be. But we always knew there was a chance she'd realise she was being watched. There always is.'

Weale looked at him through the cloud of smoke, one eye now half-closed.

'What about the boyfriend? What was he playing at? And how the hell did he get hold of a helicopter?'

'We don't know,' said Makuba.

Weale sighed. 'How are the targets now? Has the boy been any trouble?'

'Not so far. We gave them sedatives on the boat and now they're in the basement with Sammy and Joshua.'

'All right, I'll go and see them and introduce myself.' He gave a sardonic smile. 'There's an SAS flight to Johannesburg leaving at eight o'clock, so we'll head to the airport shortly. But first, I'm going out to report to the Commander.'

Tandi and Makuba nodded, an informal salute. Weale took the cognac into the kitchen and placed it out of sight, then grabbed a chunk of loose change and let himself out of the flat. The men visibly relaxed once the door had clicked shut, and seated themselves on the sofa. Makuba drew the trestle table nearer and removed a deck of cards from his jacket, smiling at Tandi.

'Okay if I deal?'

Chapter 17

The door opened and two men carrying Beretta machine-pistols entered the cell. They prodded him down a corridor into another room, which was empty but for a desk and two chairs bolted to the floor. They indicated he sit in one of the chairs. Dark thought of a field on an estate in the Scottish Highlands, and a man with a high-pitched voice and tattoos on his forearms. He had still been in his teens when he'd first encountered the fearsome Tommy MacFarlane, and in the following months he and the other SOE recruits had learned more from him about the techniques of violence than most men did in a lifetime. But even MacFarlane would have counselled caution when faced with two heavily armed men in a closely confined space. Dark seated himself.

Several minutes passed, and finally another man walked into the room. He was in his early forties, in a crisp white shirt and lightweight grey woollen suit, with very fair, almost white, hair brushed over his forehead and heavy-framed tortoiseshell spectacles.

His muscular forearms were tanned and overlaid with the same whitish hair. A Browning Hi-Power was pushed into his waistband, and he gripped a slim brown leather briefcase in his right hand.

Dark disliked him instantly: the vanity of his clothes, the unholstered gun, the irritatingly placid expression on his blandly handsome face – he looked more like an architect than an interrogator. Dark imagined he went for long bicycle rides in the forest with his impossibly blonde wife and their impossibly blond children. Thoughts suddenly crowded in on him, of Ben on a plastic tricycle, and of Claire running behind him in the park . . .

The man gave instructions to the others in Finnish and they left the room: Dark wished he had understood what had been said, but it wasn't a language he knew or even had a foothold in – it was utterly unlike all the other languages in the region. The fair-haired man strode over to the table and seated himself in the chair opposite. He took something from the briefcase, and Dark saw that it was his wallet, taken from him when his clothes had been searched. The man removed his identity card and held it up to the light, reading from it.

'Erik Daniel Johansson—'

'Sorry, but who the fuck are you?'

The man glanced down, his expression blank. Then his features settled and a half-smile crossed his face, as though amused at being pulled up for his manners.

'Detective Heikki Kurkinen. I'm investigating today's events on Utö.'

He spoke Swedish with a strong Finnish accent. Dark nodded at the wallet. 'You don't have to tell me my name – I already know it. Let me out of here. I need to do some investigating myself.'

'I'm afraid that's not possible at the moment.' Kurkinen replaced the identity card in the wallet, taking his time, letting Dark know that interruptions were not going to hurry him. Then he tossed the wallet lightly onto the table and leaned forward, his pale blue eyes under the ash-white eyebrows reminding Dark of a small, furrowing mouse.

'First I need some answers from you, Herr Johansson.' The stress on the surname suggested that he didn't believe it was genuine. He reached into the briefcase again and removed several items, each of which he placed carefully on the desk in a row. Dark gazed at them impassively. They were the passports he had been carrying, their pages wet and clumped together.

Kurkinen prised open the cover of one of them with his fingers. A photograph of Dark's face stared up, and beneath it was typed the name 'Eduardo Ballini'.

'Five passports, all containing your photograph, showing you with Swedish, Italian, Swiss, Spanish and American nationalities.' Kurkinen leaned forward again. 'So perhaps I can ask: who the fuck are *you*?'

Chapter 18

Weale walked across the square and into the telephone booth outside the cinema, then took the coins from his pocket and lifted the receiver. He dialled the number in Rhodesia and waited for it to connect.

'Campbell-Fraser.'

Weale fed some coins into the slot.

'Leopard One.'

He read out the number that was printed above the slot, then hung up. Two minutes later, the telephone rang and he snatched at it.

'You're late,' said Campbell-Fraser. 'What's going on?'

He listened in silence as Weale explained what had happened.

'How did the boyfriend get out there so fast?' he asked when he had finished. 'I thought he was some sort of vagabond.'

'We don't know. I haven't put any surveillance back on their flat. Should I?'

'No. Leave that now. Did he see anything that could help him identify you?'

'The men insist he didn't. They say they had their masks on the whole time.'

'I see. But they also missed that he spotted them.' There was a moment's silence, and Weale understood the implicit accusation – he had also missed it. 'Is there any indication you're under surveillance yourselves?'

'None. Shall we exfiltrate as planned? There's a flight out in a few hours.'

'Yes, get on it. And Johnny – no more mistakes.'

Weale replaced the receiver and started walking back to the safe house.

Chapter 19

Kurkinen didn't seem to be in any hurry with his interrogation, and in his mind Dark was running through every combat position he'd ever come across. But he wanted to escape, not get killed, and there were armed men outside: two at the most, possibly one. If there were just one, he might be able to—

'Where did you learn to fly a helicopter?'

Dark snapped back to reality. 'Bromma flying school.'

Kurkinen nodded. 'I spoke to them half an hour ago and they claim never to have seen you before.'

He feigned surprise. 'Really? Well, it was a few years ago. I imagine they have a lot of people passing through.'

'Yes, but they also keep records, and they don't have any of you.'

Dark didn't reply. Kurkinen scratched his chin and frowned, as though concerned for Dark's welfare.

'Herr "Johansson", you left a trail of destruction this evening and two people are dead, so I need to know what your role in all this was. Why did you steal the helicopter?'

'I wanted to reach my girlfriend and son before the men in the boat did – the men you let get away.'

'My officers say they saw no such men when they reached the scene. What did they look like?'

'There were four of them. All wore dark clothes and masks over their faces. But their hands were exposed – they were black men. Africans, I guess.'

Professionals, he might have added. Not simply because of the way they had dressed, but also the economy and speed of their movements and the total silence they had operated in. These weren't common or garden criminals. The shots fired and the grenade thrown might have killed him, so they weren't looking for ransom – at least, not from him. Everything pointed to their being government operatives, soldiers or special forces of some kind.

Kurkinen was looking at him sceptically. 'I see,' he said. 'So you are asking me to believe some mysterious black men kidnapped your family, then vanished into thin air.' He tapped the passports on the desk. 'And of course we have these – a getaway option. It doesn't look good, does it?'

'Are you saying I'm a suspect in this? That I've somehow *staged* the kidnapping of my girlfriend and son?' Dark dug his nails into the palms of his hand to abate some of the fury pulsing through him. In Kurkinen's position he would probably have reasoned much the same way – but he was now beyond reason.

'It wouldn't be the first time such a thing has happened,' Kurkinen said. 'But no, I'm not saying that. I'm saying I'd like to know more about why you have these passports.'

'And I'd like to know why you're asking me these idiotic questions and not trying to find my family.'

Dark felt like a fly trapped in a bottle, bashing his head against the sides. If he told Kurkinen who he was, he'd run his name through Interpol's systems and the British embassy would be informed and he'd never see daylight again. But he couldn't see how to persuade the man to act when the forged passports lay between them.

Sensing the impasse, Kurkinen tried again.

'Why did you steal the helicopter?'

'What would you have done if you'd realised your family was about to be kidnapped?'

'If I were an ordinary citizen? Called the police, of course.'

'Even if you thought it could happen at any moment? I didn't have time to waste hoping that a patrol might arrive in ten minutes. I don't have time to waste now, either.'

'How did you know they were about to be kidnapped?'

'Claire was taking my son out to Utö to visit some friends of ours, the Hanssons, who are . . . were . . . the lighthouse-keepers there. I was going to stay in Stockholm for a few days and then come out to see them. As they left I looked out of the window of our flat and saw a car had started following them. I couldn't think of how to catch up with them. Then I remembered the helicopters at the flying school.'

A flicker of a smile appeared at the corner of Kurkinen's lips.

'You presumed from looking out your window that someone was following your girlfriend's car so you decided to steal a motorbike and then a helicopter and fly out to the lighthouse to get there before them?'

Dark nodded, noting that he seemed well briefed on what had happened in Stockholm. That meant he had probably spoken to the Swedes, which might make things trickier if he ever managed to get out of here.

'What if you'd been mistaken,' Kurkinen said, 'and the car hadn't been following your girlfriend and son after all?'

'I'd have been relieved, of course. I'd have flown back to Bromma and returned the helicopter at once, with apologies.'

'Instead of which it's now a ball of ash. They're quite expensive machines, you know, helicopters.'

'They're also hard to control when you're being shot at. I was right: the men I'd seen did mean my family harm, and now I'm sitting here talking to you while God knows what happens.'

'I understand—'

'Do you?'

'You need to stop treating me like a fool, Herr Johansson. Your story isn't just thin – it's absurd. You can't have known that someone was following your family and intended to kidnap them simply by glancing out the window!' He tilted his head slightly and gave an encouraging smile. 'Is there anything in your past that made you think that was likely? Or in your girlfriend's past, perhaps?'

Dark stared ahead, his face stiff. *I also have secrets.* Yes, there was something she had hidden from him, something he had missed. He placed his elbows on the desk and leaned forward.

'Listen,' he said quietly. 'My girlfriend and son have been kidnapped by men in ski masks. I think they'll head back to Stockholm, as that was where they were based. Can we please stop wasting time and start trying to find them? Get on the phone to your friends in Sweden and tell them to put out an all-ports alert for four black men travelling with a young African woman and a three-year-old boy. They should also be following up on the transport. They used at least two cars. One was a dark green Opel Käpitan, I'd guess six or seven years old. If they visit the main dealerships in Stockholm I suspect they'll find a lead pretty quickly. Also tell them to check the harbour. The kidnappers either rented or bought someone's boat in cash, and the owner shouldn't be too hard to find. What did they look and sound like, what language did they speak to each other? These are the questions you should be looking into.'

Kurkinen didn't blink. 'Thank you for the suggestions. But I need to know what you're not telling me.'

And I need to get out of this room, Dark thought.

From the way the men had operated he doubted they were after money. It was worse than that: they might not want anything. It could simply be a hit squad, for whatever reason, something from Claire's past, and they intended to kill them both as soon as they could.

The door opened and one of the men who'd escorted him earlier walked in and approached Kurkinen. He whispered in his ear and Kurkinen nodded a few times, then left the room again. The detective looked up at Dark and smiled, revealing regular white teeth.

'We don't often have reason to contact the Zambian authorities,' he said, 'but they've been rather helpful. They've just informed us that they have no record whatsoever of your girlfriend.'

Dark stared at him, taking this in. So she had a false identity, too. Why, he wondered. Who was she? And how had she managed to obtain a Swedish *personnummer*? An idea was forming in his mind. He looked at Kurkinen and smiled back at him.

'Tell me, Detective, why are you so scared of me?'

Kurkinen raised his eyebrows. 'Of you? What the hell are you talking about?'

'All this security seems very elaborate. Yes, I stole a bike and a helicopter, but you've placed me in a holding cell, had me escorted everywhere by men with machine-pistols, come in here with a Browning in your belt and placed two armed men outside the door to protect you.'

'To protect me!' Kurkinen laughed. 'Don't flatter

yourself. This is standard procedure. And there's only one man outside—'

Dark rose from the chair and propelled himself towards Kurkinen, his right hand lunging across the table to grab him by the throat. Kurkinen was slow to react, but when he did it was with surprising force, sweeping his fist round and bringing it down onto Dark's wrist. The jabbing pain made Dark drop his hold, but he used the momentum of his movement to push away from the desk and then charged low into the other man's legs, rearing his head up like a bull at the last moment and punching up into his stomach.

Kurkinen staggered back, groaning, and Dark knew he had to act very fast or the man outside would hear and come in. He circled behind Kurkinen and took him in a stranglehold with his right arm, avoiding the Finn's increasingly frantic kicks as he did. Dark kept the crook of his elbow in position and drew his hand back to his own shoulder, placing more pressure on Kurkinen's windpipe.

Straining from the effort, he reached down with his left hand and took the Browning from Kurkinen's waistband. He raised it to the Finn's head, pressing the barrel into his temple.

'Be very quiet, Detective,' he said. 'Don't make a sound.'

Kurkinen let out a grunt of frustration, but then was silent. Dark loosened his grip around his neck a fraction of an inch, enough to allow him to breathe easily but not enough to give him any doubt that the pressure could be applied again instantly.

'If you make a move or a sound without my say-so, I'll pull the trigger. Nod if you understand.'

Kurkinen nodded.

'Good. Now we're going to move together towards the door. You're going to move your arse forward an inch, then me. Nod if you're ready.'

Kurkinen nodded again, and they bumped along, inch by inch, until they were within a few feet of the door. Both men were pouring with sweat now, and Dark's forefinger was turning red from keeping the pressure on the trigger. He took a deep breath.

'Now tell your colleague to come in here, and make it convincing.'

Kurkinen hesitated and Dark pushed the gun against the bone.

'Mäki!' Kurkinen called. 'Get in here!'

Dark watched the door.

Nothing.

He could hear Kurkinen's breathing, feel the rise and fall of his chest, and smell his sweat.

The door started to open. Dark leaned forward and smashed the butt of the Browning into Kurkinen's jaw, let go of him so he slid to the floor, then lunged forward with his other hand and grabbed at the stunned Mäki's machine-pistol. Before the other man could react, Dark had hit him in the solar plexus with the stock. He groaned in pain and started falling forward. Dark caught him in his arms and dragged him into the room, kicking the door closed behind him.

Both men were out cold, but he didn't have long. He quickly emptied Kurkinen's pockets, and took his wallet, money-clip, wristwatch and car keys, noting the Saab emblem. He stripped both men to their underpants, then undressed himself. He tore his shirt sleeves into strips and tied their hands up with them, using one of Gunnar's sailing knots. Once he felt they were secured tightly enough, he balled up the remaining shreds of cloth and gagged them both, then hurriedly took Mäki's uniform from the floor and dressed in it. He stuffed Kurkinen's clothes in the briefcase with the passports and his own wallet, picked up the Browning and headed for the door.

He opened it slowly and peered out. An empty corridor. To the left, a sliver of weak light reflected against the surface of the floor. Dark ran towards it and shoved open the door with his shoulder. He was in front of the station, a row of cars parked on the asphalt ahead of him, their bonnets gleaming faintly. Dark walked rapidly towards them, clutching Kurkinen's keys in his hand and searching for a Saab.

Chapter 20

'How long are we staying here, Mamma?'

Ben was swathed in blankets in her arms, staring up at her.

'Not long, darling. We're just going to rest for a while.'

'Where's Pappa?'

'He will be here very soon.'

The men had so far kept contact to a minimum and hadn't shown their weapons in front of Ben, but she wasn't sure how much longer she could keep what was happening from him. She wondered what he was thinking. Those enormous eyes of his saw everything – like his father, Ben was an observer.

She wasn't all that sure what was happening herself. What did they want? They could have killed them both already if that had been the plan, but they didn't seem to want to take them anywhere, either. They were being kept in this soundproofed cellar, guarded around the clock, but she couldn't see the purpose in it.

There were rumbling noises from the ceiling: they'd

taken her watch, but she guessed it was time for them to change shifts. She sat up a little straighter, adjusting Ben in her arms. A man entered the cell, and she stared at him, recognition gradually dawning.

'Joshua! Is it really you? What are you doing here?'

Ephibe's mouth twitched in a smile. 'Hello, Hope,' he said. 'It's been a long time.'

Another man stepped into the room and locked the door behind him. He was a few years younger, she saw, and carrying a small suitcase.

'The lovebirds reunite,' he said with a nasty chuckle. 'A touching scene. But let's not play it now.'

He placed the suitcase on the floor and opened the lid, revealing two tape reels.

'No,' he said, 'now we're going to have a little talk. Joshua, take hold of the microphone, please.'

Chapter 21

Friday, 22 August 1975, Helsinki

Paul Dark parked the Saab outside the ferry terminal and walked into the departure hall. It was crowded: it seemed a lot of people were heading out of the city for the weekend. He looked up at the display and saw a ferry was due to leave for Stockholm in half an hour, at just after midnight. He took Kurkinen's money-clip from his pocket and counted the notes in the wad. A thousand Finnish marks. That was around four hundred kronor: it wasn't a fortune, but it would do for the time being.

He followed the signs to a kiosk servicing waiting passengers. He bought a small 'travel' cosmetics bag and a box of disposable razors, then retreated to the public washrooms and locked himself into one of the stalls. He removed the nail scissors from the bag and started to cut away at his beard, using the reflection of the aluminium door-lock as a mirror. Once he had hacked off most of it, he shaved the rest away, going through three razors in the process.

He decided it was too dangerous to continue impersonating a Finnish coastguard as he didn't speak a word of the language, so he undressed and changed into Kurkinen's clothes, then put the uniform into the briefcase. He slipped the Browning into his waistband, obscured by the jacket.

Fifteen minutes later, he emerged and washed his face in the basin, the hot water stinging his pores. The smooth-cheeked face that stared back at him in the mirror was older than when he had last seen it, but unmistakable.

Erik Johansson was gone, and Paul Dark was in his place.

Chapter 22

Her eyes widened when the door opened. He was older, of course – a decade older, almost to the day. In different circumstances, she might not have recognised him, but his expression was the same as it had been that night he had raided the farm with his colleagues. He had cornered her in one of the outer huts, and she had known from the look in his eye and his scythe of a smile what he planned to do to her. In desperation, she'd lashed out, catching him in the face with a flailing foot, and as he'd screamed in pain she'd run and run and run until she had reached the wagon as it was leaving the gates of the compound, climbing into a sea of familiar warm bodies, into humanity.

'Hello, Hope,' said Pete Voers. 'I think we have some unfinished business.'

She shuddered with disgust. In the corner of the room, Ben was sleeping, the top of his head emerging from the thin blanket. Did the man intend to assault her with her own child in the room? She looked frantically around for a weapon but of course there was none. Everything in the room was chained to the floor.

'Stay away from me!' she hissed.

Voers grinned.

She closed her eyes and breathed deeply, waiting for him to come closer and trying to keep her thoughts calm. Should she wake Ben? Would that stop him?

Footsteps. She opened her eyes. The door opened, and another man came in, also white, but younger, wearing shirtsleeves and slacks.

'What the hell's going on here? Voers?'

'Nothing, Captain. I was just checking up on our prisoners.'

Weale glared at him. 'You didn't have my permission to do so. Leave us, please.'

Voers nodded, gave an insincere smile and left the room.

Hope let out a deep breath of relief and felt the thumping in her chest gradually slow. Ben stirred on the bed, and she went to him, taking his face in her hands, reassuring him all was well.

'Miss Charamba,' said the captain.

She didn't reply. The voice was solicitous, but had an unpleasant edge to it – was he about to take over where the other man had left off?

'I'm not going to hurt you,' he said. 'Let me explain the situation.'

He walked over to the bed and looked down at Ben, a friendly smile on his face.

'Have you ever been on an aeroplane, little man?'

Ben shook his head slowly. 'Well, you will soon. Your mother will go on board first, and then you'll come along a bit later with some other men.' He saw the look of fear cross the boy's eyes. 'Don't worry, it's best that way. Just do as I say and nothing bad will happen.'

He looked back at her, smiling. She nodded, stiffening as the man reached out and ran his hands through her son's hair.

Chapter 23

Paul Dark joined the queue and bought a ticket with some of Kurkinen's marks and boarded the ferry. The passengers were a mix of rowdy party-goers, elderly day-trippers returning home and young families. The ferry was still in the harbour, but the line of slot machines was already occupied, the players' expressions grimly focused on the rows of spinning fruit.

Dark followed the signs to the cafeteria, a large low-ceilinged hall decorated in lemon yellow and blue with a thick green carpet and strip lighting. He dreaded to think what effect the décor would have when the passage was rocky. At the far end of the room, a low plastic wall and long stuffed leather cushions partitioned off a small playroom, and children were driving around it in bright plastic toy trucks and cars, their parents watching nervously from nearby tables.

He paid for a black coffee and a limp-looking sandwich at the counter and found a table around the corner from the playroom – he didn't want to see other people's children. The floor juddered for a moment, and he watched through the windows as the harbour gradually retreated from view.

He sipped the coffee, then took a deep breath and leaned back against the chair. His neck and forearm muscles still ached from the fight with Kurkinen, but his mind was now operating in two very different modes. Part of it was focused on his immediate surroundings, his eyes surveying the other passengers, looking for any discrepancies in appearance or behaviour – a professional calculating the odds. But this was almost a mechanical reflex, and beneath the surface another part of him was in freefall, nightmare images of what might be happening to Ben and Claire flashing through his synapses before he could stop them, horror and despair churning inside his guts.

He was still struggling to believe that it had really happened, that he hadn't simply imagined it all and at any given moment he would emerge from the nightmare to find them with him again. At the same time, he had accepted reality enough to blame himself for having been so careless. All the signs had been there, and he'd missed them. He'd been trained to spot omissions in people's stories, and there had been several in Claire's. She'd never discussed her family, always avoided politics, changed the subject when it came to life in Zambia, and avoided other Africans in Stockholm. And yet he hadn't noticed anything, presuming instead she had fled hardship and simply didn't want to be reminded of it. He had been so intent on looking over his own shoulder that he hadn't even considered looking over hers.

But none of that mattered now. Whoever she was, whatever her past, she was the woman he loved, and the mother of his child. He would do whatever it took to get them back.

The ferry would take fourteen hours to get to Stockholm. It seemed an eternity in which any number of horrific things could happen, but he'd passed the stage of panic. At least he was out and looking for them now – and he knew just where to start. As soon as he landed, he had to find out who Claire really was.

Chapter 24

Friday, 22 August 1975, London

As the train entered the tunnel, Rachel gazed through the glass, her eyes following the latticework of wires and pipes along the blackened walls. She blinked, refocusing, and saw her own reflection instead. She looked tired, she thought. Tired and rather miserable.

The train emerged at Lambeth North and she minded the gap and walked briskly up the stairs. She turned left out of the station and within a few seconds reached the entrance of the tower-block with no stated occupants and the sign reading 'No Entry. Permit Holders Only.' She fished her pass-card from her purse and held it up for the uniformed guard to see, then pushed open the doors and walked into the lobby.

She presented her card to Cyril, the night porter. He pressed a switch beneath his desk to let the guard on her floor know she was coming up, and she unlocked the lift door with her key and stepped inside.

She loathed the weekend night shift, but knew she

should count her blessings. Her attempt to bring Tom Gadlow back from Kuala Lumpur to face justice nearly six years earlier had ended in his death, and she'd been hauled over the coals for it. A known traitor had slipped through the Service's fingers, and she alone was responsible. There had been talk of her getting the sack, and for a horrible couple of weeks even that she might have somehow colluded in the murder – was she perhaps also working for the Russians, and had deliberately let Gadlow out of her sight so the assassin could kill him before he returned to London and revealed all under interrogation? The inquiry had cleared her of that, but the blame for his death was still firmly affixed to her and she had been reprimanded and returned to the same rank and pay grade as she had been on when she had joined the Service.

But she'd been lucky to survive at all. The doomsday scenario Edmund Innes had outlined to her in 1969 hadn't quite come to pass, but the Service was now a shadow of its former self. She was one of the few survivors of what was still referred to, on the rare occasions it was referred to at all, as 'The Purge'. The prime minister had been unimpressed by Review Section's report into Dark and the other traitors and had decided immediate root and branch reform was needed. Dozens of officers had been discreetly 'retired' as a result. A Conservative government had been elected a few months later, but any hope it might take a softer line had soon been dispelled by the new prime minister's insistence that the agency immediately inform him of all the remaining skeletons in its filing cabinets or face the possibility of a full parliamentary inquiry.

Seeing no alternative, the Service had supplied the PM and senior members of his government with information about various 'unfortunate episodes', but not everyone had been persuaded. The new foreign secretary had been particularly persistent in questioning Innes about his predecessor's assassination. In the end, Sandy Harmigan had come to the rescue, taking the floor from a flustered Innes one hot Tuesday afternoon in the Cabinet Office. In a virtuoso performance, he had deflected all the foreign secretary's complaints, saying that it had been a horrendous, unprecedented and tragic sequence of events but that he knew from agents in the field that the terrorist responsible had been killed in a clandestine operation in Rome and the group he represented 'cauterised'. It was one of those words that tended to brook no further questioning, and Harmigan had applied his very best evocation of Dirk Bogarde's insouciance when delivering the line.

Concern over the Service's record had fizzled out soon after: the country was facing more pressing issues than the spooks' ancient history. Grave errors, it was decided, had been made, but there was nothing to be gained by harping on about them and one simply slept better if one accepted that, after all, these chaps were fundamentally decent people who knew what they were doing. In this way, the Service's deeper secrets had been protected. The occasional lurid story had appeared in newspapers, notably pursued by the *Daily Express*, but were shrugged off as conspiracy theory.

Before long, though, trouble arose again. Edmund Innes had become increasingly prone to speaking his mind, and the corridors were abuzz with tales of his inappropriate outbursts. Some thought it was simply the irascibility of old age, others that it was a nervous breakdown. The nadir was said to have occurred during a JIC meeting: Innes had insinuated that Harmigan was so keen to whitewash the record on Paul Dark that he must be some sort of double himself.

Rachel found the image hard to reconcile with the quiet, polite man she'd met, but the rumour had been confirmed to her by Sandy. In late 1971, Innes had curtly announced to the staff that he was taking a sabbatical. He had retreated to his cottage in Swanwick, and Harmigan had been appointed acting Chief. Nobody was under any illusions about the 'acting' part of the title: Innes wasn't coming back. Harmigan immediately created a new department to oversee delicate matters such as negotiating severance and pension packages and tightening Official Secrets Act obligations. By the time Labour regained power in the spring of 1974, questions over the Service's future had finally faded from view.

Within the upper echelons of the agency, The Purge had been felt a necessary emergency measure: better to remain a stripped-down core than be packed up entirely. Had they not brushed the worst horrors under the carpet, so the reasoning went, several of them might have been disgraced, or even imprisoned. Harmigan was seen as not simply a war hero, but as the Service's saviour.

He had been Rachel's saviour, too. Despite the Gadlow fiasco he had kept her on, and with the current state of the economy that was no small matter. The previous summer, Danny had found a job with the Public Record Office and had moved into a studio flat in Chancery Lane, leaving her to pay rent on the place in Holborn alone. She was barely scraping by, but as long as she was picking up a pay cheque she counted herself fortunate.

She stepped out of the lift, nodded to the bored-looking guard and took the corridor leading to the duty room. She knocked on the door and walked in. Tombes looked up.

'Hello.'

Keith Tombes was a 54-year-old Yorkshireman, bearded and podgy and notoriously messy – the desk next to him was a pile of scattered papers. But Rachel knew his habits masked an exceptional mind, and she had insisted that he be on her team in Review Section. Now he was back on night duty with her, not that he seemed to mind: if Tombes had ever had any ambitions, they had evaporated decades ago. Rachel lived in fear of his discovering her relationship with Sandy, because she knew he would be devastated – he was devoted to her, and had an intense dislike of Sandy, who he referred to as 'His Lordship'.

'Anything interesting come in?' she asked him.

'Not a lot.' He fished up a piece of paper from the pile and scanned his scrawled notes. 'Tehran sent a report on this palaver over the Americans' profile of the Shah. The long and short is they still don't know who leaked it to the press. Let's see . . .' He peered at his handwriting. 'The South Africans have sent us a confidential briefing about the talks they've set up with the Rhodesians. I've forwarded it to the Foreign Office so their bods will have it before they go out. Oh yes, Rouse in Paris checked in. He still hasn't heard from his asset. It's been three days, so I suspect we might be out of pocket there. I've prepared a memo on it to Western Europe, so that'll go as soon as the secretaries are in.' He tapped a buff envelope in the out tray, then returned to his notes. 'Oh, and Five sent over a telex from Interpol about an hour ago, via the Finns. Two dead and two missing in an apparent hostage situation on some bloody island in the Baltic. The coastguard brought a fellow into Helsinki for questioning and he managed to escape. Looks like a professional. All ports have been alerted and we're to keep an eye out, for what it's worth.' He placed the paper back on the desk. 'That's it, my girl. Want the chit?'

Rachel shook her head, and took off her jacket. Tombes was about to walk out the door when something stirred in the back of her mind and she called out to him.

'Hold on. Where in the Baltic, exactly?'

Chapter 25

Dark was thinking of getting another coffee when he looked up and saw a group of men walking steadily down the passage leading to the cafeteria.

There were four of them. They were well built, wearing dark blue woollen uniforms and with thick truncheons hanging from their belts. One led an Alsatian that was struggling against its leash, and as they made their way down the corridor they glanced each way, studying the faces of the passengers.

Dark's skin bristled. Kurkinen must have recovered and got the message out. The security crew of every ferry leaving Helsinki tonight would have been provided with his description and told to comb every inch of their boats looking for him.

He didn't like his chances. He'd lost the beard, but he was still a dark-haired, middle-aged Caucasian male, around 185 centimetres tall and weighing 80 kilograms, travelling alone. And if Kurkinen had been clever, he'd have added a description of his own clothes.

He reached for the Browning. It was still secure in

his waistband, but using it would be a last resort, as there would doubtless be other crew members and weapons on board, and he was essentially trapped on the boat. But where to go? He could perhaps find a lavatory, or hide somewhere in the car deck, but he suspected that in the course of the journey these men were going to search every inch of the ferry, and rather than hiding his only real chance of avoiding them was to stay in plain sight.

He slid out of his seat and walked towards the children's area: the low cushioned wall shielded it from view unless you were at one of the surrounding tables. The small space contained about a dozen children, running around, squabbling with each other, crying, or sitting alone preoccupied with a toy. A couple of adults were also roaming the area: a mother trying to cajole her twins into coming to have some dinner in the cafeteria, another breastfeeding her baby. One wall was taken up with a primary-coloured painting of a ferry in simple geometric shapes, a Finnish flag on its bow.

Dark glanced behind him and saw that the crew members had now entered the cafeteria, and that one of them was talking to the kitchen staff while the others were walking among the tables. The man with the Alsatian looked to be heading straight towards him.

Dark stepped into the playroom, bobbing his head as though he were a parent looking for one of his brood. A girl with plaited hair, aged nine or ten, wearing a pink skirt and striped T-shirt, approached and tapped him on the leg. She said something to him in

Finnish, then pointed at a wooden shelf with rows of tiny shoes just outside the room.

Dark quickly took off his shoes. He placed them with the others and walked back into the playroom, narrowly avoiding stepping on the fingers of a crawling toddler. The girl with plaits nodded approvingly.

'Do you speak Swedish?' he asked her. Finland was bilingual and the boat was heading to Sweden.

'Yes.'

'What's your name?'

'Saga. But my mother said I wasn't to talk to any grown-ups.'

'She's right, of course. Where is she?'

'She went to the shop. She'll be back in ten minutes, she said.'

On the way to the cafeteria, Dark had passed a small kiosk selling duty-free cosmetics.

'Have you seen my son, Ben?' he said. He hardly knew why he had said it, but he wanted to engage the girl in conversation. The crew would be looking for a man travelling alone, not a parent.

The girl looked up at him, wondering about her mother's advice but intrigued by the question.

'What does he look like?' she said, finally.

'He's younger than you. Three years old. Curly hair.'

The girl's saucer-like eyes appraised him. 'You look sad,' she said. 'Have you lost him?'

Dark nodded, and something in him nearly cracked as the girl reached out and touched his arm in reassurance.

'Don't worry. He can't have gone very far.'

Dark managed a smile.

'Can you help me find him?'

The girl nodded firmly.

'Perhaps he's in there.' She pointed at the painting of the ship, and Dark saw that the portholes were small cubbies that had been carved into the wall for the children to explore.

'I'll check,' said Dark, and dropped down to the floor. Saga laughed as he tried to crawl into the space and butted heads with a small boy in dungarees. He stretched his hand out and she pulled at it. Dark got to his feet and thanked her. He looked across and saw the man with the Alsatian standing by the entrance to the space, scanning everyone in it. Dark gave a sheepish smile, a hapless father overwhelmed by chaotic children. The man nodded and smiled back, then pulled at the leash and walked on.

Dark sat on the floor of the playroom and let his breathing return to normal.

Chapter 26

A telephone chirruped in the office at the rear of the house in the outskirts of Lusaka. On the third ring, it was picked up by the small, slim man in the black satin dressing gown reading a newspaper at his desk in the corner of the room.

'Yes? Matthew Charamba speaking.'

'Hello, Professor.'

The voice was strangely disembodied and metallic, and Charamba realised it had been put through some sort of machine. But even with the disguise he recognised the flat, terse accent typical of white Rhodesians.

'Who is this? How did you get this number?'

'You don't know me, but I have something of yours you might wish to see returned safely. Or, rather, someone.'

'What do you mean?'

'As you will no doubt be aware, some of your former colleagues will soon be taking part in talks with the Rhodesians.'

Charamba had heard of the South Africans' plans

for a summit from a paid informant within ZIPRA. Evidently someone somewhere – perhaps the same informant – had talked.

'Who is this?' he repeated, his voice now more insistent.

'Patience, Professor. All will soon be clear. I represent a group of men who want those negotiations to take place, and to be fruitful. And we want you to take a leading role in them.'

'What? You must know my position – no negotiation with the whites on this. Majority rule is not something to debate—'

'I'm very familiar with your position, Professor, but we want you to . . . *adapt* it.'

'And why should I do this for you, a total stranger calling me up at my house?'

'Haven't you guessed yet?' the man on the other end of the line taunted. 'I want you to dismiss everyone from your house. Your sentries can continue to patrol the grounds, but there must be nobody in the house when I call you back in precisely one hour from now. Do you understand?'

'Yes, but why should I—'

'Because we have your daughter and grandson, Professor.'

There was a clunking sound and then another voice came on the line, its urgency breaking through a field of static.

'Father, it's me, Hope! I'm here with my son, Ben. We're both scared. Please – do whatever these men say.'

There was a click and the line went dead.

Charamba rose from his chair, his face drawn, and opened the door of his office. Phillip Gibo, his chief bodyguard, looked up in surprise.

'Get everyone out,' Charamba said quietly. 'Get everyone out of the house at once.'

Chapter 27

Rachel took the paper from the terminal and read the message from the Interpol bureau in Helsinki. It was to the point:

SUBJECT ERIK JOHANSSON. MASEL.

She found the Interpol sheet on top of a filing cabinet and ran her finger down the codewords. There it was. 'MASEL: We are sending photographs and finger-prints to you by teleprinter immediately.'

She put the sheet down and reached for the pack of cigarettes and lighter in her purse. She lit one and leaned back on the table, enjoying the rush of nicotine. She had taken three puffs when the machine started up again, and she crushed out the cigarette in an ashtray and watched as the photograph came through.

Chapter 28

Matthew Charamba took a deep breath and picked up the telephone.

'Is the house clear?'

'Have you hurt them?'

'*Is the house clear?*'

Charamba's flesh crawled at the menace in the voice.

'Yes.'

'Good. No, we haven't harmed Hope or Ben, and have no intention of doing so provided you co-operate. Would you like more confirmation that we're holding them, and of their identities?'

He thought about it. He hadn't had any contact with Hope since she had left that terrible day, so he hadn't even known she had a son, but he didn't doubt it was her for a moment. Even ten years on, he would have recognised her voice anywhere. He could ask them for some kind of confirmation – the name of her favourite song as a child, perhaps, something like that – as a way of stalling them so he could make some investigations, but he couldn't think of anything, and something told him it wasn't a good idea to try to fool the man behind the voice.

'No,' he said, finally. 'I believe you.'

'That is also good. Now understand this, Professor, because it's very important. You can tell no one about this. Not the newspapers, not your aides – nobody whatsoever. If we have any indication that you have told anyone, or indeed have even considered telling anyone, your daughter and grandson will die. If you don't follow our demands to the letter, they will die. If you don't agree to all of the conditions we have set out for the summit, they will die. If it becomes clear in the summit or at any other time that others know of this, they will die.'

Charamba took a tissue from the pocket of his dressing gown and wiped away the sweat from his face.

'Your idea can't work. Even if I can arrange to be invited to the summit—'

'Oh, we think you can, Professor. We think they'll be glad to have you there.'

'Perhaps. But only because they know my position. If I weaken it at all, they'll know at once I have been pressured.'

'We don't think so. I think you'll see that our conditions are more than reasonable. We have even made some concessions from the last round of negotiations, which we think you can successfully argue for.'

'The last . . . !' He tried to contain his anger. 'You're crazy if you think I'll go along with this. The last round of talks put off majority rule for a century!'

'We're not at the negotiating table now, Professor. I'll call back later to explain to you precisely what we expect. You mustn't speak to anybody about this, remember.'

The line went dead.

Chapter 29

The telephone rang in the bedroom of the large Georgian townhouse in Mayfair. In the antique four-poster bed, Sandy Harmigan groaned and opened his eyes. He reached for the receiver on the side table, his mind quickly registering that the call must mean an emergency of some kind. As Chief of the Service, he was rarely woken by the telephone unless it was to herald death or disaster.

'Yes?' he said, glancing at his watch on the table as he did so. The luminous hands told him it was just after three o'clock.

'I'm sorry to bother you, sir – it's Reception. I have an urgent call for you from the night desk.'

He sat up with a jolt. Rachel was on duty tonight. He suddenly felt his heart hammering in his chest. On the other side of the bed, a body stirred.

'Who is it?'

Harmigan looked across at his wife. She was wearing a black silk eye-mask and her skin was very pale without its customary coating of make-up. She looked, it struck him, like an embalmed corpse.

'The office,' he said.

She shifted her weight and turned her back to him. 'Would you mind taking it downstairs?'

It was a strictly rhetorical question. Harmigan told the operator to hold the line, replaced the receiver on its cradle and climbed out of the massive bed. He slid into his slippers, closed the bedroom door behind him and padded downstairs, where he picked up the telephone on the dresser in the hallway and told the operator he was ready. There was a brief pause while the signal was scrambled, and then a woman's voice came on the line.

'Sandy?'

'Rachel – are you all right? What's going on?'

'Me? I'm fine.'

Relief surged through him. Nothing had happened to her. He could have dealt with anything at all but that. He realised that he'd been terrified of hearing of her death without his even being consciously aware of it. Then there was a constriction in his chest again, as he redirected his mind to finding out whatever other emergency was taking place instead.

'You nearly gave me a heart attack,' he said. 'What is it?'

'I'm sorry to call you at home.' They had agreed long ago that she would never do that, and there was an awkward silence at her tacit acknowledgement of their affair. Then she cleared her throat and went on. 'Something's turned up – or rather, someone has. I've just received a photo-telegraph from Interpol in

Helsinki and I've compared it to the ones we have. He's got a beard now and has aged a bit, of course, but I'm sure it's him.'

'Rachel, it's three o'clock in the bloody morning. You'd better be talking about Lord Lucan or I won't be very happy.'

'It's Paul Dark.'

Harmigan pressed the receiver closer to his ear.

'What?'

'The Finns took him into custody a few hours ago after he stole a motorbike and a helicopter, leaving two people dead. He then escaped from custody and Interpol have issued an alert as a result. I followed up and asked them to send me a photograph, and it's definitely him.'

'That's not possible. The bastard's dead, frozen solid on some shitty island. As you well know.'

But even as he said the words he knew they weren't true. Six years ago, Rachel had been insistent Dark might still be alive, but she had no reason to lie to him about the Finns or Interpol's photograph. Helsinki was also just a few hours from where Dark had last been seen – but no body had ever been found. He'd even sent Sudbury out to have a look, but he'd just been met by blank stares from the local fishermen.

'I'll be there in an hour,' he said. He hesitated for a moment, other words on his lips, then hung up.

He stood in the darkness of the hallway for a few seconds, then lifted the receiver again and dialled a long-distance number. Campbell-Fraser picked up on the second ring.

'Roy, it's Sandy in London. I've just had a rather alarming call from one of my subordinates about a development in Finland. Please tell me this has nothing to do with your little operation.'

Campbell-Fraser noted Harmigan's phrasing – the last time he had spoken to him it had been 'our' operation, and there had been nothing 'little' about it. The substantial costs involved in mounting the job had forced him into calling on Harmigan for help, but he had judged the opportunity too good to miss. Failure would have serious repercussions, both from the international community and closer to home – Smith would sack him, perhaps even gaol him. But he had it in his power to secure Rhodesia's future.

'I was about to call you,' he said. 'I've just got off the phone with my team leader, Weale. The boyfriend got involved somehow, but it's under control now. We have the girl and her son—'

'It's the boyfriend I'm worried about right now. Didn't you think to look into his fucking background?'

Campbell-Fraser was taken aback by the ferocity in the other man's voice. 'We did. He's just some middle-aged Swedish hippy. Works nights for a charity. What's going on?'

Harmigan sighed deeply. 'That is *not* who he is, Roy. He's a highly trained Soviet agent by the name of Paul Dark.' He ran a hand through his mane of hair, thinking. Part of him wanted to give Campbell-Fraser an almighty bollocking, but other than relieving him of his anger he knew there would be little point. Time was of the essence. 'When you say the situation's under control, what do you mean, exactly? How are you proposing to exfiltrate your men? Interpol's slapped an alert on Dark and the Swedes will be looking out for your lot by now, too.'

'They're heading back on a flight in a few hours. As far as we know, none of the passports has been compromised. Weale has already called Charamba and informed him of the situation, and I'll take over as soon as they arrive.'

'Good,' said Harmigan, relieved. 'But tell Weale to stay in Stockholm. I need him to find Dark.'

There was a moment's pause on the other end of the line. 'And how do you propose he does that, exactly?'

Harmigan considered the question, looking at his own reflection in the darkness of the hallway mirror. 'The Swedes have a counter-intelligence unit,' he said. 'This will be their job. I'll let them know one of my men is in town and will come to be briefed on their operation as there's a British national involved. What name is Weale using?'

'Frederick Collins. But, Sandy, I don't think this is a good idea. Why not have one of your people there handle it?'

Harmigan laughed bitterly, thinking of Maidment, the 58-year-old Etonian who ran Stockholm Station. 'None of them has your little crew's particular brand of . . . *expertise*, let's say. Anyway, I don't want to drag my people into this. The entire point was for Service personnel to remain uninvolved precisely in case the wheels came off. Now thanks to your team's sloppiness a wheel *has* come off, so I think it's perfectly reasonable you're the ones to put it back on again.'

'I appreciate that, but John isn't trained to—'

'Oh, please. He spends his life impersonating wogs in the bush – he can certainly pretend to be one of my men for a few hours. He's British-born, if I remember. We need this mess sorted out immediately, and he's there. What's your comms setup?'

Five minutes later, Harmigan replaced the receiver and walked back upstairs. Celia's bedside light was on and she was sitting up reading a paperback, her eye-mask pushed up over her forehead.

'What is it?' she said. 'You look like death warmed up.'

'Paul Dark's alive.'

She closed the book and placed it on her bedside table.

'Are you sure?'

'I'm going into the office to find out more – but it fits. He's in Finland. Well, probably Sweden by now.'

'Who's discovered it?'

'The night officer . . . Rachel Gold.'

She raised an eyebrow. 'The Jewess? Well, she did claim he was alive before, didn't she?'

He sighed, knowing what was coming. 'Yes.'

'But then there was that business with Gadlow in Malaysia. And she's not in the circle. Do you think you can afford to have her deal with this?'

'Dark's a completely different kettle of shit from Tom bloody Gadlow. Dark knew pretty much everything we have, and Gold knows more about him than anyone in the world.'

'More than you, even?'

'Much more. So yes, I'm going to use her on this.'

Celia Harmigan placed a hand to her mouth and yawned widely. 'Well, it's your agency, Sandy.' She plumped up the pillows behind her, then squinted at him. 'You've got your shifty look on. Is there something else?'

'Yes. Dark's got in the way of the Charamba job.' He explained the situation, and she listened, her face cold and thin-lipped.

'I see. Well, you'd better make sure you get hold of him before he can cause any more mischief. I don't want the plan ruined because of your incompetence.'

She leaned over and switched off the light, then pulled down the eye-mask and disappeared back beneath the sheets on her side of the bed.

Chapter 30

Weale circled the telephone booth and consulted his watch again. The Commander was three minutes late with the call. It was an eternity in a situation like this, and he was beginning to worry that something had happened. Was the operation in danger of being exposed, or had Campbell-Fraser decided to cut off all contact because it already had been? That was the nightmare scenario, as they had to get out of the country within the next few hours – if they didn't they'd be on the run from the Swedish authorities with no way out, and with two hostages to keep them company . . .

The telephone rang and he grabbed at the receiver.

'Leopard One here.'

'Hello, Captain Weale. We met last year in London.'

It took Weale a moment to recover, but then he recognised the voice: it was the overly suave Chief from British intelligence, Harmigan. The Commander had dragged him along on a 'fact-finding mission' to meet him and a few others in the Service last year, but the only facts he had found were that England was still as cold and dreary as it had been when he had left it as a child and that British intelligence was run by pompous asses.

'Yes,' Harmigan said, as though reading his thoughts, 'you didn't much like me. Well, the feeling's mutual. I suspect you thought me a dull old stick with no idea of the harsh realities you deal with when operating behind enemy lines.' Weale didn't say anything – that was precisely what he had thought. 'You're mistaken. I was in your boots, or ones rather like them, not so many years ago, and I have a very good idea of what your work entails. And you have utterly fucked this operation up by not carrying out more thorough checks on the boyfriend.'

Weale had heard enough. 'I've no idea what you're talking about,' he growled, 'but I don't have to listen to this crap. I take my orders from—'

'Major Campbell-Fraser, I know.' Harmigan laughed unpleasantly. 'But I'm afraid you do have to listen to me, Captain. Thanks to your carelessness, we've had to change plans. Campbell-Fraser gave me your number because, you see, he takes his orders from me.' Weale drew his breath sharply, and Harmigan went on. 'Yes, I've been running this operation and now you're going to take your orders from me directly so we don't have any more cock-ups and jeopardise the whole thing.'

'I don't believe you. The Commander hates the Brits.' As do I, he felt like adding.

'He doesn't usually stand for "God Save the Queen", it's true, but Roy and I go back a long way. And we happen to have complementary aims here, which is of course the continuation of white rule in Rhodesia. Strange bedfellows and all that. He came to me with this operation and I provided a great deal of the money and logistics for it. You can call him to check if you like, but we don't have much time thanks to your errors, and if you think about it for a minute you'll see that the only other way I'd know to call this number at this time, or the fact you're travelling under the name Frederick Collins, or that you're holding Hope Charamba and her son in a flat just off the central square in Vällingby, would be if your operation was entirely blown, in which case I doubt we'd be chatting on the telephone, don't you?'

Weale had fallen silent.

'Good. I'm so pleased we understand each other. Now, let me hear you speak in a British accent. You're going to have to fool a few Swedes, and they're not as stupid as they look.'

Harmigan sat in his office smoking for a few minutes, then pushed back his chair and got to his feet. He walked across the carpeted corridor and took the lift down to Rachel's office. Papers were spread across her desk and she was reading them with an expression of intense concentration.

'So you found the files.'

She looked up. 'Yes, Archives dug them out for me.'

'Good.' He walked over to her desk and perched himself on the corner. 'You'll soon remember most of it, I expect. I need you to present to the JIC in . . .' he looked at his watch '. . . an hour from now. Think you can manage it?'

She nodded slowly, controlling her breathing with an effort. He had offered her no congratulations on her discovery and no apology for having ignored her suspicions nearly six years earlier. She knew that wasn't his way of doing things, and that her vanity wasn't the real issue at stake, but she resented it nonetheless. He always managed to avoid giving her any professional credit, perhaps because he felt it would alert others to their relationship or perhaps because he never thought to.

Still, he was giving her a chance. If she impressed now – and if they managed to bring Dark in – she was sure he'd find a way to promote her that nobody would question. If only she had picked someone else to fall in love with, she thought. But then perhaps that was the whole point: the self-sabotage had itself been part of her attraction to him. In the weeks after she had returned from Kuala Lumpur, a physical tension had built up between them. She had lain awake at night applying obscure cipher pattern theories to his most offhand remarks to try to work out if he felt as she did or if she was simply imagining it. She had finally received her answer in a taxi-cab after a boozy Service dinner at the Garrick, when he'd wordlessly slid his hand across the leather seat and intertwined his fingers with hers. The chaste gesture had been the starting gun for their affair.

Nearly six years later she was still deeply in love with him, even though she knew it couldn't end well. She spent her days perpetually on stand-by, waiting for him to whisk her off to his room at his club for a hurried half-hour of sex and whispered promises he wouldn't keep. She'd drifted – no, she had leaped headlong – into the classic scenario: the affair with the boss who would never leave his wife.

It was especially unlikely in his case as Celia was fabulously wealthy, having inherited a mining consortium from her first husband, David Meredith, a Service officer who had been killed in a car crash in the late sixties and who had been one of Sandy's best friends. As well as the very comfortable lifestyle this situation afforded Sandy – and he enjoyed the finer things in life – his position as Chief would be in jeopardy if Celia and he were to divorce, especially if there were any indication of impropriety with a member of the Service. Her career would also be in tatters if the affair ever came out.

At least, this was the reasoning Sandy used on her, and which she had come to accept. She'd lived with the secret of their affair for so long that it had become cover for her, an instinctive lie she didn't need to think about any more, like telling people she was an archivist in the Foreign Office – although that one felt increasingly close to the truth. On a weekend visit the previous summer, her mother had found her crying in her bedroom, but hadn't pressed her for the reasons behind it. She hadn't been able to bring herself to tell her. Mum was the daughter of Lithuanian immigrants, but the English habit of avoiding all emotional matters had slowly seeped into her until it had settled. The only living soul she had confided in, and even then without mentioning his name, was her brother, Danny. But despite his own chaotic love-life he'd been appalled she was seeing a married man and had pleaded with her to call it off. She now pretended it was over just to avoid hearing his lectures, especially since she had once referred to Sandy in passing in another context and he'd rolled his eyes theatrically: 'Oh, the old war hero.' He was nearly twice her age, in fact – and yet still she hung on. Her life was taken up on the surface with work, and beneath it the questionable drama of minuscule oscillations in her relationship with Sandy.

She closed the folder she had been reading, distracted by his presence next to her.

'Will Bradley be there,' she asked, 'and if so do I need to keep anything back?' Since the war, the head of CIA's London Station sat in on all Joint Intelligence Committee meetings, and Harry Bradley was the current incumbent.

'Yes, he'll be there, and he should know everything. In fact, let's stress that Dark has damaged Washington as much as he has us. We need all hands on deck to catch him, so let's put the frighteners on.' He gave a mirthless smile. 'Shouldn't be too hard.'

Chapter 31

Hope Charamba sat in the passenger seat of the car, her jaw clenched. She was wearing a nun's wimple and clutching a passport in the name of Sister Emily Sempewa. Next to her, Peter Voers stared at the road ahead as he drove. Hope thought the dog collar in his shirt clashed obscenely with his brutish soldier's face, but she knew her emotions coloured her view of him – the customs officials would simply see two members of a Jesuit Catholic church in the outskirts of Salisbury.

Voers looked across at her, and she turned away. She knew he was angry that he had been interrupted by his leader, the one they called Captain, when he had wanted to assault her. Angry and resentful and ashamed – a volatile mixture. But they were under a tight schedule to catch a flight leaving the country, so she felt that she was at least safe from that horror for the time being. Wherever it was they were taking her was a different matter.

For the hundredth time, she glanced in the rear-view mirror. The blue Vauxhall was still five cars behind them. Ben had become hysterical at being separated from her for the journey, but she had managed to calm him down. There hadn't been any choice. The Captain had made it plain that if she caused any trouble on the way – attracted the attention of a passer-by, alerted a customs official – the men behind would simply stop following, and Ben would be killed. She had no reason to doubt him.

They arrived at Arlanda airport, and Voers parked the car in the long-term area. He turned to face her and smiled – oh, how she loathed his smile.

'I wonder what food they'll serve on the plane,' he said, stroking his moustache with his forefinger and thumb. 'I'm famished.'

Chapter 32

Saturday, 23 August 1975, Lusaka, Zambia

It was approaching dawn when the driver of the black Fiat saloon took the turning into the city's Roma suburb. Matthew Charamba peered through the rear window of the car, searching for any signs of life. This was the first time he had left the house in weeks and his mind was hungry for something to feed on other than the fears that had been occupying it for the last three hours. But all he could make out was a row of greyish houses and dense foliage.

At the end of the avenue, a large villa was set back from the road with a surrounding fence covered in hessian. This was 'The Vatican', the secret headquarters of the Department of National Security and Order – ZAPU's spy agency. It made for a more discreet location for a rendezvous than Zimbabwe House, ZAPU's headquarters in the city, which was believed to be under constant surveillance by the Zambian authorities and perhaps others.

The Vatican was an anonymous-looking four-bed-room villa, but several sentries were positioned just behind the wrought-iron front gates. As the car drew in, one of the guards called through their arrival on a radio set. Once given the all-clear, the men began checking the car for weapons.

'Only you go through,' the lead sentry said when they were done, pointing at Charamba.

'Impossible,' said Gibo. 'He's not going in there alone.'

Charamba held up a hand. 'It's all right, Phillip.'

'Are you sure about this, sir?'

Charamba nodded. He hadn't told Gibo the real reason for his visit here tonight, that Hope and her son had been kidnapped. He had been too frightened to. The man with the metallic voice had been very persua-sive on that point. In his last call, he had changed his demands: he now had to confirm by noon the next day that he would be participating in the talks. Charamba had tried to explain that he wouldn't be able to push Nkomo and the others in such a time frame, and his first call to them hadn't been promising – Nkomo had claimed they already had enough people for their dele-gation. But the Rhodesian hadn't listened. He hadn't allowed him to speak to Hope or her son, either. What if something had happened to them? The man insisted that if Charamba agreed to their demands they would be released as soon as the talks were over, but how could he trust this would happen? The caller had simply reiterated his demand and hung up.

So here he was, at Nkomo's door to beg. But if he was going to walk straight into the lions' den it was vital that he gain the lions' trust, and he wasn't going to do that bringing his bodyguards with him. Nkomo and his men could simply kill him, of course – take him somewhere and shoot him as a traitor to the cause – but he didn't think they would. It would rid them of a potentially dangerous rival, but it would only serve to make him a martyr and was too risky for their own reputations: anyone thought to have been involved in such an act would be cast out forever. Well, so he reasoned. He might have failed to consider all the angles of the current power dynamic, in which case he could be in serious, possibly mortal danger. But bodyguards would send the wrong message, and unarmed they wouldn't be able to stop anything from happening anyway.

He climbed out of the car and allowed himself to be escorted through the gates and into the villa. On the ground floor, the living room had been converted into an operations room, and a few serious-looking men were loitering there huddled over telephones. Charamba had a pang as he saw how much better equipped they were than his own group, and that they were still working at this time of night.

He was led upstairs and ushered into a windowless room. Five men wearing fatigues were waiting for him around a bare conference table. He saw with relief that none of them was armed, either. One of the men stepped forward. It was Nkomo, whom he hadn't seen since he had left the party just after their release from prison. He looked at ease, and well fed.

'Hello, Matthew.'

Charamba took his hand. 'Hello, Joshua.'

Nkomo gave a wary smile. Charamba shook hands with the others, and they seated themselves around the table. The atmosphere was loaded with unspoken tension for a minute, and then Nkomo asked the question all of them were thinking.

'We were surprised to hear from you. You say you want to join us in these talks. What do you hope to gain?'

'Nothing personally,' Charamba lied. 'I think it is a chance for peace, and I want to help influence our country's future in any way that I can.'

The men nodded, but looked unconvinced. Charamba tried again.

'I think we can work better together, but also that it is important that we are seen to be working together. A more united African front will be more appreciated in the international press, and it will put more pressure on the whites to listen to us. I am also confident that if we were to reach an agreement with Smith, we would be able to win the vote in the country.'

He delivered the final point very lightly, as it was a matter of significant resentment with Nkomo and the others that he had become a more popular figure with the public, but he had carefully rehearsed the speech before leaving the house.

The men asked him some more questions about

how he saw his role at the summit, and he answered as best he could. He didn't reveal the position the metallic Rhodesian voice had ordered he should adopt – that would have to wait for the summit itself, if he ever got that far.

After fifteen minutes, Nkomo made motions to finish the meeting.

'You have some very interesting ideas, Matthew,' he said. 'And you seem sincere. I think some good could come of you partaking, but you must understand there is resistance to your presence. We need to discuss this further among ourselves, but we will contact you to let you know our decision.'

'Soon, please,' said Charamba, straining to keep the desperation from his voice.

Nkomo nodded. 'Of course.'

Charamba was escorted downstairs again and trudged back to the waiting car. He climbed in reluctantly – all that awaited him at the end of the drive was a sleepless night as he worried about Hope and the grandson he had never met.

Chapter 33

Saturday, 23 August 1975, Whitehall, London

Rachel followed Harmigan down the narrow corridor. One part of her mind was still sifting through the dossiers on Dark, while another part was wondering if she was appropriately dressed. Sandy had told her to keep her outfit 'sober', her make-up light and to avoid high heels – he had said the latter because Wilson was short, but she suspected it was also because he wanted to tower over everyone in the meeting, her included. Obedient as ever, she was wearing navy flats and a pale cream blouse, but she was having second thoughts about the skirt, a Prince of Wales check number that probably showed off a little more of her legs than 'sober' accommodated.

But perhaps nobody would notice in the mounting atmosphere of tension, which was now bordering on outright panic. Scarcely half an hour had gone since Sandy had persuaded the prime minister that he needed to be informed of developments. As a result, the meeting had been moved from a boardroom on the fourth floor to the main Cabinet Office Briefing Room, known as COBRA, a small crisis operations centre that had been set up three years earlier amid fears the country's infrastructure might collapse if there were widespread strikes. It seemed a little like overkill even for Dark coming back to life, but Sandy was fond of grand gestures.

They came to a staircase and walked down it until they reached a steel blast door guarded by two uniformed guards. One of them took their passes and let them through into a long low-ceilinged room with wood-panelled walls, a large mahogany table that barely fitted into it and dim lighting. She was pleased to note the latter, as now her skirt would be less conspicuous. And the room wasn't as disturbing as she had expected – talk of it in the office usually brought to mind apocalyptic science-fiction films, but while strikes hadn't brought the country to a collapse they had led to the three-day week, and having gone through the hunt for paraffin and candles to see her own dinner by, COBRA's furnishings didn't seem much bleaker than anywhere else.

There were a few *Dr Strangelove* touches nevertheless: part of one wall was taken up with an array of radio and communications equipment, and at the far end of the room there was another blast door. This, she knew, led to the Nuclear Release Room, where the prime minister would use the codes in its safe to give the order for a missile strike if the time ever came.

Rachel removed the dossiers from her briefcase and placed them around the table, then helped set up the projector screen with a technician from the Cabinet Office while the room filled up. There were five spooks: the heads of Five, DIS, GCHQ and the JIC, and Harry Bradley from CIA. It was, as Sandy had promised, a crowd of abbreviations. Rounding it out were the home secretary, Roy Jenkins, and the foreign secretary, James Callaghan, the latter of whom had apparently been very annoyed to have been called in as he was about to set off on a trout-fishing holiday in Ireland.

The prime minister was the last to arrive. He was a more formidable figure than Rachel had expected from seeing him on television and from Sandy's pre-meeting rehearsal, and his every gesture seemed crisp and decisive. He lit a small cigar – his pipe was his trademark, but he smoked cigars in private – and nodded at Harmigan, who quickly got to his feet.

'Good morning, gentlemen; Prime Minister. We're against the clock so I'll spare the chit-chat. We're here to discuss this man.' An image appeared on the wall-screen. 'I'll allow my colleague, Rachel Gold, to explain.'

Rachel scraped back her chair and approached the screen.

'Good morning. This is Erik Johansson. A Swedish citizen, he works for a haulage company in Stockholm. However, he isn't who he seems.' She nodded at the technician, and the photograph was replaced with another of Dark, smooth-shaven and several years

194

younger – it was from his 1964 pass-card for Century House, which Rachel had found in Archives. 'In fact, we've ascertained that he is the former British intelligence officer Paul Dark.'

Jenkins was the first to speak, his mellifluous voice dripping with scepticism.

'And just how have you "ascertained" this?'

Rachel smiled politely, determined not to be intimidated. 'The camera never lies, Home Secretary. Interpol sent us a photo and we compared it with all the images we have on file.' She raised a hand, and with a loud click the photograph of 'Johansson' reappeared, now laid over the photograph of Dark. 'As you can see here, the position of the eyes, mouth and nose in relation to each other, the eyebrows, eyelids, the angle of the forehead, the size of the jaw – all are identical. His face has become fractionally narrower in the last six years, but it's definitely him.'

Jenkins peered at the picture through his thick spectacles. 'Yes, I'll grant it looks like him, but how sure are you?'

'I'm afraid the answer is "very". You can find all the details between pages three and nine of the dossiers. We used a graphics tablet to input the photos into our facial recognition system and our calculations are that the chances of this being anyone other than Paul Dark is around five billion to one – more people than there are on the planet.'

There was a respectful silence in the room as this sank in. Rachel took a breath and continued.

'Dark turned up on Interpol's radar a few hours ago, following a violent incident off the coast of Finland. It seems that he's been living undisturbed in Stockholm, where he has a girlfriend, Claire Nsoka, who holds a Zambian passport but who the authorities in Lusaka have no record of, and that they have a young son. Both Nsoka and the son have apparently been kidnapped – we don't know who by – and Dark has resurfaced to try to get them back.'

She looked up at the men facing her. 'There's a full account of Dark's activities in your dossiers, but the thrust is this: six years ago, a KGB officer walked into our Station in Nigeria and claimed to know the identity of a major Soviet double agent working within the Service. Dark, who was head of Soviet Section at the time, realised at once that he was about to be exposed and went on the run. He eventually wound up in Moscow, where it seems the Russians threw him in the Lubyanka, perhaps having decided that even they couldn't trust him any longer. Dark managed to escape from there, which is some feat, but was killed by Soviet special forces in a remote area between Sweden and Finland in October 1969 – or so we believed until today. Clearly, we were mistaken.'

'Clearly,' said Callaghan, who was now foreign secretary but had been briefed about Dark when he had been home secretary in the government's previous term. 'Didn't that information about Dark's death come from a Russian defector? One you lot swore blind was the genuine article, if I remember correctly.

Have the Soviets fooled us all this time, and if so does that mean Dark is still working for them?'

Rachel shot a look at Harmigan, who glared back: he had warned her before the meeting that she was not under any circumstances to mention that she had previously suggested Dark might still be alive, as it would put them under far too much pressure in the room. They were to present a united front.

'It is indeed the case that we learned of Dark's supposed death via a document passed to us by an agent-in-place in Moscow. This was a report written by Alexander Proshin, who we believe was Dark's handler in London for many years. In our view, the most likely explanation for this is that the Russians *meant* to kill Dark, but Proshin or someone in his team didn't finish the job properly and his report was an arse-covering exercise – if you'll pardon my language.' The men in the room smiled at her tolerantly. 'It might be that Dark was badly wounded enough that he seemed dead, or that they thought he had no chance of surviving in the open. Whatever the case, it's now clear that he did survive and made it to Stockholm. Once there, it wouldn't have been very hard for him to establish a new identity, especially as he speaks fluent Swedish on account of his mother. We're still looking into this, but it seems that for the last eleven months he's been working as a manual labourer during the daytime and at a homeless shelter a few nights a week.'

At this, Harry Bradley let out a derisory snort. 'So

he's got an African girlfriend and works at a soup kitchen – did you trace him through his subscription to the *Guardian*?'

There was an uncomfortable silence, and Jenkins rolled his eyes. Bradley was a 'good ol' boy', and relished it. A stocky, bear-like man with a crest of dyed black hair, he had disappointed his family by going into the espionage game – his uncle had been a senator and his father had been the 'Dixiecrat' candidate for president in 1952. Further back, the family had been staunch segregationists. He was well known for airing controversial views to provoke, and Rachel decided the best way to respond was to pretend it had been a serious question.

'No, sir, we traced him because he escaped from custody in Finland and Interpol issued a notice as a result. The location rang a bell, so I looked into it.'

Bradley folded his arms, his expression mock-chastened. 'Smart girl. By the way, how old is Dark? Judging by that first photo you showed us, he looks like he's getting on some.'

'He's just turned fifty.'

Bradley gave a low whistle, milking it. 'Shit – I'm forty-eight and can barely finish a round of golf.' He peered over his spectacles at the others, looking for a supporting nod or smile, but nobody gave it. Unbowed, he leaned back in his chair and played with his dossier's treasury tag, twisting the bright green cord in his fingers. 'I guess I don't get the flapdoodle. Dark's on the most wanted list, but is he a serious threat now?'

Rachel looked at Harmigan, who nodded and turned to Bradley.

'Harry, this isn't a "flapdoodle". In my considered view' – he placed enough emphasis on 'considered' to remind Bradley and the rest of the room of his own war record – 'this man is the worst traitor this country's ever had. His actions make those of Philby, Blake and the rest of them seem like . . . well, a child stealing candy from a baby would perhaps be the simile in your idiom. He was head of our Soviet Section and, for a brief time, deputy Chief. As far as we can determine, he betrayed every secret he came across between 1945 and 1969 – and I'm afraid he had full Five Eyes clearance.'

'I heard enough about all that when he went missing. But that was six years ago, Sandy. It's not like he can tell Moscow any more secrets than he already has.'

'No, but if the Russians get hold of him again they might decide to go public this time. The papers would jump with joy, and we'd all be up against it.' He looked around the room, and waited as everyone imagined the headlines if Dark's treason was unveiled at a press conference in Moscow, and the resulting pressure they would all be under to explain it. 'There's also a question of justice,' he went on. 'Dark's actions led to the deaths of dozens of our agents, assets and officers – in some cases he did the deed himself, at point-blank range. We're very keen to see him brought to account, and I trust your government is, too.' A facsimile of a smile flickered across his face, then vanished. 'We also still don't know precisely what he betrayed. Miss Gold wrote an excellent damage assessment at the time, which we've included in your dossiers for reference, but it would be more useful to hear it from the horse's mouth. Unfortunately, we're not the only ones interested in that. Dark is a walking intelligence gold mine. Any foreign government or group that manages to get hold of him might be able to squeeze him for everything he knows. That could be Peking, the Cambodians, Middle East terrorists . . . you name it. We have to stop that from happening at all costs. The reality is that every moment he's out there creates the potential for another catastrophe.'

Bradley frowned. 'Okay. So bring the bastard in. You have photographs of him, Interpol's sent out an alert. Presumably you can just arrest him the moment he tries to leave Finland.'

Harmigan steepled his hands together and smiled benignly, his long face taking on an almost priestly demeanour. 'The Finns already took him into custody and he escaped, knocking out the head of their coast-guard in the process. He's probably already left the country by now. The border controls on the boats there are practically nonexistent – you just need to buy a ticket. Our best guess is he'll have boarded a ferry back to Stockholm, as that's the direction the kidnappers took, and one of my men in the city is making contact with Swedish intelligence as we speak. We hope to pick him up soon, but I'd caution against complacency when it comes to this man. We don't know where he is, what identity he's using or what emergency measures he has in place. He's successfully evaded the attentions of every major intelligence agency in the world for six years, and has three decades of experience as an operative and officer. He's highly trained in escape and evasion techniques and has even worked as an assassin, killing an exceptionally unpleasant individual in Hong Kong. And as Miss Gold has just explained, he broke out of the Lubyanka, which as you know is a prison *within the KGB's own headquarters*.'

Bradley's lips twitched, but he fell silent. Harmigan raised his eyebrows as if to say, 'Any more for any more?' Rachel was considering what he had just said when she realised there was a stirring to her left, and that the prime minister was addressing her.

'Miss Gold, or Sandy if this isn't Miss Gold's domain, can you explain to us how the Swedes didn't realise Dark was living there? They have checks, don't they – identity cards and so on? My impression's always been that it's a fairly enlightened democracy.'

His tone was friendly, the Yorkshire lilt to his accent more obvious than on the television or radio. She smiled. 'A little too enlightened, perhaps, Prime Minister. You're right, of course, but their "open society" model cuts both ways, and has unfortunately been rather useful to terrorists. So far this year they've expelled two Japanese Red Army members, and you may remember there was a group who staged a siege at the West German embassy in Stockholm in April and killed two diplomats in the process. Associated with the Baader-Meinhof gang, we think. It also looks like members of Black September were hiding out in the city before the Munich massacre.'

Wilson took a long draw of his cigar, then tipped it against a glass ashtray on the table. 'I see. Have the Swedes been turning a blind eye to all this, or are they incompetent in some way?'

Harmigan stepped in again. 'I suspect a little of the latter, Prime Minister. There has been talk of Soviet infiltration of Swedish intelligence in the last couple of years, but to date it seems to be just that. And as I understand it from colleagues in Stockholm, while they have some knowledge of these terrorists and radicals, in practice they are extremely hard to pin down. Some operate under cover at legitimate organisations while others simply lie low in flats in the city, either having cash funnelled to them through a network of contacts in the region or by robbing the occasional bank to top up funds.'

Wilson leaned back, staring at the ceiling. 'Could one of these groups have helped Dark?' He sat up again and turned to Rachel, fixing her with his gaze. She froze for a moment before regaining her composure.

'That's certainly a possibility, Prime Minister. It could be that he became involved with a terrorist group and they've turned on him and kidnapped his family, or something along those lines. The ballistics experts in Finland have told us that the kidnappers used nine-millimetre Makarov cartridges, which are standard issue within the Warsaw Pact, but also a US Army-issue M26 hand grenade. Those are more commonly known as "fragmentation" grenades, because an indented liner fragments when they explode. Baader-Meinhof stole a large cache of them from the American base in Miesau four years ago, and we know the Japanese Red Army used them when they held up the French embassy in the Hague in September.'

'Well, that narrows things down,' said Bradley. 'We're dealing with a radical leftist group who hate America, right?'

Rachel tried not to react to the naked self-interest and smiled politely instead. 'It's really too early to say. It might be that, or even a directly Soviet-sponsored cell, but a group on the right could also have captured some of the Miesau stock and used it to frame leftists, for example.'

Harmigan broke in again. 'Oh, I think that's a little far-fetched. Let's not start seeing elaborate conspiracies until we have a little more to go on.'

She bristled at the public dressing-down.

'Just keeping an open mind, sir,' she said, with a tight smile.

Wilson appeared not to have noticed the momentary crack in their united front.

'All right, Miss Gold, Sandy – I've heard enough. What is it you want from us, and from me in particular?'

Harmigan was waiting for the opening, and pushed a sheet of paper forward on the table. 'I'd like you to sign this, Prime Minister. We need to set up a security cordon very quickly, but we're going to have to persuade Interpol and everyone else to go along with it. Your signature would speed up the process considerably.'

Wilson reached for the form. He read it in silence, his brow furrowed, then he peered up at Harmigan.

'I appreciate all you've just said, Sandy, but isn't this still rather over the top for one man? You're asking for troops with automatic weapons at every customs post, port and airport across the whole of Western Europe.'

Harmigan nodded. 'If you remember, last year you authorised the deployment of four hundred troops to Heathrow, backed by tanks. Security was tightened in airports all around the world.'

'Yes, but that was because we were worried there would be terrorist attacks.'

'Prime Minister, Paul Dark *is* a terrorist. Six years ago, he murdered the Chief of my agency in cold blood. We have the ballistic evidence to prove it. He was then directly implicated in the assassination of two further Chiefs. He also tried to assassinate you.'

Wilson's head jerked up. 'What did you just say?'

'I'm afraid so. It was on your visit to Nigeria in 1969. I've brought the dossier on the incident.'

He passed a buff folder to Wilson, who flicked it open. Three minutes and some seconds later, he closed it and turned back to Harmigan.

'Pardon my French, Sandy, but why the fuck am I only being told about this now?'

The atmosphere in the room had now changed – everyone was finding pieces of lint on their trousers or a spot on the ceiling to examine. Harmigan smoothed his hands over the leather sleeve of his chair. 'Well, sir, because Dark was initially exonerated of any involvement in this by my predecessor. I did consider raising the topic with you at our first meeting, but due to the passage of time and the importance of establishing trust I felt it was best to let sleeping dogs lie.'

'And sleeping traitors! Lying to my face seems a mighty peculiar way of establishing trust. You carefully skimmed past all of this, as I remember it. There had simply been some "suspicions" about him, you told me. You also told me he was dead. Now I learn he was some sort of KGB assassin intent on killing everyone in Britain, me included, and that he's alive and kicking and perhaps getting ready to do it all over again. It's a bit much, Sandy, really.' He threw the dossier onto the table and pointed at it scornfully. 'Did you brief Heath about this?'

'No, sir. I didn't feel it was relevant.'

'Oh. Did he try to kill him, too, then?'

'No, sir.' Harmigan bowed his head. 'I understand the frustration, sir, and I apologise for not disclosing this earlier. But we really do need to find this man at once.'

Wilson took a sip of water from a glass in front of him, then set it down.

'What about the Russians, and the Chinese? They're

hardly going to miss it if every airport and harbour in Western Europe reinforces its security, and they'll want to know why.'

'I'm afraid that can't be helped, sir. We're just going to have to get hold of him before they do.'

Wilson took a pen from his pocket.

'Well, make bloody sure you do.' He signed the paper with an angry flourish and handed it back to Harmigan, then levered himself up from his chair. 'Thank you for the briefing – I'm afraid you'll have to finish without me as I have another appointment I must attend.' He nodded curtly at the figures around the table. 'Gentlemen. Miss Gold.'

He signalled his aide by the door, and walked out.

'Drink?'

'Thanks. A small one.'

Harmigan strode to the glass-topped trolley and surveyed the collection of bottles.

'Scotch do you? I've a twelve-year-old Laphroaig if you fancy.'

'Perfect. No ice, your way.'

Harmigan smiled to himself. For all the supposed pedigree of his family, the man was a philistine. He took out the bottle, selected one of the stippled glasses from the tray beneath and poured a measure into it, then walked over to the wingback chair and handed it to Harry Bradley.

'Went well, I thought.'

The American took the glass and nodded his thanks.

'Yeah, though Wilson didn't seem to appreciate that file you gave him too much.'

'No, but it did the trick. Desperate times call for desperate measures.'

'Sure.' Bradley grunted. 'Trust Dark to take up with a nigger.'

'Looked rather pretty, from the pictures.'

'Well, he always had a way with women, let's give the fucker that.' Bradley took a sip of the whisky and glanced around the massive office. The neighbourhood was a dump, but Harmigan had certainly made the most of his penthouse suite. He set the glass on the small table next to him and leaned forward in his chair.

'Let's not beat about the bush, Sandy. Your men royally screwed up here, and we need to get things back on track right away.'

Harmigan nodded. 'I have it in hand.'

In hand, thought Bradley. It was like stepping back in time with these guys.

'How, exactly?'

'The cell leader has stayed in Stockholm and is now acting under my personal instructions to find and finish Dark.'

Bradley smiled at the euphemism. 'And you're sure he's still up to it?'

'Yes.'

Bradley turned and picked his glass up again. 'He'd damn well better be. By the way, what's the deal with the Gold girl?'

Harmigan froze for a fraction of a second, then

recovered and looked across at him with a perfectly level expression. 'What do you mean?'

'I mean all that shit she spouted about framing leftists. A little close to the knuckle, wasn't it?'

Harmigan felt his heart return to its normal rate.

'That wasn't my doing.'

Bradley raised his eyebrows over the rim of the glass. 'You mean you haven't brought her into this? Don't you trust her?'

'I trust her to do her job, yes – she's an exceptional analyst. But this isn't for her. The fewer people who know the better.'

Bradley leaned back in the chair and felt the warm glow of the whisky radiate through his chest. 'I hope she isn't *too* exceptional an analyst, Sandy.'

'It's all under control.'

Chapter 34

Saturday, 23 August 1975, Salisbury, Rhodesia

'I'm having second thoughts about the South Africans' plan for a conference.' Ian Smith looked at the men around the table. 'The sticking point, as most of you know, has been that several of the guerrilla leaders fear they'll be arrested if they re-enter Rhodesia. Rightly, I might add!'

There were chuckles around the room.

'Their new proposal is for us to meet in a South African Railways' dining car at Vic Falls. The carriage would be positioned very precisely on the bridge so that their delegation would be seated on the Zambian side of the border and we'd be on this side.'

There was a murmur around the table. 'We could use the opportunity to bring the lot back over here and apply the screws,' said Shaw. 'We might learn a thing or two.'

Smith frowned, but there was a hint of a smile behind it. 'That's not especially helpful, Willard.

Tempting, but rather counter-productive in the longer term, I suspect.'

'What does Kaunda make of this?' asked Riggs, head of Special Branch.

'He's keen,' said Smith. 'The idea is that he would attend with Vorster, both of them acting as observers.' He pursed his lips in a small, cynical smile. 'Nkomo and Sithole would have a few of their people with them. Mugabe has refused to take part, claiming the others are selling out, but I don't think we need shed any tears over that. Zambia, Botswana and Tanzania would send a few delegates for form's sake, and BOSS would oversee the security arrangements. I don't object to any of it on principle, actually: it's an ingenious solution, and just the sort of dramatic stunt the international press eats up. I naturally want any summit we participate in to receive as much attention as possible. But my feelings haven't really changed on the futility of talks right now. Vorster is threatening to withdraw more material support, but I reckon we can manage pretty well even if he does – and as I've said before, I don't take kindly to being blackmailed.' He leaned back in his chair and lifted his hands towards the others. 'But I'd like your views on this.'

Three seats to Smith's left, Roy Campbell-Fraser was frantically thinking how to deal with this development. The last time he had spoken to Matthew Charamba he had given him a deadline for noon tomorrow to accede to his demands and arrange with Nkomo that he would attend the conference. But that deadline might now be too late. Campbell-Fraser had been sure Smith would bow to the South Africans' pressure to take part in the summit, and indeed had believed it was a done deal, but the man was even more stubborn than he had thought possible. He cleared his throat and Smith turned to him, his eyebrows raised.

'Roy?'

'Well, I may have something for you, Prime Minister – although I must stress that it's highly provisional, based on talk from some of our recently captured terrs.'

'Oh, yes? What have they been saying?'

'That Matthew Charamba might be joining the African delegation.'

Smith rolled his eyes. 'Charamba? That thug's made his position clear: he wants us to specify a precise time-frame for black rule. That is totally unacceptable. He's just the sort of leader we can't do business with.'

'I'm aware of all that, Prime Minister, but we're hearing that he's now thinking of abandoning that position and coming into the negotiations to argue it would be better to postpone talk of majority rule until peaceful transition looks like a realistic prospect.'

'What? That's a complete U-turn! Why on earth would he do that?'

Campbell-Fraser shrugged. 'We don't really know at the moment. This is just what we're hearing. It might be that his inner circle have persuaded him his previous position was futile. If one were of a more cynical frame of mind, one might suspect he's changing his strategy so he can position himself as a potential leader instead of forever being in exile.'

'A power-grab, you mean, uniting all the factions?'

'Perhaps. Anyway, I don't think we care too much why he's changed his mind, do we, as long as he turns up and argues it that way?'

Smith pressed his forefinger against his lower lip. After a few seconds he smiled. 'This might be very good news, Roy. Charamba has massive support among the blacks so he would be able to swing any arrangement if he came to the talks. How sure are you of these rumours?'

'At the moment, I'd say we're about eighty per cent sure. I hope to firm things up very soon.'

Smith nodded, taking this in. 'Excellent. Let me know the minute you hear anything further. Call my office directly.' He looked around the table. 'Now, do we have any other business to attend to?'

Chapter 35

The counter-intelligence unit of Sweden's Säkerhet-spolisen, informally known as Säpo, operated out of offices in the large police station in Bergsgatan on the quiet island of Kungsholmen. John Weale approached the concrete shed in front of the station, where a sentry asked for his name, consulted a docket and then let him past.

He walked through the gates feeling uncharacteristically anxious. As soon as he had got off the phone with Harmigan he had broken protocol and called the Commander, who had tersely confirmed that the orders were genuine: he was to meet with Säpo and discover what they knew of Dark's movements, then find Dark and 'silence' him.

Weale had spent his life taking orders, including to kill in cold blood, but he was reluctant to do so in this case, and not just because they came from a Brit. Despite Harmigan's blithe claims this would be a walk in the park, it was an extremely risky idea to impersonate a Service officer at the drop of a hat to another intelligence agency. Weale had meticulously prepared a legend for Frederick Collins as a British fabric sales-man, not as a spook based in Sweden. His knowledge of the country was related to the operation at hand, and if anyone scratched at the surface it would fall apart. Harmigan had assured him the Swedes wouldn't be looking for anything out of the ordinary and that if he encountered any trouble he was simply to insist on placing a direct call to his office in London, but that was scant comfort. He knew he had no choice, and Campbell-Fraser had made the operation's importance clear: the very fate of white rule in Rhodesia was at stake. He had decided to take him at his word and act accordingly. It would make the job a hell of a lot easier.

The marble-floored lobby of the building was deserted except for an overweight man in a brown suit and maroon shirt smoking a cigarette. He had shaggy greying hair and lonely eyes with large bags beneath them. Seeing Weale approach, he crushed his cigarette out in a nearby stand and ambled towards him.

'Frederick Collins?'

'Yes, I'm here to see Iwan Morelius.'

'That's me.' He stuck out a large hand.

Weale took it. 'A pleasure to meet you, Iwan. I take it Sandy Harmigan has explained to you our interest in this matter?'

Morelius nodded. 'Broadly speaking, yes. A Soviet agent in your service, I understand.'

'*Formerly* in our service,' said Weale, wincing. He hoped he wasn't overplaying it – his accent didn't take

much modifying but he had to be careful not to cari-
cature the tight-arsedness too much and come over
like Terry-Thomas. The key to cover was not to bow
too much to expectation, and he'd decided that the
best way to avoid tripping up was to stick fairly closely
to his own personality.

'I understand,' said Morelius. 'You come highly
recommended by Sandy, incidentally. How is he these
days?'

'I wouldn't know,' said Weale, his tone airy. 'I haven't
seen him in more than a year. He still knows how to
give orders over a telephone, though.'

Morelius smiled, the bristles of his moustache falling
over his lip as he did so. 'Where is it you're based, Mr
Collins? You aren't on the Service's declared list here.'

'Ah, yes, sorry about that – I'm not at the embassy,
more of a roving man in the region.'

The Swede nodded. 'I see.'

They walked to the lift, and a minute later emerged
into a modern open-plan office, where Weale was
introduced to a group of neat young men with
side-partings and, in several cases, horn-rimmed
spectacles.

'They dress better than I do,' Morelius said with a
smile. He turned to the men. 'This is Frederick Collins
from British intelligence. He's here to tell us what he
knows about Herr Johansson, and in turn you will tell
him what we've discovered.'

Chapter 36

Harmigan rapped on the door of Rachel Gold's office and, without waiting for an answer, stepped inside. He closed the door and drew the blinds with a swift pull of the sash, then took her in his arms. She felt her breathing tighten as they kissed, his skin scratching against hers. Then he drew away, his eyes sparkling as she hadn't seen them do for months.

'Oh, you were glorious, my dear! Wonderful. I've just had a little chat with Bradley and he's given us the go-ahead to use KH, with all the bells and whistles.'

KH was Kinnaird House, a CIA command centre in Pall Mall that was rigged up with powerful radio receivers, computers and other state-of-the-art equipment. It had briefly been used during the Penkovsky operation, and senior members of the Service still waxed lyrical about it.

Harmigan was holding a straw hat in one hand, which he placed on his head gingerly. 'I'm heading over there now to get things going. Want to take the car with me?' She didn't reply and he looked at her, puzzled. 'What's wrong? Darling, this is rather a hefty promotion. And it's well deserved, believe me. Nobody will question it.'

She slumped into her chair and folded her arms, incredulous at his apparent ignorance of the cause of her anger.

'Who's the officer you sent to talk to the Swedes?'

The penny dropped as Harmigan completed the sentence in his mind: . . . *and why haven't you sent me out there to work with him?* This was why you should never fall in love with your subordinates, he thought. He took the hat off and tried to think how to calm her down.

'A very good chap, Fred Collins. He's one of our alongsiders in the region. I don't want to involve the Station if I can avoid it. Darling, you've read the files backwards and forwards so you know I wasn't telling tales in there – Dark's a very dangerous man, and will very likely try to kill anyone who gets in his way.'

She gave him a savage look. 'So you can't send this delicate little flower to help find him, is that it? Come on, Sandy, you know I'd be better use on the ground in Stockholm than watching it all unfold from here.'

He flicked at the ribbon of his hat, and she clenched her fists unseen beneath the desk. The ghost of the Gadlow operation had risen between them, as she had been afraid it would. He claimed to trust her judgement, but when it came to the crunch he didn't trust it enough to send her out in the field again.

Harmigan took a deep breath. 'Dear heart, be

reasonable. This might get extremely hairy, but it's not only about that. I know you feel Dark's your bag, but this is a team effort, remember, and I need your analytical skills here. Dark might not even be in Sweden, and even if he is he may well turn up somewhere else before long. KH is where we'll gather all the intel, and I can't afford to have you incommunicado on a flight to Christ knows where when the shit hits the fan. But one of our ground rules was you wouldn't question my judgement like this.'

An invocation of the famous ground rules. They never seemed to suit her much, she thought. But his voice had now taken on its familiar commanding air and she knew he intended to cow her with it, as he had cowed the prime minister and Bradley, and as he had previously cowed Whitehall into appointing him Chief. She knew all his tricks. He wanted her to feel like the hysterical woman making unreasonable demands, seeing attacks where there were none. Instead, his response had brought home the reality of the situation to her: it wasn't just that he still blamed her for Gadlow, but that he blamed himself for ever thinking she might have succeeded. There would be no second chances in the field because he had decided she was inherently unsuited to it – she was only any use as an analyst, a back-room digger helping out the blokes, good old Rachel in HQ.

She tried to calm herself. She knew there was no advantage in pursuing the complaint, either personally or professionally. He had made up his mind so she had better make the best of a bad lot, at least for the time being. She dropped her gaze and gave the tiniest of nods to show her acquiescence.

Harmigan smiled reassuringly and placed a hand on her arm. 'That's my girl. You're under a lot of pressure, of course – we all are. But let's try to stay calm and not turn on each other and read false motives into things. Speaking of which, you said something interesting in the meeting.'

She smiled from one corner of her mouth, giving what she knew was a good impression of coquettishness in their own private language. 'Just the one?'

He laughed, pleased she had snapped out of her mood. 'Don't fish too much! I mean that theory you floated that the kidnappers might not be left-wing terrorists but part of a feint by someone else, framing them for it. Did I follow that correctly?'

'Yes. What about it?' She studied his face for clues as to what he was after, remembering how he had contradicted her in the meeting.

He waved a hand casually. 'I was just wondering what had led you to believe it was a possibility.'

'Nothing concrete. It was more of an instinctive reaction. It just all seems rather too neat, don't you think? Something doesn't quite fit. It's a little too . . . ambitious, if you know what I mean.'

He smiled. 'No, I don't. What do you mean?'

She got up and walked around the desk, thinking it through. 'Well, according to the Finns, Dark claimed the men who kidnapped his family were black. His girlfriend has a Zambian passport, and even though that seems to be forged it rather suggests they were Africans rather than, say, Americans.'

'Yes, but what does that prove? There are plenty of African terrorist groups – pick a country, my dear.'

'But African terrorists don't usually operate in Europe like this, do they? I can't think of a single other case, actually.' A thought struck her, something that had been nagging at the back of her mind. 'By the way, what was all that stuff about Dark trying to kill Wilson in Nigeria? I never saw that in his files.'

Harmigan gave an apologetic smile. 'Yes, I'm afraid we did have to hold that one back.' He looked down at his shoes, Oxfords polished to a military sheen. 'As for your other idea, well, it's an interesting thought but let's take care not to get side-tracked. You were right about Dark being alive, but this isn't really time for feminine intuition. It's terribly easy to get caught up in byzantine theories and see complexities that aren't there, but if it walks like a duck, quacks like a duck and is carrying Soviet weapons, it's probably a Soviet-sponsored duck.' He smiled again and clapped his hands together so they made a dull thud, indicating that the subject was closed. 'Anyway, let's bring the car round, shall we?'

Chapter 37

John Weale accepted the mug of coffee from Morelius's secretary and settled into his chair. 'Do you have any leads on where he went after escaping from custody in Finland?'

Morelius gestured at one of his men, older than the others and with a leathery complexion and shrewd eyes.

'Yes, we think he's either on his way back here or already in the city. It could be he has an emergency cache of papers here, but even if not we believe this is where he will look for the clues as to who took his family.'

Weale took a sip of coffee. 'And do you have any ideas who that might be?'

'Well, he told the Finns the kidnappers were black, but as I'm sure you can appreciate that isn't especially helpful. He may have been lying, or just mistaken. And we can hardly stop every black man leaving the country, especially as they might already have done so.'

Weale nodded. This was very good news – by his

calculations Voers and the rest of the team should be boarding their plane right about now, and as the Swedes didn't know who they were looking for there was a very good chance they would make it out.

'So how do you plan to find him?'

'Well, we've put alerts out to the police and military with complete descriptions and photographs, and all ports and airports now have armed troops on the lookout for him in line with your Chief's recommendations to Interpol. We've also informed television, radio and the press, both here and across the Nordic region. They are running bulletins every hour – a dangerous killer on the loose and so on. He should be in all the evening papers, we hope front-page. In the meantime, we're putting together a map of all known friends and associates of the girlfriend, Claire Nsoka. She worked as a picture researcher for one of the papers, so we're interviewing people there, as well as talking to her son's kindergarten and of course interviewing neighbours.'

Weale was heartened. These were precisely the measures he would have implemented, and he wouldn't have fancied his own chances against such a manhunt. 'What about the flat? Were there any clues there?'

Morelius turned to a colleague and rattled off instructions to him in rapid Swedish. The other man left the office and came back a minute later clutching a dusty-looking holdall in one hand and a rifle in the other.

Weale stood and looked both of them over carefully.

The holdall was empty, but presumably had been where Dark/Johansson had stored his emergency supplies. He picked up the rifle and stared down it, then weighed it in his hand.

'Not a bad weapon. I can imagine he could have done some damage with this.' He turned to the Swedes. 'Any idea where he might have got it from?'

'We're investigating that, too,' said Morelius. 'It could be that he simply bought it over the counter somewhere, as it's easy to do with cash if you have the right papers.'

'How did he get his papers in the first place? I understand he had five passports on him. Presumably he used a forger – are there such people in Stockholm?'

Morelius nodded. 'Our colleagues in Finland noted down the details on those passports, so they are of course all on the alert notice. But as you say, he must have had them made somewhere. If the five were his complete collection, he may try to get another one made from whoever created those. There are very few people we know of here who are capable of such a thing.'

Weale glanced up. 'How few?'

'Well, we already checked out most of them and turned up nothing, but there is one person we haven't yet visited. Would you like to come along with us?'

Weale smiled.

Chapter 38

The city was a horror. Young women with figure-hugging jeans and Sunsilk hair clung to men with even glossier hair and even tighter jeans as they strolled carelessly through the streets. And everywhere there were children, most of whom seemed to be small boys of around three years old.

In the rear of the taxi, Paul Dark closed his eyes and leaned back against the headrest. He'd managed to shut down his racing mind only long enough to catch a few minutes' sleep on the bus ride from the ferry into central Stockholm: abstract shapes redolent of despair had flitted beneath his eyelids, coalescing and hanging just out of his reach. At T-Centralen, he had changed Kurkinen's marks into kronor, then found a telephone booth and looked up the address. When Kurkinen had questioned him, he'd urged him to investigate car dealerships and the harbour in Stockholm, but it could be that the Swedish authorities were in the midst of doing just that and if he tried the same he would simply walk straight into their cordon. But he doubted they would know where he was headed now.

The car came to a traffic light and he forced his eyes open again, worried he might nod off. His body had initially reacted to Claire and Ben being taken with the classic acute stress response, fight-or-flight: accelerated heart-rate, nausea, sweating, tunnel vision, the lot. But now he'd both fought and fled, his body had hit a brick wall and he was in a state of hypo-arousal, overcome with a feeling of lethargy and unreality, almost as though he were watching himself from outside.

He sat up straighter. He didn't want to return to fight-or-flight mode, but he had to regain his energy and lucidity. The first thing to do was address the fears he was trying to suppress head on. Chief among them were the recurring visions of Claire and Ben either dead or being subjected to torture. If he were going to be any use, he had to accept that both were possible, but that neither were likely. If the men in the masks had wanted them dead, they would have shot them on the island when they had the chance. They'd shot at him, and they had killed the Hanssons without any apparent compunction, but they hadn't aimed their fire at Ben or Claire. So they must want them alive. Hold on to that fact. Hold on to it, and don't let go. It means this is a kidnap, which means there's a very good chance they're still alive and being kept in good health. It means the men want something. You just have to find out what it is.

He smiled bitterly at his optimism. *Just.*

The car was approaching the address he'd given
and Dark asked the driver to let him off on the corner.
He paid him and waited until he had left the area,
then walked up to the apartment block. He scanned
the names on the push-buttons until he found the one
he was looking for and pressed it firmly. Thirty
seconds passed, and then a voice came through the
small speaker.

'Hello?'

'It's Erik Johansson. Please let me in. It's an
emergency.'

A moment later, he was in the lobby of the building
and bounding up the stairs.

Weale went with Morelius and two of his men in an
unmarked Saab. Twenty minutes later, they parked
opposite the bakery in Gamla Stan. The younger officers marched towards the building and Weale followed
with Morelius, his right hand reaching to check his
Makarov was in place behind his jacket.

Karl Vesterlund was a small man with piercing blue
eyes, somewhere in his seventies. He showed no
surprise or even anxiety at being raided by the security
services, and Weale wondered if he might no longer
care whether the authorities questioned him. They
walked into a small, cluttered living room, but there
was no sign of any forgery work being done.

'Where's your office?' Morelius asked in an even
voice. 'We can tear down the walls, you know.'

Vesterlund shrugged, and Weale realised he was

simply resigned to having been detected – he had expected the day to come eventually and was mentally prepared for it.

He unhooked a lever from a bookcase and it slid away, revealing a doorway, then led them down a small flight of steps into a cramped room that contained a desk, a chair, several bright lamps, ink, tape, scissors, a microscope and disordered piles of paper, many of them small, familiar-sized booklets.

'My study,' Vesterlund said with a rueful smile.

Morelius showed him the Finns' photograph of Dark, and he leaned down and peered at it. He shuffled over to a filing cabinet and took out a ledger, which he placed on the desk and started leafing through until he found what he was looking for – a small stamp-like photograph that he offered to Morelius.

'Here he is.'

In the apartment block in Hägersten, a lanky young man stood on the landing peering out of the flat. He was dressed in nothing but a pair of white underpants. Dark recognised him: it was Jonas, the boyfriend Marta had supposedly broken up with so disastrously that Claire had needed to rush round to offer comfort. So perhaps that had been a lie, though to hide what he didn't know. But Claire had consulted with Marta about that, so hopefully it wasn't the only thing she'd taken her into her confidence about.

Jonas started to speak but Dark lifted a finger to his lips and hurried him back into the flat. The living room was small but well ordered, with orange and pink Marimekko curtains and two lounge chairs in birch, chrome and leather. Expensive, tasteful stuff, confirming his suspicion they were middle-class dropouts, no doubt funding their rebellion with their parents' money. He walked through to find Marta Österberg standing in the kitchen in her nightdress.

'Erik? You look different. You've shaved. You said there was an emergency?'

'I need to talk to you about Claire. She and Ben are missing.'

She stared at him. 'What do you mean?'

'Someone's kidnapped them, and I need to find out who. Claire had a false passport, and I think you or someone else in your organisation arranged it for her. I know we've never seen eye to eye, but I need your help. I need you to tell me her real name and anything else you know about her past. Please.'

Marta met his gaze with an appraising one of her own. She had indeed never liked him: he was arrogant and apathetic, and she couldn't understand what Claire saw in him. But his desperation rang true, and she couldn't think of any plausible reason for him to invent such a story anyway. Jonas was trying to catch her attention out of the corner of her eye, but she decided to trust her own instincts.

'Her name is Hope Charamba. That's all I know.'

'Is she Zambian?'

'I don't know, I'm sorry. Who's taken her and Ben? Have you informed the police?'

Dark ignored her, his mind racing ahead.

Hope Charamba.

It meant nothing to him, and could be from any country in Africa for all he knew. He needed someone who did know. His mind suddenly grabbed at a memory – a large reddish face in the Lagos heat. Yes. Of course.

He did some swift calculations. After Kurkinen had dusted off his pride and the bruising around his wind-pipe, he would have sent Interpol all the names on his passports as well as the photograph they had taken of him. There was a chance Interpol would have sent out a wide enough alert that someone in London could have recognised him. If so, the Service would now also be looking for him. It was a slim chance, but he had to consider it nonetheless. And if it were the case, they would have provided the Swedish authorities with a photograph of him unshaven.

He probably had a window of only a couple of hours to get out of the country before the newspapers and radio and everything else conspired against him making it out without being spotted, but he had a major problem without a passport. It would be rela-tively easy to visit another Scandinavian country – he wouldn't have to show a passport at either end – but that wasn't going to help him get to Belgium. One solution would be to find the old chap in Gamla Stan and ask him to make him another passport, but that would be time-consuming and potentially very risky.

'Who made Hope's passport?' he asked Marta.

She threw her hands up and shook her head. 'Why does it matter?'

He glared at her.

'A man called Vesterlund.'

'An old man, lives above a bakery in Gamla Stan?'

She nodded, and Dark swore under his breath. But perhaps there was a chance.

'How well known is he?' She peered at him, not understanding, and he tried again, willing her to follow the speed of his own thoughts. 'Is it possible the authorities know about him?'

She hesitated for a moment, then shook her head – but the hesitation had given him all the information he needed. She wasn't sure, so Vesterlund was out. Even if Säpo didn't already know about him, they might be able to track him down and apply some pressure until he told them about his most recent visitor, and the name on the passport he had made for him. He thought for a moment, staring into Marta's puzzled, almost angelic-looking face. She was beautiful enough in the classical Scandinavian way, but did nothing for him and apparently the same applied in reverse as he'd never had any inkling she found him attractive. That didn't surprise him, but he couldn't for the life of him understand what she would see in someone like . . .

Jonas. He looked over at him, still standing by the door in his briefs, watching. He was in his early thirties, pigeon-chested and with a weak chin. But his colouring and the general set of his features were close enough.

'Where's your passport?' Dark said. 'Your emergency one, I mean. You must have one.'

The young man glared at him. 'I think perhaps it's time you left.' He looked across at his girlfriend, his arms folded.

'Claire and Ben are missing,' Dark said, also looking to Marta. 'Please.'

She took a deep breath, and then nodded. 'Go and get it, darling. Quickly.'

The office in Kungsholmen was thick with the fug of cigarette smoke, and some of the men were rubbing their eyes, the hours of concentration taking their toll. Weale, paradoxically, felt more awake than he had done in days. His concerns about his cover had faded now he'd passed muster with the Swedes, and his focus had become more intense. He was starting to panic that he'd lost Dark.

The old forger Vesterlund had been turned over to the police to be arrested and charged, but he hadn't given them any serious leads. He had admitted to having made Dark the five passports he'd had on him in Helsinki, but claimed to have had no other contact with him. Weale was an expert in weighing the reliability of such testimonies from his work with captured terrs, and in his judgement the man was telling the truth.

Morelius had placed a couple of his men on watch outside Vesterlund's flat in case Dark came calling, but Weale's instincts also told him that that possibility wasn't on the cards now. Dark might have used more than one forger, or be visiting another one at that very moment. He might already have left the country. Weale hoped to hell he hadn't – he didn't relish the idea of having to tell Harmigan he'd lost sight of the target.

He tried to think through what he would do in the other man's shoes. Dark's overriding concern must be to find out why his family had been taken, and from there try to figure out by whom. But Weale had no idea how much the girl had told him of her past life, and she would be up in the air with Voers and the others by now so he had no way of checking.

'We'll find him,' said Morelius, sensing Weale's frustration. 'We're watching the ports very closely.' He indicated the banks of computer screens his men were huddled around, most of which showed closed-circuit television stills.

'We're linked to every customs post in the country here, and they all have the photographs of Dark that Interpol and your colleagues in London provided. We've also tightened the usual restrictions on travelling within Scandinavia at the request of your prime minister, so even within the region he would have to show a passport – provided he hasn't already got through, of course.'

Weale wanted to ask why the hell they had such an idiotically lax system in the first place, but bit his tongue. His eye had been drawn to one of the screens, which had just started showing images of passports in rapid succession.

Morelius followed his gaze. 'Yes, that's something new from the customs people at the airport. They have it in Berlin, too, and a few of the larger American cities. Each customs official has a glass plate under their desk, and they place passengers' passports on it when they go through.' He mimed the movement with one hand. 'A linked computer in their control centre scans the page, rather like a photocopy machine, and we can access the resulting image from here. But it doesn't help us much in this case because it takes twenty minutes or more for the images to get here. Even if we did happen to spot Dark's photograph among them, by that time his flight would already have left. Perhaps in a few years this system will be of use, but today . . .' He shrugged his shoulders.

'But we have access to all the flight manifests,' said Weale. 'So if we match the name on the passport with the manifests we can figure out where he's heading. Do you get every single one of these photographs sent here as a matter of course?'

'From Arlanda airport, yes. But we're talking about thousands of passengers. Are you proposing to look through them all to try to spot him? If I can be direct with you, the idea seems a little desperate. This isn't something that can be done with the naked eye.'

'Why not? That's how the passport officers are doing it. I suggest we set up what is in effect a separate customs post here, double-checking every scanned passport image as fast as we can manage. Dark will know we're looking for him by now, and he'll also know that to get out of Scandinavia he'll have to use a photograph that looks enough like him to get through customs, but not enough like the photographs we've circulated to have him stopped. But with all due respect to your customs officials, I think our judgement as to how he might disguise himself is probably more sophisticated. We can also order the information here: start with the easiest and work outwards to the harder stuff. So let's filter out all Caucasian male passengers between the ages of, say, thirty and sixty, and start looking at those.'

Morelius clicked his fingers at one of his men.

'Not bad, Mr Collins,' he said when he had given the instructions. 'I'm starting to understand what Sandy Harmigan sees in you.'

Chapter 39

Paul Dark paid the taxi driver and walked through the revolving door into the main concourse of Arlanda airport. He quickly found an overhead monitor and saw that SAS had a direct flight to Brussels departing in three hours. He was about to approach the airline's desk when he sensed something strange about the space directly around him. It took him a few seconds to see them – uniformed soldiers were discreetly patrolling the perimeter of the concourse, armed with machine-pistols.

His stomach tightened. The coincidence was too great: they had to be here because of him, and that meant someone had worked out who he was. And to get the usually placid Swedes to bring troops in, it had to be someone who had a hell of a lot of clout. CIA? Or Service? The latter was the most likely explanation, as they had the most information on him. Who was Chief now? Still Innes, perhaps. He was a safe choice.

He turned away from the desk. Airline check-in

staff usually just glanced at your passport photo as they tapped in your details, but the soldiers meant full measures were in place, so they would also have been put on the alert for him. There would probably also be passport checks at both ends now. So he had to think again. Could he take a non-commercial flight – sneak onto a freight, perhaps? He quickly dismissed the idea. Fewer people meant identifying himself would be even more difficult. His one advantage was the crowd: those chasing him had to find him in the haystack of the hundreds of thousands of people travelling around Europe.

Further down the concourse he spied a bookshop with a stand outside containing the day's newspapers, and he walked towards it to put more distance between himself and the soldiers. He was stopped short by a frame on the wall that featured enlarged reproductions of all the front pages. The British and other international papers were running with two stories: the Portuguese had lost control in eastern Timor, and three people had been killed in an explosion in a pub in Armagh. But the Nordic evening papers and late editions were leading with a different story: him. The front pages of *Expressen*, *Ilta-Sanomat*, *Aftonbladet* and *Aftenposten* all featured the same two photographs of his face: the one taken just hours earlier in the coastguard station in Helsinki and one of him clean-shaven – an old Century House pass, he thought. The headlines in each language proclaimed he'd murdered his girlfriend and son and was now on the run and might kill again at any moment. *Aftonbladet* had the most striking cover, making the most of the fact Claire had worked for them by using a smiling photograph a colleague had taken of her at her desk with Ben seated on her lap making faces at the camera. '*HAN DÖDADE DEM – HITTA HONOM!*' was the headline: 'He killed them – Find him!'

So they were playing it like that. Not 'sought for questioning', not 'a prime suspect', but that he'd actually killed them. His jaw clenched at the tactic, but he could hardly expect Queensberry rules.

He retreated to one of the seating areas, his mind racing through his rapidly narrowing options. After he'd given Marta and Jonas a graphic description of what might happen to their friend and his son if they didn't give him all their assistance, he'd persuaded them to part with two spare passports, a fresh set of clothes, an attaché case, some cosmetics and enough of their parents' kronor to buy him the plane ticket and anything else he needed for the next few days. But it had taken him time to persuade them, valuable time, and after a while he'd felt he couldn't afford to spend any more of it in case he missed a flight.

So he'd taken the taxi here. He'd been right about the flight, because if he had delayed much longer he'd have missed it, but the security cordon was much tighter than he'd bargained for. They'd set up the sort of measures reserved for a terrorist on the loose: armed troops and a major media alert. No doubt they had arranged radio and television broadcasts, too, in which case he'd been lucky the driver hadn't heard or seen any and driven him to the nearest police station.

The check-in time for the flight was in just over an hour, and he didn't even know if there were any seats left on it. But the next direct flight to Brussels wasn't for another couple of hours, and indirect routes would take even longer. And the more time he took, the worse his odds of getting through. It was now or never.

He stood abruptly and walked to the bathroom area, locking himself in one of the stalls. He removed Jonas's leather jacket and shirt and hung both on the door hook. Then he took Marta's box of Jane Hellen hair bleach from the attaché case, and as he leaned over the basin applied a dose of the bleach into his scalp and eyebrows. The instructions said it would take forty-five minutes to turn him into a 'platinum blonde', but his hair was too dark for that to work and it wasn't what he wanted anyway. He estimated fifteen minutes should be enough for the desired effect, and noted the time on Kurkinen's wristwatch, which he was still wearing.

Reaching over to the door, he removed some items from the pocket of the jacket, then flipped down the lid of the toilet and seated himself on it. The first item was his wallet. The leather had been damaged by the water, but the photograph in the inside pocket was still dry, and there he was, looking down at a newborn Ben cradled in the arms of Claire. Or

Hope, as he now knew was her real name. He traced a fingernail across her face and thought of the way she tasted when they kissed, and the way the tiny crevices of her lips would sometimes catch his. He remembered the morning of his birthday when she had given him the wallet, and Ben bounding onto the bed to give him his card, and then the three of them in Haga Park. He bit into his cheek unconsciously, his ribcage thumping as the shame and guilt and rage coursed through him.

He snapped the wallet shut. All his training said he should destroy the photograph, as it could ruin his cover if found on him, but it was the only concrete link to his family he had left. Besides, he told himself, he might need it later to help find them. He spent the next five minutes thinking up a legend that would at least sustain initial interrogation in the unlikely event it came to that. So the man in the photograph was his brother, Karl. He was two years older than him, a dentist in Gothenburg, and this was his family: Karl's wife Ingrid and their son Nils. The Swedish word for dentist was *tandläkare*, so shorten that to 'TAN' to remember it. Make Gothenburg 'GO', and he was two years older, so the phrase to remember was TWO TANGO, as in 'It takes two to tango'. And the first letters of Karl, Ingrid and Nils spelled 'KIN'.

Having committed this to memory, he reflected how deluded he'd been to believe he had left his past behind and become a peaceful Swedish citizen called Erik

Johansson. Within a matter of hours, he'd reverted to the dedicated operative preparing a cover story without a second thought. A few hours too late, he thought bitterly. He'd meant to investigate Claire's past when they had met as a matter of routine, but he'd been swept up by the thrill of new love and before he had managed to catch his breath she'd become pregnant and all his remaining caution and tradecraft had deserted him, his mind preoccupied with the prospect of bringing a new life into the world.

There was little point in dwelling on the error now. He turned to the other items he'd taken out: Jonas's two spare passports. One was in the name of Per Sundqvist, a pharmacist from Uppsala, and the other was Henrik Jansson, a primary-school teacher from central Stockholm. After examining them both, he replaced the Sundqvist passport in the jacket. Jansson was a much more common name, meaning it would be harder to run checks on, and his Swedish accent was a Stockholm one.

But a problem remained: the photograph was of Jonas. Would it be good enough? The man had rather bland, forgettable features, but looking at the photograph now Dark only saw the differences between them and his own. Jonas's hair was a dun straw colour, and he was confident the peroxide would make for a reasonable pass there, but the eyes now seemed very far apart, the ears sticking out . . . the whole idea suddenly seemed much less workable than it had done with his brain working overtime in Jonas and Marta's flat.

In normal operational circumstances he would have replaced the photograph with one of himself – he'd spotted a few booths in the concourse. But affixing a new photo to a passport properly required the expertise and tools of a specialist, and he didn't have either, nor the time to find them. So there was no choice. He would simply have to hope the customs officials didn't examine the passport too closely, even though they would no doubt have been instructed to watch for all Caucasian males travelling alone and been given the two photographs of him for reference.

He put the passport and wallet back in the jacket and sat there going over the situation in his mind until the dial-hand on the watch had reached the fifteen-minute mark. As soon as it had, he placed his head under the tap and rinsed the peroxide out, then did the same with his face to get it out of his eyebrows. He'd taken a small bottle of Jonas's cologne from their bathroom cabinet, and now he dabbed some of it on his wrists and under his armpits to mask the smell of the peroxide before putting the shirt and jacket on again and opening the door. The main area of the bathroom had a hair-dryer attached to the wall, and he blasted the hot air onto his scalp, fixing the style and parting so it matched Jonas's in the photo. When he was satisfied he had as close a likeness as he could get, he walked back out to the concourse and strode confidently to the SAS desk.

He queued for a further ten minutes until finally he reached the desk. The flight was only half full, and he paid the teller with Marta's cash – she barely glanced at the photograph in the passport.

Ticket in hand, he walked towards the terminal's bar. He had a sudden craving for an ice-cold beer. He bought a pack of cigarettes but opted for a glass of orange juice instead. Alcohol would be dangerous in his current state of mind.

The bar had a small terrace overlooking one of the runways, and he went onto it so the breeze would dissipate the scent of ammonia faster. He found a chair in a secluded corner and tried to calm his nerves.

He was on his third cigarette when the announcement for his flight's boarding came over the small Tannoy above the door of the bar. He crushed out the cigarette and walked to the passport counter, making sure to keep his gait unhurried. He handed the booklet to the customs official, allowing his back to stoop and his chin to droop a little as he did. The more hapless he seemed, the less likely he would come across as the world's most wanted traitor. The official examined the photograph and then peered at him.

'Look at me, please, sir.'

Dark did so, gazing ahead with a pasted-on smile as the man studied him and then looked down at the photograph of Jonas. Was this going to be it? Would he be discreetly taken to one side and handed over to a member of the British embassy, then on to London and the rubber room in the basement of Century House? He had a sudden vision of the entrance of the building and wondered if the old porter Cyril still worked there, with his Webley hidden beneath his copy of *Sporting Life* . . .

The official pushed the passport across the desk to him.

'Have a pleasant journey, sir.'

Chapter 40

Saturday 23 August 1975, Pall Mall, London

Harry Bradley was waiting in the lobby of Kinnaird House, running a comb through his great pompadour crest of hair. The CIA man bounded over as soon as he caught sight of them, kissing Rachel's hand solicitously and congratulating her on her performance in the COBRA meeting. 'I reckon the prime minister liked you,' he said with a knowing smile.

She was worried he might follow it up with a wink, but instead he whisked them upstairs to show off the goods. As they emerged into the vast hangar-like space Rachel couldn't help being taken aback. Review Section's operational base in Warren Street had been a small, gloomy affair, with partitioned rooms and ancient radiators that creaked through the night. In contrast, this was a huge complex of glass and brushed steel – she almost expected to turn a corner and bump up against a lunar module. Bradley noted her expression with undisguised glee.

'Oh, this is nothing,' he said with a grin. 'Wait until you see our toys.'

He led them across a gangway overlooking the central hall, which was filled with shirtsleeved technicians attending to dozens of clean, brightly coloured machines: switchboards, teleprinters, computer terminals, satellite-linked telephones. Rachel recognised several Harvests, powerful cryptanalysis computers specially built for the NSA by IBM, but most of the models were new to her. Bradley pointed out a few that were directly connected to Interpol's headquarters, while another grouping banked a wall of radio equipment, below which men were seated in tubular steel chairs, wearing heavy padded headphones and sombre expressions.

'They're monitoring radio frequencies across Scandinavia in case anything interesting turns up. Anyway, come down and meet the team.'

They descended a staircase and crossed the floor of the hangar. Bradley had assembled around fifty officers to hunt Dark, and Harmigan had seconded a further twenty from the Service, most of whom she had recommended from the Review Section days.

'This is a joint operation,' Bradley said, addressing the throng as they gathered around, 'but the Brits have a head start on us, so without further ado I'll hand you over to the esteemed Sandy Harmigan.'

Harmigan smiled. 'Thank you, Harry. It feels rather like old times.' He turned to face the team. Other than Rachel, they were all men. With the exception of Keith

Tombes and a couple of others, most were in their twenties, all of them pale-complexioned despite the long summer in London. The sobriquet 'spook' had never struck Rachel as being so apt, and she wondered, not for the first time, why she hadn't chosen a profession with more attractive men.

She tuned in to Sandy's speech. He spoke with great care but very quietly, and the Americans in particular were leaning forward to catch his words. He started by stating that the operation to find Dark had been assigned a codename, and then used it in his next sentence as though they were all already aware that it was PHOENIX.

Rachel looked across the room at Tombes, who was raising his eyebrows at her theatrically. She smiled, knowing what he meant. Sandy's convolutions were no accident: he liked to keep people on their toes, and specialised in this sort of minuscule mind-game. Tombes was probably also unimpressed by the codename, which she agreed was bloody silly, both glorifying its subject and sloppy as a piece of tradecraft. If intercepted by the Soviets, and they knew Dark was now known to be alive, it could be a giveaway. But she had learned not to speak such thoughts, and to pick her battles carefully. These routines and rigmaroles, like the stale biscuits and the weak coffee in the canteen, were felt to be necessary, part of the mystique of the Service. Codenames were meant to be assigned randomly, which would have thrown up BANANA or GRENADINE or something similarly mundane – but secure. Presumably Sandy had decided on PHOENIX, which sounded more exciting and made them all feel like they were at the pictures.

And there it was. It had taken her a few seconds, but she had found his purpose: the codename was to build morale, and this was a rallying of the troops, Americans and Brits, all in it together. She glanced at the others: they were hanging on his every word. For the Yanks, seeing Sandy in the flesh was more significant: they were in the presence of the Chief of the British Service, and a war hero to boot.

Sandy finished up his introduction and handed over to her. All the Service's files on Dark had been packed into boxes and sent over by Station 12 in a secured van before they had left Century House, and she took out the folders and distributed them to the men.

'These are our Bibles from now on,' she said. 'When we looked at Dark's career nearly six years ago, we were trying to figure out what he had betrayed to the Russians. Now we want to know rather different things: where he is right now, and of course where he might be headed. There might be valuable clues in these files. I suggest we start by compiling a list of all the identities Dark has ever used, and all his known contacts. Let's see if we can get that done in the next couple of hours.'

As the men went scurrying off, eager to complete the tasks, she looked around at the huge hall and the weight of technology and expertise devoted to tracking down this one man. It was all very impressive, but she knew she was in the wrong place. She should be in Stockholm.

Bradley was showing Harmigan around the office he had set up for him next to the hangar. 'All the mod cons,' he said, his salesman's routine still in place. 'Secure phone, bed in the closet if we need to go all night on this, and of course –' he walked over to the corner of the room – 'a bar. Fancy a snifter?'

Harmigan smiled, and made a note in his mind to have someone check whether Bradley had a drinking problem. 'No, but thank you once again for the use of the facilities. It's much appreciated.'

Bradley waved it away. 'Sure.' He lowered himself into a chair and swivelled around on it impatiently. 'What's the deal with your guy? Has he "finished" Dark yet?'

Harmigan had been waiting for the question. 'He's checking in with me at six. I take it you don't mind if I arrange for Century House to transfer him directly here?'

'Go right ahead. The scramblers are all G-16s, best around. I'm keeping my fingers crossed your man will deliver, Sandy. As you argued so convincingly just now, Dark is a walking grenade.' He abruptly got up from the chair and strode towards the door. 'So he'd better not fucking go off.'

Chapter 41

'How about him?' said Weale.

He looked over at Morelius. The Swede's expression was placid, but Weale knew he was becoming irritated. This was the fifteenth photograph he'd queried, and all of them had proven to be innocent passengers. Nevertheless, Morelius now gestured at one of his technicians, who brought the passport into closer view on the screen.

'Henrik Jansson,' Weale read out. 'A teacher.'

'It doesn't really look like him,' said Morelius. 'He has the wrong hair colour and no beard.'

'We've been through this, Iwan. He could easily have shaved by now, and he's had time to dye his hair. If he wore the right clothing I think he looks enough like him that he could have used it to get through – can we just run a check on the number, please?'

Morelius stifled a sigh. 'All right.'

'No need,' said one of the technical analysts at his side. 'I know that face, and he isn't a teacher. His name's not Jansson, either. He runs a small organisation here in Stockholm called the Swedish Committee for Refugees.'

He strode to a filing cabinet in the corner of the room and rummaged around in it until he had found a dossier, then walked back to the others holding it up.

'Got it. Jonas Frids. Twenty-nine years old. Was in Paris in '68, then worked with the Anarchist Black Cross in London, providing food parcels and other support to prisoners in Spain. After that, he became involved with various liberation movements before turning up here. He now heads the refugee committee with his girlfriend, Marta Österberg. It's privately run, but we've long suspected it provides cover and aid for radical leftists, including terrorists. We've never had enough on them to kick them out.'

'Until now,' said Morelius. 'By God, this must be him! I take it back, Frederick.'

But Weale's mind had already moved on.

'Where's he heading?'

The analyst tapped at a computer keyboard for a minute until the flight details for Henrik Jansson, passport number 88465602, appeared in flickering typeface on the screen:

JANSSON.H......SK415/STO-BRU

Ten minutes later, the telephone rang in the office in Kinnaird House, and Sandy Harmigan listened as Weale debriefed on what he'd discovered at Säpo.

'When does that flight land,' asked Harmigan, 'and how soon can you be on the next one?'

'Dark's arrives at a quarter to ten. There's another leaving at half past eight, but—'

'We've no time for buts, Captain. If the wrong people get hold of this man, we're all in the shit – you, me, Campbell-Fraser, and several others. Catch the half-eight flight. As soon as you land, head for our embassy and ask for a Sebastian Thorpe. I'll try to figure out what's going on while you're in the air. Call as soon as you're in the Station.'

Harmigan replaced the receiver, opened the door to the office and strode out to the hangar, indicating that everyone should gather round.

'We have a lead: he's on his way to Brussels. An SAS flight.'

Rachel, seated with some of the Americans, stood at once. 'Shall I signal the Belgians to tell them to bring him in as soon as he lands?'

Harmigan considered this for a moment. 'No. That side of things is under control. What we need to know now is *why* he's heading there. Where's he going in the city, or is it a transit point for somewhere else? What's he after? A month's salary for the first person to tell me.'

He headed back to his office. Rachel quickly followed him in. To her surprise, she saw he was putting his jacket on.

'Sandy, what's going on?' she said. 'What do you mean it's under control? Where are you off to?'

'It's being dealt with. And I'm going home.'

'Now we know where he's headed? I'd have thought you'd want to be here until the kill.'

Harmigan looked up at her and smiled. 'Dark's flight doesn't land for a few hours yet. This is as good a time as any to grab a hot meal. I'm only round the corner – call me the moment you hear anything, or if you figure out what the hell he's doing heading to Belgium.' He raised his eyes to the ceiling. 'Belgium! Of all places.'

She nodded, and as he walked past her he pecked her on the cheek.

From one wife to another, she thought, walking out behind him.

Chapter 42

'I think I'll get a coffee and bite to eat. Anyone want something from the machine downstairs?'

Nobody did, so Iwan Morelius left the room alone. He took the lift, but once he was in the lobby he walked past the vending machine and out into the evening sunshine. He walked briskly down the street, heading east until he came to the gates of the yellow-painted church. A few people were milling around the gravestones. Checking he hadn't been followed from the office, Morelius walked past them and into the church.

It was dark and cool inside. He let his eyes adjust as he walked rapidly around the perimeter. Once he was sure it was empty, he slid into the pew furthest from the altar on the left and removed a small notepad and pencil from his pocket. After checking he was unobserved once more, he wrote in minuscule but very neat letters in Swedish:

'SUBJECT LEFT ARLANDA ON SK415, ARRIVING BRUSSELS 21.45. TRAVELLING AS HENRIK

JANSSON, SWEDISH PASSPORT 88465602. BRITISH OPERATIVE FREDERICK COLLINS IS FOLLOWING.'

He looked around again. The church was otherwise perfectly still, the sole movement motes of dust floating in shafts of sunlight.

Morelius turned to the back of the notepad, where tiny numbers were listed in groups of five. He picked a line, then spent ten minutes encoding the message on a fresh page. When he'd finished, he crossed out the numbers he'd used and tore the completed message from the notebook. He folded the page in half, and again the other way, then reached for the pale green hymn book from the pew. He checked it was the right copy – there was a small pencilled asterisk on the bottom corner of the front page – and placed the piece of paper in the small pouch attached to the inside of the back cover.

Then he closed the book and put it back in the pew. He stood, nodded at the altar reflexively, and walked back out into the street. On the next corner was a telephone booth, and he slipped into it and dialled a local number. He let it ring four times, then hung up and redialled. This time he let it ring twice before hanging up again.

Less than a mile away in Södermalm, a young woman walked rapidly to the hallway of her apartment and fished some car keys from a bowl on the dresser.

Chapter 43

Rachel found the memorandum a few minutes after eight. It was just a couple of paragraphs long, but it told her everything she needed to know. Triumphant, she had dialled Sandy's house, but nobody had picked up. She had got Tombes to keep trying, but after half an hour there had still been no answer. Deciding to bite the bullet, she'd prised the page away from its folder, placed it in her attaché case and marched out to her battered but trusty little Austin 1300.

She had driven past the Harmigans' house countless times, but usually averted her eyes from it. She knew it was absurd, but she found that if she ignored Sandy's life away from her she could almost convince herself it didn't exist. But she knew the address, a discreet square in Mayfair with its own padlocked garden. She felt like a Dickensian orphan with her nose rubbed up against the window just looking at it. She parked in an illegal spot opposite and ran up the steps.

A woman answered the door a few seconds after she had rung the bell. Although she had never met her,

Rachel knew at once that it was Celia Harmigan. She looked pretty much exactly as she'd imagined her: crimped hair, almost blue-black and falling to her neck, heavily kohled eyes in a pale face with a wide, almost masculine jaw, high cheekbones, a slash of red at the mouth, and a dark gown draped over her tall and terribly slender figure. Around her neck she wore a silver necklace with a striking pendant, long and thin and ending in a sharp tip, like the nib of a pen.

'I'm looking for Sandy Harmigan. It's urgent. I'm Rachel Gold, from the office.'

Celia Harmigan's lips parted slightly. 'Oh,' she said, 'I know who you are.' Her voice was lower pitched and more attractive than Rachel would have thought possible from her ghoulish appearance. Celia drew the door wider. 'Do come in,' she cooed. 'You'll have to wait, I'm afraid, as Sandy's in a meeting.'

Rachel stepped into the hallway. Here she was, then, in the heart of Sandy's private world. It was, of course, immaculately tasteful. Directly ahead of her was a spiral staircase with gleaming banisters, and to the right an antique dresser and large gold-framed mirror. She suddenly had an image of her parents walking in, and cringed. Mum would have 'oohed' and 'aahed' like she had when she'd visited her rooms in Cambridge, and Dad would have nodded approvingly at Celia. 'Nice pile you have. Very nice.' And then at the first opportunity he'd have leaned in and whispered in Rachel's ear: 'Stay close to this lot, Rach – how the other half live, eh?'

She dismissed the thought and took stock of the rest of her surroundings. To the right of the mirror a door was slightly ajar, a sliver of pale yellow wallpaper visible through it. Had Celia just come out of that room to answer the doorbell? Was that where the meeting was being held? And *what* bloody meeting? Sandy had told her he was going home to eat.

'I just need to talk to him for a couple of minutes,' she said to Celia Harmigan's skeletal back. 'Can he not come out?'

The older woman turned, then leaned in so her face was hovering over Rachel's. 'I was wondering if you'd ever dare show your face in this house,' she said. Her voice was as calm and polite as it had been before.

'I'm afraid I don't know what you mean.'

Celia registered the look of apprehension on Rachel's face and smiled. 'Oh, don't be scared, I'm not going to scratch your eyes out. A few months ago I might have, yes, when I still wasn't sure if you were screwing him.' She laughed as Rachel flushed. 'Oh, come now. You surely didn't think I wouldn't find out?'

'Please, I don't know what you think you know, but—'

Celia raised a hand. 'I had you followed by a grubby little man from Shadwell. You were rather careful, I'll give you that, but then of course you've been trained to avoid tails. But once he showed me the photographs, I felt strangely empty, actually. All that hatred I had built up for you just wasn't there any more. "My rage is gone, and I am struck with sorrow." Everything's in Shakespeare, don't you find?'

Rachel felt the blood rush into her eardrums and something rising in her throat, a mix of shame and horror. This woman had seen photographs, of her . . . She wanted nothing more than to turn round and leave the house, but at the same time she was glued to the spot. She couldn't leave. She had to speak to Sandy.

'I think . . .' she said, 'I think perhaps you've misunderstood.'

Celia Harmigan's eyes flashed at her. 'Oh, no, Miss Gold, I've understood perfectly. It's an *adventure*.' She said the word with a sneer, her nostrils flaring. 'Perhaps he's even convinced himself he loves you.' Her eyes flickered over Rachel. 'Well, I'm sure you're perfectly . . . lovable. But he won't leave me, do you understand?' Her jaw tightened. 'That won't happen.'

Rachel was conscious of a soft, padding sound somewhere nearby. The door across the hallway had widened and someone was coming through, a man, brogues stepping over the thick carpet. Sandy. She caught a glimpse of a polished conference table behind him, and the dim shape of several figures seated around it, the one directly ahead of her wearing a dark checked jacket. She couldn't see his face, but she was sure she recognised the jacket from the COBRA meeting – it belonged to Harry Bradley. What the hell was he doing here?

The door closed with a discreet click, and Sandy strode up to her.

'Rachel? Has something happened? More news of Dark?'

She looked up at him. Her head was still dizzy from the onslaught by Celia, whose face remained glacially calm, for all the world as though she hadn't just confessed to hiring a private detective to trail her.

'Yes,' Rachel managed to get out. 'Can we talk?'

'Of course.' Sandy took Celia by the arm and whispered something in her ear. She nodded, and glided towards the door. Sandy turned back to Rachel.

'Wait in there,' he said, gesturing to a door on the other side of the hallway. 'I'll be back in a minute and you can fill me in.'

'What's the meeting about? I saw Harry Bradley.'

'Yes, I'm smoothing things over with the Yanks. It just came up, and I wasn't near the phone.' He touched her arm. 'Sorry. I'll be back in a minute.'

She nodded and, half-dazed, walked into the room he had indicated, which appeared to be his study. It was a near-replica of his office, with the same clubby furniture and gleaming dark wood. There was a large leather armchair in a corner of the room and she walked quickly to it and collapsed into its embrace. She realised her hands were shaking. She took a deep breath and tried to think through what had just happened.

Celia knew. All right. She knew. She had followed her, she had photographs, and she was staying by Sandy anyway. And yet, despite the shock of this, her mind was already racing elsewhere. There was something else going on here. She had the peculiar feeling she had not just stepped into a private world, but a secret one. And something about it was wrong, somehow. She needed to grasp it before the thought left her. Yes, Celia knew about the affair, but leave that to one side. What was her *role*? Harry Bradley was here, and several others, apparently having some sort of conference with Sandy. This was strange enough in itself. But Celia also seemed to be involved in some way – she had just walked back into the meeting room and Rachel felt sure she had emerged from it to answer the front door.

Did Sandy keep her so well informed of Service business that he let her sit in on meetings with the head of CIA Station?

She got to her feet again and walked around the small space thinking, her eyes taking in the bookshelves as she did. It was a fairly predictable collection, she saw: leather-bound editions of Dickens and Hardy sprinkled with some non-fiction about the Second World War. All very respectable, but she doubted Sandy had much time for reading. She stopped as she reached a spine that read 'HARMIGAN' in large typeface.

Intrigued, she picked it from the shelf and saw the title. *Safe Conduct*. Of course, his memoir. She'd read a cheap paperback edition of it years ago, but the film stuck out in her mind more – it had become a staple of Sunday afternoon television. The edition she now held in her hands was a hardback, a first edition by the look of it. The jacket featured a striking watercolour of a man creeping along some docks, presumably representing Sandy on his mission in Saint-Nazaire. It was a key scene in the film, too, she remembered. Beneath the title, a line of blocky text read 'The Most Extraordinary Memoir to Emerge from the War'. The back cover was taken up with a black-and-white portrait of the young author, his dark hair severely parted in the style of the day as he gazed confidently at the camera. He'd been a handsome devil, and hadn't he known it.

She opened the book and it fell open at the illustrations, most of which were photographs of him throughout his life. There he was training with his parachute regiment as a sombre-looking 21-year-old, followed by a snapshot of him in the back of a Sunderland flying boat, a jaunty smile and his thumbs aloft as he prepared to fly into Norway. What a war he'd had, and now he was here in Mayfair with that harridan . . . She flicked the page over and stopped short.

It was a photograph, sepia-toned and grainy like most of the others. The sun shone down on a group of men seated in a stone courtyard. Bamboo poles were visible behind them. In the centre of the group Sandy peered out from beneath a straw hat, wearing a white shirt, baggy trousers and some pointed leather slippers, his face deeply tanned. To his left was a younger man, Asian, with delicate features, and to his right was another white man wearing shorts and holding an old-fashioned pistol. The caption read: 'Irregular warfare school, Kelantan, December 1958'.

The man directly to Sandy's right was Tom Gadlow.

She closed her eyes and tried to picture the photograph anew. It was something she had done for many years, since a day in *shul* when she was in her teens. It had been a warm morning and her mind had been drifting. She had glanced up and seen a woman seated a few feet away who she hadn't recognised. Then with a start her features had somehow rearranged themselves and she had realised it was her aunt, Hannah. But that fraction of a moment when she had seemed a stranger had troubled her. She had always been very close to Auntie Hannah and previously would have sworn she'd have recognised her anywhere, at once. The moment had taught her that even if you thought you knew something or someone completely, early impressions could shape your perception of them and as a result you could miss things – data – that had been sitting there in front of you all along. You had to look at everything through fresh eyes, especially if you were convinced you already knew the full story.

Over the years, the creation of such 'Auntie Hannah moments' had become part of her working methodology. Sometimes when she was looking at ciphers she tried to visualise them in her mind as concrete images, floating pictures she could travel around and examine until the solution eventually presented itself to her. But now her mind stubbornly refused to co-operate – she remembered the photograph of Gadlow, but however hard she tried she couldn't manage to summon it up as a detailed image and felt overcome by frustration.

There was a noise from just outside the room and Rachel opened her eyes with a start. She quickly shut the book and replaced it in the shelf, then turned to the door as it swung open. Sandy stood there, his hands clasped together expectantly.

She smiled faintly, wondering whether she should ask him about the photograph or tell him that his wife had followed them and claimed to have photographic evidence of their affair. But what would be the point in either case? She had to think things through first, away from here. Right now she felt out of her depth, and almost claustrophobic. So instead she just nodded and with an effort dragged her mind back to the reason she had raced over here in the first place.

'I think I know why Dark has gone to Brussels,' she said.

'Excellent. What have you found?'

She smiled, despite herself, at the flattery. 'Well, he's been there once before, but it was nearly fifteen years ago and it was a very brief diplomatic mission, smoothing relations with the Sûreté after one of our agents was caught trying to frame a government minister in a honey trap.'

'I remember that. Johnson, wasn't he called? Quite a palaver.'

She nodded. 'We looked at every scrap of paper about it in the files, but it looks like a dead end. So I approached it from another angle, trying to put myself in Dark's shoes now. He doesn't know who's taken his family, but we know from the Finns that he's convinced they were African. So if I were him, I'd want to start by finding out more about that. But he's at a serious disadvantage. He was always a Soviet expert – he knows bugger all about Africa. In fact, it turns out he has only visited the continent twice: Egypt when he was a child, and Nigeria in 1969.'

'The Wilson incident.'

'Yes. And when he was in Lagos then, the Head of Station was none other than Geoffrey Manning. Who moved to Brussels three years ago.'

Harmigan rolled his eyes at the mention of the name. 'Christ! That crank. But would Dark know about his new mission in life?'

Rachel took her bag from her shoulder and drew out a single piece of paper. She unfolded it and passed it to Sandy, who eyed it sceptically.

'What am I looking at?'

'About halfway down,' she said, unable to keep the glint of triumph from her eyes. 'It's a translation by BBC Monitoring of a documentary about Manning, broadcast by Swedish radio last year. Conducted in his flat in Brussels.'

Harmigan walked over to the armchair and seated himself in it, crossing his legs, then started reading the paper. Rachel watched nervously.

'It's the country's most listened-to programme—'

Harmigan raised a hand. Thirty seconds passed before he looked up at her. He was smiling.

'Well done. I knew I could rely on you, my dear. Yes,

this is it. He must have heard it and thought "Hello!" And now he's remembered, and off he's gone. Very well spotted. Now let's think. Actions.' His eyes travelled around the room as though seeking inspiration from it. 'We need to send another signal to Brussels right away. Tell Thorpe to wait for Collins, and as soon as he arrives to drive him straight to Manning's – is he still at this address?'

Rachel gave a small nod.

'Good. Tell Thorpe to hold back himself, though. I don't want the Station directly involved in this.'

She nodded again, but didn't move or otherwise respond. The moment stretched out between them. Finally, she glanced over at the bookshelf.

'I had a look at your memoir while I was waiting for you.'

He tilted his head and smiled. 'Oh? Awful load of crap, I'm afraid. The film was rather better.'

'There's a photograph in it of you with Tom Gadlow.'

He raised his eyebrows. 'Yes?'

'It's at a training school in Malaya. You never told me you'd worked with him in the Far East.'

He smiled again, but now more coldly. 'No. I haven't told you lots of things about my life, I'm sure. It's hardly a secret, as you can see. It's been public knowledge since that book was published in 1961.' He tilted his head back and examined her. 'And I'm not sure I much like your tone, my dear.'

She stared at him, weighing his own tone. He didn't appear nervous, but then it would take a lot to catch Sandy off guard. He was the definition of unflappable.

'Sorry,' she said. 'But you can see why—'

'I've told you before to resist this temptation of seeing conspiracies behind every corner. There was no reason to tell you this. None. I was briefly in SOE with Philby during the war, too. And Dark, for that matter. So was half the Service. You can play that sort of connect-the-dots all day long, but the result is you'll conclude that everyone is some sort of double agent.' He paused for a moment. 'Edmund went barmy pursuing that sort of thinking. I suggest you steer clear unless you want to end up in the sabbatical game, too.'

'I'm sorry,' she said again. 'Getting carried away.'

He gave a curt nod. 'Accepted. Now can you get back to the office and send that signal to Brussels? We don't have time to mess around on this. Dark is due to arrive –' he checked his watch – 'within the next forty-five minutes.'

'I'm on my way,' she said. 'But aren't you putting a lot of faith in this Collins chap? What if Dark gets away from him?'

Harmigan cocked his head and sighed. 'I imagine I'll consider involving the Station if it comes to that. But let's not go through this again, Rachel. I told you why I need you here—'

'Think about it, Sandy!' He flinched, and she realised it had come out more aggressively than she'd meant. She tried again, lowering her voice. 'Think about it. Dark's desperate to find out who took his family. He evidently believes he can get some answers from Manning. He's a crank, yes, but a well-informed one. Dark will leave Brussels the moment he has his take from Manning and head for wherever it indicates. So let's think a step ahead. Say he manages to do that without Collins stopping him. To figure out where he's gone and why, we'll need to find out what it was he got from Manning. Are you sure you can rely on this Collins to do that?'

Harmigan closed his eyes to think. If it had been anyone else making the argument, he'd have agreed at once – she was right. He needed a back-up option: someone who could debrief Manning if necessary and who had all the background on Dark at their finger-tips. She was the best person for the job, but if there were any chance she might run into Dark . . . He real-ised even as the thought formed that resisting the idea was futile. This was no time for sentimentality – there were far greater issues at stake. There was an element of risk, yes, but he hadn't become Chief without a fair amount of gambling and, besides, she *wanted* to be in the field again. She was practically begging him to give her the chance.

'All right,' he said finally. 'Go. Drive to Northolt now and I'll ring and tell them to get you in the air as soon as you arrive.' He added, almost as an after-thought, 'But please, be bloody careful.'

She adjusted her bag and he escorted her out – the meeting room door was now firmly shut, she noticed – and they said goodbye soberly and without any emotion, as though Celia were watching them. Perhaps she was, Rachel thought.

She walked across the street and unlocked her car. As she squeezed in behind the wheel a picture emerged in her mind, as though released by her having left the house. It floated in her consciousness like a three-dimensional tableau: Tom Gadlow's body splayed out at the bottom of the garden in Kuala Lumpur, his eyes rolled up into his head.

Chapter 44

Saturday, 23 August 1975, Moscow

Colonel Sasha Proshin of the GRU's Second Chief Directorate sat with his hands on his lap, staring at the small tear in the corner of the baize-topped desk. It was shaped, he thought with sudden clarity, precisely like a miniature sea-horse – he could even make out the serrated shape of a mouth in the far north of the tear before it joined the cloth. He remembered the real sea-horse he'd found on the beach at Sukhumi that summer with his father when he was – how old? He must have been eleven.

Proshin had never been in this room before, but was unsurprised that it was decorated in the usual over-the-top manner, with a crystal chandelier hanging from the high ceiling, dark red wallpaper and a massive baize-covered desk in the centre of the room. The chair he was seated in was preposterously ornate, with veneer marquetry spiralling across its back and armrests plated in red leather and canted with shiny gold tacks. But despite the room's stagy grandiosity it had very poor ventilation, and his nostrils were filled with the tang of the sweat of the two other men in the room, unsuccessfully masked by the smell of cologne. The scent seemed rather more delicate than the usual foul stuff one found at GUM, so he guessed someone had been on a trip to the West and brought back presents as *blat* for the big guns. He wondered who, and where they had been – Paris? How he missed Paris.

Directly opposite him was seated General Ivashutin, the head of the GRU, barrel-chested, staring glassily ahead. To Ivashutin's left sat Borzunov, head of the agency's foreign counter-intelligence directorate, a small-shouldered man with a deceptively gentle demeanour. Although it was being presented as an informal meeting, complete with a large samovar on the table and painted porcelain cups, Proshin was anxious. Ivashutin and Borzunov's expressions were inscrutable, but something about the setup reminded him of a tribunal and he knew that at any moment he might find himself fighting for his career, or his life.

That was, if it hadn't already been decided. A few years ago he had been severely reprimanded when old Victor Kotov, the security chief of his directorate, had been discovered passing documents to the British, some of which he confessed to having stolen from the safe in Proshin's office. Proshin himself had eventually been cleared of any involvement, but it had been a very unpleasant few months and he knew that the black mark would forever remain on his file. As for being made a general, well, it had been made plain to him that that was out of the question.

He was now, he knew, never more than a step away from being disgraced. He had a surveillance team of three tracking his movements, and a listening post was stationed above his flat. His greatest fear was of being slipped a dose of the new psychotropic drug that had been developed by the scientific directorate. While it wasn't quite the 'truth serum' beloved of late-night spy films, it came alarmingly close, transforming you into an eager-to-please blabbermouth within minutes. It had no taste, colour or odour and, terrifyingly, subjects were left with little or even no recollection of having been under its influence. Proshin had come across it a few months earlier in the case file of a dangle they'd sent to French intelligence who, after a decent interval, had been 'kidnapped' back to Moscow. On arrival at headquarters, the agent had been debriefed about everything he had learned in Paris, then taken to a safe house to be awarded a medal in secret. After a sombre ceremony, his colleagues had toasted him with a bottle of Kubanskaya. The freshly minted hero had eagerly drunk up, not realising that his glass alone had been prepared in advance. An hour later he had been sprawled out on one of the armchairs in the living room of the safe house talking about how the French had persuaded him to confess he was a plant and turned him. He had been executed a few days later.

For Proshin, this incident was more horrifying than all the stories of rats being piped into cells in the

Lubyanka. For one, he knew it to be true, having read the transcript of what the agent had said under the influence of the drug. But it was also the idea of it, the principle. Like all GRU officers, he had become used to living under constant surveillance, watching his every move and utterance. The sole surviving area of freedom was his mind, and the knowledge that this could also be breached, and without his ever even being aware it had happened until it was too late, chilled him to his core.

'Alexander Stepanovich,' said Borzunov, and Proshin looked up with a guilty start. 'We've asked you here to clear up some discrepancies in the record of one of your agents.'

He shifted in his seat. 'I will of course do my utmost to assist in any way, comrades.'

Borzunov nodded, somehow contriving to make even that tiny gesture seem sarcastic. 'We would like to talk to you about INDEPENDENT. I've just been reviewing your handling of his case, for reasons that will soon become clear.'

Proshin stiffened. So he hadn't been imagining it – his apprehension was wholly justified. Try as he might, he could think of no good reason why they would summon him to discuss Paul Dark on a Saturday evening.

The samovar was singing, a long note that to Proshin's ears sounded like a cry of despair, and Borzunov poured three cups and passed them round. Proshin dutifully took a sip and for a moment forgot himself in the richness of the flavour, a mix of wood-smoke and pine cones. It was one thing he had never understood in all his years in London – how the English could possibly think the weak concoction they drank deserved the name of tea.

Borzunov also took a sip, then glanced down at the bulky dossier open in front of him.

'Between June 1954 and March 1969, you operated as the case officer for this agent. Is that correct?'

'Yes, comrade.'

'And how frequently did you meet with him?'

Proshin was sure there was a trap secreted somewhere in the question, but he answered it honestly.

'Usually once a month, but there were some unscheduled contact breaks.'

Borzunov replaced his cup on the desk. 'So that would make – allowing for such breaks – well over a hundred and fifty meetings with him. Would you say you grew to know him well during that time?'

What a question, thought Proshin. Yes, he'd come to know Paul Dark. He had been his confessor, his chess partner, his taskmaster – and, finally, his executioner. But the question wasn't a sincere one, and he'd be a fool to treat it as such. He was now certain he was being led into an ambush. If he denied he had known Dark well, he would be admitting he had been an incompetent case officer who hadn't managed to get close to his agent despite running him for nearly fifteen years. But if he claimed he had got to know him well, Borzunov might just as easily accuse him of being incompetent for having failed to foresee Dark's subsequent actions. He thought for a moment before settling on a line that might sidestep both pitfalls.

'I think I got to know him as well as one can with such a man.'

Almost as if he were a cuckoo clock stirring into motion at the top of the hour, Ivashutin abruptly cocked his head and leaned forward, propping his elbows on the table. 'What does that mean?' he asked brusquely. The two of them were playing off against each other, Proshin thought – it was straight out of the interrogation manual.

'I mean, sir, that there was a detachment to him – a certain coldness, shall we say. I never felt that he fully confided in me, but we had some form of understanding.'

Borzunov picked up an ugly bronze paperweight in the shape of Sputnik from the table, turning it in his hands. 'Did that understanding extend' – his voice was now a soft purr – 'to your collaborating in falsifying his death?'

Proshin felt a little queasy.

'I have no idea what you mean, comrade.'

Borzunov placed the paperweight back on the baize and gave a broad smile. His teeth were small, sharp and yellowing. He rummaged in the dossier and took out a slim black-banded file. He held it up with two fingers, as though it were contaminated.

'This is the report on Operation ROOK you wrote at the time, in which you claimed that you shot him and left his body in the Finnish archipelago.' He placed the file on the table, flipped it open, and started to read aloud. '...When it became clear INDEPENDENT was determined to fight to the bitter end, I shot him in the stomach and he fell to the ground. My radio operator, Lieutenant Cherneyev, took his pulse and determined he was dead, after which we carried my father's body to the helicopter and left the area. We crossed the border at 0300 hours.'

He glanced up at Proshin.

'But he is evidently *not* dead.' There was a brief, loaded, silence. Then he took a sheet of paper from beneath the folder and spun it round with his hand. It was a photograph of a middle-aged man with long hair and a beard.

Proshin recognised him at once. He felt a crawling sensation in the crown of his head, like a tumour suddenly blooming in his brain, and for a moment he thought he might black out. He looked up to see Borzunov speaking into the intercom device on the table, and he heard the doors behind him swing open and the sound of heavy footsteps thudding against the hardwood floor, then softer as they reached the thick carpet. A fair-haired man in camouflage fatigues came into view. He walked up to the table and saluted.

Proshin did his utmost not to show his distress, but the blood was drumming in his ears and he could feel his heart jolting madly beneath his shirt. It was Cherneyev. He had been in his early twenties at the time of the operation, but in the years since his face had taken on a harder look: his cheekbones were now more pronounced and his blueish-grey eyes seemed deeper set and more penetrating. From the uniform, it seemed he was now a member of the KGB's Directorate A, the counter-terrorism *spetsnaz* group Andropov had set up the previous summer. It looked like they'd lifted him straight off the parade ground at Kirovograd.

Borzunov smiled at the newcomer.

'Thank you for coming here at such short notice, Dmitri Ivanovich. We would like to ask you a few questions about Operation ROOK in Finland. Do you remember it?'

Cherneyev nodded. 'Yes, Major.'

Borzunov smiled. 'No need to stand on ceremony, Cherneyev – "comrade" will do here. We're just having a friendly discussion.' He looked back down at the file. 'According to this report, the British agent was shot in the stomach, and you then checked him for signs of life.'

'Yes, comrade. I felt no pulse at all.'

'How strange.' He indicated the photograph of Dark. 'So this is someone else, then, do you think? An identical twin, perhaps. Or does the man have super-natural powers, to rise from the dead like this? What is your explanation?'

Cherneyev looked at the photograph, but didn't flinch. 'I was clearly mistaken. I remember that he had no pulse at that moment, but perhaps if I had tried again some seconds later it would have returned.'

'And why did you not do just that?'

'I was following orders, sir. I asked Comrade Proshin if I should dispose of the body, meaning I should throw it into the water, and he told me to leave the man there for the birds to feed off. So I did, and we left immediately after.'

'Thank you, Lieutenant-Colonel.'

Ivashutin trained his eyes on Proshin.

'Well, comrade? Do you dispute this account?'

'No, but you heard what he said – he felt no pulse. What would anyone think in such a situation other than that the man was dead?'

'Did you not think to simply wait a few moments and check again? It was rather unprofessionally done, surely.'

He considered lying, suggesting that he had made Cherneyev carry out a further test, but decided it was too risky – it was his word against the other man's but these men weren't fools, and if they didn't believe him things might become very difficult for him indeed. Better not to risk angering them further and simply play as contrite as possible.

But his professional pride needled at him. Why *had* he left Dark there and not simply kicked him into the sea? Or, better still, simply leaned down and shot him through the forehead? It hadn't crossed his mind. Cherneyev had told him he couldn't feel a pulse, so he had presumed he was dead. He had been fatigued, freezing cold, and he had just witnessed the devastation of his father's death, and he had wanted to leave the place as soon as he could.

But it was unforgivable nonetheless – he accepted that. You never leave a loose thread. He wondered if he had perhaps subconsciously wanted to leave Dark alive. But no, that was absurd: he had most definitely wanted him dead. He had wanted him dead for some time.

Ivashutin spoke. 'I won't waste words, Alexander Stepanovich – this operation gives a very poor impression. You were this man's case officer, and yet he escaped from London without you even alerting anyone at our Station there of that fact. He then escaped from you in Italy, and once again here in Moscow. Finally, you tracked him down to Finland, where you claim you killed him. And yet he is still alive. So the question troubling us both is whether you were merely incompetent – or if you made sure this man could escape? Perhaps you are not working for us at all, but another intelligence service.'

'Comrades, what can I say to prove my innocence? I've served this agency all my adult life, as did my father before me.'

Borzunov frowned in mock-disappointment. 'Please, Alexander Stepanovich, save us the impassioned pleas. You spent a great deal of time in the West. You speak fluent English, you attended the opera in Covent Garden, you even had a suit made for you in Savile Row.'

'That is a lie! I bought a suit during my first year in London, yes, but it was not made for me, and it was at the request of the ambassador!' The two men looked down at him, their eyes devoid of any sympathy. Proshin thought rapidly – the key to surviving any interrogation was to change its focus. An idea flashed through his mind. He gestured at the photograph of Dark on the table. 'Where is the photograph from?'

Borzunov sneered. 'You think to challenge its authenticity? There can be no doubt it is him. This is from an intercepted Interpol alert.'

'No, it is clearly genuine. But why has Interpol placed an alert on him now – he must have done something.'

Borzunov glanced at Ivashutin, who nodded. 'This is not of your concern, comrade, but it appears that since you "killed" him, the Englishman has been living in Stockholm, and he has a girlfriend and young son. They were kidnapped yesterday by a group of black nationalists. The girlfriend is African.'

Proshin took this in, thinking. He wondered who the Interpol source was in Stockholm for them to have such detail – he didn't know of any such agent, but then it would be compartmentalised, probably something for the Fifteenth Department. More significant was the African connection.

'How has it been established that she's African?' he said. He was gratified to see a look of puzzlement cross Borzunov's face – Ivashutin's expression remained unchanged.

'She has a Zambian passport, although it appears to be forged. Do you have intelligence relating to this woman, Proshin? If so, I advise you to speak up now.'

He had used his surname. This was a good sign, as it meant he was interested enough to have forgotten they were all meant to be having a little tea party together.

'I don't know anything about her,' he said. 'But as you've just read the dossier on INDEPENDENT, perhaps you remember that he confirmed our earlier intelligence about a conspiracy within the British Service.'

Now Ivashutin's eyes glittered, and he leaned forward. 'You are referring to the faction at the top?'

Proshin nodded. 'What if that group is involved now?' he said. 'Could they not have arranged for the kidnapping of the girlfriend and son in order to draw INDEPENDENT out of hiding? By using a team made of Africans, or at any rate blacks, that would provide them with cover.'

He knew at once he'd hit his mark. He could almost see the two of their minds turning over his suggestion – they had forgotten all about his supposed failings. He remembered a favourite expression of his father's: 'To an officer, fresh intelligence is like a drug. We will chase it to the ends of the earth, even if it is false.' He hadn't provided fresh intelligence so much as a sketch of a theory built on the foundations of old intelligence, but the drug was taking hold nevertheless.

'Please leave us for a moment, comrades.'

Proshin got to his feet and followed Cherneyev into a waiting room encased in lacquered wood panelling. They sat there in silence on a low sofa that needed upholstering. After ten minutes, the intercom sounded on the secretary's desk and she waved at them imperiously to go back in.

Borzunov was still seated at the table, a self-satisfied look on his face, but Ivashutin had taken his jacket off and was standing by the window. He spoke with his back turned away from them, gazing down into the courtyard that nobody ever used.

'Operation ROOK was a disaster, and the two of you are to blame. It needs to be finished, and it needs to be done quickly. Our latest intelligence is that INDEPENDENT is currently on his way to Brussels. If it is the case that the British are involved in kidnapping his family, we must intervene.'

He turned on his heels and looked directly at Proshin. 'I want you to go there and complete the work you should have done six years ago. You know the man, and you know at least some of his ways. But as you're not to be trusted on this alone, Cherneyev will go with you. I would like to see this man dead within the next twenty-four hours. If you fail, there will be consequences for you both. Your flight leaves in precisely –' he looked at his wristwatch – 'forty-seven minutes. A car is waiting for you downstairs with further instructions.'

He nodded to indicate they were dismissed, then poured some tea from the samovar into his cup and took a sip.

Proshin and Cherneyev took the lift together, both men staring sightlessly at the dulled metal of the doors as they closed in front of them.

'Did you bring any other clothing with you?' said Proshin. 'I suggest you change before we get in the car.'

The other man didn't answer.

'Did you hear me, comrade?'

Cherneyev slowly turned his head and looked at him with his hard grey eyes. 'Oh, I heard you, old man. Now you hear me. I don't appreciate being fished out of my unit because you weren't thinking straight six years ago, and I don't intend to risk my neck on your say-so again. I'm making sure Dark is killed this time, and you're not going to stop me with your effete little ways. So I'll be giving the suggestions from now on, are we clear?'

His hand shot out and grabbed Proshin by the throat.

'I said, are we clear?'

Proshin nodded, and the hand relented.

Chapter 45

Sunday, 24 August 1975, Salisbury, Rhodesia

Ian Smith waited for his wife to climb aboard the Command Dakota before following her up the ramp to take a seat next to her. Once they were securely in place, the pilot pressed a button that sent a prepared encrypted message to Air Force headquarters: 'DOLPHIN 3 DEPARTING'. Then he ran through one last check of his controls.

A few minutes later, the Dakota was in the air and heading for Victoria Falls.

Chapter 46

The DC-9 skidded onto the runway at Zaventem at a quarter to ten. The cabin lights came up and Paul Dark joined the crush of passengers hurrying down the staircase. A thin veil of fog swirled across the tarmac and the sky spat rain. Dark had the urge to turn up the collar of his jacket, but that was one thing you never did when trying to remain inconspicuous – even a glance at a distance could have people humming the tune from *The Third Man*.

At the foot of the staircase a stewardess was pointing passengers towards a bus parked about fifty yards from the plane, which was waiting to take everyone to the arrivals terminal. Dark stepped onto the tarmac and leaned down as if to tie his shoelaces, but his peripheral vision was waiting for the fraction of a moment he needed. After several agonising seconds, it came – the stewardess turned away from him to answer a question from a young woman holding a baby in her arms. Dark, still crouched down, scuttled his feet backward like a spider until he was under the fuselage. He closed his eyes so the whites of his eyes wouldn't be visible in the darkness, and held his breath, expecting to hear a call from the stewardess any moment to ask him what he was doing. But it didn't come, and after a few seconds he heard her speaking to another passenger.

He had spent most of the flight wondering about his options on landing in Belgium. He'd made it through passport control and security at Arlanda without any trouble, but he knew that the agency or agencies searching for him wouldn't have given up simply because he had managed to evade them once. They would have people working around the clock, glued to computer screens, searching for any sign of him in the haystack of radio-waves and electronic communications. And if any of those worker bees had managed to figure out which identity he was using in the three hours since he had boarded the flight in Stockholm, the authorities here would have been alerted and 'Henrik Jansson' would be picked up the moment he showed his passport.

With this in mind, he'd roamed the check-in area at Arlanda looking for someone he could impersonate on arrival in Brussels, but there had simply been no suitable candidates. He had searched again on the flight, walking up and down the aisle, but he had struck lucky with Jonas and the bar had now been raised for how much he had to resemble his mark. Because if he had been detected, the men hunting him would be furious that he'd given them the slip and the customs officials would have been given instructions to be even more rigorous. He had decided he didn't fancy his chances trying the same trick again.

Dark sat beneath the plane and listened until the last passenger had come off and the stewardess had walked back up the staircase. He opened his eyes and saw the doors of the bus close and then head off.

He took a deep breath. He could hear the low chatter of the crew above him, perhaps discussing their plans for a night in the city. He'd gone out with a BOAC stewardess for a few months once and had spent many an evening waiting for her in airport bars: he doubted the drill she'd described would have changed much in the intervening years. They'd be cleaning the aisles and packing up their gear now, and would be coming down the staircase themselves in a few minutes. The pilot and co-pilot had less to do but usually waited until the crew were finished so they could all leave as a group. Not always, though.

He stepped out of the shadow and walked across the tarmac towards a parked Sabena jet in the next bay. He'd spotted a small flickering glow beneath one of the wings that he thought he recognised. As he drew near, he saw that he'd guessed right: a member of the airline's ground crew was seated cross-legged on the rear of his service truck, smoking a cigarette.

He was alone.

Dark marched up. 'What the hell are you doing?' he called out to him in French, his voice terse and authoritative. 'You should be working.'

The man stood and arched his shoulders back, peering into the darkness. Dark stepped forward and punched him in the solar plexus, thrusting his fist hard into the flesh. The man doubled over, winded, and Dark followed through with a knife-hand strike to the vagus nerve behind the ear. The man slumped to the ground like a puppet with its strings cut. Once Dark had checked he was unconscious, he removed the cigarette from his fingers and crushed it beneath his shoe. Now the darkness was near-absolute. He quickly began stripping off his clothes.

Five minutes later, dressed in the man's yellow and blue overall, he parked the truck in the Sabena bay outside a low boxy building adjacent to the terminal. He descended and followed a group of men wearing Alitalia insignia who were heading towards the building. One of the men held the door open for him, and he nodded his thanks. He walked into the baggage handling area, busy with men unloading cases. He found one of the carousels that was deserted and, glancing around, stepped over it, then ducked and crawled through the plastic curtains. A small boy clutching a balloon was staring at him. Dark smiled at him and stood, wiping the dust off his knees, then headed purposefully into the body of the arrivals hall.

Soldiers were patrolling here, as they had been in Stockholm, but none of them paid him any attention. Dark located the *bureau de change* and exchanged his kronor for francs, then took the escalator down to the railway station and bought a ticket into the centre of Brussels.

A quarter of an hour later he walked out of the Gare du Nord and was greeted by a throng of taxi drivers wanting his business. One of the men, burly with wild grey hair, caught his eye, and he nodded at him. The man gestured obscenely at his disappointed colleagues and then opened the passenger door of the cab with a flourish.

'*On y va, m'sieur!*'

Dark climbed in. The car stank of cigarettes and the driver's body odour.

'*Rue de Stassart soixante-quatre, s'il vous plaît.*'

The man nodded and roared off, forcing Dark's spine into the back of the seat.

He had a hollow feeling in his stomach, only partly caused by the man's driving. He was hoping Manning lived at the address directory enquiries had given him, but if he didn't he'd just wasted several hours flying out here and he'd be no closer to finding out who had taken Claire and Ben, or where they were now. Somewhere in the world, men with guns were holding them both. How were they dealing with it? Had they been hurt? Did Ben understand, was he scared . . . ?

The city flashed by in a succession of tunnels and intersections and sparks flashing on tramlines. He saw a billboard reading 'MAES PILS', and remembered steins of cool beer in a darkened bar. He licked his lips unconsciously.

The driver took a turn and Dark had a sudden

intuition he was being duped – that it was a deliberate detour to increase the fare. He leaned over and glared at the man.

'*Qu'est-ce que vous faites?*' His nails were digging into the palms of his hands, and he realised his nerves were drawn so taut that even a delay of a few seconds might make him snap. Perhaps sensing this, the driver sped up.

'*Ne vous inquiétez pas, m'sieur,*' he said, raising his palms fractionally on the wheel. '*Nous sommes presque là.*'

They came into the African neighbourhood. Dark wound down his window to get some air and the smells of grilled fish and plantain drifted in from a nearby restaurant. The taxi slowed for the lights and a young woman in a bright green dress came to the crossing. Time stilled. *Claire.* He was reaching for the handle of the door and was about to tell the driver to stop the car when she turned and stared straight at him and he realised his error.

She crossed the road, and he leaned back against the leather seat. Cold sweat licked his forehead, and his heart was thumping.

Pull yourself together, man.

The driver veered into Rue de Stassart. It was a narrow street, a mix of shabby nineteenth-century houses and concrete office blocks: it looked like someone had taken all the ugliest parts of Paris through the ages and smashed them together while wearing a blindfold. They passed a group of young Africans dressed up for a night on the town – Dark registered the insistent thump of music from further down the street – and then he saw number 64: a massive and monstrous red-brick house that occupied an entire corner, with a four-floor turret uniting both sides like the spine of a book.

'*Juste ici, s'il vous plaît.*'

He paid and climbed out, gulping air. The taxi sped off and he walked up to the house and peered at the list of occupants next to the door. One of the place-holders read 'MANNING, G. – AFRICA TRUTH'. Dark pushed the button beneath it and stepped back.

A couple of minutes later the door opened and a neck craned out, watery eyes peering from a crumpled face. He looked like a frightened turtle. Dark pushed at the door and stepped into the stairwell.

'Hello, Geoffrey,' he said. 'I've come to pick your brains.'

Chapter 47

Cherneyev and Proshin were the first two passengers off the plane. They were both tired and irritable, but Proshin knew he was lucky to have been given this option at all – he could have been sent in disgrace to the provincial office in Kuibyshev, thrown into a cell in the Lubyanka or worse. And he had no doubt what the 'consequences' Ivashutin had mentioned would be if he failed now: the firing squad.

Despite the unpleasantness in the lift in Moscow, Cherneyev had recognised the impossibility of travelling in his fatigues and had told Proshin to take him to his office. 'It's not Savile Row, is it?' he had sneered when Proshin had shown him the brown cotton suit he kept in his wardrobe, but he had put it on nevertheless. It was two sizes too baggy for his muscular frame, but he was passable.

They now made their way through customs without any difficulties, and were greeted on the other side by a young man in a leather jacket and jeans holding a sign bearing their assumed names. This was Yuri

Diadov, the communications man for the GRU's illegal *rezidentura* in the city. After establishing identities with the phrases they'd been given, they followed him out to where he'd parked his car.

Diadov got behind the wheel and the other two climbed into the back. Once they'd all squeezed in, Diadov reached under his seat and took out a parcel, which he passed wordlessly to Proshin behind him before starting up the engine. As they came through a tunnel, Proshin unwrapped the oil-cloth and found two Browning Hi-Powers nestled against each other. Cherneyev put out a hand, and Proshin dutifully handed one of the guns to him. Cherneyev examined it in the glow of the streetlamps, checking the magazine and inspecting it for markings – there were none.

'Where did you get these from?'

'A personal contact.'

Diadov glanced in the rear-view mirror and noted the wintry expression on Cherneyev's face. He recognised the type: he was what was known euphemistically as an 'executive agent', a special forces operative trained to hunt and kill the enemy, and to follow orders unthinkingly and to the letter. The other man was an officer, a flabby functionary rather than a killing machine, but he was perhaps more dangerous, as he would be watching his every move and then reporting back to headquarters. He decided a little more information might be advisable. 'One of our agents bought them from a Belgian who assists the mercenary community here,' he said. 'We've used him before and he's always been reliable and efficient. To our knowledge, the authorities here have no records of him or these weapons.'

Cherneyev gave a curt nod. 'I hope your evaluation of that is accurate, as it's we who will pay if it isn't. What about INDEPENDENT? Have you established where he's headed?'

Diadov showed no surprise that the younger man appeared to be in command even though the signal he'd received had indicated that the older one would be. 'I made some enquiries, but I hope you can appreciate that I haven't had a lot of time. However, I did manage to discover that a man broadly matching INDEPENDENT's description took the train into the city about an hour and a half ago.'

'How broadly?'

'Same height, weight and general appearance, but no beard and he had fair hair. He's dressed in some kind of uniform, perhaps airport ground crew.'

'How many stops are on that train?'

'Just two – the northern and central stations.'

Cherneyev exhaled, making a noise somewhere between a sniff and a grunt. As he'd suspected the moment he had seen the man, he was an incompetent novice. How did these people get posted into the field? Perhaps, like Proshin, he'd landed the job through family connections.

'"Just two",' Cherneyev repeated, his voice laden with sarcasm. 'That's one too many, Diadov, because he could have got off at either of them and we don't know which. In fact, he could be anywhere by now. He could be in Antwerp, or Ghent, or got off the train and taken another straight back to the airport and caught a plane somewhere else.' He slammed his fist into the headrest of the empty seat in front of him, shaking the car for a moment.

Diadov stiffened. 'My instructions were to arm you, drive you into the city and go home. No more than that.'

He took the turning onto the motorway and the three men fell silent, each of them resenting the others for different reasons.

Chapter 48

The flat had once been rather a grand affair: the ceilings were high, the floor was parquet and there was a marble fireplace in the living room. But the glory years were long gone now. The paint was flaking from the walls and the frames of the windows, and a smell of mould hung over everything.

Manning had done his best to liven the place up with the décor, which had a somewhat contrived African theme: garish paintings featuring zebras, toucans and flame trees and a few fierce-looking tribal masks hung from the living-room walls. In one corner was a teak bookcase and next to it a small desk, on which rested a typewriter, piles of paper and an open bottle of Johnnie Walker. Behind that were two battleship-grey filing cabinets and a rickety chair in which a pyjama-clad Manning was now seated on Dark's instructions. Funny, thought Dark, he had been wearing pyjamas the first time he had met him, too. Perhaps it was the same pair. The bags under his eyes were more pronounced, but otherwise he looked much the same as he had when Dark had last seen him, six years ago in a clinic overlooking a courtyard in eastern Nigeria.

'How's Marjorie?' Dark said. 'This place doesn't really look like her style.'

Manning's jaw hardened. 'She left me, as I'm sure you know.'

Dark hadn't, but he wasn't surprised. He had forgotten all about Geoffrey Manning until he'd happened to catch the end of a programme on P1 one Sunday morning and had been astonished to hear his plummy tones emerging from the transistor. The programme had naturally made no mention of his time in the Service, referring to him simply as a 'former British diplomat', but that confirmation of his identity had alone been enough to make Dark's jaw drop. The Colonel Blimp who had laughed along with the good old boys in the Lagos Yacht Club had apparently had the most unlikely of Damascene conversions, as well as reserves of political nous and organisational efficiency Dark would never have suspected of him in a million years.

Sitting at his kitchen table, Dark had stared at his radio set in wonder as Manning had explained to his earnest Swedish interviewer how he had gradually become disillusioned by the British government's role in Africa and had resigned from the 'Foreign Office' in protest as a result. In 1970, he had moved to London and taken up with Biafran activists there, but he hadn't lasted long – Dark presumed the Service had told him to clear out or they'd find a way to charge him under the Official Secrets Act. He had then moved to Johannesburg and become involved in the anti-apartheid movement, but the South African authorities had been about as welcoming as the British so he'd upped sticks for Paris, where he had worked for Amnesty's press office. In 1972, he had left to set up his own organisation, Africa Truth, which campaigned 'to end racist colonial rule in the continent'. It did this by publishing a newsletter of the same name, petitioning governments and mounting publicity stunts: ambushing delegates with photographs of massacred children at a conference in London, protests outside embassies, marches and sit-ins. Manning and his small team were forbidden from entering any of the countries they wrote about, but relied on insider sources, mostly liberal whites.

In late 1973, Manning had relocated again, this time to Brussels, where he had continued to run the organisation from this very flat and, the documentary had implied, regularly flew to African countries to meet with sources. Manning had boasted that he had a comprehensive database on Western subterfuge across the continent, and one of his cohorts had called him 'the Simon Wiesenthal of Africa', the thought of which had nearly put Dark into hysterics and had brought Claire running from the bedroom to see what had brought it on.

He felt like laughing again now, but this time out of despair. If he wasn't mistaken, the vaunted database looked like it was the two filing cabinets in the corner of the room.

'It played better on the radio, Geoffrey,' he said, more to himself than Manning.

'They blamed you for Wilson, you know.'

It took Dark a moment to catch up to what he was saying, and then the penny dropped.

'Yes,' he said, 'of course they did.'

'That was where it all started for me. A couple of blighters from London barged into my office a few days after it happened. No signal, no call. Just turned up out of the blue and told me I'd seen Paul Dark with a sniper rifle, nobody else, just Dark.' He looked up, anger blazing in the bloodshot eyes. 'Told *me*, Head of Station! You were a traitor, they said, a Russian double. You'd been planning to kill our prime minister. They had a whole story worked out. But I'd been there. I'd been in that god-awful little room with you and seen it all with my own eyes, so I knew they were lying. Traitor you might well be, yes, but assassin you were certainly not. And if we were prepared to stitch someone up for that, where did that leave me? In the final analysis, who was I? The more I thought about it – and by Christ did I think about it – the more I realised that I didn't really know the answer to that one. So I resolved to find out.'

Dark stared at him. Well I never, he thought. Manning had set out on his voyage of self-discovery as a result of what had happened in Nigeria. He would have called it shell shock, only it seemed to have woken the man up.

'I take it they blocked your pension?'

Manning glared at him. It was an old Service aphorism that the few who left its ranks and then attacked it publicly were usually motivated less by a newfound conscience and more by revenge.

'It's not about my bloody pension. But yes, they took it away. I handed back the OBE before they could strip me of that. I didn't deserve it anyway. "Other Buggers' Efforts".'

Dark nodded in pretended sympathy. 'Are you alone here?'

Manning grunted, but Dark sensed a lie. He crossed the floor to the kitchen and looked out the window at a higgledy-piggledy landscape of back gardens, rooftops, washing lines and pylons. A set of double doors leading off to one side were half-open, and he walked through to find a young girl lying on her side on a mattress on the floor, sleeping. The coverlet was turned back and the imprint of Manning's body was still visible on the sheets next to her. She was naked, and Dark winced at the sight of her pale ribcage. He leaned down to the mattress and shook her shoulder. She awoke, a startled look dawning in large grey eyes.

'Time to leave,' Dark said, and walked back to the living room. A minute later she emerged, now dressed in denim shorts and a T-shirt. Manning nodded at her in a silent signal, and she slipped out the front door without a word. Dark listened as she descended the staircase and, once he heard the front door shut, walked over to Manning. He crouched down and stared into his face.

'I need you to tell me everything you know about Hope Charamba.'

Chapter 49

The embassy was cloaked in darkness by the time Weale reached it. He showed the sentry at the door his 'Frederick Collins' passport and was escorted up a narrow flight of stairs to the secure room, which was a sparse soundproofed space only slightly larger than a prison cell. Waiting for him behind the barrier was Sebastian Thorpe, a small, pink-faced man in his fifties wearing a ruffled shirt and a pale-blue suit that made him look like a villain in a light opera.

'Welcome, Mr Collins. How was your flight? Did you fly direct from Stockholm?'

'I need a gun,' said Weale. 'A semi-automatic if possible.'

Thorpe froze for a moment, then gave a steely smile. 'I see. Delighted to meet you, too. Do you have a chit for it?'

Weale couldn't tell whether he was being serious. They had to produce signed forms to gain access to weapons at Inkomo, of course, but this man had been given direct orders by his Chief. What the hell did he think he'd come here for?

'I don't have time for this crap. Our target might leave the country any moment. Call Harmigan – he told me to check in as soon as I got here.'

Thorpe stared at him for a moment, his arms folded. He'd received the Cat A flash that this man was due to arrive just a few hours earlier, and he hadn't been pleased: it had essentially ordered him to act as his butler. The message had also indicated that Collins was an alongsider, a freelance operative working in tandem with the Service but not officially attached to it. Thorpe didn't like alongsiders at the best of times, as they often had their own agendas and could muck things up as a result, but Collins made him feel especially uneasy. From the way he carried himself, he guessed he was a former soldier or mercenary, and he was perturbed by his casual use of the word 'target'. But after a few moments he walked to his desk, connected to the secure line and dialled the number in London.

'It's Thorpe,' he said, when he'd been put through. 'Your Mr Collins has arrived.'

Chapter 50

Manning was refusing to co-operate. He looked like a bruised boxer, slouched back against the chair. Dark had tied him to it with the sheet from the mattress to stop him trying anything.

'Torture me if you like, old horse,' he said, jutting out his chin. 'I'm not helping a traitor.'

Dark nodded. The old Manning was still in there somewhere. Dark didn't have any scruples about torturing him if it would get him closer to finding Claire and Ben – but he thought he spied a quicker method.

'How old was that girl I saw when I came in, Geoffrey? Thirteen, fourteen?'

Manning glared at him. 'Elise is eighteen.'

'Really? She looked a lot younger than that to me. I wonder if she'd be able to prove her age in a courtroom. Shall I call the news desk of *Le Soir*? Or perhaps Reuters?' He walked over to the telephone and lifted the receiver. 'There must be an enterprising journalist in this town who'd look into it if I gave them the nod. You're a dab hand at this sort of thing nowadays, what do you think? "Former British Diplomat in Child Prostitute Disgrace – Sentencing Tomorrow". Would that work as a headline?'

'I'm fond of her. Leave her out of this.'

Dark ground his jaw. 'I'm fond of my family, Geoffrey. So enough of the bullshit and start talking. Hope Charamba.'

Manning looked up to the ceiling, his Adam's apple bobbing frenetically in his throat. Then his shoulders abruptly sagged in defeat. 'I've not heard of her, but I'd guess she's related to Matthew Charamba.'

Dark replaced the receiver and walked back to the armchair.

'Good. And who is Matthew Charamba, exactly?'

'He's a Rhodesian nationalist. Or Zimbabwean, I should say. He was a village school-teacher who rose through ZIPRA's ranks and—'

'I'm rusty on these acronyms, old horse.'

Manning nodded. 'ZIPRA's the military wing of ZAPU and ZANLA's the equivalent for ZANU. There are also a couple of splinter groups. They're all supposedly united now – there was an agreement in Lusaka last year – but there's still a hell of a lot of tension below the surface.'

'Main cause?' Dark willed Manning to hurry along – his politics might have changed but his lugubrious way of speaking hadn't.

'Tribal differences, mainly. ZANLA are primarily Shona, while most of ZIPRA are Ndebele.' Manning caught Dark's look of impatience. 'Charamba is

Ndebele. A few years ago he was being tipped to take over as ZIPRA's commander-in-chief but he was arrested before that happened.'

'What was the charge?'

'Oh, the usual – "conspiring against the state". The trial was held *in camera*. He spent three years in prison but was released with a few other revolutionary leaders last year as part of Smith's supposed softer approach. Within a few weeks he'd left ZIPRA and set up a new group, the Zimbabwean People's Party.'

'Moscow-backed?'

'I doubt it. ZIPRA is heavily funded by the Kremlin, but Charamba seems to be independent of foreign influence. He's managed to draw some people from ZIPRA and even a few from ZANLA, but otherwise it hasn't really gone anywhere. Might not stay that way for long, mind. Our sources indicate it's pretty much just him and a few aides working out of a heavily guarded villa in Lusaka. The Zambian government turn a blind eye to his presence there, as they do with ZIPRA. A lot of Zambians support ZIPRA, either tacitly or directly, and a few of them have aligned with Charamba's group.'

Dark took this in, marvelling at how he had under-estimated Manning all those years ago. He might not be the Wiesenthal of Africa, but his grasp of the politics was impressive. Dark would never have guessed the man had such talents, but even his unpredictability had a predictable side: once he'd persuaded himself he had no option but to co-operate, the expert's zeal to share his knowledge had overtaken him and the information had started tumbling out. The trick now was to gather as much of it as he could in case he had second thoughts.

'Why did Charamba leave ZIPRA?' he asked. 'And why didn't he join the other lot, ZANLA?'

'Oh, he has no truck with them, either. He came to the conclusion in prison that there's no point in negotiating with the white regime in the way they've all been doing because it's taking place entirely on the whites' terms. He's right – those bastards have no intention of ever letting go of power. Charamba's position is that the starting point for them coming into talks should be setting a fixed date for majority rule. He argued that should be within a year – Mozambique's just done it in nine months – but Ian Smith has repeatedly said he doesn't believe majority rule is even possible in his lifetime, so the others rejected the idea. Unworkable.'

'And now he's in exile in Zambia and no longer at the top table, is that it?'

Manning pursed his lips. 'For the time being, but I wouldn't rule out his making a comeback, as turnarounds are very common in these movements. These new talks are unlikely to progress very far without him. I rather suspect that at some point they'll get desperate and reconsider, especially as anything they agree at the negotiating table has to go to a national poll – that's what went wrong last time. That gives Charamba a lot of power. His time in prison sealed his reputation as a revolutionary for a lot of people, and there are now songs about him sung in the villages.'

'Hang on. Slow down. What new talks?'

Manning frowned. 'I thought you knew. Smith is holding constitutional talks with ZANU and ZAPU on Monday. On Victoria Falls Bridge.'

'Will Charamba be there?'

'Not as far as I know. But I haven't listened to the World Service yet. They were due to have a report on it later.'

Dark absorbed the information. It was too much of a coincidence not to be relevant. The talks had to be why they had taken Claire and Ben.

'Does Charamba have any children?'

Manning peered at him, puzzled. 'Not that I know of. I think he was briefly married, but his wife died in a raid by the authorities several years ago.'

Dark considered this. Either Manning's expertise had its limits, or a gigantic set of coincidences had taken place. On balance, he decided it must be the former. He looked at the filing cabinets in the corner of the room. Both of them had locks on. He grabbed Manning by the chin and forced his head to face them.

'I'm going to need your help opening those.'

Chapter 51

Diadov dropped his two sullen charges outside the Gare de Midi, and Cherneyev headed straight for the taxi rank. Once he had taken out his wallet, the drivers soon crowded around him. He showed each of them the photograph of Dark and asked in broken French if anyone recognised him. No one did. He turned back to Proshin.

'Come,' he said, as if addressing a pet dog who needed to be taken for a walk.

They climbed into one of the taxis and Cherneyev directed it to the Gare du Nord, where he repeated the procedure. Ten minutes and a thousand francs later, he had found Dark's driver and they were in his car speeding towards Rue de Stassart.

Chapter 52

The photographs were spread across the desk: a few were in colour but most were black-and-white Xeroxes, or Xeroxes of Xeroxes, the features of the men – they were almost all men – lost in the contrast of deep shadows. Dark sifted through them, frustrated. There were a couple of images of Matthew Charamba, newspaper clippings at the time of his imprisonment, but they were too grainy to be any help, and there was no mention of his having a daughter.

Dark willed himself not to panic. He didn't yet have enough to go on. It seemed pretty likely that Claire – Hope – was Matthew Charamba's daughter, but he still had no idea who had kidnapped her, or why. There was a bewildering array of leaders in the guerrilla movement, and he had no idea how to navigate the spider's web of their connections to Charamba to find who had the strongest motive.

'Is this it?' he asked Manning. 'Is this all you have?'

'On the Zimbabweans? Yes.'

Something stirred in Dark's mind, phrasing Manning had used earlier. Dark turned to face him.

'How about on the Rhodesians?'

Chapter 53

As Thorpe turned his white Sunbeam Rapier into a cobbled street, Weale caught the scent of grilled fish on the air. He peered out of the window: Africans, dozens of them, walking around like they owned the place.

He glanced down at the gun Thorpe had retrieved for him, after a great deal of tutting, from a safe in the Station. It was a Walther 7.65 automatic that looked as if it hadn't been used this decade. But he'd checked the mechanism several times, and it would do the job.

'Let me off on the corner,' he said.

Chapter 54

Dark took a sharp breath when he found it. There were half a dozen men in the photograph. All had beards and wore ramshackle camouflage and caps, and all were holding rifles, leaning on them like Greek shepherds clutching their crooks. The man on the far left of the picture was a few years younger, but the nose – the skin a shade darker than the rest of his complexion – the shape of the face, the piggish little eyes . . . he was unmistakable. It was the birdwatcher from Haga Park.

Dark held the photograph up to Manning, stabbing a finger at the man.

'Who is this?'

Manning squinted at it. 'I don't know.'

Dark glanced meaningfully at the telephone on the desk.

'I don't, I swear! All I know is that they're Selous Scouts.'

Dark's head cocked. There had been a faint noise from the street, something out of place with the other sounds. He crossed to the window and drew the curtain to one side. A building at the next corner was lit by two spots of bright light. A car had just turned into the street and was inching along it. It was a taxi, and Dark could see part of the driver's face in the windscreen. Grey hair, burly . . . it was the man who'd brought him here earlier.

Dark quickly walked through to the bedroom where he had found the girl earlier. He stepped over a pile of books and papers and opened the wardrobe. The trousers all looked far too big for him, but jackets were more forgiving. He picked one out and put it on over the Sabena overall. It looked incongruous up close, but it changed his outline. He placed the photograph in an inside pocket and went back into the living room.

'What the hell are the Selous Scouts?'

Manning hesitated and Dark leaned in with his right hand and grabbed his throat. Manning's eyeballs bulged, red veins scribbling across them, and he strained to breathe.

'Rhodie . . . special forces,' he whispered, and Dark relaxed his grip slightly. Manning's head tottered forward in the chair and he gasped for breath.

'I've never heard of them,' said Dark. 'A new outfit?'

Manning didn't answer and Dark stepped forward.

'Yes!' he said, his voice a notch higher than it had been before. 'Set up a couple of years ago. They turn Africans and use them back out in the field.'

Dark nodded. That fitted with Claire and Ben's kidnappers. The birdwatcher – his accent had been

Rhodesian, of course, not Dutch – had conducted the surveillance, then they'd carried out the actual snatch using black Africans, meaning nothing led back to them. Clever.

Another noise from the street. He would have to leave in a few seconds. But not yet. Part of his mind was screaming *get out get out get out*, but the professional instinct overrode it. In here, he had access to specialised information – to intelligence. Out there, he'd be blind again.

He strode to the filing cabinet and rifled his fingers through the section on Rhodesia. There were dozens of dossiers, and to save time he took them all out and splayed them across the floor, then kneeled down and started looking through them until he found the one with 'Selous Scouts' typed on the front panel. He glanced across at the attaché case, which he'd left by the door when he came into the flat. He decided to leave it. He needed to be fast on his feet. He picked up the Selous Scouts dossier and took the papers from it, then folded the bundle and stuffed it into the pocket of his jacket, next to the photograph.

He glanced around again. Was he forgetting anything? Yes. Money. He rushed back to Manning and searched his pockets. He had a couple of hundred francs in notes.

'Is that it?'

Manning nodded. Dark looked around for a safe, but didn't see one. Perhaps behind one of the paintings? But he could hear the taxi's engine in the street

– there was no time. He went to the door. Manning grunted, writhing in the chair.

'For Christ's sake, you can't leave me like this, Paul!'

Dark closed the door behind him and ran down the staircase. As he came out onto the street he saw the taxi turning the corner nearest him. He started running in the other direction. Further up the street, a figure on the same side of the pavement was walking towards him, the soles of his shoes echoing against the cobblestones. He passed under a streetlamp and Dark caught a better look at him: a white man with a tan and fair, short hair, dressed in slacks and shirt sleeves, peering up at the street numbers. As if conscious of being watched, the man abruptly lowered his head and looked across at Dark. Their eyes locked, and Dark knew in his bones he was one of the Rhodesians, and that he'd come here to kill him. In the same instant, the man started running towards him.

Dark froze, suckered by having two pursuers suddenly appear either side of him. Behind him, he could hear the taxi slowing – had they seen him yet?

He had just two options: keep going in his current direction and meet the man rushing towards him, or turn and head towards the taxi. In a flash he decided the man was less of a threat than the car, because whoever was in the latter hadn't spotted him yet – if they had, they'd have already speeded up to reach him, or he'd be hearing a car door slam by now. The decision made, he started running again, heading straight for the Rhodesian. In his peripheral vision, he registered a low doorway a few feet ahead of him and to his left, and he slowed as he neared it. A printed sign on the door read 'ACCES/INGANG'.

He veered left and flung his weight against the door. The body of it shook for a moment, but then bounced back onto the hinge.

He glanced up at the street. The Rhodesian was now less than twenty feet away and he'd removed a gun from his jacket, its barrel catching the light from the streetlamp.

Dark threw himself at the door again as the shot rang out, and this time as his shoulder slammed into it the hinge gave and he stumbled into darkness, nearly losing his balance. A moment later he clasped his hands over his ears as the shrill screech of an alarm rang out.

Rachel searched the street for a white Sunbeam Rapier. After she'd threatened to cable London and have him sacked, the security officer at the embassy had given her the model and licence plate. She was about to find a phone box to call and ask again when she saw it parked opposite an African restaurant. Thorpe looked up in alarm as she rapped on the window.

'I'm Rachel!' she shouted at him as he wound it down. 'From London. Sandy signalled I was coming?' There was no response. 'Phoenix!' she called out. Thorpe nodded and opened the door. She bundled in.

'Where's Collins?' she asked.

'He went to Manning's. My instructions were to wait for him here.'

'When did he leave you?'

Thorpe looked down at his watch. 'About ten minutes ago.'

Rachel stared at him. 'How far away is Manning's?'

Thorpe was about to tell her when the sound of an alarm broke through the air. Rachel jerked her head towards the street.

'Shit.'

She opened the door and started running towards the sound. Thorpe watched her, stunned for a moment, then opened his door so he could follow her.

The alarm was ringing on a single high note, and Dark felt like it was tunnelling into his brain. He reached a hand out to right himself against the nearest wall and searched around, blinking rapidly so his eyelids moistened, improving his vision. He was in a tiny hallway and just ahead of him was a glimmer of light. As his eyes adjusted he saw it was reflective glass: another door.

He groped forward and grabbed at the handle. It, too, was locked. His pulse was pounding furiously now, panic rising as he realised he had nowhere to go and just seconds before the Rhodesian arrived. He threw his shoulder against the door's upper window until the glass cracked and then shattered, shards crumpling in a shower over him. He braced himself and hurtled his entire body forward.

Once through he righted himself again. The temperature was a little cooler here. He saw a long marble-floored corridor with iron grilles running along the walls, a strip light flickering from the ceiling. It was a shopping arcade, closed for the night, the shops locked away, the shoppers all gone home, just him and a mad Rhodesian commando chasing him.

He edged around the door and flattened himself against the grille directly behind it, trying to calm his breathing. His entire body was now tensed, from the trapezoid muscles in his neck to a clenching in his abdomen. His hands were sweating as he glared at the door, waiting. He wiped them against his trousers and blinked away the droplets stinging his eyes. He strained his ears to catch the sound he knew was coming, but the peal of the alarm was near-deafening. He could sense something, though. Vibrations thudding beneath him. Footsteps.

Dark leaped on Weale as he came through the door, chopping at the back of his neck with his left forearm and punching down into his stomach at the same time, releasing all his pent-up rage and letting out a scream as he did. Weale groaned and keeled forward, his gun falling from his hand and clattering to the floor. Dark caught him by the neck with his forearm and took him in a chokehold, then moved his other hand up to cover his mouth and nostrils before pulling him down to the floor. He kept his grip steady, and time slowed as the sweat dripped down his throat and into the other man's hair.

Then the moment passed, as the Rhodesian kicked out wildly and clawed at Dark's forearm. Struggling to keep the chokehold, Dark clamped his fingers over the man's nostrils with more force, both to inflict more pain and to make his breathing harder. When the man's legs started jerking a little less insistently and Dark felt there were only a few seconds of life left in him, he pulled his hand away and threw him against the metal grille draped against the wall.

'Where are they?' he screamed, and the vibration pulsated in his eardrums. The Rhodesian had slumped back to the floor. Dark repeated the question but the man didn't answer so he lashed out with his foot, catching the man on the jaw and sending him flying.

Dark realised he needed something to convince him, something greater than mere pain. He scoured the surrounding area for the gun, but most of the area was in shadow and he couldn't see it. He turned to the Rhodesian again. He was breathing hard and his jaw was lolling to one side, dislocated. Trickles of blood ran down his neck. He looked a mess, two beats from death, but there was also a glint in his eye. It was defiance. The man was a professional, and he would rather die than give him anything. He grinned as Dark realised this, drooling pinkish red liquid.

Dark felt another surge of rage come over him, almost overpowering in its intensity. The thought of Gunnar and Helena, mown down like animals. His family taken from him, his Claire, his little boy . . .

And this bastard had been involved. Had perhaps even planned it.

Dark drew his leg back to kick him again, but as he did the alarm abruptly stopped. His eardrums pulsed, and as the ringing subsided he picked up new noises: the faint sound of traffic, the soft thump of the music from the discotheque, and something else beneath it all. A low, gravelly sound.

He looked around frantically, confused, and then he saw it. Just a couple of feet away, a small air-conditioning unit was attached to the wall. The alarm must have triggered a generator that had switched it on, but the machine was making a noise like it had something caught in its blades and it was also leaking, a shallow pool of water gathering on the floor beneath it.

Dark leaned down and grabbed the Rhodesian by the feet, then wheeled around and dragged him across the marble. The man let out a low groan. Dark reached the puddle. It was dirty, with greyish flotsam floating on the surface. He pulled the man forward until he was lying face down in it and then pushed his head into the water, hearing the crack of a bone as he did and continuing to exert pressure, forcing the man's mouth and nose into the puddle until his movements slowed and his spine shuddered and squirmed and finally there was a muffled gagging sound from below and then just quiet and stillness.

Dark withdrew his hand, and an ache pulsed through his forearm. There was a new sound in the

small space, and he looked around to locate it.
Footsteps, a colliding mess of them. The door opened
and Dark caught sight of two figures, a young woman
with black hair and a man in a ruffled shirt, a face like
a bloated fish, who he recognised from some distant
time, some distant file.

Service.

They ran forward, and the woman leaned down to
pick something off the floor. The gun. It had been lying
there within his grasp all along and he hadn't seen it.
Dark got to his feet and started running from them,
taking a turning into a long corridor of shops selling
hats and carpets and televisions. He heard a shot being
fired behind him but he hadn't been hit and he kept
running until he came to the main entrance and
emerged onto a wide, tree-lined boulevard. His teeth
were chattering and his whole body was shivering. He
stood for a moment, catching his breath, then gathered himself together and started walking rapidly
down the street.

The taxi driver parked the car outside 64 Rue de
Stassart. As Proshin paid him, a sharp sound emanated
from somewhere in the street.

'Was that a shot?'

Cherneyev opened his door, loading a round into
the chamber of his Browning as he did so.

'I'll handle this,' he said.

The door of the house was ajar, and Cherneyev
strode through the hallway, Proshin following a few

feet behind. They climbed the staircase three steps at a time. Manning jumped when he saw them, his eyes now popping out of his skull with fear.

'Who the fuck are you?'

Cherneyev ignored the question and raised the Browning.

'Where is Dark?' he said in English.

Manning looked like he might pass out, but managed to nod his head at the open door. Cherneyev was about to ask another question, but before he could a small hole opened up in the back of his skull, and a fraction of a second later the sound of the shot echoed through the room. He fell forward and crashed into the desk, making the typewriter jump and emit a high pinging sound that hung in the air. Then the body slid away and fell to the floor, the face buried into the parquet.

Proshin lowered his gun and turned to Manning.

'I am sorry to disturb,' Proshin said quietly.

Manning stared at him, dazed. Proshin walked over to Cherneyev and crouched down next to him. He pulled his jacket roughly from his torso, making Cherneyev's head bounce against the floor, then reached into a pocket and turned it inside out. He leaned over and bit into it with his teeth, tearing the fabric. A small brown packet, no larger than a cigarette, fell onto the floor, and Proshin picked it up and stared at it. Then he placed it in his own pocket and went to the desk in the corner of the room. He picked up the telephone and, in bad French, asked the operator to connect him to the British embassy.

'I am Paul Dark's case officer,' he said once the switchboard had answered. 'I am at number 64 Rue de Stassart, and I wish to defect.'

Then he slumped into the chair behind the desk, leaning his head back as the sweat poured down his face. It was done, he thought. He had done it. His fate would be in the hands of the British now. He just had to hope he'd made the right decision.

Chapter 55

As Sebastian Thorpe speeded his Sunbeam through the outskirts of Brussels, Rachel focused on the corona of light around each passing streetlamp. They looked like small nooses, she thought.

The stench of death filled her nostrils, but she was thinking about the living, too. Less than two hours ago Paul Dark had been just a few feet away from her, his face contorted in a savage grimace in the half-light, a wild animal having just killed its prey. She had taken a hurried shot and followed him through the corridors of the arcade, but she'd been too far behind and had lost him. Downhearted, she'd trudged back to Thorpe, who she found staring down at the body of Collins in the same position she'd left him. 'He's dead,' was all he had said, a stunned look on his face. She had felt she might panic then, but an unexpected sense of calm had come over her and she had known what to do, or thought she had.

They'd left Collins and trekked up to Manning's flat, only to find more surprises in wait for them.

Another body, this time a Russian, shot through the back of the skull. And seated behind the desk had been none other than Alexander Proshin, leading light of the GRU's Second Chief Directorate, spy-runner . . . Paul Dark's handler.

She hadn't recognised him at first, slumped against the chair with his eyes dazed. But at Review Section, they'd found a couple of photographs taken by UCL staff – summer barbecues on campus, a picnic at the beach – in which he had been lurking in the background, and after a few moments she recognised him from them. She had leaned down to check she wasn't mistaken.

'You must interview me now,' he had whispered.

His English was good – well, he'd spent fifteen years as an illegal in London – but his accent was still strong and he strangulated the words in the Russian way, so it had taken her a moment to understand what he was driving at.

'Of course,' she'd replied evenly. 'But we need to get you to somewhere safe first, Mr Proshin.'

He'd smiled at her then, pleased that she knew his name. Then his eyes had flashed with desperation and fear. 'But it must be here, you understand? Not in London.'

Her ears had pricked up at that. Defectors were usually a lot keener on getting safely to Britain and arranging the terms of their new lives there than the inconvenient business of revealing secrets about their former colleagues.

'What's the hurry?' she'd asked.

'My life is in danger. It must be here.'

She'd stared at him, puzzled by his insistence. 'Why?'

'London isn't safe for me. It may be that your superiors try to persuade you it is better if I am not interviewed at all. Don't allow it. You must interview me, and you must do it here – do you promise me this?'

She had nodded dully. Perhaps it was for the best, she'd thought. At least that way she wouldn't have to face Sandy's wrath quite yet. Proshin had looked at her like she was his saviour, but she felt a long way from that. Sandy had been right to hold her back in London searching through old files. That was all she was good for, and even there she wasn't so sure. Would he ever forgive her for this? Professionally, perhaps. But personally? She doubted it.

She glanced in the rear-view mirror. Proshin was in the back seat, apparently lost in thought. Seated next to him, shivering under a blanket, was Manning, still looking shell-shocked. He had initially been reluctant to come back into the bosom of the 'hatefully corrupt' Service, as he'd kept referring to it, but after she had explained that a hunter-killer unit could soon be on its way from Moscow to find out what had happened to their two-man cell, the virtues of hiding out in a safe house until the coast was clear had come back to him and he'd allowed himself to be bundled in.

Thorpe took the turning onto the motorway leading out of the city, and the streetlamps gradually became sparser. She breathed a small sigh of relief: the chances of their being stopped by the police were now less likely. It didn't bear thinking about what might happen if they were: as well as a Soviet agent in the back seat, the boot contained two corpses rolled up in a couple of Manning's rugs. It had then taken her and Thorpe over an hour to get both bodies into the car, all the while anxious that at any moment they might be seen or interrupted by the authorities.

But they weren't safe yet. She fiddled with the dial of the radio to see if there was anything on the news or the police scanners. There was nothing, and she left it tuned to a local rock station. Sandy rarely listened to anything but Haydn, and as a result of spending so much time in his company she had largely missed out on her own generation's music. A mournful male voice was singing, and the lyric suddenly seemed like it was addressing her directly. It was an adaptation of Thoreau, she realised: 'The mass of men lead lives of quiet desperation.' And women, she thought. Look at her: here she was in a car with Paul Dark's handler and all she could think of was how her married lover would react. It was all she could ever think of. She knew in her heart of hearts that Celia was right – he would never leave her – and yet still she hung on. It was bloody pathetic.

Fields flitted past, and after a few minutes she spotted what she was looking for by the side of the road: a telephone booth. She told Thorpe to slow down and asked him to hand her all his loose change. It was time to face the music, and call home.

Chapter 56

Paul Dark ordered a Virgin Mary with an added dose of spices from the stewardess. She prepared the drink and passed it to him with a wide empty smile, then took the next passenger's order.

Dark gulped down the contents of the glass, the fiery familiarity of the Tabasco making up for the lack of alcohol, and reflected on what he had discovered in Brussels. He had read through Manning's file on the Selous Scouts three times before visiting the bathroom, tearing the papers into strips and flushing them down the toilet bowl. The file had only been a few pages long, but from the description of the regiment's methods, capabilities and previous operations, Dark was sure that they had carried out the kidnapping, and that the creature he'd met in Haga Park had been their spotter. The head of the regiment was Major Roy Campbell-Fraser, and there was a separate file on him: he was ex-SAS and had served in Malaya. A ruthless sort of man, Dark thought, and one very capable of planning such a job. Presumably he planned to use Claire and

Ben – or already was using them – to exert pressure on Charamba and his group, most likely in connection with the talks about to get under way in Rhodesia.

Dark's first instinct had been to fly straight to Salisbury, because the file showed that the Selous Scouts had their headquarters just outside the city, in a place called Inkomo, and that seemed the most likely place for them to be holding Claire and Ben. But there hadn't been any direct flights there from Brussels, and the hitch made him realise he hadn't really thought it through. Even if he took several legs to get there, Rhodesia was well known to have some of the tightest customs controls on the continent. And if he managed to get through, what would he do then? He could hardly single-handedly storm a special forces base, especially as he was unarmed and had no way of knowing where to find weapons in Salisbury, let alone pay for them.

But Manning had told him that Matthew Charamba lived in a heavily guarded villa in Lusaka. That meant weaponry. And if Claire was his daughter, as he thought she must be, he would have some very good motivation to use that weaponry.

Chapter 57

Rachel Gold dropped the francs in the slot and dialled the number. An operator answered on the fifth ring.

'Savage and Cooper, how may I help you?'

'Hello, I'd like to speak to a manager, please. I have a terribly urgent complaint about my Phoenix policy.'

There was a slight pause on the line as the operator registered the phrase 'terribly urgent'. In Service field terminology, it was DEFCON 1, and required informing Chief at once. The operator asked for her number and she read it out from the card next to the slot and hung up. Ninety seconds later the receiver chirruped back into life, and she picked up to hear Sandy's voice.

'Rachel, what the hell's going on? Where are you? Do you have Dark?'

'No. I'm with Thorpe in a call-box outside Brussels – we're on the way to the Château. And we're two men down.' She rapidly explained the events of the previous few hours, leaving nothing out. She was expecting him to explode, but he didn't speak for several seconds and when he did his voice was very quiet.

'Am I to understand that you and the Head of Station are driving around the Belgian countryside with two corpses in the boot of his car?'

The coldness of his tone was more shocking than if he'd screamed abuse at her. She told him Thorpe had called in a favour with a long-term asset in Antwerp and that as soon as she and Proshin were safely ensconced in the Château he would see to the cremation of both bodies.

Harmigan went silent again. Then he asked whether Collins' passport had still been on him when they'd searched his body.

She had been waiting for the question and reached into her jacket. 'Yes. I have it here. Frederick Collins, an independent fabric salesman.'

'Destroy it,' said Harmigan. 'Did Dark take any passports from Manning? I imagine he has a few stashed away.'

'Manning says he didn't, but it might be that Dark was carrying more than one.'

'Yes, that's quite possible.' Harmigan let out a heavy sigh. 'I do wish you'd called me earlier. He'll almost certainly have left the country by now.'

I couldn't call you earlier. I had to dispose of two bodies before I was arrested for aiding and abetting murder.

As if sensing her thoughts, Harmigan asked if there had been any sign of the Belgian authorities.

'Nothing so far, and there was a nightclub open nearby that probably masked most of the noise. It might be a different picture come morning, though.' She glanced down at her watch. It was approaching three o'clock. 'Come daybreak, I mean.'

'But nobody saw you?'

'I don't think so.'

'You don't *think* so?' Now his anger was coming through openly and she could picture him seated at the desk in KH, the veins on his neck pulsing. She didn't respond, as she knew from experience that doing so usually enraged him even more.

'All right,' he said finally. 'I'll call my contacts in the Sûreté and have a discreet word. What about Dark – any idea at all where he's headed?'

'From what Manning told me, it sounded like he's on his way to Rhodesia. By the way, he's shaved off the beard and dyed his hair blond, so the alert description needs to be altered.'

'Fine. What makes you think Rhodesia?'

'Well, Manning was still rather shaken up when I spoke to him, but he claimed Dark wanted to know about a black Rhodesian woman by the name of Hope Charamba. That must be the girlfriend's real name.'

'Did Dark tell Manning that?'

'No, but why else would he be asking after her?'

'Let's not make any grand assumptions quite yet. It hasn't got us too far.'

She ignored the rebuke. 'Well, if she is his girlfriend it might be important – her father's Matthew Charamba. He used to be one of the nationalist leaders there, but he's currently out of favour and living in

Zambia. Dark also reacted to a photograph of a white Rhodesian who works for one of their special forces outfits.' She looked down at the note she had made for herself. 'The Selous Scouts. A bloodthirsty lot that make the SAS look like the Boy Scouts, apparently. They capture guerrillas and turn them, sending them back into the bush to gather intelligence on their former comrades. I think this must all be related to these talks the South Africans have set up. Perhaps the Rhodesians took the daughter to pressure the father at the negotiating table, using black Africans as cover.'

'Your pet theory,' he said, and she remembered his objections to the idea during the COBRA meeting. 'Do we know where this Charamba lives in Zambia? Dark might be headed there instead of Salisbury.'

'Manning said Lusaka.'

'All right. Christ, what a fiasco.' She didn't reply. 'What about Proshin? Have you spoken to him?'

She considered mentioning the remarks he'd made in Manning's flat, and decided not to. 'Just a few niceties so far.'

'Has he said why he wants to defect to us, or what he's bringing with him?'

'Not yet. I'll ask him all that as soon as we get to the Château.'

'No, don't. Leave him there with Thorpe, please. You need to get back here at once.'

'What?' She could scarcely believe her ears. 'Surely you don't want *Thorpe* to interview Proshin? He has no knowledge of the man at all!'

'He's not to interview him either – just tell him to keep Proshin on ice for the time being. Leave Manning there, too. They can play Scrabble together, or whatever the Belgian equivalent is. Manning can head back to Brussels in a few days, and we can fly Proshin over here and question him until we know what he had for dinner eighteen months ago. But he isn't our priority right now. Dark's still out there, and I need all the help I can get to find him. I'll see if we can lay on a flight for you. Don't go away.'

The line suddenly went silent, and she took the opportunity to switch hands – the one holding the receiver was slick with sweat. She looked out at the car and Thorpe raised his hand to her. She raised hers back to indicate that all was well, but her throat was dry and her stomach had coiled in tight. She couldn't see Proshin's expression in the rear of the car, but she felt he had played some bizarre version of the old 'pick a card, any card' magic trick on her, and she imagined he was smiling smugly at having pulled it off.

It may be that your superiors try to persuade you it is better if I am not interviewed at all.

Four long minutes passed before Sandy came on the line again, his tone now brisk and businesslike. 'Right, I've just spoken to Harry and he's willing to play ball. There's an airfield at the NATO base in Chièvres, about an hour and half from the Château. Be there at seven o'clock sharp. That's in just over four hours, which gives you ample time to get to the Château, make sure Proshin's tucked up safely with Thorpe and then to head back again. You can sleep on the flight.'

'Why don't I just bring Proshin with me? It's not ideal, but I can at least conduct a preliminary interview with him on the plane—'

'Rachel, just do as I fucking say for once!'

She drew the receiver from her ear for a moment to gather herself, the blood pulsing at her temples. When she replaced it he was speaking in a more conciliatory tone.

'I'm sorry, but I've had enough of the second-guessing my decisions now. This entire operation has been jeopardised.'

The phrase 'because of you' hung in the air.

'But you still love me, don't you?' She had meant it to sound like a flirtatious joke, but her voice caught on the sentiment and it came out as more of a whimper.

'For Christ's sake, pull yourself together,' he hissed. 'Not now. We have to behave like professionals and sort this out. So don't interview Proshin, make it clear to Thorpe he's not to, either – and then get on that plane at seven. Understood?'

Not now? *Yes, now!* she wanted to scream down the line at him. *Especially now.* But instead she simply said, 'Understood,' replaced the receiver, and walked back to the car.

Chapter 58

Rachel sat in the tiny observation room and stared through the one-way window at Alexander Proshin. He was seated in an armchair in the living room, looking down at his hands clasped together in front of him. Where was the anxiety he had shown in Manning's flat, she wondered. Had it all been an act? But then she noticed that his feet were twitching, a couple of tremors every second. So he was still nervous, but just trying to keep it under control.

The Château was a flat overlooking the beach in Ostend. The nickname was ironic, as when the Service had bought it just after the war it had been the height of luxury, but it was now rather grim, with flyblown lampshades, a low ceiling and stains on the carpets. It was looked after by two officers who posed as a married couple, and the husband of the team, Sawkins, a six-foot-five officer who had trained with the SAS, was now standing outside the door of the living room with a machine-pistol by his side. His 'wife' was in the kitchen, washing up the remains of coffee and an omelette Rachel had devoured on arrival. In one of the bedrooms, Manning was already asleep.

The flat was nothing to look at, but it had been given a very careful makeover by the boffins. Dozens of miniature microphones had been placed in the walls and beneath items of furniture, giving a crisp sound to recordings. At the moment there were eight microphones within a five-foot radius of Proshin.

Rachel glanced at her watch. It was coming up to four, the fag-end of the morning. If she wanted to make the flight from Chièvres at seven, she should leave within the next hour.

But still she stood fixed to the spot. Something was very wrong, and no matter how she approached it, everything circled back to Sandy. He had repeatedly deflected her requests to go out in the field to find Dark. Admittedly, quite a lot had gone wrong since she had, but now that the shock of it had worn off she didn't feel it could justifiably be laid at her door. Now Dark's handler wanted to defect – a chance to salvage at least a small victory from the jaws of defeat – and yet Sandy had ordered her to fly back to London, not even bringing the man with her.

It was mystifying. Troublingly so. Leaving an asset of the magnitude of Proshin behind simply to have her analytical skills on tap didn't make sense to her. Dark was heading for Africa now, and she didn't see how she could help with that.

Might it be that he was simply being protective of her? Perhaps, she thought – he had warned her Dark might kill anyone who got in his way, and he had done just that, drowning Collins in a pool of dirty water barely an inch deep.

But this didn't feel like protectiveness. It felt more like Sandy simply didn't want her to interview Proshin. She remembered the instructions he had given her to pass on to Thorpe and corrected the thought: it looked like he didn't want *anyone* to interview Proshin.

She was also perturbed by his reaction when she'd told him about the Selous Scouts, and how they looked to have been behind the kidnapping of Dark's family. Her pet theory, he'd sneered. She thought back to the conversation they'd had in her office, when he'd asked about her false-flag remark only to dismiss it in similarly snide terms. What was it he'd said? 'If it walks like a duck, quacks like a duck and carries Soviet weapons, it's probably a Soviet-sponsored duck.' She'd found it a little peculiar at the time, but now the entire exchange rang alarm bells. It *hadn't* been her pet theory, merely a possibility that had occurred to her, and a standard consideration in such circumstances. His dismissal of it stank of protesting too much, and the duck joke felt forced. It looked like he had wanted to drive her away from the idea. Why? Had he known right from the start that the kidnappers were Rhodesian? If so, how – and why hadn't he told her? And later, when he'd found out Dark was heading for Brussels, he hadn't wanted the Belgians to intervene, claiming he had things 'under control' – what had that meant?

Most troubling of all was the prediction Proshin

had made. He'd warned her that her superiors might try to dissuade her from interviewing him in Brussels, and Sandy had then done precisely that. She could think of no good reason not to interview such a potentially valuable defector straightaway – and she could think of one very bad one. It was an absurd idea: monstrous, unthinkable. He was Chief of the Service. But the idea had invaded her thoughts and now she found she couldn't dislodge it and it played over and over in her head like the tattoo of a drum.

What if Edmund Innes had been right? What if Sandy was a Soviet agent?

It would explain why he was so determined Proshin shouldn't be interviewed. She knew from the files that Dark had done something similar, delaying the interviewing of a KGB defector who knew about him until he could arrange for counter-measures to be put in place.

Well, there was only one way to find out, and if she was going to do it she had to do it now. She checked that the recorders were turning and left the observation room. She walked down a small corridor and came to the door leading to the living room. She told Sawkins that he and his 'wife' could now clock off for the night.

'Yes, ma'am.'

She watched him walk towards the kitchen, then turned and faced the door. This was the point of no return. If she were wrong, she could kiss any idea of promotion goodbye. Indeed, whatever happened on the other side of the door, she was almost certainly kissing goodbye to her job, and to Sandy, too. But quiet desperation wasn't going to cut it any more – she had to act.

She took a deep breath and opened the door. Proshin looked up in surprise as she entered and gave a laugh of seemingly genuine pleasure.

'I am very relieved,' he said. 'I was starting to worry you might not keep your promise.'

She walked across the threadbare carpet to the corner of the room, where she took a folding wooden chair from beneath its dust covers. She carried it over to where Proshin was seated, unfolded it, and seated herself opposite him. She peered into his face, thinking of the hours she had spent studying him in London, the cigarettes she had smoked down to the butts while trying to piece together the information they'd gathered on him. The grand spymaster, Paul Dark's handler . . .

But now she was finally face to face with him, she was disappointed. He looked like any other middle-aged Russian official. Hair cropped very close at the back and sides, stocky and squat, wearing a poorly tailored blue serge suit. Five-o'clock shadow complemented his already greyish pallor. His eyes were perhaps the most interesting thing about him, she thought: they gave an impression of cool intelligence, but there was something perturbing flickering in them. He reminded her of a toad seated on a lily pad, and she tried to compose her face so as not to give away her visceral dislike. She had to find out why the hell Sandy had been so determined to stop anyone talking to this man.

'Are we alone?' Proshin said, breaking into her thoughts.

'Yes. I've dismissed the housekeepers.'

'What about your colleague?' He tilted his head towards the large mirror on the wall, behind which the office was hidden.

'There's nobody in there.'

He stared at her intently and then leaned forward, his knees almost touching hers.

'Can I trust you?'

His breath smelled strongly of garlic, and she leaned back in her chair fractionally. 'I think the question here is more whether I can trust *you*,' she said. 'You called the embassy to announce that you wish to defect to us having just killed one of your colleagues in the home of a British citizen. So right from the start you've forced us to cover up a murder you've committed. Why shouldn't we simply turn you over to the Belgian authorities? Or to the Soviet embassy?'

He didn't answer for a moment. Then he smiled again. 'I'm so glad Sandy Harmigan sent you here. I'm sure Mr Thorpe is perfectly competent, but I don't think he would have been as appreciative of what I have to tell you.'

She bristled instinctively at both names being said aloud in a Russian accent, but of course he would know about them. She knew the names of senior intelligence officers in other agencies, and it was natural that someone of Proshin's seniority in the GRU would know the name of their Chief and the Head of Station in a European capital. But it was disconcerting nevertheless. Coupled with his earlier warning, it felt eerily like he had been listening to her private conversations.

'I apologise for the inconvenience,' he went on, sounding less like a man who had left a corpse bleeding over a parquet floor and more like a British Rail driver announcing a delay. Perhaps that was where he'd picked up the expression, she thought. 'It wasn't my intention to cause trouble for you. Shall we start again?' He extended a paw of a hand for her to shake. 'Alexander Proshin. But you can call me Sasha.'

'Sarah Severn.'

She wasn't sure what reaction the name would elicit, but nothing immediately registered on his face. He simply replaced his hand on his lap. She decided to press.

'I've read the memorandum you wrote about Miss Severn in 1969. I presume you were referring to her, anyway, and that she really is dead?'

Proshin shifted in his chair. 'Yes,' he said finally, his voice barely above a whisper. 'But this was my father's doing, not mine. A very regrettable matter, I am sorry to say. When she became involved with Paul Dark, her fate was effectively sealed.'

'But in the report you said you had killed her. Did you lie then or are you lying now?'

He clasped his hands together. 'I was lying in the report. This was to protect my father's good name.'

'By taking the blame for it yourself?' Proshin didn't respond. 'You also claimed that you killed Dark. Again, why did you lie?'

He sighed, thinking of the cross-examination he'd gone through in Moscow the day before. 'At the time I was convinced that I *had* killed him. My radio operator, Cherneyev, felt his pulse and assured me Dark was dead. He was wrong. Cherneyev is the man I shot tonight. What have you done with his body?'

'How nice of you to take an interest. Cremation. Let me see if I follow what you are telling me. This Cherneyev knew you lied about Dark being dead six years ago, so you killed him?'

Proshin flinched. 'No. That is not it at all. But there are more important subjects for us to discuss. I must—'

'Mr Proshin, I'm afraid I do need an explanation for why you murdered this man.'

He sighed again, then nodded and held up the palms of his hands in a gesture of surrender. 'Yes, I will answer. The fact are like this: I recently came under suspicion in Moscow. I realised I had only one choice: to defect at once. I had a chance to do this because I was sent here to find and kill Dark, accompanied by Cherneyev. This was the only way I could escape him to reach you.'

'By killing him? There were easier ways, surely? You could have lost him somewhere or simply made an excuse, then jumped in a taxi to our embassy.'

Proshin shook his head. 'Cherneyev was *spetsnaz* – special forces – and he was under orders not to let me out of his sight. I had no choice.'

'What were you under suspicion of in Moscow?'

'I have been under surveillance for some months, I do not know why. But yesterday Ivashutin's chief investigator accused me to my face of being a British agent. Once such an idea is uttered, it is impossible to escape, believe me. It follows you wherever you go, it crawls its way into everything.'

Rachel wrinkled her nose, unimpressed. 'And yet they let you travel to the West.'

'Yes, but this was my chance to prove my loyalty, by finding Paul Dark. They evidently felt that Cherneyev's watch on me would be sufficient. In most circumstances, it would have been, but I had no other options. I had to choose, as you say, between the devil and the deep blue sea. It will now take some time for Moscow to realise he is dead and send some other dogs to hunt me down. But by then I very much hope they will be too late and that you will have taken me from here and secured me a new life under a new name in England.'

She frowned. 'But you told me London wasn't safe for you.' He didn't reply and she leaned forward to press her point home. 'I wonder if you can understand why I'm struggling to trust you, Mr Proshin. Nothing ever seems to be your fault, and your story is alarmingly inconsistent.'

'I've risked my life to be here,' he said, 'and I'm

risking it talking to you now. London is not safe for me at this very moment, no, but I am hoping that as a result of this conversation it will be. Once you understand the situation and have taken all the steps to deal with it.' His eyelids flickered at her doubtful expression. 'I understand your scepticism, and I respect it – it is of course the correct attitude. But you must realise that I am no ordinary defector.'

Rachel groaned inwardly. Would-be defectors were often self-important: if they could convince you their intelligence was crucial to the fate of the world you would whisk them away to safety and a new identity, pay them handsomely and – perhaps most importantly – they could convince themselves that their betrayal of former colleagues had been a matter of great principle overriding all patriotic considerations.

'You're far from ordinary,' she said, humouring him, 'but I need to establish some facts about you first.'

'You already think you know all about me,' he said, almost sneering. 'You don't. I see how you are looking at me, with this typical Western complacency. Is it because I have an accent when I speak your language? And how good is your spoken Russian, please?'

She didn't say anything.

'Well, then. I suppose you regard me as a dull, boastful Soviet with a narrow view of the world.' He smiled as she squirmed. 'Let me explain about my time in London. I was not a tourist travelling on the top of a double-decker bus with my camera poised to photograph Big Ben – I *lived* there. Over time, I came to love England. I do not mean in that silly way Americans love it, obsessed with shooting grouse or seeing Vivien Leigh at the Royal Court, although I did both of those. No, the real England for me was the jazz clubs of Soho or the beer at The Mayflower!' His eyes gleamed. 'On Friday nights, I used to treat myself to a packet of fish and chips from that little place in Tottenham Court Road. Do you know it? I can still taste the vinegar on my lips. Ah, your food, which people like to chastise so much. For me, it was a miracle. Do they still make Polos?'

She stared at him, not understanding for a second. 'The mints, you mean? Yes, I think so.'

'Ah.' A wistful look came into his eye. 'You don't happen to have any on you now?'

She shook her head.

'No matter. Something to look forward to. But please, I implore you to discard these prejudices and listen very carefully to what I have to say. I've been studying your agency for decades, and I know more than you can imagine. But if you and I work together, we can shatter the established order of intelligence in the West.'

She resisted the urge to stand and leave the room. For a few seconds, he had almost succeeded in luring her in – she did in fact know the chippie he meant, and had found herself licking her own lips at the mention of it – but his seduction had fallen at the final hurdle. This was far worse than delusions of grandeur, it was loony stuff, a train headed in the wrong direction.

'That's an unusual pitch, Mr Proshin,' she said, picking her words carefully, 'but I'm afraid I'm not especially interested in shattering intelligence in the West. In case you hadn't noticed, I work for a Western intelligence agency, and it's the Soviet Union we want to shatter. I'd rather hoped you'd tell us more about the workings of the GRU. Incidentally, I don't dream for a moment that I know everything about you. Far from it. However, I think I do know a fair amount. I've studied your career in great detail.'

'And I have studied yours, Miss Gold.'

A shiver ran through her.

'Oh, yes,' he said. 'I know "a fair amount" about you, too. You're the protégée, shall we say, of Sandy Harmigan, and a gifted analyst. I could not have requested a better choice to receive me – sincerely. But your vision is clouded by unwarranted suspicion. You know I am a very high-ranking officer in the GRU and that I was Paul Dark's case officer. For fifteen years, everything he gave Moscow went through me, and of course I have studied his entire dossier. I suspect you would like to know more about that.'

She didn't like the way he had turned the tables on her, and she especially didn't like his 'shall we say' in reference to her being Sandy's protégée. What exactly did this man know about her, and how did he know it?

'Once upon a time we would have wanted to know all about that,' she said coolly. 'But I'm afraid you're six years too late. Dark is on the run and at the moment what we want is *him*. And you have no better idea where he is than we do, Mr Proshin.'

'Please, call me Sasha.' He looked down at his shoes, then glanced up at her again and smiled. 'You may have a point. I don't know where Dark is and you may well now have better information. I understand the man in Brussels is an Africa expert, so I imagine Paul will now have figured out which country on that continent this relates to. My guess would be either South Africa or Rhodesia.'

'What makes you say those two?'

He tilted his head. 'Considering those involved, I think it is clear this concerns a white-majority nation, don't you?'

She had no idea what he meant, and was growing irritated at his intimations that he was privy to information beyond her ken. She suddenly felt claustrophobic, shut up in this stuffy little room in Belgium with this ghastly Sov. To give herself time to think and to reassert her control, she took off her jacket and hung it over her chair, then stood and walked to the window. The curtains were drawn, but she peeked through them. The sky was black and starless, but down below she could see a thin stretch of beach, cold and grey and lit by the neon from the nearby casino. She turned back to Proshin. He was watching her deflection with an amused glint in his eye. She strode back towards him.

'Mr Proshin – Sasha – I confess I'm still confused. A man of your experience must know that we aren't looking for defectors. We want agents. Every minute you're in the West is a minute you're away from the centre of action, and a minute more that your intelligence is out of date.' She wandered back to her chair and sat down. 'But some of what you say is intriguing. You might be of use to us if you were to return to Moscow on our behalf. Is that something you would contemplate?'

A smirk played around his lips. 'No, that is decidedly *not* something I would contemplate. Photographing documents in Moscow is nothing compared to what I can offer you *right now in this room*. Besides, I value my health.'

'Meaning?'

'Meaning that your agents-in-place in Moscow have the unfortunate habit of ending up dead. Penkovsky, Kotov . . .'

'Kotov's dead?'

He let out a hollow laugh. 'What do you think they did, awarded him the Order of Lenin? Yes, they narrowed the field of suspects, gathered evidence, extracted a confession, then shot him.' He spread his hands out in a gesture that said this was self-evident. 'There is no way for me to return to Moscow again safely. I must get to England. But first I need to make you understand the situation so you can take all the steps necessary to deal with it.'

'What situation?'

'That the Service is under fascist control.'

Chapter 59

Rachel's heart sank. *Fascist control!* She might as well wrap everything up now. For a minute she'd bought into his talk of being an all-knowing spymaster, but he must just have had some lucky guesses. The man was simply a nut.

She cursed herself for not having considered the possibility earlier, but the fact that he'd run Dark combined with Sandy's forbidding her from interviewing him had blinded her. But it made all too much sense. The Russians had a conspiratorial mindset, but even experienced Service officers occasionally went potty like this. Too much time spent in the world of shadows and it could become hard to distinguish truth from lies. Indeed, Sandy had himself warned her several times of succumbing to it. With good reason, as it had led to her countermanding his direct orders and suspecting he was a traitor. What an idiot she'd been! Now she'd have to find a way of withdrawing from the situation, preferably without alerting Proshin that she wasn't interested. Perhaps it was a blessing in disguise that Thorpe would play host to him for a while. Then they'd find a quiet little bungalow somewhere in Surrey where he could quietly nurse his madness.

As if reading her thoughts, Proshin shot out an arm and grabbed her sleeve.

'You must listen to me,' he said, and now his eyes were blazing with desperation. 'Your life and mine, they depend on it.'

She broke free of his grip and stared at him. 'Fascists? Really, Mr Proshin, I was expecting more from you than this. If you really believe that's the case – and I can assure you it isn't – why didn't you defect to the Americans? Or the French?'

'A good question.' He said it as though he had been disappointed by her previous efforts. 'I considered both of those options, but rejected them for two reasons. Firstly, I work – or rather, worked – in the British department of the GRU, and ran British agents, most notably Paul Dark, so naturally this dictates that my intelligence is most attractive to your Service. But secondly, I prefer fascists to Communists.'

She wanted to put her head in her hands and cry at how badly she had misjudged the potential worth of this man.

'You think the French and Americans are Communists?'

He gave her a patronising smile. 'You misunderstand me, Miss Gold. The GRU has penetrated the CIA and the SDECE at a high level. I know this very well, but I do not of course know the names or positions of most of the agents, as that is strictly compartmentalised. But I know they exist. So yes, I would certainly have enjoyed living in New York or the Côte d'Azur, but before that happened I might have found myself being interviewed by the wrong person, in which case they would have arranged for my convenient disappearance.'

'But how do you know I'm not a Soviet agent? Or that whoever had come to interview you wouldn't have been?'

He smiled. 'I don't, and I didn't. I told you: I am risking my life. But as I have worked in the British department for many years I have an extremely good idea of who our agents are in your service. At the moment, none of them is in a position that would make it likely they would be sent here to interview me. As for the KGB, that is certainly possible, as I don't know their agents, but I decided I must take the risk. I thought it was the best chance I had.'

'Unless you were taken to London,' she noted. 'You were very insistent on that point.'

Proshin nodded, but didn't speak. She felt that he was toying with her, as if his daft conspiracy theories were a puzzle for her to solve. Part of her wanted to leave him. She could take the safe-house car to the airfield, catch the flight home and pretend that none of this had happened. But she knew she wouldn't. She was here now, and she had to see it out. Besides, Proshin had just claimed – almost in passing – to have information about Soviet penetration of the CIA, SDECE and the Service, and even if he were a complete madman it was at least worthy of probing. But before she got to that she had to dig into his most sensational claim so far.

'These fascists you mentioned. What do you mean? What fascists?'

He nodded eagerly. 'There is another service within your service: a faction at the top, controlling things. Ivashutin is the one who discovered it, about twenty years ago now.' He caught her expression, and misinterpreted it. 'Yes, it has been going on for a long time. Ivashutin was in the KGB then, and when he was appointed deputy chairman many agent reports crossed his desk. These included those of Kim Philby. He became intrigued by the excellent quality of Phiby's intelligence and decided to review all of his reports, dating back to his recruitment as a student at Cambridge. He became fixated by one report in particular. When Philby had joined the Service during the war, he had informed his case officer in London that everything seemed so quiet there that he had the peculiar feeling that he'd been recruited into a front organisation – that the real Service remained hidden from him.'

Rachel shrugged, perplexed. This was the big mystery he thought would shatter Western intelligence?

'It was clearly a joke,' she said. 'Philby had that sort of humour.'

He shot her a sour look. 'Naturally, this possibility

was considered. But what if it were *true*? What if we were fighting the wrong enemy in England, cardboard cut-outs as with your famous tanks in the war, and all the while the real Service was hidden from us entirely, working on other operations we knew nothing about? This kept Ivashutin awake at night. He tried to raise it within the KGB, but nobody there was interested.' He shrugged as if to say this was to be expected from the KGB. 'At that time, Philby and other agents were providing a wealth of evidence to show that the Service not only existed but presented a serious threat to our activities. But when Ivashutin became head of the GRU, some other agents in Britain provided us with intelligence that corroborated Philby's initial suspicion.'

'Which agents?'

'Pritchard, Gadlow and Dark.'

Rachel was sitting bolt upright now. 'What did you say?'

Proshin smiled at her. 'Yes, Paul Dark told us this, too.'

'No, no, before that, the second name. You said Pritchard . . .'

The Russian raised his eyebrows. 'Gadlow? Yes, he was an agent-in-place we had in Malaysia, your Head of Station there. I was his case officer briefly, just before I was recalled to Moscow to take up a new position in the directorate. It was presented to me as a promotion, but in reality I was being removed from fieldwork as I was no longer to be trusted.'

Rachel took this in, absorbing its implications. It

made sense. It explained why the papers Kotov had taken from Proshin's safe and photographed had included documents that had been seen by Gadlow. The pieces of the puzzle were slowly fitting together, but in a horrifying way. She registered, as if it were happening to someone else, a crawling sensation along her forearms. She closed her eyes, gathering her thoughts, then opened them again and looked at Proshin.

'What intelligence did Gadlow provide about this, exactly?'

'He informed us that he had been recruited into this faction when he worked in the Far East after the war.'

'In Malaya,' she said dully, fearing she knew what was coming next.

'Yes. Gadlow had been in Singapore during the war, with your military intelligence. A "stay-behind" group, as they were known. But the Japanese invaded before they were ready and he was stranded in the jungle with his cell until 1945, when they were all taken out by submarine. That was when it happened, in the jungle. He was working alongside Malayan Communists against the Japanese and he became very close to them. By the time the war had come to an end he was a committed Communist, and when he returned to London he approached us, through an attaché at the embassy. Then in 1948 you will remember that the Malays turned against the British. The same guerrillas Gadlow had trained and befriended in the war had now become the enemy. After your High Commissioner was assassinated, he and several other

British operatives were sent back into the jungle to fight them, now helped by . . . the Senoi Praaq.'

He said the last words as though he were pulling a rabbit from a hat. She looked at him, perplexed.

'*Safe Conduct*,' he prompted her with a smile. 'Harmigan's memoir. You've read it, I presume.'

She felt her neck muscles tensing. 'Yes, a few years ago. What of it?'

'Perhaps you remember that the last chapter but one is about his work alongside the Senoi Praaq.'

She looked at him blankly. Proshin straightened his shoulders as he took this in.

'I see. It was published with a lot of restrictions, of course, but for us it has been an extremely valuable text for many years. The Senoi Praaq were an anti-Communist resistance army made up of native Malay tribesmen. The British had to remain in camps in the jungle because of their conspicuous appearance, while the Senoi Praaq went into the villages to buy food and supplies and to gather intelligence.'

Rachel nodded. It rang a vague bell. She felt something give way in her stomach, and a sense of shame and anger at herself for having missed part of the puzzle. Details of Sandy's secret life had been hidden in plain sight all this time and she hadn't even considered it. *It's hardly a secret . . . It's been public knowledge since that book was published in 1961.* Of course the Soviets would have pored over every word of his memoir! Had she not looked more closely for fear of what she might find? If only she'd taken the blasted thing when she'd had the chance, instead of returning it to the bookshelf. She wondered for a moment if there might be a copy somewhere in the safe house, but decided she didn't have time to search for it.

She turned back to Proshin. 'How well do you remember that book?'

He scratched at an eyebrow. 'Very well, I would say. In our directorate, all new officers are examined on its contents within their first six months, and I often write the questions for this test. We provide them with a specially prepared Russian version, but I have read it in English several times.'

'There's a photograph in it. It shows Harmigan and a couple of other men in some sort of training establishment in Malaya. One man is Gadlow, the other is an Asian, I suppose one of these Senoi . . .'

'Praaq.'

'Yes. Do you know who that man is?'

Proshin shook his head, but Rachel realised the moment the words had left her lips that she had answered her own question.

The waiter.

Of course, the bloody waiter from the party in Kuala Lumpur, walking past her on the grass like butter wouldn't melt. He was the man in the photograph with Sandy. She thought of the photograph again, and recalibrated. No, the waiter was too young, but the resemblance was too close. He must be related to the man in the photograph in some way. Had Gadlow recognised him, perhaps, the man who had come to deliver his death? Or perhaps in the darkness, in a very different environment years later, and in his own desperation to escape, he hadn't.

'What do the Senoi Praaq have to do with fascists? What's the connection?'

'Not the Senoi Praaq, but the British who trained them. Gadlow was among them, but most were of course extreme anti-Communists. This was a difficult time for him, especially as we lost contact for several months. But soon he discovered that there was a secret group within the British force. He gradually earned their trust, and they invited him to join. Over the years, the group expanded and became more influential.'

'How?'

'The members assist each other in their careers, like the Freemasons, or Etonians or other groups. This was how Gadlow was appointed Head of Station, for example. But the main purpose is to protect their own fascistic interests.'

She sighed. 'And you actually believe this?'

Proshin nodded. 'Yes, I do. Four agents told us about it, and I have reviewed all the intelligence. First, Philby, who I admit may have been joking, as you suggest. But sometimes the truth is revealed in jest. Then Gadlow, as I have just explained. Then our agent Pritchard, who managed to infiltrate the group in the early sixties. Then Paul Dark, who found evidence that some of the most senior members of your service were working in this way, alongside similar groups in other countries. Finally, Gadlow's own fate sealed it.'

'*Gadlow's* fate?'

'Yes. He felt that his knowledge of this faction would protect him. He called it his insurance policy. "If they ever come for me, Sasha, I have my insurance." This is what he used to say to me.'

Rachel looked at him with horror, as the impression of Gadlow, even with the tinge of a Russian accent, was striking. He had to at least have met the man.

'He often spoke of it,' Proshin went on. 'He was convinced that if he were ever exposed as working for us, his information about this group's members and activities would be a very strong bargaining tool.' He smiled grimly. 'Now Gadlow's insurance policy has become mine. He never received the opportunity to test it, of course, because someone made sure that he was killed before he returned to London to tell anyone.'

She stood again, partly so he couldn't see the expression on her face, and circled around the chair, tempering her breathing as she thought through what he was saying. She turned back to face him, leaning over the chair.

'How do you know *I'm* not part of this faction?'

'I don't,' he said. 'But I am taking an educated guess.' He reached into his jacket and she froze for a moment, trying to remember how thoroughly she'd frisked him and wondering if she could have missed a gun or some other weapon. But instead he brought out what looked to be a cigarette, which he passed to her.

As she took it, she realised it was a piece of paper

that had been rolled tightly into a narrow tube and secured with a strip of tape. She tore off the tape and it uncoiled, nearly leaping from her fingers. It was two pieces of paper, in fact. The first was a copy of a message typed in Russian, the second was in English. She read the latter:

'THE SPEAR', AS IT IS KNOWN TO ITS MEMBERS, IS A GROUP OF WELL-CONNECTED FIGURES IN THE BRITISH ESTABLISHMENT WITH FAR-RIGHT SYMPATHIES. AMONG THEM ARE POLITICIANS, JOURNALISTS AND INTELLIGENCE OFFICERS. MOST MEMBERS HAVE LIVED IN THE COLONIES, MAINLY AFRICA AND THE FAR EAST, AND HAVE WORKED IN INTELLIGENCE OR SPECIAL FORCES. AS PREVIOUSLY DISCUSSED, I WAS INVITED TO JOIN IN MARCH 1954 WHILE IN MALAYA, AND I ACCEPTED WITH YOUR APPROVAL.

THE LEADER OF THE GROUP IS DAVID MEREDITH, WHO IS ALSO ITS MAIN FINANCIER THROUGH HIS AFRICAN MINING CONCERNS. HE IS ASSISTED BY HIS WIFE, WHO IS AS FANATICAL AS THE REST OF THEM. THESE ARE ALL THE CURRENT MEMBERS THAT I KNOW OF.

A list of around thirty names followed. Rachel barely took them in, her eyes swimming. She looked up at Proshin.

'When did Gadlow give you this?'

'He passed it to his case officer in Bangkok in February 1958, through a dead drop. The original message was of course encrypted using a one-time pad. This is the decrypt and the Russian translation of it, both copied down by me directly from his file, which I had access to when I was running him from the GRU station in Kuala Lumpur in late 1969.'

'But you could simply have fabricated this,' she said. 'Typed it out at your desk in Moscow.'

Proshin unclasped his hands. 'That is true, of course. But I have not. Listen to what I have said, read what is written, and judge for yourself. It is genuine.'

She looked down at the note again, taking the names in one by one. In the intervening years, several had become Service old hands, one of them even briefly serving as Chief. He and a couple of the others were now dead. She recognised one name as that of a journalist at the *Daily Telegraph*, another from *The Times*. Three were backbench Conservative politicians who she knew held hard-right views. But could Moscow know that, too? Easily enough, surely. And if so, they could use it. The Soviets were avid propagators of precisely this sort of disinformation, and Proshin could be part of an operation to discredit all these people, either wittingly or unwittingly.

But she didn't think so, in her bones. Something deep within her told her it was just as he said, and that one night in 1958 Tom Gadlow had written this down and placed it in a dead drop in Bangkok. It was partly because she knew of previous groups along these lines. In the thirties, there had been The Nordic League and The White Knights of Britain and Mosley's 'dining society', The January Club. Groups with a similar bent had appeared sporadically since the war, most recently fuelled by fears that the Labour Party was penetrated by Communist agents and would lead Britain into anarchy. Rachel was only an occasional visitor to the notoriously macho basement bar of Century House, but even so it had been impossible to miss in the last few years that many of the older officers had very right-wing views, and on several occasions she'd sat through whisky-fumed rants bemoaning the loss of the colonies or advocating the need for a military reserve in the event of society breaking down.

So the existence of such a group wasn't implausible. Proshin's claim that it *controlled* the Service had seemed absurd to her, but even that now didn't seem as unlikely as it had done a few minutes earlier. This was because one name on Gadlow's list appeared to her eyes to be written in bolder ink than the others: Sandy Harmigan. As Chief of the Service he was an obvious candidate for such a smear, but could he be a fascist? He was right wing, of course, a Conservative through and through, but nothing more sinister than that as far as she knew. And yet it made sense. Snatches of conversation over the years came back to her, the way he had rolled his eyes at certain remarks, or let others pass . . .

And then there was Celia's inclusion. David

Meredith had been her first husband, and she had inherited his mining fortune after his death in a car crash. Rachel had a sudden vision of Celia standing at the door of the house in Mayfair, the slash of red at her mouth and the silver necklace flashing around her throat. At the time, the tip of the pendant she had worn had reminded her of the nib of a pen, but it had been thicker than that. The front section of her scalp tingled as she realised that it much more closely resembled the head of a spear.

It was an Auntie Hannah moment, but she took no pleasure from it. And it immediately raised new questions in her mind. Was the pendant a talisman of some sort, perhaps a private signal used to identify her to other members of the group? Or a brandishing of status? Perhaps Celia had taken over her husband's role as leader of the group. If so, that might be why she had been present at the meeting with Harry Bradley. She hadn't been acting as Sandy's aide or errand girl – she ran the whole bloody show. And perhaps her former husband's financial interests in Africa still needed protecting.

The thought reminded her of something else in the message and she glanced back up at Proshin. 'What do they need financing for? What are they spending it on?'

'Operations. Unofficial ones that serve their political purposes, and which they execute through deniable partners. They have framed us or our allies for several terrorist atrocities in Western Europe, for example. A few years ago, they tried to make it appear that Paul

Dark wanted to kill your prime minister. Perhaps you know of this already.'

She nodded dully. That supposed assassination attempt in Nigeria. She guessed that Sandy had held back the information on that from her for the same reason he had held it from Wilson: any mention of it in its immediate aftermath would have led to it being thoroughly investigated, with potentially dire consequences for the conspirators. But six years later, it was a fair bet that while Wilson would be momentarily furious to learn he had been in danger, his anger wouldn't burn intensely enough to set up an inquiry into such ancient history, especially with the culprit apparently a traitor on the run. Presumably, the file Sandy had given Wilson to read had been doctored to blame it on Dark.

She closed her eyes, blocking out the room and Proshin and urging herself to think of an alternative explanation. Start again, she thought. Let's say it's true, all of it. Does it hold together? Gadlow joined this group as a Soviet agent, and planned to cash in his 'insurance policy' if exposed. That held, she thought. Facing a life sentence for treason, it was plausible he would have tried to bargain by dropping the bombshell that a far-right faction was working in the upper reaches of the Service, and that Sandy was its leader. But how would Sandy have reacted? The moment she had shown him the documents proving Gadlow was a Soviet agent, he would have realised the problem. She tried to imagine what his thought processes must have been. First, horror that his group had been penetrated in this way, which meant that Moscow knew all about it. But that must have paled into insignificance at the thought of what could happen if Gadlow managed to tell anyone important about it. Anyone not in the group, that was.

On the other hand, she thought, why would he panic? If Gadlow made this claim, he could simply deny it. Why should anyone believe a Sov agent about such a thing? But Sandy knew that Gadlow would be convincing. He had been in Malaya with him and several of the others, some of whom would be shown to have far-right links if investigated. Gadlow would also presumably have been able to give details of their meetings and plans. So Sandy would have soon realised that he had no choice: he had to make sure that Gadlow never spoke of it to anyone in the upper ranks of the Service. That he never reached London at all. But he also had to stay at one remove from it. If *he* had flown out to Kuala Lumpur to fetch Gadlow and the man had died within hours of his arrival, suspicion would fall on him – as indeed it had on her. She had been cleared of any involvement partly because she was young and inexperienced, with no links to Gadlow and no motive for wanting him dead, but also because Sandy had argued that case for her.

She steadied herself against the table. He had sent her out there to take the fall. It wasn't the Russians who had arranged for the waiter to kill Gadlow – it was Sandy. It took her a few seconds to order it in her mind, but she had no doubt she was right. Her feminine intuition, she thought bitterly.

Proshin was peering at her. She knew she should be believing Sandy more than this strange Russian she had never even met before tonight, but try as she might she couldn't. The scales had fallen, and she tried to absorb her dismay. As well as the personal betrayal, she realised she had been seduced by a false image. Sandy had seemed grand and irreproachable to her, an ideal figure, a statue. She had foolishly confused him with the noble version of him played by Dirk Bogarde – the famous scene in the film in which he stalked the streets of Saint-Nazaire with his pistol at his side, his eyes glinting in the darkness, like a modern Knight of the Round Table. She'd fallen for the idea of him as a leader and a man of integrity simply because he was in that position, because he looked the part and, she supposed, because she had wanted such a figure to look up to.

But he wasn't a knight. Nothing like. He was just a shabby little fascist playing games with people's lives. And he had lied to her, all down the line.

Proshin was right. She had to take the necessary steps, and she had to take them now. She turned to him, her jaw set.

'Wait here,' she said, and walked to the door. She took the passage to the back of the flat and pushed open the door to the bedroom. Manning was asleep beneath a pink duvet cover, snoring. She turned the light on and walked over to him. He rubbed his eyes and stared at her.

'What the hell's going on?' he asked.

'You're right about the Service,' she said. 'It's corrupt to its core. I need you to help me fix it.'

Chapter 60

Without warning, a sea eagle plummeted from its perch three hundred feet above the Zambezi River to snatch a fish in its talons, its strange laughing cry echoing across the still air as it swooped back up with its prize. It was just before sunrise at Mosi-oa-Tunya, 'The Smoke That Thunders' – Victoria Falls – and the greatest spectacle in Africa was rapidly revealing itself, the spray from the waterfall pluming into the air in a constant cloud.

On the 650-foot-long steel bridge spanning the second gorge, a South African Railways diesel engine inched five carriages towards the white line painted across the midpoint of the tracks. The central carriage of the five, Car 49, had an ivory and gold exterior. It had been built and fitted in England, and apart from a few small repairs looked the same as it had done in 1947, when it had been part of the 'White Train' used by the British royal family on their visit to South Africa. Inside, it was air-conditioned, with beige carpets and walnut and chestnut panelling. A long polished stinkwood table had been set with carafes of water and vases of fresh flowers placed at both ends of the carriage. Lunch would be crayfish, specially imported for the occasion.

On the veranda of his suite at the Elephant Hills Hotel just above the Falls, Ian Smith sat in his dressing gown and looked out at the view, his heart rising with the beauty of it. He glanced down at the golf course directly below his room and smiled as a warthog emerged from the undergrowth to run across one of the Gary Player-designed fairways.

He took a deep breath, then stood and walked back inside. It would have been a lovely morning for a round of golf, but he had greater problems to deal with than calculating how to direct a small ball into a hole. It was time to get dressed and prepare – it would be a long day.

One floor beneath, Roy Campbell-Fraser stood on the veranda of his room, watching the carriages being positioned on the bridge through binoculars. He was pleased. Smith had initially thought to take Willard Shaw with him as part of his retinue, but Campbell-Fraser's information about Charamba's decision to join the talks had turned the tables and he'd been invited as the intelligence representative instead. He now had the ideal opportunity to see his plan in action at close quarters. And Charamba would have no idea he was sitting opposite one of the men he had spoken to on the telephone.

Chapter 61

Paul Dark disembarked from the plane and walked into the main terminal of Lusaka airport. A fan moved slowly in the ceiling, its blades creaking. The heat felt like an iron placed against his face after the air conditioning on the plane, and his clothes hung on him like chain mail. Adding to his sluggishness, he had barely slept on the flight and his muscles still ached from his struggle in the shopping arcade.

He didn't regret killing the Rhodesian – the man had been a professional and wouldn't have hesitated to kill him if he'd had the opportunity – but he was perturbed at how easily the violence had come to him. He had almost *enjoyed* it. The red mist had descended at the thought of the man being involved in kidnapping Claire and Ben, but the transition to his old brutal self had been seamless. Well, it was too late to do anything about it, he thought. Once he got them back he could put the monster away again. For now, he'd use it.

Something else was nagging him about Brussels: the

couple who had appeared in the arcade after he'd killed the Rhodesian. He was certain they had been Service. The man had been based in Paris in the mid-sixties, he thought, though his name escaped him. He hadn't recognised the woman at all, but she had been dressed in a very English way, in stockings and a sober skirt. If his instincts were right, it meant the Rhodesians *and* the British were chasing him – or that there was some sort of co-operation between them. He wasn't sure which prospect was worse.

He loosened the collar of his shirt as he took his place in the queue for the counter. A single official was inspecting passports, a young man in shirtsleeves. Despite his youth, he looked like he was taking his task very seriously and Dark felt the familiar knot in his stomach tighten. He was using Jonas's other passport now, Per Sundqvist, the pharmacist from Uppsala, but he wasn't sure it was going to work. Perhaps he should have tried to find Manning's safe, after all. But that wouldn't have helped him either: even if he had found another passport there, the Service would simply have put an alert out for it.

He reached the front of the queue and the official beckoned him forward. Dark handed him his passport and he opened it up and looked at him.

'Is this your first visit to Zambia, Mr Sundqvist?'

'Yes.'

'Business or pleasure?'

'Pleasure.'

It happened very quickly after that. The official

simply glanced up and nodded and a moment later Dark felt his arms being taken behind his back and metal pressing into his spine. He was marched away from the queue and through an unmarked door, where he was shoved into a chair in a corner. A dead rat lay against one wall, and flies were buzzing around it. Dark felt like retching, but held it in.

A few minutes passed, and the young official walked in. He lit a cigarette slowly, and Dark revised his view of him as he did.

'You have no smallpox or yellow fever certificates, Mr Sundqvist,' he said finally. 'Can you explain this, please?'

Chapter 62

Monday, 25 August 1975, Chièvres, Belgium

The sky was a sheet of pale grey. Rachel parked at the airfield and walked, buffeted by a wind, up the tarmac to the C-47.

'I was told just one passenger,' said the pilot as he took in the two figures standing next to her.

'There's been a change of plan,' she replied. She gestured to Manning and Proshin, and they climbed aboard.

Chapter 63

There was a knock on the door and Charamba looked up. It was Gibo.

'What is it, Phillip?' he said, irritated at the intrusion. He wanted time alone to think before they set out for the talks.

'I've had a tip-off. A white man has arrived in town and asked to see you.'

Charamba peered at him. 'When did you hear this?'

'Just now. They're holding him at the airport. He said you would know what it was about.'

Charamba stood. 'Get the car,' he said.

Chapter 64

'He's tired a lot,' said Jessica Innes, as she led them through the front hall. 'And he has dreadful nightmares. A couple of months ago he woke up at two in the morning and just shouted the word "Traitors!" over and over.' She gave a small smile, apologetic and ashamed and yet stoic at the same time.

'I understand,' said Rachel. 'We'll be very careful.'

She had driven here straight from Northolt with Proshin and Manning squeezed in the back seat of the Austin, two defectors in their own ways – traitors, too, depending on who you asked. It had taken her a while to find the village but Manning had helped, having visited it many moons ago when it had been occupied by a previous Chief.

Jessica Innes rapped on the door of the study.

'Edmund? I have some visitors here to see you. From London.'

There was no response, and they stood in awkward silence.

She was about to knock again when the door

opened, and Innes stood there in his dressing gown and slippers. He seemed to have shrunk since Rachel had last seen him. His face was narrower at the cheek-bones but his jowls were still there, as if Giacometti had started work at the top of his head but abandoned the job halfway through.

He shuffled out of the room, peering through his spectacles with watery eyes.

'I wondered if it might be you,' he said. 'I see you've brought some friends.'

Chapter 65

The door of the room in the basement of Lusaka airport swung open and five men marched in. All wore fatigues, and were armed. Dark didn't offer any resistance as they escorted him from the room and bundled him into an unmarked station-wagon outside. Someone placed a blindfold over his eyes and tied his wrists together, a voice called out 'Go!' and the engine started up.

Half an hour later, he was roughly dragged out and taken into a cool house. They led him down into a basement and tore off his blindfold – the room was empty. They left him, and he paced the concrete floor. The summit was due to start later that morning, but the thugs at the airport had taken his watch so he had no idea how much time he had left. Two hours? Three? Finally, the door opened and a small, neat-looking man entered. He wore a short-sleeved white shirt, slacks and sandals, and he had glasses and a neat beard. He approached Dark and stared down at him.

'I'm Matthew Charamba,' he said. 'I'd very much like to know why you are looking for me.'

Dark breathed out in relief. 'My name is Paul. I have a son with your daughter, Hope. I think I know who's taken them, and I've come to try to get them back, with your help.'

Charamba looked at him, his expression impassive. 'Why should I believe you?'

Dark took a step closer to the man. 'Because it's the truth. I knew her as Claire. She has a birthmark inside her left elbow, the shape of a teardrop. She has a smile that makes you think someone has turned the lights on. She has tiny dimples in her cheeks that you only see if you're very close. We love each other, and we love our son, Ben.'

Dark had spoken without altering his voice, as though reciting a poem. But now he saw that Charamba was crying softly. He had opened up Dark's wallet and found the photograph of the three of them. He waved a hand at Gibo and the others.

'Get out,' he said. 'Leave us.'

Chapter 66

Rachel asked Innes if she could use his telephone, and he took her into the conservatory. She dialled, her hand trembling.

'Savage and Cooper.'

'Phoenix,' she said. 'It's terribly urgent.'

There was a pause on the line and then a familiar voice came on. 'You looking for His Lordship?' said Tombes, ignoring protocol. 'He's not here, is he? Buggered off to leave us plebeians slaving away.'

She pushed her fingers into her temple in frustration. She couldn't really face calling his house and having Celia pick up instead of him. 'When did he go home?'

'Home? He's gone out to Rhodesia. Left about an hour ago.'

It came like a punch to her chest. She hadn't seen that coming, but of course. Of course he bloody had.

'I need you to make some calls for me, Keith,' she said. 'Several calls, in fact. Do you have a pen handy?'

Tombes laughed. 'I've been waiting for you to ask, Your Highness.'

Rachel replaced the receiver and stood for a moment, thinking. Then she picked it up again and dialled a number in Chancery Lane.

'Good morning, Public Record Office.'

'Good morning. I'd like to speak to Daniel Gold, please.'

Chapter 67

'You haven't told them?' said Dark, surprised. 'Your men.'

'I haven't told anyone. They said if I breathed a word of it they would kill them both, and I believe them.'

'I see. And what exactly have they demanded of you?'

Charamba explained the script he was to read from at the summit and Dark listened in silence. It was much as he had suspected.

'The first thing you have to understand,' he said, 'is that they have no intention of letting them go after the summit. Far too risky. They'll kill them both.'

Charamba looked at him, his face frozen in shock at the words.

'How can you be so sure?'

Dark didn't reply for a few seconds. Then he said: 'I have experience of operations like this. We need to formulate a plan and we need to do it now. How large is your delegation?'

Charamba grimaced. 'Two. Just me and my body-guard.' It had been a deliberate attempt to put him in his place by Nkomo and his cronies, but he'd had no choice but to accept.

Dark took this in. 'Do you have any maps?' he asked. 'The more detailed the better.'

Charamba stared at the strange man who had dropped into his world, and weighed the way he had acted and spoken. Then he glanced back down at the photograph still in his hands and made a decision. He stood and walked to the door.

'Phillip, come in here. And bring the others. Everyone in the house.'

Chapter 68

Monday, 25 August 1975, Victoria Falls

It was a quarter to ten in the morning. From the Rhodesian border post, Ian Smith walked slowly onto the bridge. He had put on a dark suit and tie, with a white shirt and matching pocket handkerchief. Flanked by advisers and security men, he squinted in the sharp sunlight and nodded at the assembled photographers and pressmen, but said nothing – he had made a statement at his hotel earlier, filled with the usual platitudes. The group walked along the platform next to the compartments, then climbed the small mobile staircase and entered Car 49.

At the Zambian end of the bridge, John Vorster and Kenneth Kaunda began their walk from the opposite direction. Kaunda, looking relaxed in one of his elegant safari suits, smiled and waved his handkerchief at the onlookers. Directly behind them were the Zimbabweans and their retinues: Nkomo, Sithole, Muzorewa and the latest addition, Matthew

Charamba. When they reached the platform, the group paused briefly as Vorster and Kaunda gave brief comments, then they too walked towards the 'peace train'.

As he made his way down to the central carriage, Roy Campbell-Fraser looked out of the window at the splendour of the Falls. The South Africans were overseeing the security with help from the Zambians so he had no say in the arrangements, but he'd had a discreet word with the officers in charge and had been impressed by their thoroughness. The bridge had several inbuilt advantages as a location: the ravines either side of it and the raging water below made for a formidable natural barrier. Security posts had been erected on both sides, and the entire area had been closed off to aircraft, meaning that any approach from the sky would be instantly detected by the South African Air Force and shot down. Tourist trails around the edge of the Falls had been cordoned off, and the South Africans had visited all possible sniper positions and reconnoitred nearby villages.

Campbell-Fraser opened the door to the central carriage and was greeted by the BOSS agent responsible for guarding it. He saw from the place-cards that he wasn't to be seated at the table itself, but directly to the right behind Smith. Still, it was a bird's-eye view. He helped himself to a glass of whisky from the bar in the corner and waited as the room began to fill up.

* * *

In the first of the Zambian carriages, a South African security officer held a German Shepherd on a short leash. As Matthew Charamba entered, he asked him to raise his arms so he could be frisked.

'It's just a formality,' he said, noting Charamba's expression.

'Are you conducting the same formalities with the men on the other side of the carriage?'

'Of course,' the man replied with restrained equanimity. 'Everyone who enters the train is being checked. This is for your own security.'

Charamba raised his arms and the man patted him down.

'And who is this?' he said when he had finished, nodding at the figure behind Charamba.

'Phillip Gibo, my private secretary.'

The South African looked down at a clipboard and then up again at Gibo.

'All right,' he said. He frisked him, too, then gestured at the attaché case in his hand. 'Open it, please.'

Gibo glanced at Charamba.

'That contains my private papers,' Charamba said.

The BOSS man glared. 'Nothing goes beyond this point without being checked.'

Charamba took a breath and nodded. Gibo placed the case on the ground and opened the combination. It clicked open, and he lifted it back up to show the South African its contents. The South African flicked his fingers over the papers, fingering the edges of the case. Then he clicked his teeth at the German Shepherd, which bounced up on its hind legs and sniffed at the case.

After a few moments the man nodded and let them through to the central carriage, where they took their seats on their side of the table.

Chapter 69

The Grumman Gulfstream II landed on the airstrip at Inkomo at just after eight o'clock in the evening. Sandy Harmigan stepped onto the tarmac and felt the heat rush over him. For a moment, he felt he was back in Malaya. He turned back to the plane and extended his hand to his wife.

'Mind your step,' he said.

She glowered at him. He hadn't wanted her to come, but she had insisted. She liked to protect her investments, she'd said, a little too pointedly for his liking.

They reached the foot of the steps. In the dim haze ahead, a large man in camouflage gear was striding towards him.

'Pete Voers,' he said, sticking out a hand. 'Major Campbell-Fraser sent me to pick you both up.' He glanced up at the jet. 'We don't get too many of these landing here.'

'No,' said Celia Harmigan with a chilly smile, 'I don't imagine you do.'

Voers considered responding, but decided against it.

They walked towards the barracks. 'I'll show you the prisoners,' he said. The Commander had said they would want to inspect the goods.

Chapter 70

Roy Campbell-Fraser was tired and angry. Despite the air conditioning, the carriage felt muggy and claustrophobic – the stale sweat of twenty men pressed against each other around the narrow table lingered in his nostrils.

The summit had been going on for nearly two hours, but there had been more breaks than actual talk. Vorster and Kaunda had given some peppy opening remarks but had left ten minutes later – the acrimony had begun within moments of their vacating the train. Now several of the delegates were openly doodling as the others spoke, and Smith was becoming increasingly irate at the lack of progress.

Campbell-Fraser was furious for another reason: Matthew Charamba hadn't spoken a word so far. He had simply sat there, stone-facedly listening to the others speak. What the hell was he playing at? Campbell-Fraser glared at him across the table, thinking about his next move.

Chapter 71

'What does your daddy do?' said the boy in English. They had quickly established it was their only shared language.

'He helps people,' said Ben.

'My daddy's a soldier,' said the other proudly. 'He will be back soon.'

'Mine, too,' said Ben.

In the small nursery section behind the barracks, Hope tried not to cry as she watched Ben playing with around a dozen other children on the linoleum floor, a ritual that seemed to take place every evening before the children's bedtime. A few other mothers looked on, but they sat apart and none of them talked to her. Joshua Ephibe stood by the door watching the scene, a machine-pistol by his side. She wondered if he would have the guts to shoot her if she just took Ben in her arms and made a run for the door, but it was an idle thought – by her mental calculations in the car from the airport, they were less than fifty kilometres from Salisbury, but the view through the flyblown windowpanes confirmed that this was a military base, and the perimeter was patrolled by dozens of armed men.

Still, they had been let out into the open air now, and were staying in a tiny but clean room that felt a little less like a cell. There was running water and food was placed under their door twice a day. The threat of physical assault also seemed to have abated, at least for now. Life almost felt normal. But that was perhaps worse, she thought, that they might become used to this situation. She also knew there was a danger in feeling grateful to her captives – there had been a famous case a couple of years earlier during a bank robbery in Stockholm when just that had happened. She and Erik had watched the news, gripped by the evolving drama. But then, his name wasn't really Erik and hers wasn't Claire, so they had been enacting their own hidden drama as they'd sat on the cramped sofa together watching the television.

But this was all too real. She had nearly given up hope of being rescued now: even her father wouldn't be able to breach such a place. She simply had to hope he acceded to their demands, whatever they were. And in the meantime, pretend to Ben that everything was normal, while reminding herself at every opportunity that it wasn't.

Chapter 72

Paul Dark wiped the spray from his face-mask and pulled at the oars. Like the man in front of him in the dinghy, he was dressed from head to toe in black, but he also wore rubber gloves and a matching mask to cover his skin.

It was coming up to nine o'clock. He'd chosen the time carefully: the sun had set three hours earlier, but tonight the moon would be close to full, which meant they might be able to see more easily but could also be more easily seen. While it wasn't quite pitch-black now, the next hour was the darkest it would get.

The dinghy hugged closer to the bank, and he let go of the oars and crouched, waiting for his opportunity. He checked the fasteners on the waterproof case strapped to his back one last time. Everything was secure. High above, he was dimly aware of flashes of light passing by and for a moment he thought of the war and the searchlights he had seen in Germany.

Forget the war. Live now.

They reached the turning, and Dark tapped his

companion on the shoulder in gratitude and then bent his legs and slipped over the side and into the black water. He shivered as the cold penetrated his body, then started swimming below the surface. It was only a few feet to the bank, but the current was strong and he couldn't crawl because the kick would stir up surf and whiteness of it might alert the men above. So instead he stretched out his arms in a wide arc, pushing as hard as he could.

He reached the bank and came up for air, grasping at the surface with his hands. He held on to a rock momentarily but then his grip failed and he slipped back into the water, the current pushing him away again. He clenched his eyes shut and pushed harder until he made up the last remaining foot again, and now he propelled himself out of the water in one smooth movement and managed to get hold of a sharp outcrop of rock. He pulled himself out of the water and began crawling up with his hands until he was over the lip and into deep foliage. He leaned back, dizzy. Squinting through his face-mask, he could make out the dinghy as it went back the way they had come, to safety and a warm bed in the hotel over the border with the rest of Charamba's group. Then he looked across at the view facing him. From this point, the ravine looked vast, and he was merely an atom on the face of the planet.

He started climbing. The moon was already brightening, and soon it would be worse than a spotlight. It took him nearly an hour to reach the small clearing he had identified on the map earlier, and his fingernails were torn and the palms of his hands bleeding by the time he did. The roar of the falls was much louder now, filling the space and making his ears pulsate. He gathered his breath and kept going. The final few feet took him nearly a quarter of an hour to crawl across, because now he could see the sentry: a man in khaki fatigues, the muscles on his forearm tensed around the trigger of a sub-machine-gun.

He was young, perhaps even thirty years younger. But Dark had the motivation, the element of surprise, and decades more training. He waited until his breathing had stilled, then silently removed the knife from its sheath and held it in his right hand, feeling its heft and accustoming himself to it. Then he crept towards the clearing until he was directly behind the sentry. He leaped forward and chopped at the back of the man's neck with his left forearm. As the man fell, Dark moved his left hand to cover his mouth and nostrils, then thrust the blade into his kidneys. It caught on something, a bone or organ, and Dark wondered if he should draw it out and attack from the front, but then it sunk in and he was pulling it free and dragging the man back and downwards into the shadow of the bridge.

He checked the man's pulse. He was dead.

The killing had taken less than five seconds.

He left the man where he was and headed for the foot of the bridge. The steel girders stretched out above him, the latticework resembling the enormous web of a spider reaching up to the long thin stretch leaping across the sky. He could just make out the carriage in the centre, the exterior of it pale grey in the moonlight, the inside of it lit like a Halloween pumpkin. He reached out an arm and gripped one of the girders, then started making his way up.

Chapter 73

Campbell-Fraser wanted to murder Matthew Charamba. The summit was now coming into its eleventh hour and he still hadn't uttered a word.

He glanced across at the BOSS man standing by the door of the carriage. Campbell-Fraser had every confidence in the South Africans, but there was still a niggling concern in the back of his mind. Harmigan had called just before he'd left Inkomo to inform him that Johnny Weale was missing in action in Brussels and that his intelligence indicated that Paul Dark was now on his way to Africa – possibly to Salisbury, possibly to Lusaka. As a result, Harmigan had decided to fly out himself. The thought had worried Campbell-Fraser until he realised it would be useful. If Dark tried to head for Inkomo to rescue his family, it wasn't a bad thing to have the Chief of British intelligence standing in his way.

But now he was worried Dark might have tried something, and he just didn't know about it. The BOSS agent had an intercom set attached to his belt, and

Campbell-Fraser wondered whether he could take him aside in the next break and call Inkomo to check. Perhaps he could also figure out a way to put further pressure on Charamba – let him listen to his daughter and her son on the intercom, perhaps?

Campbell-Fraser looked up as he registered the sound of breaking glass. One of the windows of the carriage was shattered and the curtain had blown into the room and draped itself over several of the African delegates. As Campbell-Fraser moved towards Smith, he saw the BOSS man in his peripheral vision moving to reach for his pistol. In the same instant, he saw that the figure tumbling through the glass was clutching something in his hand, a greyish-white object.

'Hold your fire!' he shouted at the BOSS agent. 'Plastic explosive!'

Chapter 74

Rachel approached the sentry hut and asked to speak to Sandy Harmigan. One of the men stepped forward and looked her over. He took in her accent and the way she was dressed – far too many layers – and smiled.

'And who shall I say is calling?'

'Rachel Gold.'

He nodded and went into the hut. She waited, gathering her thoughts. There was no wind, and sweat was sticking to her blouse. Beyond the barrier she could see a constellation of corrugated-iron buildings in the midst of the forest plantation, with clusters of aerials extending from rooftops like metallic branches. The sentry emerged from the doorway and walked back towards her.

'Wait here,' he said.

Ten minutes later, she saw a tall figure walking towards her. It was Sandy, wearing his pale-grey linen suit and his straw hat. He looked like he was about to go punting.

'You found it, then!' he said. Now he reminded her

of her father, greeting a guest for lunch. 'Sorry about not being able to warn you in advance, my dear. By the time I decided to come out, you were already in the air from Belgium. I take it the flight was all fine?'

She nodded, noting the lie, and followed him up to the barracks. He led her through a deserted, darkened operations room, past radio sets and walls covered in maps and pins. Rachel was reminded of the early days of Review Section. She'd come a long way since then.

Sandy ushered her into an office that had a sign reading 'MAJ. CAMPBELL-FRASER' on the door. The air conditioning was on full blast. The room was sparsely decorated, with a filing cabinet, a small refrigerator and, positioned diagonally, a long desk. Seated in a low chair at the far end of it was a slim figure in a severe dress, wearing a pendant around her neck.

'Hello, Mrs Harmigan,' Rachel said.

Chapter 75

Car 49 was silent now. Each of the delegates had a wire leading into a small putty of plastic explosive attached to his forearm. All the wires were connected, and led to the small device held in the hand of the man in the black mask. Matthew Charamba had disarmed the BOSS agent, and now held his pistol out in front of him, his jaw clenched.

Ian Smith was the first to speak. 'This is madness,' he said. 'If you kill me or anyone else in this room, it'll set your cause back decades.'

The man by the window drew back the mask to reveal his face. 'I don't intend to kill you, Prime Minister. My name is Paul Dark. You might not have heard of me, but some of your party have.' He nodded at Campbell-Fraser, whom he recognised from Manning's dossier.

'I don't know this man,' said Campbell-Fraser. 'I have no idea—'

There was a burst of crackling static and a tinny voice echoed around the room. 'De Bruyne – everything okay in there?'

It was the BOSS agent's walkie-talkie.

'Answer it,' said Dark. 'Tell him all's well.' His eyes flicked to the detonator in his hand. 'Make it convincing.'

De Bruyne spoke rapidly into the mouthpiece. 'Everything's fine here. Someone just dropped their glass.' He signed off.

Dark nodded. 'Good.' He turned his attention back to Smith. 'Just so we know where we stand, Prime Minister: on Friday, a group of Major Campbell-Fraser's men kidnapped Matthew Charamba's daughter and grandson from Sweden, on your instructions. The idea was to manipulate Professor Charamba into appearing at this summit and arguing, without seeming to, in favour of your government's position. With his popularity across the country, he'd be able to secure the votes needed to push through the resolution with the black population. But the result would be an indefinite extension of white rule. It was a clever little plan. Ingenious. But it had a flaw, didn't it? Unfortunately, Campbell-Fraser's men didn't realise Hope Charamba's boyfriend was not all he seemed.'

'Dark?' said Smith. 'Wasn't there a Soviet spy with that name?'

'Yes. When Campbell-Fraser realised who I was – or perhaps when someone realised for him – he tried to have me killed by sending one of his thugs after me. And now here we all are.' He looked around the carriage, and the frightened group of men staring at him.

'I assure you I had no knowledge of this, Mr Dark,' said Smith, his voice quiet but determined. 'However, I've no doubt we can come to an amicable arrangement.'

'We'd better,' said Dark. 'Whether you knew about it or not, the plot has failed. There isn't going to be any resolution here except for our family being returned to us, along with a guarantee of safe passage into Zambia. Otherwise, we'll release the tape recordings of the telephone calls Major Campbell-Fraser made to the professor here, and even with his voice disguised I think you'll both find it rather difficult to explain to the world's press. And we also, of course, have other options.' He glanced down at his hand again.

'But if anything happens to us, your family will die anyway,' said Smith.

'If you refuse to release them, it won't matter, will it? The professor and I are in agreement about this.' He nodded at Charamba, who nodded back.

'Your threat is meaningless,' said Smith. 'If the press see all this commotion they'll want to know what the hell's going on. So the story will get out anyway.'

'You will deal with that now. You and Professor Charamba will go out and make a brief statement together saying you're very close to reaching agreement but that the pressure of everyone waiting for it is off-putting so both delegations have asked to continue the talks in complete privacy tonight. If they don't leave at once, they're in danger of scuppering a deal for the future of Rhodesia – that sort of thing. Dismiss the security detail for the same reason.'

'They won't like that,' said Smith.

'They won't be able to do much about it – a request from the negotiators themselves, one of them the leader of Rhodesia. I'm sure you can make it convincing, Prime Minister. I presume there's a no-fly zone over the area?'

Smith nodded.

'Stand that down, too, effective immediately. And if you try to give any sort of signal something is wrong, the professor will shoot you through the back.' Dark glanced at the opposite end of the carriage, where a small clock hung from the wall. 'You've got three minutes to clear everyone away and get back to your seat or I flick the switch on this thing.'

Smith made to object, then changed his mind. Charamba walked towards the Zambian end of the carriage and gestured with the pistol in his hand. Smith stood and joined him.

'After you,' Charamba said grimly, and Smith opened the door. Charamba followed him out, and a few moments later the sound of Smith's voice floated up to them.

'Gentleman, we have a brief announcement to make . . .'

Dark looked around the compartment until he found what he was looking for: there was a telephone on one of the side tables. He carefully handed the detonator to Phillip Gibo, then picked up the receiver:

the connection was live. He gestured to Roy Campbell-Fraser to leave his chair and come to sit in the one next to him.

'We need to make a call, Major. I want my family placed on a flight here at once.'

Chapter 76

Celia Harmigan returned Rachel's greeting with a look of barely disguised loathing. Sandy strode across the room and settled into one of the other chairs, folding his legs. It was a swift, casual movement, as debonair as ever, but Rachel sensed an unfamiliar awkwardness.

'We flew here in one of Celia's planes,' he said airily. 'Considering the urgency, it seemed the best option. Celia insisted on coming along for the ride.' He looked towards her and smiled forgivingly. 'A little African adventure.'

Rachel took in the false jollity, and Celia's continued silence.

'Has Dark turned up yet?' she asked.

'No,' Sandy said, sitting up. 'And with any luck, he won't. In the meantime, the summit is continuing, and I'm using this spot as an observation post. I know the chap who runs the place.'

'Yes,' Rachel said quietly. 'From Malaya. I know.'

He looked at her for a long moment, then leaned

back in his chair. 'All right,' he said. 'You've flown all this way, so let's hear it.' His voice was steely and hard now, the pretended air of friendliness suddenly gone.

'It's over,' she said. 'Us, of course.' She glanced at Celia. 'But also the two of you. Edmund is back as Chief.'

Celia Harmigan looked up. 'Christ, Sandy,' she said. 'Can't you keep your little bitch under control for even a few hours?'

Sandy Harmigan didn't speak for a few seconds.

'She's bluffing,' he said, finally.

Rachel shook her head. 'I'm afraid not, dear heart. I interviewed Proshin in Brussels – yes, against your orders – and he told me all about your little gang. "The Spear".' She turned to Celia, nodding at the pendant. 'Lovely piece. It's not silver, is it?'

She had fallen silent again, and Rachel went on.

'Platinum, I expect. But that's not where the big business is, of course. The big business is chrome. Geoffrey Manning told me about it in vivid detail.'

'Manning!' said Sandy, and laughed. 'Rachel, I'm disappointed, really. You shouldn't believe a word that fool says. As for Proshin, I've no idea what he's told you, but you should know by now that a potential defector will claim just about anything under the sun. Especially if he's been ordered to by Moscow.'

She walked towards the table and sat on the end of it. 'You're not understanding me. It's over. It's not just me who believed Manning – Edmund did, and so did the JIC. They met to discuss it all this afternoon.' She looked down at her watch. 'The PM should also have been informed by now.'

'Well, well.' Sandy placed his hands on the table and spread them out. 'While the cat's away, the mice do play. Look, I've no idea what you think you're doing, but if anything you've just said is true you've wasted a lot of people's time and they won't be very pleased when I get back to London and clear it all up. Manning's a traitor to the Service, and Innes is mentally deranged – howling at the moon I'm a double agent, for God's sake! As for Proshin, well, he's clearly a Soviet plant spreading disinformation on Moscow's orders. Some rather peculiar stuff, by the sound of it. How were you taken in by all this nonsense?'

Rachel nodded – she'd expected him to try this line. 'You can't smooth-talk your way out of this,' she said. 'Even to me. You're too late. Innes, Proshin and Manning each have credibility problems, but put them together and they're a formidable team. Proshin had the documentary evidence about your group. Manning had the expertise to explain it. And Edmund had the ability to decipher it all, and the clout to make sure it was listened to. A shower, a suit and personal vindication can do wonders for a man's persuasive talents. And he never accused you of being a double agent – at least, not for the Soviets. Because your allegiances lie elsewhere, don't they?'

'Sandy, I think I've had enough of this now,' said Celia. 'Can you get rid of her?'

Rachel turned to her and smiled. 'It won't go down

very well if I disappear. Unless you fancy facing murder charges. It'll be easier to prove than with Gadlow, I expect.'

Sandy suddenly stood and walked towards her. She thought he was about to hit her, but he stopped when he was about a foot away. 'You're being offensive now, Rachel,' he said. 'And I'm not sure it's wise.'

'What, for my career? Who's bluffing now?' She smiled. 'Edmund didn't accuse you of working for Moscow. You just let me think that. No, he discovered you were running private operations on the side with your friends, and he told you to stop it or he'd sack you. You denied it all, of course, and there was sweet eff-all he could do. But then I looked through the stuff Kotov had passed us and found the evidence that Gadlow was working for the Russians. That changed the situation rather drastically, because he could blow your little gang's existence and activities to Innes. And then you'd not just be sacked, but you and several others would be in gaol with a D-notice having been slapped on the trial. So you stalled. You huffed and you puffed that the evidence against Gadlow wasn't conclusive, all of which gave you enough time to arrange for someone to kill him. Who was the assassin, by the way?'

'Don't answer her,' said Celia.

'I suspect he was related to someone from your Malaya days,' Rachel said. 'Anyway, it doesn't much matter – he did his job. Of course, by sending me out to fetch Gadlow you'd put me in the frame to take the fall for it, though you did your best to rectify that after the fact. Sweet of you. But you did it for tactical reasons: it protected you, but also held my "failure" to protect Gadlow over me and used it to make me loyal to you. Then you used his murder – the murder you'd arranged – to oust Edmund. He was unprofessional for having let me out in the field, a traitor had been lost on his watch, and so on. You played it very cleverly. The final straw was making out he was losing his marbles. And whoosh ... you were Chief.' She took a breath. 'And now you're here, having flown out on a Meredith Mining jet.'

She walked to the fridge, crouched down and opened its door. She took out the bottle of champagne and turned, holding it up.

'On ice!' she said. 'Christ, you really are a pair of shameless little crooks. It took a while to figure out, listening to Proshin and Manning yapping away, but we got there eventually. I thought it was about ideology at first. This whole thing – the summit, the kidnapping of Charamba's daughter – but that's only part of it, isn't it? It's also about money. And metal. Ferrochrome is used to make stainless steel, and you need lots and lots of it to build fighter jets, and tanks, and missiles. Rather unfortunately, thirty-three per cent of the world's chrome is in the Soviet Union. But seven per cent is in Rhodesia, most of it from mines Celia owns. Sanctions be damned! And, of course, as Chief it's been terribly easy for Sandy to make the right introductions in the defence industry. I take it the

Americans are a major client, which is why Harry Bradley was invited round.'

The Harmigans didn't respond.

'Yes, I thought so. But, of course, your business is largely dependent on Ian Smith's regime. The day the black Africans take over this country you'll have a serious problem. It's a safe bet that they won't want white foreigners exploiting their natural resources, and they'll requisition the mines from you. So you need this place to be ruled by whites for as long as possible.'

She walked over to the table and took a chair, crossing her legs in a parody of Sandy's style. 'For all these reasons, Major Campbell-Fraser's plan was rather up your street, wasn't it? Yes, Geoffrey told me about him, too. It turns out the leader of the Selous Scouts served in Malaya. That seemed a little too much of a coincidence. The operation must have cost a pretty penny, but Christ, what a prize – the guarantee of white rule in Rhodesia for decades to come. So here you both are, Sandy pretending to be on Service business keeping an eye on the summit, but in fact both of you waiting for Charamba to do your bidding and deliver the goods. I presume his daughter and grandson are being held somewhere on the premises? And then, when the summit is over, you were going to toast all that lovely cash continuing to flow into your bank accounts, before ordering them killed. Bit of a blip in your planning that Paul Dark got involved. I suppose nobody knew his identity. The best-laid plans, as they say. You must have been livid when you found out. It was like Gadlow all over again, only worse. Dark knew *far* too much. He might tell the wrong person what had really happened in Nigeria, for example. Yes, he's a Soviet agent, but he could provide a lot of convincing information about it. And while Wilson was fairly angry when you told him Dark had tried to bump him off, he would have been rather more so if he was informed that a cabal of fascists in the Service had been behind it. So you wanted Dark out of the way, to become as dead as he had been before. Only you needed deniability, as you had done with Gadlow. So this time you used an 'alongsider', Collins. Who was he? Someone else from your Malayan days – or a Selous Scout? Both, perhaps. And you wanted him to kill Dark very quietly, which is why you didn't want the Belgians involved once you figured out he was heading their way.' She stopped and looked up. 'How am I doing?'

Sandy Harmigan laughed quietly. It was a dry sound, like leaves rustling. 'So you're the great spy-catcher now, is that it?' Rachel winced: in an intimate moment she had once told him about her childhood fascination with puzzle-books and Oreste Pinto. 'Well, I don't know why I'm surprised – I always said you were an exceptional analyst. Collins was a Selous Scout. And yes, I knew Roy Campbell-Fraser in the Far East: "C" Squadron of the Malayan Scouts were mostly Rhodesians. A very good soldier, and we had many adventures together. Gadlow's assassin was a young man by the name of Udah Atnam. I worked with his father and saved his life one night, rescuing him from a Communist camp in the jungle. Udah was repaying his father's debt. But broadly speaking, you got it all. Most impressive, especially as you had to collate it all from three unreliable sources. But analysis is useless without an operational plan, and I'm not really sure what yours is. How are you intending to stop Charamba from doing our bidding and delivering the goods, as you put it?'

Chapter 77

Hope sat up in the bed, all her senses primed. She looked across to the cot and in the moonlight streaming through the curtains saw the rise and fall of Ben's chest. Her shoulders lowered in relief. But what had woken her? Her eyes turned to the far wall.

The figure of a man stood in the doorway. He placed a finger to his lips and grinned.

'Shhh,' said Peter Voers. 'Be careful not to wake the boy.'

He began walking towards her, his hands already unbuckling his belt.

Chapter 78

Rachel stared at Sandy Harmigan, momentarily stunned by his response. Running over the scenario in her mind on the flight she had expected him to deny it to the end, not flatly confess like this. And she had expected to fly into a rage, to scream and kick and shout and throw things. But instead she merely felt emptied out and numb, and she now understood why Celia had been so cold when she had seen her arriving at her front door. It was the suspicion of betrayal that drove you mad – once confirmed, it felt like it had always been there.

'You're going to stop this,' she said quietly. 'You're going to release Charamba's daughter and grandson and then you're going to contact the train and tell whoever you have in there – Campbell-Fraser, I suppose – that it's over.' She nodded at the telephone sitting on the desk. 'Then you're going to fly back to London on that fancy jet of yours and present your-selves at Carlton Gardens, where you'll both sign full confessions.'

Celia Harmigan laughed. 'Have you gone mad? Why should we do any of that?'

Rachel nodded. 'You've no choice. Once you've confessed, you'll both be arrested for conspiring against the state – that's what your little gang of fascists have been doing – but your trial will be held in secret. Your assets will be stripped, and you'll both be imprisoned . . .'

'If this is an attempt to convince—'

'I've not finished,' Rachel said coldly. 'You'll both be imprisoned for a few years, but then you will be freed. You and the other members of The Spear will be kept under observation, but your reputations will remain intact. You won't be invited to the Queen's garden parties any more, but you'll be free to live as you wish.' She steepled her hands together, a gesture of Sandy's she had picked up. 'But if you *don't* co-operate now, the situation will be very much worse. If you fail to turn up at Carlton Gardens in the next couple of days, or if anything happens to me, Edmund will pull out all the stops. Interpol will issue a red notice for the two of you, wanted for sanctions busting, kidnap and the murder of a British civil servant in Malaysia in 1969. Your photographs and descriptions will appear in newspapers and bulletins across the world, from the *Cape Times* to the World Service. No expense or effort will be spared to find you. Wherever you run, you'll eventually be arrested, brought back to England and tried on those charges. But the trial will be public, and in the meantime we'll have leaked as much as we can about your activities to the press.'

Harmigan shook his head. 'I don't believe you. That would only damage the Service.'

'Not as much as you've done already. Edmund's prepared to ride this out. We will simply wipe our hands of you. "One rotten apple" and all that. Your reputation in particular will be utterly destroyed – especially after we strip you of your Military Cross.'

There was a moment of silence. 'You can't do that,' Celia said. 'There'd be outrage. He's one of the country's most loved war heroes.'

Rachel shook her head. 'The *film* character is, yes. But Sandy isn't Dirk Bogarde. Anyway, you know how the press are – fame simply makes the fall all the more newsworthy.' She looked at Sandy and gave a rueful, almost pitying smile. 'I should have spotted it earlier, really. I happened to mention *Safe Conduct* was on the telly to my brother one afternoon and he was strangely dismissive. "Oh, that old war hero." I thought he was making a crack about Sandy's age, but he wasn't. Danny works with war archives at the Public Record Office and he'd read the correspondence of the Military Cross Committee, including the discussions around the awarding of your medal in 1943. Two of the committee's members were extremely reluctant to believe your conveniently unverifiable story of derring-do in the back streets of Saint-Nazaire, pointing out that the intelligence you'd presented from it on returning home had proven faulty. One of the committee, a general no less, was convinced you'd been intending to desert before you had been picked up by your colleagues.'

Sandy Harmigan's jaw was locked. 'But they were overruled. I was awarded the medal.'

'Yes,' said Rachel. 'They were overruled by men who went on to join The Spear. We have the names.' She let it sink in. 'So you see, your memoir, the film, your name . . . all of it would be in tatters. Even if you somehow found a place where nobody reads the newspapers, you'd be living on the run, never able to show your faces in polite society again and in constant fear of arrest and lifelong imprisonment. And you'd be remembered not as a hero but as a coward and a traitor to your country.' She spread her hands out on the desk. 'It's your choice.'

A low keening sound erupted from Celia Harmigan. When she looked up her make-up had smeared horribly, her face like a hideous Noh mask that had collapsed in on itself. Sandy seemed numbed, his eyes glazed.

The desk started to vibrate and all three of them jumped. The telephone was ringing.

As if waking from a dream, Harmigan reached across to pick up the receiver.

'Yes?'

'Hello, Sandy,' said the voice on the other end of the line. 'It's Paul Dark here. I want my family back.'

Chapter 79

'I'm begging you. Don't.'

Hope's voice was barely audible, and her eyes were flickering between Voers and Ben in the cot. He was still asleep, but for how long?

'You owe me,' Voers said. 'I've waited long enough.'

He leaned over the bed and placed a large hand against her cheek. His skin was rough, calloused. She knew that in a moment he would bring his other arm across to pin her in place, but also that if she struggled she would certainly wake Ben. She closed her eyes and tried to clear her mind . . .

She felt Voers' chest drop onto her, heavier than she had been anticipating, and for a moment she was winded. Then the bed frame started to shake and her ears were filled with a horrendous cracking sound. She realised his weight had lifted from her and opened her eyes.

Joshua Ephibe was standing over Voers' body, which now lay half-twisted off the bed. The front of his head was smashed into the corner of the wall, and a pool of dark blood was leaking from it. More blood dripped from the floor and her eyes followed it up to the machine-pistol in Ephibe's hands.

'I saw him come in here. Listen, we need to go. Bring your son.'

She stared up at him, not understanding.

He leaned down and whispered into her face, his eyes wide.

'I can help you get out of here. But it needs to be now. Hurry!'

She nodded dully, then sat up and reached for her clothes.

Chapter 80

In Car 49, the delegates sat frozen in their chairs, most with sweat pouring from their faces as they watched the second hand creeping inexorably around the face of the clock on the wall.

Two minutes and twenty-five seconds had gone by since Ian Smith and Matthew Charamba had left the carriage. Through the smashed window behind Paul Dark, the roar of the falls seemed to become louder by the second as everyone strained their ears for any sound of the two men.

Dark looked down at the object in his hand. It was a small ugly piece of grey plastic encasing some wires, but it could kill everyone in the room. He lifted the cover to reveal the switch beneath. Had Smith decided to call his bluff? Could he have a pre-arranged signal with the security men on the bridge to indicate there was a problem?

He glanced back up at the clock. Thirty seconds left.

'You have to give them more time!' one of the delegates blurted out, his voice strained with desperation.

Dark ignored him. Twenty-nine seconds.

There was a screeching sound as the door slid open and Smith and Charamba entered the carriage. Groans of relief echoed around the room.

Dark replaced the cover over the switch. 'All okay?' he asked Charamba.

'Yes. Everyone's now vacated the bridge.'

'Any funny business?'

'No. Did you make the call?'

Dark nodded. 'They should be here within the next two hours.'

He told Smith to resume his seat at the table, which he did without speaking. Dark realised his hands were slicked with sweat and that his muscles were in a spasm from keeping so still. He called Gibo over and handed him the detonator again, then took a napkin from the table and wiped his hands with them, letting the circulation return to normal.

Something moved in his peripheral vision and he jerked his head up. It was Charamba. He had walked past the position he had been in before and was now marching determinedly towards him. His eyes were bulging, and they were fixed on the man seated directly next to Dark: Roy Campbell-Fraser.

'Professor—'

'I know what I'm doing.' Charamba reached Campbell-Fraser, drew the pistol from his belt and placed it against the back of the Rhodesian's neck. Campbell-Fraser didn't flinch, but his nostrils flared fractionally.

'Killing me won't get your family back.'

'He's right,' said Dark, taking a step forward so he could lead Charamba away. 'We discussed this.'

Charamba glared at him and flexed his gun hand in warning. 'That was before I'd seen the bastard in the flesh.' He looked down at Campbell-Fraser again. 'I just want to make sure of this. You admit you planned the kidnapping of my daughter and grandchild?'

Dark took a breath. It sounded ominously like he was reading him his last rites.

'Yes,' Campbell-Fraser said. 'And I'd do it again.'

As he spoke the last word, he thrust his body back in his chair, throwing out his right arm at the same time and smashing his elbow into Charamba's jaw. Almost in the same move, he swung the arm back down again and grabbed hold of Charamba's drooping hand, twisting it in a single sharp move and catching the pistol as it fell from it. Charamba collapsed to the floor, crying out as he landed in the field of glass fragments by the shattered window. Campbell-Fraser heaved forward again in the chair, swivelling his body until he was in the same position he had been a second earlier. Only now both his hands were around the butt of the pistol.

Chapter 81

The room was empty.

Sandy had given her directions to it and she had watched as he and Celia had walked across the airstrip and climbed aboard their jet. Had he tricked her and told her the wrong place? Surely they couldn't have decided to try their luck with fleeing, after all she had outlined?

Then she saw the body by the bed. She ran over and saw the wound in the head. The blood looked fresh. The bed was also unmade and the pillow still had the indentation of someone's head. They must have just left.

Rachel ran back to the door and out into the field that surrounded the base. She started running back towards the main compound, looking for any sign of a woman and a young child.

Dark ducked as Campbell-Fraser fired, and as he did he caught the expression on the face of Phillip Gibo, holding the detonator on the other side of the table.

Dark shook his head furiously at him to signal he mustn't hit the switch, then reached out and grabbed Campbell-Fraser by the legs, yanking at them with all the strength he could muster.

Campbell-Fraser cried out as he fell and reached out for the table with his spare hand, but he missed and lost momentum. He landed on his back with a thud and the sound of crunching glass. Dark was about to reach over to grab the gun when he realised the man's body was somehow still moving. He looked down and saw that Charamba had wrapped his arms around Campbell-Fraser's chest and was pushing his feet against the legs of the table so they were both sliding along the sheet of glass fragments towards the hole in the window. Dark watched as, with a howl of rage in his throat, Charamba gave another heave and the Rhodesian overtook him and hurled towards the empty space. Campbell-Fraser's scream faded as he hurtled into the darkness and joined the roar of the falls below.

Chapter 82

Rachel had found the two of them with one of the black Selous Scouts by the edge of the base, crouched down in a hole in the fence. The man had drawn his weapon on her, but it had taken just a few words to make them realise the true situation. 'Your husband has taken some men hostage,' she had said. 'I'm to take you to him.'

The man had dropped his weapon then, and they had come willingly with her. Rachel had considered countermanding Dark's orders by trying to persuade the South Africans to intervene, either from a distance via sniper rifle or by invading the carriage from the air, but all such ideas were useless, she knew, as there was too great a risk that Smith and other delegates would be killed. Sandy had told her Dark was prepared to blow everyone in the carriage to smithereens if his demands weren't met, and it sounded more than plausible.

She had immediately told the Harmigans she was commandeering their jet and pilot. Celia had tried to kick up a fuss, but Sandy had calmed her down.

Rachel had quietly repeated the consequences if they didn't turn up in Carlton Gardens within the next forty-eight hours, and then boarded the plane. She hadn't glanced back.

At Victoria Falls airport, she found a taxi driver who had insisted he couldn't drive anywhere until he saw the roll of bills in her hand. He parked at the foot of the bridge and she helped her passengers climb out. There was nobody at the barrier, just the moon shining above and the lights from the central carriage blaring and the roar of the Falls.

It was time.

Chapter 83

A woman walked into the carriage, slender and pale. Dark recognised her at once from the arcade in Brussels, but it was the two figures directly behind her that captivated his attention.

'Pappa!' Ben cried, and Dark took him in his arms as he raced across the carriage. Then he walked towards Claire – Hope – who simply leaned against him, sobbing gently with relief. She turned and saw her father and embraced him, too.

'Mr Dark.'

He looked up. It was the Englishwoman.

'My name's Rachel. I've been looking for you.'

Dark took a step towards her. 'Have you arranged for safe conduct for me and my family through Zambia?'

'For your family, yes. But not for you, I'm afraid. I have instructions from London and they're adamant you face justice.'

Dark stared at her. He moved his head slightly and glanced back at the carriage. Gibo was still standing there, the detonator in his hands as if glued to them. But Dark couldn't tell him to set it off. Not now.

He turned back to the woman, Rachel, whose eyes were fixed on him. He didn't need the detonator, he realised – he could kill her with his bare hands. She didn't even seem to be armed. Within a matter of seconds he could strangle her as he had done the sentry, and then take Hope and Ben and run, using her father's contacts across the border, and then on to another destination, away from all this.

But what would be the point? The Service would only send others to look for him, as would the Russians, and who knew who else.

Face justice. What would that entail, he wondered. He very much doubted anyone would wish to see him tried in public. More likely a long and nasty interrogation followed by the rest of his life in solitary confinement. That was what traitors deserved. He thought back to the day four years earlier when he'd stood across the street from the British embassy in Stockholm and contemplated walking in. Instead he had kept running, and as a result he'd met Hope and they'd had Ben – *created* him, a new being in the world with his own mind and soul. But he'd been living on borrowed time nevertheless. They could hide somewhere and change their names every year – but he couldn't change his past. Wherever he went and whatever he did, the people he'd betrayed would remain dead.

He glanced across at Hope and Ben. Could he bury his old self so easily now? And could he spend the rest of his life looking over their shoulders as well as his own? They didn't deserve that. They'd have a better chance without him. Her father would protect them, he was sure, using all the power he had at his disposal. And he would be more powerful after today – if the others had any sense, they'd appoint him their leader.

Dark walked towards Hope and took her face in his hands. 'I must go,' he said. 'Do you understand?'

She caught herself in a sob, but then nodded, and he kissed her on the lips, long and hard and savouring the sweetness of her. Then he crouched down and hugged Ben, squeezing tight and feeling the soft warmth of his cheek.

'Will I see you again soon, Pappa?'

'Mamma will take care of you,' he said. 'I have to go to England now.'

Ben took this in, then nodded slowly. He lifted a hand and placed it over his heart. Dark closed his eyes and took a breath, then in one movement stood, turned and began walking towards Rachel Gold.

Author's Note

A summit between Ian Smith and black nationalist leaders did take place in railway dining car 49 on Victoria Falls Bridge on 25 August 1975. However, there was no siege. It was instead a short-lived affair that achieved very little and broke up in acrimony. I've created a fictional version of the summit, compressing some events and altering others entirely, but I've also incorporated many real details, drawing on contemporaneous reports, memoirs, declassified government files and other sources. Talks between the two sides eventually led to Rhodesia becoming Zimbabwe in 1980, with ZANU's Robert Mugabe being elected the country's leader, a position he still holds.

Ian Smith, Harold Wilson, James Callaghan, Roy Jenkins, Ndabaningi Sithole and Joshua Nkomo were of course all real people, as is Kenneth Kaunda. Pyotr Ivashutin was in the KGB and then in the GRU, but I've imagined that he took Kim Philby's impish suggestion about SIS being a front for another service seriously. Matthew Charamba shares similarities with several Zimbabwean leaders of the era, but isn't intended to represent any one of them. The character Iwan Morelius is named after the Swedish thriller connoisseur who died in 2012, in tribute to his friendship and encouragement and a memorable meeting in Stockholm. *Skål*, Iwan.

The Selous Scouts existed and operated much as I've described within Africa, but not (as far as is known) in Europe. My main sources on this unusual regiment and its methods were very generous feedback from veterans and the memoirs of its leader, Lieutenant-Colonel Ron Reid-Daly. Roy Campbell-Fraser is my invention, though, as are his politics and motives.

The document mentioned in Chapter 8, 'Towards the Summit: An Approach to Peaceful Change in Southern Africa', was real, and I've drawn on the discussion of its contents in David Martin and Phyllis Johnson's *The Chitepo Assassination*. That book also concludes that Rhodesian intelligence was responsible for assassinating ZANU leader Herbert Chitepo, a theory supported by several other sources, including the memoirs of Reid-Daly and the book *See You in November* by Peter Stiff, which purports to be a biography of one of the assassins.

The Spear is inspired by several clandestine and private intelligence groups of the era, notably The 61, an alongsider organisation to SIS; GB75, established by Colonel David Stirling, the founder of the SAS; and Tory Action, set up by George Kennedy Young, who had been deputy director of SIS.

British special forces did co-operate with Malays during and after the war, including with the indigenous Senoi Praaq. Tom Gadlow's conversion to Communism is partly inspired by George Blake's in North Korean captivity, but also by the experiences of John Cross, whose memoir, *Red Jungle*, shows his empathy for the Communists he lived and worked with in Malaya during the war. Cross never became a Soviet agent as a result, but I've drawn on his experiences and also extrapolated from Nigel West's fascinating entry about him in his *A to Z of British Intelligence*.

Select Bibliography

Declassified files

'Rhodesia: Sithole's Views on Victoria Falls Meeting', confidential cable from US embassy in Lusaka to the Secretary of State, Washington DC, and other embassies, 21 August 1975, US National Archives, 1975LUSAKA01593, US National Archives.

'Rhodesia: Gabellah's Views Before Bridge Meeting at Livingstone', confidential cable from US embassy in Lusaka to the Secretary of State, Washington DC, and other embassies, 22 August 1975, US National Archives, 1975LUSAKA01597, US National Archives.

'Vorster–Kaunda Meeting at Victoria Falls', secret cable from the US embassy in Lusaka to the Secretary of State, Washington DC, and other embassies, 24 August 1975, US National Archives, 1975LUSAKA01612, US National Archives.

'Rhodesia: Grennan Sees 50-50 Chance For Settlement', confidential cable from the US embassy in Lusaka to the Secretary of State, Washington DC, and other embassies,

27 August 1975, 1975LUSAKA01642, US National Archives.

'Rhodesia: Botswana's Version of Victoria Falls Talks', confidential cable from the US embassy in Gaborone to the Secretary of State, Washington DC, and other embassies, 29 August 1975, 1975GABORO01150, US National Archives.

Books

Christopher Andrew and Oleg Gordievsky, *KGB: The Inside Story of its Foreign Operations from Lenin to Gorbachev* (Sceptre, 1991)

Christopher Andrew and Vasili Mitrokhin, *The Sword and the Shield: The Mitrokhin Archive and the Secret History of the KGB* (Basic Books, 1999)

Christopher Andrew and Vasili Mitrokhin, *The Mitrokhin Archive II: The KGB and the World* (Allen Lane, 2005)

Tennent H. Bagley, *Spy Wars* (Yale University Press, 2007)

Tennent H. Bagley and Peter Deriabin, *The KGB: Masters of the Soviet Union* (Robson, 1990)

John Barron, *KGB: The Secret Work of Soviet Secret Agents* (Bantam, 1974)

Tim Bax, *Three Sips of Gin: Dominating the Battlespace with Rhodesia's Elite Selous Scouts* (Helion and Company, 2013)

George Blake, *No Other Choice* (Jonathan Cape, 1990)

Jonathan Bloch and Patrick Fitzgerald, *British Intelligence and Covert Action* (Brandon, 1984)

Genrikh Borovik, *The Philby Files: The Secret Life of the*

Master-Spy – KGB Archives Revealed, ed. Phillip Knightley (Little, Brown, 1994)

Gordon Brook-Shepherd, *The Storm Birds: Soviet Postwar Defectors* (Henry Holt & Company, 1989)

John Cross, *Red Jungle* (Robert Hale, 1957)

Andrew DeRoche, *Black, White and Chrome* (Africa World Press, 2001)

Stephen Dorril, *MI6: Inside the Covert World of Her Majesty's Secret Intelligence Service* (Touchstone, 2000)

Stephen Dorril and Robin Ramsay, *Smear! Wilson and the Secret State* (Grafton, 1992)

Ken Flower, *Serving Secretly* (John Murray, 1987)

Fodor's Guide to Europe (Hodder and Stoughton, 1969)

Paul French, *Shadows of a Forgotten Past: To the Edge with the Rhodesian SAS and Selous Scouts* (Helion and Company, 2013)

Anatoliy Golitsyn, *New Lies for Old: The Communist Strategy of Deception and Disinformation* (Dodd, Mead & Company, 1984)

Keith Jeffery, *MI6: The History of the Secret Intelligence Service, 1909–1949* (Bloomsbury, 2010)

Roy Davis Linville Jumper, *Death Waits in the 'Dark': The Senoi Praaq, Malaysia's Killer Elite* (Greenwood Press, 2001)

Roy Davis Linville Jumper, *Ruslan of Malaysia: The Man Behind the Domino That Didn't Fall* (CDR Press, 2007)

Christer Leijonhufvud, *Stockholmarnas 70-tal* (Trafik-Nostalgiska Förlaget, 2013)

Judith Lenart, *Berlin to Bond and Beyond* (Athena Press, 2007)

David Martin and Phyllis Johnson, *The Chitepo Assassination* (Zimbabwe Publishing House, 1985)

Martin Meredith, *The Past Is Another Country – Rhodesia: UDI to Zimbabwe* (Pan, 1980)

Paul Moorcraft and Peter McLaughlin, *The Rhodesian War: A Military History* (Pen & Sword, 2011)

Jan Morris, *Destinations: Essays from Rolling Stone* (Oxford University Press, 1982)

Malcolm Muggeridge, *Like It Was* (Collins, 1981)

Joshua Nkomo, *The Story of My Life* (Methuen, 1984)

John Parker, *Rhodesia: Little White Island* (Pitman, 1972)

P.J.H. Petter-Bowyer, *Winds of Destruction: The Autobiography of a Rhodesian Combat Pilot* (30° South Publishers, 2005)

Kim Philby, *My Silent War* (Grafton, 1989)

Michael Raeburn, *Black Fire! Accounts of the Guerrilla War in Rhodesia* (Julian Friedmann, 1978)

Ron Reid-Daly and Peter Stiff, *Selous Scouts: Top Secret War* (Galago, 1982)

Ron Reid-Daly, *Pamwe Chete: The Legend of the Selous Scouts* (Covos-Day Books, 2001)

Ian Smith, *Bitter Harvest* (John Blake, 2008)

Claire Sterling, *The Terrorist Network: The Secret War of International Terrorism* (Holt, Rinehart and Winston, 1981)

Peter Stiff, *See You in November: The Story of an SAS Assassin* (Galago, 2002)

F. Spencer-Chapman, *The Jungle Is Neutral* (Lyons Press, 2003)

Viktor Suvorov, *Aquarium: The Career and Defection of a Soviet Military Spy* (Hamish Hamilton, 1985)

Richard Thurlow, *Fascism in Britain: From Oswald Mosley's Blackshirts to the National Front* (IB Tauris, 2006)

Anthony Verrier, *Through the Looking Glass: British Foreign Policy in an Age of Illusions* (W.W. Norton and Company, 1983)

Robert Wallace, H. Keith Melton and Henry Robert Schlesinger, *Spycraft* (Bantam, 2010)

Nigel West, *The A to Z of British Intelligence* (Scarecrow Press, 2009)

Nigel West and Oleg Tsarev, *Triplex* (Yale University Press, 2009)

Terry White, *Swords of Lightning: Special Forces and the Changing Face of Warfare* (Brassey's, 1992)

Acknowledgements

My thanks, as ever, to my family for bearing with me; my editor Jo Dickinson; my agent Antony Topping; everyone at Simon & Schuster who worked on the book; and those who asked not to be named here.